PHILIP—He was famed as the "Prince of Sea Captains." He ruled his ship with an iron hand, and was worshipped by the crew. But he could not rule his own destructive passions, or hide from himself his secret shame . . .

CARTWRIGHT—His domain was on land, in the jungle of commerce. Men feared him, and he had given them ample cause for that fear. But now he was on strange territory, on the pitching deck of a storm-tossed ship, and for the first time he knew the chill touch of terror . . .

JENNY—Her vivid red hair was the color of passion, but her mind was cool and calculating. She was the final prize of this dangerous voyage, as with full sails and a wake of bubbling white foam, the *Calcutta Eagle* moved ever closer to incredible riches—or shattering disaster . . .

THE LADY AND THE DEEP BLUE SEA

BY GARLAND ROARK

CURTIS
BOOKS

MODERN LITERARY EDITIONS PUBLISHING COMPANY,
NEW YORK, N.Y.

To Sally Burk

PART ONE

1

□ The big clipper was slanting her masts alee when the captain's wife appeared on the quarter-deck and braced herself for the snap roll to windward. As the ship roared on for Boston harbor, Jenny Broadwinder found her sea legs, moved to the lee rail, and stood gazing out over the water.

At a glance, one might believe her sea-weary and dreaming of land and flowers after a long voyage from India; or one could imagine that she was thinking of a home which the handsome captain on the weather side might have promised her after four years of married life at sea.

Her stance, the tilt of her head, seemed copied in a way, reminding one of a proud woman posing for a full-length portrait against a background of open sea and sky. On this May afternoon of 1856 she wore a dress and matching bonnet of royal blue; above the full skirt a corseted waist accentuated the lines of bosom and hips and added breadth to shoulders already extended by puffed sleeves. Blue whipcord and lace closeted her wrists and throat, and the white lace edging the hood of her bonnet, together with a large cerise bow at her neck, framed a small oval face.

Perhaps the mouth was a trifle generous, nostrils sensitively thin for an upturned nose, the forehead rather high and her blue eyes unduly large. Individually they fell short of artistic perfection; collectively they gave the face a great deal of character.

Missing in her expression was the expected stamp of endured emptiness that marked most seafaring women. At best, a woman's life at sea was confinement few could endure for long. Seas and oceans and more of the same days and weeks on end, small quarters, one's out-of-doors limited to the length and width of decks, often with only men for company and, always, danger, lurking over every horizon provoked crankiness, fear, and sudden outbursts of temper. Jenny Broadwinder had fought with these things and more during her first years afloat, though in her own mind her greatest achievement had been less a partial victory over boredom and fear and more in accepting the challenge of ship and seas. All in her own way, all in secret.

On the surface she maintained her position as the captain's demure lady, made it her business to win the love and respect of every man aboard. She dressed meticulously, appeared on deck at regular intervals, regardless of weather, read or crocheted under the awning on balmy days, spoke cheerily to all, and accorded her husband and the officers the proper nautical address. All the while, even at times when she instructed the cabin boy in mathematics and spelling, she kept a finger on the pulse of the ship without seeming to do so.

And now, under her attitude of quiet dreaminess, Jenny was conscious of all about her. Her glance lifted inquiringly to the lookout in the foretop and dropped to her husband. Supposing she had entertained the thought of living ashore a moment before, she knew it to be purely transient, for since dawn, port entry and the maze of events likely to separate husband and wife had dominated her.

The ship rocked along, tossing up spray as it gave to the scend of the waves. Masts played a wider arc against the sky, falling from port to starboard with rhythmic grace. The ship's bell announced the half hour with a single sharp note that rolled off across the ocean. The rent healed and the creaking of blocks and the voice of the wind eddying down through cavities of sail once again blended peacefully with the swish of water down the runner's sides.

Jenny walked to the taffrail, looked into the hooded binnacle, and smiled at the helmsman spinning the big double wheel. "Our lookout has us on tenterhooks," she said.

"Aye, Mrs. Broadwinder, that 'e has."

"Anxious to see the new little Murphy, aren't you?"

The big redhead grinned. "For the wings of a gull, ma'am, I'd soon know whether 'tis girl or boy."

"Well, Johnny Baker will cry land soon or this ship will see the master's lady joining the lookout."

She moved slowly to the weather side and stood at the rail just abaft her husband. Port entry always evoked in her a certain uneasiness which she was forced to contain under a guise of excitement. An admiring public expected Captain Philip Broadwinder to open the harbor in the usual spectacular fashion, all sails full and yards lined with men putting them in harbor stow. However, the deck watch seemed asleep. Furthermore, the captain's coat showed the marks of salt spray and a thin stubble shaded his weather-tanned cheeks. She sucked in her nether lip and thought of all that should be done before the tower watch at the Hull station brought the ship under his telescope. Then she was thinking Philip might need a reminder.

At his side, she said, "I told the steward to send warm water below and I laid out your razor, Captain Broadwinder." As he touched his cheek, she added, "Also a new coat. And since you're going below, send up my reticule please."

"Since I'm going?" A wide grin broke the repose of his face. "You're a remarkable woman, Mistress Jenny."

Sending his glance aloft, he ordered the lookout to sharpen his eyes, then turned to his chief mate. "Mr. Fortune, when Baker cries the land, you'll break out the fore and main royals and run out the studding booms." He glanced in the direction of Boston. "And have every hand show presentable when we dock."

As he moved toward the after companionway, Jenny fell in step beside him. "I recall your saying something about a new flying jib."

"Aye. Will you tell Mr. Fortune to fly it?" His broad mouth pursed and he gave her a brief kiss. "And remind me to sail in this direction ashore."

"Meaning me? That I shall, sir," she replied, meeting his gaze. "If I can locate you once we touch land. Now along with you, Captain. And don't forget my reticule."

Broadwinder had scarcely left the deck when the lookout cried: "Land ho!"

Instantly, the chief mate's hands cupped at his face. "All hands!" The "fo'c's'le" gang poured out. Orders deafened ears and strong, red-faced topmen scrambled aloft to fling canvas to the wind. High up, they were soon loosening gaskets to a rousing chorus of "Sir, I'll choose your daughter Alice to a sperm whale any day." Then the royal sails blossomed white in the blazing sunlight. Out ran the booms beyond the yardarms. "Stun's'ls all!" Clews were hauled out and, there, the *Calcutta Eagle* was "wearing bonnets." And crawling up the flying-jib stay was a spanking-new triangle, white as the fresh wake boiling under the ship's counter.

As more sail was added, Jenny felt the ship surge forward.

Smiling now, she clung to the forward poop rail, murmuring as she gazed Boston way, "Here we come, in true Broadwinder style."

West by north over the clipper's horizon lay the town of Hull with its signal station on Telegraph Hill, where, from a small tower on this bright afternoon, a lookout searched the unbroken chop of water all the way to the indefinite blue rim of sea and sky.

His gaze slowly swept the horizon until a faint speck of white above Scituate Neck caught and held his attention. Through the telescope he made out the fore royal and topgallant sails of a ship lifting fast from under the curve of ocean. With her identity cloaked in the haze of distance, the lookout checked a list of the ships expected by the merchants of Boston who maintained the station in order to obtain advance notice of the arrival of vessels, and waited for the hull to break horizon.

Minutes later, the vessel rose up full, a tall three-master heeling for Boston harbor under a great press of canvas. In quick time the vessel took on shape and dimension, and the pennant apeak was magnified into a white swallowtail bordered in blue, with a red letter C central. The lookout not only recognized the famous house flag, but found it relatively easy to identify the ship by the way she was handled, for only one captain sustained such an approach.

The lookout knew the old sea was not kind to all ships. Many vessels limped in under jury masts and many more arrived too weary to emulate this flash packet's entrance.

The ship roared closer, slicing the seas into fans with her cut-water and spreading foamy lace far out from a tea-colored hull and on into her long wake. On the springs of the sea she rolled her masts from port to starboard, throwing up the burnished copper of her hull to flash golden in the sunlight. Then she was dipping her colors in a singular fashion, further proving that the celebrated captain stood her quarter-deck. The salute was his trade-mark, and the very fact that he did not confine his courtesies to only the big ships of the stream further set him apart from the run of clipper captains.

As though a notable's fair lady had just honored him with a graceful curtsy, the lookout smiled and forgot that sailing ships no longer stirred up boyhood enchantment in an old man. A moment of his youth recaptured, he formed the message which was quickly relayed to Boston by magnetic wire:

"The India Commercial Line's *Calcutta Eagle* opening the harbor at a fast clip."

The wire was no sooner acknowledged in Boston than the firm's house flag was hoisted to the signal tower atop the Merchants Exchange. It flattened in the breeze to give Boston advance notice of another clipper homing her way into port. The news spread quickly along State, India, and Broad streets, into countinghouses and lofts and onto the slip piers, where an errand boy in the service of the India Commercial Line heard it and broke into a run for the firm's headquarters on Merchants Row. That he was the first to break the news there was made evident by what followed his earsplitting cry of:

"Cap'n Broadwinder's crowding sail for Commercial Wharf!"

The white-headed cashier came alive and darted excited glances at long rows of desks where clerks were getting to their feet. Business was forgotten. The cashier grinned, stepped out of his cage, and moved briskly toward the private office of the shipowner. The door was opened before he reached it by the man whose initial decorated the house flag.

"I heard, Samuel. The lad has a foghorn voice."

"Yes, sir. Now, do I humor the clerks, and shall I order a carriage for you?"

"Perhaps I should warn Captain Broadwinder to enter port after office hours in the future. But let them go. I'll trust you to deliver my compliments to our captain and his lady, as well as my regrets at being detained."

"But, sir, it's Captain Broadwinder! You know how he comes in."

"Yes, yes, I know."

George Cartwright re-entered his office and stood before a water color between two oil paintings of ships. Sketched was the full masculine face of a big man with cap set at rakish angle. There was a devilish smile on his wide mouth, and in his eyes there seemed enough energy for two men. Yes, George Cartwright knew how Philip Broadwinder came in. Small wonder he caused such to-do in harbors the world over, or that men called him the "Prince of Sea Captains!"

George Cartwright could scarcely contest the opinion of men, since merchants clamoring for quick deliveries of cargoes and return goods liked Broadwinder's speed and luck. He doubted if there was a master from Maine to Florida who inspired such confidence. A paradox of the first water, indeed, for the face in the ebony-and-gilt frame was not a prudent one.

Which was neither here nor there, the shipowner admitted. Prudence, skill, or luck—they were all the same in effect —were in this case submerged by a personality, dwarfed by a paragon of sail. And Captain Broadwinder would continue his merry, ostentatious way, as he was probably demonstrating at that very moment, until some impulsive act stripped him down to a mere man capable of error. On the other hand, there was no sane reason for circumspection, Cartwright admitted.

Comical, in a way, he thought. How his friends and rival shipowners would laugh at this analysis of his most profitable captain! Touched by the humor of it, he smiled wryly, thinking it odd indeed that a popular asset should be catalogued in his mind a secret liability. However, as with other matters in the past, his private opinion justified a feeling of chronic uneasiness. To his way of thinking, the honors bestowed upon Captain Broadwinder were greater than he deserved, for Philip had so long walked arm in arm with luck that his ability to cope with real trouble seemed a virtue untested.

The thought trend led to Philip's wife, and Cartwright was aware that seldom had he glanced at the picture of her husband during the four years it had hung there without recalling the day in Medford when the *Calcutta Eagle* was launched in the Mystic River. The daughter of Nathaniel Cornish, a fourth-generation shipwright, and the former Molly Penhallow, of an old and respected seafaring family of Bath, Maine, Miss Cornish was considered a spinster and excellent schoolteacher at twenty-five. Although Jenny had never so much as seen Philip Broadwinder until that day the schools let out, as they did for launchings in Medford, she permitted him to escort her home after the ceremony.

George Cartwright walked to his desk and sat down.

Prior to that day in Medford, Jenny had drawn his own glances with something more than a pretty face. Lurking in her eyes had been a quality that both attracted and puzzled him. There was no explanation for it unless one believed in the existence of some strange harmony that is born of a mere glance. He enjoyed thinking this was so, despite its visionary aspect and despite the fact that she became Philip's wife before they rigged the ship in Boston a few weeks later.

He gazed at the papers on his desk and tried to concentrate on the cargo aboard the *Calcutta Eagle,* only to find himself thinking that a long voyage was rather hard on a pretty woman. Then he was walking toward a window, passing a mirror, he paused to study inquiringly his own reflection—a man of slim figure and a touch of gray at the temples, one whom few had ever called handsome. Every once in a while someone used the word distinguished, and he was agreeably pleased to rate that much.

His glance shifted again to Captain Broadwinder's picture, then back to the mirror. In the frame was dash. In the mirror was dignity. Cartwright's father had been a proper Bostonian, after the usual creditable adventures in sail. The shipping business had been handed down to him by his father also. Three generations, one line, one name, one house flag, one pattern of living. There was little a Cartwright of Boston could ask for. Why his sister, Julia, had spoken those very words last evening.

Poor, precise Julia. The various methods she employed in her reach for some relation of harmony with her own empty social position. How she would stiffen if he should so much as hint that there was one thing a Cartwright might ask for; that being the winning manner of Philip Broadwinder where one woman was concerned: Philip's wife.

His brow lifted. The fact exposed took on an ugly countenance. In self-defense he returned to his desk and fell to work in earnest. When, two hours later, Samuel entered his office, it was the Yankee merchant who slowly pushed his chair back and said, "Well, Samuel, I suppose he put on the show for which he is famous."

"To the credit of the house, sir. Scarcely paused to pick up the pilot, and swung his yards around to the other tack in record time. But begging your pardon, sir, Mrs. Broadwinder is waiting to see you."

Cartwright suppressed a start. "You mean Captain Broadwinder?"

"No. His friends carried him off in a victoria."

"Hmmm. You gave him my message of course." Thinking of Jenny Broadwinder and preparing himself for the meeting ahead, he scarcely heard the cashier's reply. Then he was bidding Samuel show her in.

On his feet before the door opened, Cartwright waited tense and expectant. Then he was looking into the serious, intelligent face of the small woman entering his office. It was the same finely chiseled face he had seen often, though he was searching it for the quiet beauty he had discovered years before in Medford.

Her glance was direct as she moved to the chair he indicated and acknowledged his greeting. Then she sat down, smiled briefly, and removed her gloves before saying, "Captain Broadwinder was unavoidably detained, sir. Knowing you were anxious to examine the papers, he asked me to bring them."

"Yes," he said, looking past her talkative eyes to tendrils of red-brown hair under her bonnet, admiring her even as he realized that she sat before him with a straight face and a falsehood on her lips.

Samuel entered with her portmanteau, followed by a clerk carrying a box which seemed uncommonly heavy for its size.

"An object Captain Broadwinder found in Rangoon," she said, before asking the cashier to pry the lid.

"For me?" Watching her as she nodded, Cartwright could not fail to notice the way she seemed to thaw out of a guarded reserve. "Now what could he bring this time?" he said, removing an object from the box.

He looked up suddenly from a small gold-plated temple statue of a supreme deity of Hinduism. Oddly enough, the captain had remembered for two years now his admiration for a similar though less imposing Siva.

Jenny smiled. "You are wondering how Captain Broadwinder could afford a piece set with gems. He couldn't and didn't. Nor can I tell you how he came by it without actually stealing it."

"Then I won't ask. I'll just admire it and say it is now the prize item of my India collection."

She was opening the case and getting down to business when he asked about the voyage. "Rather uneventful," she replied. "The captain figured his monsoons correctly. The ice drift slowed us on our easting down. But it is all recorded."

One by one, she placed papers before him; all in relative importance from manifest down to disbursement vouchers. "You will notice," she was saying, "Captain Broadwinder effected a substantial saving over the last voyage. He sailed with fewer men before the mast. Victualing bills were reduced. Also repair cost was kept at a minimum."

"Yes," he said, meeting her raised glance. "Excellent," he added, breaking his stare.

"Here are the articles, light certificates, bills of health, deviations from voyage—the latter due to icebergs and a Chilean bark flying her union down—in distress, sir—under Africa. Now let's see, clearance labels and certificates of pratique, and the log, of course."

He examined each item briefly with concealed appreciation for her businesslike dispatch and knowledge of each subject.

"One other item, sir. Captain Broadwinder asked that I explain the alteration in the logbook. Under the date of April tenth you'll note small damage to tea cargo. Poor battens on a hatch. Estimated damage is listed."

"This isn't the captain's handwriting," he said.

"I was in need of some responsibility. Crocheting became dull after a time." What she said next seemed to take the crochet needle out of her hands. "Captain Broadwinder, incidentally, is interested in stepping the ship with teakwood masts. They seem to defy the typhoons of the China Sea."

He said, to cover his thoughts, "Eh? a costly proposition."

She argued well, however, and left an impression that her husband might be maturing. At thirty he should. She was one year younger, though perhaps a dozen years his senior in wisdom. A most unconventional and fascinating woman.

"Oh yes," she said. "As usual, Captain Broadwinder took advantage of his privilege of sending ventures to foreign ports. There was room to fetch back cheroots, Manila indigo, and sandalwood." Handing over the papers, she said, "He wishes to apply the proceeds once more to his accumulated fund for the purchase of a greater interest in the ship."

"Splendid. At this rate, he'll soon own half of her."

"God speed the day, sir. It is too bad he doesn't own half of her now while he is favored with good fathoms between ship and reefs. It can't last forever, you know."

"No," Cartwright said thoughtfully. "But Philip sails in luck and skill. And popularity. I remember when your husband was just another captain."

"He's fast changed our skies," she replied.

"Indeed he has." Feeling her bid for that exra quarter interest in the ship, he thought to forestall her trading instincts. "Of course," he added lightly, "we have the utmost faith in Philip, whereas with another captain we might wonder if his popularity loomed as a threat to his vigilance as a sailing man."

She caught the meaning in full. Her face softened into a

smile that did not reach her eyes. "Only a Yankee ship-owner could so discount an asset, Mr. Cartwright."

He tried to cover his annoyance. Men didn't deal with one another in this manner and he, quite unused to this sort of thing, felt an upsurge of resentment toward Broadwinder for sending her here. Now were the captain himself in her place, he could open up and say:

"Look here, Captain, aren't you forgetting a few little incidents that are best summed up as popularity misplaced—for example, that it was I and not you who set the precedent for sailing on or before the advertised day instead of keeping valuable cargo tied up, to the loss of shippers?"

Other examples likely to debate the captain's ego raced through his mind. But they were for a man's ear. And he had been too long in replying to her thrust. So he merely smiled it off.

Then she was standing to take her leave. The interview had ended.

"May I drive you to the hotel?" he said, suddenly anxious to lengthen his moments with her.

"It would be very kind of you, sir."

He called Samuel, ordered a carriage, and placed the ship's papers in the vault. In the interval of waiting she browsed about his office looking at this picture and that. Pausing before a painting of the firm's ill-fated *Bengal Runner*, she said:

"Struck a reef." Turning to him, she added, "See what I mean?"

He did. This was intended to remind him that the luck of even a Broadwinder would run out sooner or later. Meeting her glance briefly, he said, more in self-defense under the guise of jest, "I see what you mean, all right. Though I refuse to admit it."

She appraised him anew, her eyes alive with challenge. "Oh, I think you'll admit it, but in the words of Captain Broadwinder, do you care to place a wager on it, that is, bet you won't admit it?"

She had him cornered and he knew it. "Why, yes," he replied with a suddenness that surprised him. "You name the amount."

"The sum that separates Captain Broadwinder from a half interest in the *Calcutta Eagle*."

He was staring intently at her when she changed the subject so adroitly that he was left far behind. Then Samuel entered and advised that a carriage was waiting. As Cartwright made ready to go, she said, "Haven't you forgotten something, Mr. Cartwright?"

His glance sharpened inquiringly.

"A receipt for the ventures, sir."

"Of course, of course," he said, feeling the color diffusing his face. Turning abruptly to the vault, he made a second attempt at humor. "Never would I have said a Cartwright tried to beat a lady in a trade."

"It's the other way about, sir." A provocative smile tugged at the corners of her lips. "I refer to our friendly wager."

As they followed Samuel outside, Cartwright grimaced. The terms of the wager were rather vague. Now it was coming back to him. He had side-stepped her bid for extra shares in the ship by refusing to trade on the assumption that Philip courted disaster at sea; a contradiction of his opinion, he mused. But it was all in fun and, of course, meaningless, more like a dare.

Soon the carriage was rolling and she was relating an incident of the voyage that had to do with a challenge dropped in Singapore by a rival shipping firm's Captain Mayo Keys:

"He publicly stated that he would race Captain Broadwinder to any place at any time, sir. Captain Broadwinder's answer was, 'At the right time and place, Captain Keys.'"

"An excellent reply. Racing is hard on a ship. I recall the time he blew the sticks out of the *Eagle* while running the bark *Panther* for San Francisco."

"But we won! And at the Parker House in San Francisco a dozen captains, including the *Panther's* master, called it skill, since Captain Broadwinder could get along without the light sails and masts he blew."

"I was speaking of damage and prudence. However, I suppose your way of looking at it is more sporting."

"Sporting?" she said, almost accusingly. "Competitive is a better word, don't you think?"

She was looking up State Street, with firmness in her voice and expression. "It is strange that you don't feel a part of it, considering the over-all effect on business."

Before he could form any answer, she said, "One's view of life and business from an office chair evidently dulls one's sense of adventure. Do you agree? Now perhaps I should ask the cause of the uneasiness you feel about your ship under Captain Broadwinder. But I won't.

"Because you are a businessman who is far from blind to the value of a good sailing captain, let alone a popular ambassador of the line. From a standpoint of money you can hardly censure sailing methods that make for speedy voyages, any more than you can doubt the broad vision of Captain Broadwinder, which, along with his quick wit and charm, has lifted him from relative obscurity to his place as the 'Prince of Sea Captains.'"

"Of course——"

"And you will agree that some few men shine as symbols of something infinitely greater than the men themselves. In Captain Broadwinder one sees ships and sails and big water and is aware of some fascinating mystery beyond one's grasp."

"I cannot argue that any more than——"

"Nor, Mr. Cartwright, can we forget that a mortal is only as strong as his faithfulness to that which he is committed to. If there is merit to that which he serves, he is all the stronger. Now if you'll pardon my long speech, sir, I'll say in the vernacular of the sea, sits the wind in that quarter?"

As though he had done the talking, Cartwright drew a deep breath and came up with a lame "To be sure."

Turning her face to him, she gave visible proof that her aroused spirit was not yet on the ebb. A touch of color still lingered under her skin and her eyes were every bit as penetrating as before. He waited expectantly.

"Mr. Cartwright, unless my judgment is in error, you took our wager lightly. I was never more serious, I assure you. Beyond this fact, I realize that from your countinghouse you can never properly visualize the dangers accompanying a ship at sea, any more than you can fully appreciate the Captain Broadwinder I just brought to your attention." Following a moment's pause, she said:

"In my opinion, sir, a voyage aboard your *Eagle* should prove most enlightening to you."

Her words, tone, and expression and outspokenness left Cartwright speechless. For an instant he looked as if she had slapped him. Then her challenge struck him in full force, and his scattered thoughts crystallized into a reply:

"Perhaps your visit today is just the tonic I needed, Jenny."

He had never called her Jenny before. As she flashed him a look of surprise, her head cocked curiously, he smiled and felt pleasantly bold about it. He thought for a moment he held the initiative and vowed to himself to cling to it. Then he realized how false and betraying one's quick judgment could be. Her quiet suggestion that he enlighten himself by going to sea paled all else.

A little later George Cartwright returned to his office with Jenny's challenge still ringing in his mind. The first object to meet his glance was the gift from Captain Broadwinder. He looked at the sketch on the wall. The expression in the Broadwinder face had not changed one iota. His cap was set at the same rakish angle, or perhaps more so since Jenny's gallant defense of his "sailing methods, broad vision, quick wit and charm"; since she created of him a symbol of the seas. He admired her courage and loyalty and, grudgingly, even her assaults on a shipowner's way of life which, up to her coming, he had thought quite unassailable.

Perhaps she was right about Philip. Totally right. He withheld judgment for the present. An idea was forming in his mind, one likely to settle the matter once and for all.

For more than an hour he checked the flow of goods from Boston to San Francisco and on to the Orient, as well as current demand cargoes from China, India, and the Dutch East Indies. The winds "blew profitable" both ways for any shipowner. Poring over maps, he routed more than a voyage. Ordinarily he took his time in advertising embarkation, since every ship required time in port for repairs and loading. But a change was taking place in George Cartwright. He was in the grip of a reckless adventure. His next move would prove it.

There was still a little daylight left when he sent for Samuel and asked him to read a letter he had written to Mr. James Oliver Barking, head of the rival firm of Barking & Pevy.

Samuel adjusted his spectacles and read:

Begging your indulgence and consideration of the proposition herein, which I am confident will arouse your interest, I submit the following in friendly spirit:

It stems from an incident in Singapore, wherein your capable commander Mayo Keys of the extreme clipper ship Emperor challenged our Captain Broadwinder of the Calcutta Eagle to a race any time to any place, to which Captain Broadwinder replied, "At the right time and place, Captain Keys."

Now since we are aware of the sporting qualities inherent

to the business of shipping, differing to horse racing only in time and distance and, I may add, the favorable effect upon shipping, I am wondering if you care to entertain the idea of a race between our captains to the extent of joining me in a discussion of ports and destinations to our mutual advantage.

With highest esteem for a worthy competitor, I am,

Your obedient servant,
George Bertram Cartwright

Samuel's jaws hung on their hinges and his old eyes danced with a mixture of disbelief and excitement. He held the letter a moment while trying to reconcile the challenge to the man who penned it. He knew that proper and staid Bostonians—Cartwrights—seldom resorted to quick decisions; rather, decisions of this nature were reached only after ample thought and no end of arguments. Which was not, could not, be the case here. But if the motive remained a puzzle, the clear portent of the letter was far from it. George Cartwright was being born all over again and in the pattern of his father before him.

Slowly forming on Samuel's face was a hard grin of appreciation. "By gadfrey, sir, we're beginning to live!"

He said more. The city would turn its pockets inside out for wager money; that he would relish the honor of rousting old Oliver Barking out of sound sleep just to see the expression of his face. That he would.

"The quicker the better, Samuel. Julia and I will be at home."

"Captain Broadwinder will sail circles around Mayo Keys," Samuel said in departing.

George Cartwright could not speak his mind in reply any more than he could advise Samuel of his decision to watch the race, should it materialize, from the deck of the *Calcutta Eagle*. All the way, if only to test the quality of steel in the captain's mainspring. And, of course, there was Jenny.

2

☐ While dining alone that evening, Jenny gave considerable thought to her recent meeting with George Cartwright. She continued to resent his vague remarks concerning Philip. His attitude in general seemed beyond the surprise it had evoked in her, the very opposite of what one might expect. Had Philip lost him money on the voyage or brought damage to the ship, one could understand, at least excuse, his strange uneasiness. She supposed she had gone a little far in defending her sailing man. Certainly she had never made such a speech before. All for dear Philip, who with perfect ease and impunity left her to shift for herself.

The memory of his departure that afternoon was poignantly fresh. His friends had boarded the *Eagle*, and the ringleaders of the welcoming committee had made much to-do over the captain's wife. Small, quick-witted, and wicked Angus McGovern, the East Boston shipbuilder, had rolled his r's against each other in praise of a woman who went to sea with such an undeserving man as Broadwinder. The big, pink-jowled cordage manufacturer, Cottingham, had been equally attentive, as had Bronson the State Street banker. They didn't for a minute fool her, not one of that guileless group, with their gifts and nice talk. It was apparent that they meant it to be a stag affair. They had come for Philip. Mrs. Bronson had extended an invitation to Mrs. Broadwinder, to be sure, and the little Scot's wife came later to offer the captain and his wife quarters in their Beacon Hill house. But the men had departed in McGovern's victoria after a rousing chorus in the ship's saloon:

> *Cape Cod cats they have no tails,*
> *Heave away, heave away!*
> *They lost them in the sou'east gales,*
> *We're bound for Californiay!*

And now in her room, facing the boxes and chests from the ship, she could easily imagine the merriment at one of Boston's exclusive clubs. Perhaps at this very moment Philip was telling another of his suspenseful but wild yarns of the sea, or making a remark that would invite rejoinders as vicious as harpoon thrusts. From Philip's accounts of these gatherings, a woman's place was out of earshot.

"Oh well," she said, with not quite a sigh, and turned her attention to the businss of emptying trunks and the maze of bags and boxes; all of which indicated an indefinite stay in port.

Several hours later Jenny brushed a lock of hair from her eyes and sat down. At last the work was done. She heard a clock tolling the hour of midnight. Suppressing a yawn, she rose wearily and crossed the room to a curtained window. There she looked out on the pale fall of moonlight dimmed by the lights of Boston.

It reminded her of the night before, when the moon dominated sea and ship. No interference from the land, no waiting up for Philip.

Drawing a deep breath, she turned away from the window. She was soon brushing her hair in long, slow strokes, trying as she did so to forget that she had spent the entire evening unpacking and making the room a tidy and friendly abode. Now everything was in order, shipshape.

And she was still alone.

This was no doubt the first of many such nights, she thought, saying aloud, "I'm half a mind to go home."

She could see in memory the moon riding high over Medford. She had entered the world to the sounds of a shipwright's adz and saw. Often she had visited the Thatcher Magoun yard on Riverside Avenue south of Park Street to watch her father work with infinite care on ships for the deep stream. She could not count the times she had crossed the square easterly to Ship Street and passed by the old rum distillery and pretty meadows in her strolls to Gravelly Bridge. There she had dreamed of the future, effortlessly, romantically, of adventures that had to do with ships, of some prince among the men who sailed them. While in the distance a blacksmith's hammer on anvil at the Medford Shipyard sounded in her visionary mind eight bells at sea as a tall vessel rolled in the waves under full sail, with shadows of the rigging moving back and forth across deck.

At such times the romantic spells of girlhood had so completely possessed her that she felt the frightening warmth of blood rushing into every fiber of her being. It was the same after she grew into womanhood.

She had walked with Philip to Gravelly Bridge on the evening of the day they had met. The moonlight made a silver ribbon of the Mystic River as it flowed placidly by on its way to the sea. Along the riverbank were surfaces of hewn logs, edges of flaring bows, a crescent-shaped rib of some future clipper ship's skeleton—a bone from Adam to create a woman, as all ships were—the anonymity of ladder rungs, taut lines of guy ropes, and the yellow pine from Maine in stacked rows together with white oak for her scantling, all these things in ghostly but sweet shimmer. How veiled and vague they had seemed, though how very real, for she had in her trance turned them into sliding ways down which dreams were launched.

Never would she forget the surge of happiness in her heart when Philip took her in his arms and kissed her there on the old bridge that night. It was the beginning, the promise of life in its fullest. Dreams were no longer idle dreams.

And now she had memories for company. The days, months, and short years of their marriage, the sweet and the bitter. There had been times when she, jealous of his duties on deck, felt as an adultress must in a dimly lit room with a man married to a ship. What was that power of sail and deck over the hearts and muscles of men? She knew, for she had shared it with Philip. It was a magic of movement, of a dream, in which the numbing bitterness of Cape Horn gale seemed as sweet as fast seas touched by tropic stars. Though a sailing adventure began in a countinghouse, a cold business proposition, every voyage remained the pursuit of a dream in the souls of men. As with Columbus, Magellan, and Drake. The world would change and ships would change, but the hearts of men would, like the sea, remain the same always.

Philip would never change. She knew this. And yet, how much change would she, if she could, make in him? Perhaps a great deal. Perhaps none. His charm and dash fed her pride and fears; his winning ways attracted women as well as men. She had been very jealous at times, and always possessive. But what wife wasn't?

Jenny listened, hoping the footsteps down the hall were Philip's. As the sound died away, she turned down the coverlet and sat on the bed, thinking this was no way for a husband to treat a wife on their first night ashore. But it was always like this. Had been since that night when he stood at a public gathering and flung a challenge across the Atlantic to capture the fancy of a nation. As brief as audacious, it had launched him in the public eye. She recalled her own feeling of excitement as his voice boomed forth with:

"You sea-minded British put to sea a ship of the class and speed of the Yankee clipper and count your pounds sterling."

It did not matter that Captain Broadwinder had been in his cups at the time or that on the following morning he scarcely remembered voicing the challenge in the presence of the governor of the Commonwealth and the visiting British ambassador, his future popularity was assured.

Staring vacantly at the door, she wondered if it had been a happy accident. In a way yes, for he could not have imagined the effect of his speech. On the other hand no, for Philip had backed up his challenge with driving sail on the high seas. Recklessly, said many. Expertly, said others. Who was right and who was wrong? It would be interesting to see.

All else followed, for he completed voyages as he talked, with abounding energy. Form that day on she became more concerned with his adjustment to fame, with helping him grow with his reputation and improved position. It dominated her, and she admitted now that her efforts in this direction had been and were selfishly inspired by a single purpose of mind, that of protecting her happiness, guarding it against the fruits of Philip's popularity.

While crawling into bed, she paused, a worried frown knitting her brow. George Cartwright had suddenly crossed her mind again; rather, the thought of Philip evoked an awareness that Cartwright intuitively felt the same undercurrent of trepidation concerning Philip that she had never been able to wholly dispel.

"The devil with Cartwright!" she said, slipping under the coverlet and snuggling down. "He's just another shipowner who thinks like one."

Jenny opened her eyes at dawn to see Philip entering the room. Piqued, she closed her eyes again and remained still and silent as he cried, "Look alive there, Mistress Jenny!"

One could not ignore a man like Philip; he would not allow

it. But she tried and for her pains she felt herself being scooped up into his arms.

"Philip!" Her sharp cry was accompanied by a futile struggle to escape. He laughed and drew her closer, then began to stagger across the room as though on a rolling deck, shouting orders fore and aft and up into an imaginary top hamper. Sail should come in at once, and two men were needed at the helm.

"Philip! You'll rouse the hotel!"

"Shall I let the poor souls drown? We're fast broaching to. And you can lay to that, me bonnie lass." His face was very close to hers when he paused in sudden intent study of her. "A right handsome woman I have here," he said. "Almost as pretty as the girl I met last night, the one with dimpled knees. Can you boast of dimples, girl?"

"Had dimples on her knees, did she?" she flared. "Just where have you been, Captain Broadwinder?"

"Captain? So ho!"

He laughed in her face, pinched her, enjoying the fire in her eyes, not knowing its depth. A man could plumb the sea, but never a woman. She was wondering if he would ever learn this when he renewed his antics, this time prancing about and whirling her in dizzy circles. Her head was spinning when he reeled to a stop and said:

"Remember the time thirty thousand people crossed over to East Boston to see McKay's *Great Republic* launched?"

Tightening her mouth into a thin line, she refused to answer. But she remembered. She had felt as a queen must, her hand tucked in Philip's arm. Someone had parodied for the occasion Cowper's poem entitled, *The Diverting History of John Gilpin, Showing How He Went Farther than He Intended, and Came Home Safe Again,* which was sung by the crowd. Then at the suggestion of none other than the famous builder of the *Flying Cloud,* McKay himself, the crowd substituted Philip's name for Gilpin's.

"Jenny girl, they sang the parody tonight." He raised his voice with it:

> "*Broadwinder is a mariner*
> *Of credit and renown,*
> *A train-bound captain eke is he*
> *Of famous Boston town.*

"Now let us sing—Long live the King,
And Broadwinder long live he;
And, when he next doth ride abroad,
May I be there to see!"

"Who sang it? The girl with the——?"

His wide mouth touched hers gently, teasingly. She squirmed and laughed above her protestations, all the while aware of his thought trend as well as her own growing desire to be crushed to him. All he was thinking was in his eyes now, in his retreating smile, and she dared not meet his full gaze. Instead, she averted her face and toyed with ideas of punishing him for leaving her alone all night. Foolish ideas, when he was so near, his lips brushing her cheeks and eyes; when such a soul as Philip's, as wild and free as the waves and winds of the seas he conquered, caused her to grow impatient of waiting for his kisses.

Her glance darted up at him and in the instant he read her mind, for her eyes were suddenly defenseless.

"I told them the mermaid yarn tonight," he said. "But you know, I almost forgot to take along the fish scale. Now wouldn't your fine captain have been thrown on his beam ends if that had happened?"

"It might teach you a lesson. But just which version of the story did you tell?"

"The one where you slipped down into the cabin and found us——" Her finger at his lips silenced him.

"Philip! You didn't!" She glared at him, then looked curious. "Or did you?"

"Well, no. I saved that one for the girl——"

"With the dimpled knees," she said for him.

She knew there had been no girl, and he was holding her near his heart now, very close to him; too close for her to just do nothing.

As she turned her face up to his, reaching for his mouth, she realized that he had purposely waited for her to do this very thing. Philip Broadwinder was a devil. But devil or saint, he belonged to her.

Then her hand was at the back of his neck and she, with the blood pounding loudly at her heartstrings, was drawing his face down to hers.

Afterward, when the morning sun sent a single bright ray through a crack in the curtains, Jenny lay very still beside him.

After long contented moments she sat up and looked down at his face in the repose of sleep. Smiling, she pushed the tousled hair from his forehead and bent to give him a gentle kiss.

3

□ Jenny Broadwinder dressed unhurriedly that morning, but with deliberate care. Though she tried to muffle the rustling of petticoats lest the sounds interrupt Philip's sleep, she thought the noise from the street below enough to wake even the dead. But this mariner, who at sea often leaped out of bed at the slightest sound, slept on as though deaf to the clatter of Boston. What a night he must have had. However, all this was beside the point. Shore attire to a woman who had spent months at sea was nothing short of a fascinating experience.

Philip had never seen her in the light blue dress she had cut and sewn between Rio and Boston. With lace of paler blue at the collar and sleeves and the blue necklace he had given her in Calcutta, she should not only look very presentable to his many friends at the Parker House dining room but strike a gleam of admiration from his appreciative eye.

A little later she sat before a mirror in critical study of herself. Her hair was carefully combed and arranged and her full mouth was generously red. Too red perhaps. She pondered this a while before toning it down a shade or two. Her cheeks had a healthy color and the blue of her eyes seemed to strike a compromise with the color of her dress and a Southern ocean.

At the very moment Jenny decided she gave an impression of ordered loveliness Philip almost frightened the wits out of her with an unexpected cry:

"Holy mackerel, a vision out of the blue!"

Her start and quick scolding glance tickled him immensely. He sat upright, studying her a minute before leaping out of bed. Despite her protest, he encircled her waist and drew her to him. Just as he seemed about to undo everything that had occupied her for more than an hour, a heavy rap sounded.

Darting him a triumphant glance, she disengaged herself and walked to the door. Opening it, she accepted an envelope from a messenger boy, returned for her reticule, and thanked the boy with smile and coin.

"Who was it, Jenny?" Philip asked, watching curiously as she broke the seal and handed him a note, which he read aloud:

" 'Congratulations, Philip. I believe you'll win by the length of a continent, but why the devil didn't you tell us about it at the party?'

"From Cottingham," he said, frowning in puzzled manner. "Maybe he's still drunk."

Jenny studied the note and eyed Philip narrowly. "Perhaps you drank a little too much yourself," she said accusingly. She stood in silent appraisal of him before saying, "Try to remember, Philip. Perhaps you made another world-startling speech last night."

"Lord forbid! Now all I said——" He rubbed the crease between his eyes with a forefinger. "No, I didn't say anything that would—let me see that paper again—'I believe you'll win by the length of a continent,' old Cott says."

"Did you by any chance mention that remark by Mayo Keys?"

Broadwinder glanced up, seeing her now as stern of face as a judge about to pronounce sentence. "No, not that I recall," he replied with marked uncertainty. "But wait a minute! Doesn't Cottingham ask right here why I didn't tell them at the party?"

Jenny raised her brows, took a step and whirled. "Where else did you go, Captain Broadwinder?"

Another rap at the door caused the anger building in her eyes to fall away. She answered the rap and returned with a somewhat similar message from Angus McGovern. As Philip read, she sat down and looked beyond him. She said nothing, though when he looked at her again there was no mistaking the quiet fury that had come into her expression.

"Jenny," he began, only to be cut short.

"Captain Broadwinder, I think I shall go to Medford. Alone."

"Medford? But why, Jenny? Just because a few friends decide to do a little rough joking? That's all it is. What else could it be?"

Her back was to him now. "I'm wondering, Philip. In fact, every time we touch the land I wonder what you'll do next. It's the uncertainty of it."

This was something new to Broadwinder. He rubbed the back of his neck and examined her with unbelief in his eyes. "The uncertainty?" he said. "What the devil has come over you, Jenny?"

She turned her face to him. "Your questionable behavior, Philip. This is not the first time."

"Nor the last," he retorted hotly. "And you can lay to that. When the time comes that Philip Broadwinder has to untie himself from your petticoat——"

"Enough, Philip!" Her chin lifted defiantly. "And don't you follow me to Medford."

The captain had been caught between wind and weather before, though not once had he resorted to luck or resigned prayer to effect a change for the better. In this instance, he took command of his "quarter-deck" in a manner that left no doubt as to who was the master. His voice was crisp and his words were clipped and brief as he told Jenny to "look alive and steer a course she would not soon regret." He added, in gentler tones, that any fool could run from the weather, though a wise seaman would check the force of a storm before risking his ship in a turn-and-run maneuver.

"The best ship can broach to, you know, Mistress Jenny. And so can a marriage."

As angry and determined as she was, she found herself in his arms before she realized what was happening to her. Then she was fighting back at the traitorous emotions that flooded her with unbidden fire. Trembling almost helplessly in his arms, she could feel the firmness of her lips dissolving under his.

"Stop, Philip!" she cried, slanting her face away from his. "Look what you're doing to my dress!"

His reply was silence, that and a sudden tilting of her head with his hand, so roughly done that she thought her neck was snapped.

Then the third messenger arrived, and Broadwinder stood with hands on hips, shaking his head. "The devil and his unholy imps!" he roared as Jenny almost ran for the door.

Soon he said, "From Bronson, the old scoundrel." Crumpling the note, he seemed by his expression to be making a choice between full-gale anger and mirth. Then he sank into a chair and laughed. Nor did he seem surprised in the least when Jenny, unmindful of her disarranged hair and dress, laughed with him.

Suddenly he sobered and gave her a fierce look. "Why the devil aren't you packing, Jenny?"

She made no reply, just eased herself into his lap and placed an arm about his neck.

"Now, Mistress Jenny, you'll listen to the captain's verdict. The next time you get any mutinous ideas, whether in Bombay, Borneo, or where, I'm going to put you aboard the first vessel bound for the States and send you straight to Medford. Is that clear?"

Jenny nestled her head on his shoulder and ran her fingers across his cheek. "Yes, Captain Broadwinder." Her face touched his. "I'm hungry. Very hungry," she said.

The captain and his lady had no sooner seated themselves and ordered lunch than old Samuel entered the Parker House dining hall grinning from ear to ear. His cheeks retained the happy, pushed-up wrinkles as he joined them, and Broadwinder thought he radiated more than a gleam of welcome from his squinted gray eyes. Samuel ordered a pot of coffee, nothing more, and continued to look as though the whole world was a huge joke designed for his amusement. After talk of this and that, he said:

"Captain, Mr. Cartwright would like an audience with you, that is if you can find time for him while in port."

Broadwinder laughed. Samuel cackled. Jenny looked curious. Then Samuel gulped coffee in amused silence. When he seemed fortified by the brew, he reached into his pocket and produced a newspaper.

"Read," he ordered brusquely.

Broadwinder did. So did Jenny. Their eyes grew wide as they fell on the bold type:

CAPTAIN BROADWINDER CHALLENGES CAPTAIN MAYO KEYS TO RACE FROM MELBOURNE TO BOSTON

As Philip demanded an explanation, Samuel said, "Now you know why Mr. Cartwright would enjoy seeing you, Captain."

"Sure, but who the devil is responsible for this?"

Samuel raised a bony finger to his lips. Leaning toward

Philip, he said in a whisper, "Doesn't the paper say you are, Captain?" His eye closed in a merry wink. "It's better for the trade that way."

Jenny bit her lower lip. Transferring her sharp glance from Philip to Samuel, she said, flashing a smile minus any humor, "You mean to say, of course, it is so typical of our dashing Captain Broadwinder that he might as well have flung the challenge himself."

"Right, Mrs. Broadwinder. So right that nobody would believe the Prince even if he denied it."

Jenny nodded, her expression sharp and wise as she confronted Samuel. "And since the race is to begin in Melbourne, I gather that the interested parties, Messrs. Cartwright and Barking, the dear souls, have figured the voyage to ensure no loss of tonnage or——"

"Freight rates," Samuel interposed. "But you meant to say your husband figured the voyage. Remember?" he said, pointing to the newspaper.

"Of course." Jenny smiled, her gaze sweeping around to Philip. "Captain Broadwinder, I owe you an apology."

"Apology? Oh yes. To be sure," he replied almost in detachment, adding contemplatively, "Melbourne to the Horn. The long, rough easting down. On up to Boston." Then he rubbed his jaw vigorously, a puzzled expression on his face. "I can understand that, but what I can't understand is George Cartwright. It isn't like him."

"No, it isn't," Samuel agreed, behind a wide grin.

"Nor Oliver Barking." Philip studied Samuel closely. "And just how the devil did either of them learn about Mayo? His challenging me in Singapore?"

Jenny dropped her glance. Samuel turned his palms up. Broadwinder frowned, said at last, "So! Seems we'll make a merry sea chase of it. You can count on that—with Mayo so far astern of me the *Eagle* will sprout barnacles in Boston before he opens the harbor."

"Aye! Aye!" Samuel's eyes glittered. "That's the way I'm betting, Cap'n. Now would you mind meeting the newspaper reporters in that frame of mind—say at three this afternoon?"

Jenny ate in silence, scarcely aware of the tremendous amount of driving canvas Philip and Samuel were volubly flinging to the big winds of the roaring forties. A strange feeling of guilt assailed her, for there was no denying that she alone was responsible for this unhappy state of affairs. Cartwright had neatly turned her defense of Philip against her by planning a race she did not in the least desire. He had seized upon her unwitting account of Philip's reply to Captain Keys in Singapore and overnight launched a great sailing adventure. Cartwright had done this! But why? As Philip had said, it was not like George Cartwright. For some reason, he had stepped out of character.

She lifted her glance to Philip, who was becoming more enthusiastic by the moment, and slowly dropped her eyes as the shipowner's remark of the day before rang fresh in memory: "Perhaps your visit today is just the tonic I needed." And he had addressed her as "Jenny."

Jenny was of a sudden minus appetite. As she put down her fork, Philip eyed her, asked why she appeared so glum. With no ready answer, she forced a smile and lifted her fork again. Then she seemed to realize that she was after all a part of Philip and therefore a person vitally touched by the adventure, which facts made demands on her. She should, must, act the part. During the next half hour she feigned a degree of excitement by remark and expression, and before Samuel and Philip departed for a meeting with Cartwright something of her pretense had ignited a real spark. It continued to burn inside her as she returned to her room, only to slowly go out under the inroads of nagging questions concerning Cartwright's motives.

As questions provoke questions, she was soon asking if Cartwright had made the bold move simply to put an end to any existing doubt concerning Philip. Or—and her eyes widened with the asking—was it actually a manifestation of something she had seen in his eyes, as when he called her "Jenny"; something she had refused to believe? Even if it were true, there was no sane adjustment of his personal regard for her to a race.

George Cartwright's uneasiness regarding his most profitable captain was something she could not put aside as an error in her judgment. She seemed to know that he was putting Philip Broadwinder to the iron test.

Several hours later Philip returned, both jubilant and contemplative. He paced back and forth from door to window, reminding her of his quarter-deck tread from weather to lee rail, face to wind and back to wind. By thunder, he had used the situation created by the shipowner to make a few demands. She asked what sort of demands, hoping strongly that he had bargained for the extra quarter interest in the ship that would make him half owner.

"New copper on her bottom and stout Manila. And"—he turned to her, face beaming—"we'll step a new mainmast and bend on fresh cotton, Mistress Jenny."

"Oh?"

"Right. And—'Since this is your proposition, Mr. Cartwright,' I said, 'there'll be no empty bunks in fo'c's'le aboard of me this run.' Of course, his purse made his tongue wag lively a while but he soon belayed. However——" He stopped short, frowning and stroking his chin and cheeks.

"Then he got red under the collar. Asked me this, mind you, Jenny, *me*, if I didn't want all the crazy high sails such as Angels' Whispers, Jimmy Greens, and Trust-in-God sails above moons'ls. Said I should not forget that it was he, not I, who had thought of sailing on an advertised date instead of when laden, that he had done as much as I toward furthering my popularity, with innovations that better served those who paid the freight rates.

"Beginning there, we had a real lively time. I blew a strong and righteous wind. I asked him if he drove the *Eagle* in the gales around Cape Stiff to record voyages while I sat smug as a toasted kitten in his office. Well, with that, he took in sail in one fine hurry."

"Good for you, Philip!" she exclaimed, eyes dancing.

"But then he handed me a jolt." Palming his chin, Broadwinder gazed thoughtfully at the floor. "He said he was boarding the *Calcutta Eagle* for the entire voyage."

Jenny felt her heart skip a beat. For a long moment she studied her husband with unbelief, then with head cocked, a sharpening and thinning intensity coming into her eyes. Cartwright's decision to sail with them seemed to upset all previous calculations. But only for the time it required to adjust the surprise in her mind. Then she was thinking that this bit of news served to prove her former conclusions—perhaps even the things she had discarded as vain thoughts, his regard for her as he called her "Jenny." And the very fact that he had accepted her challenge to go to sea did nothing to alter it.

4

□ The weeks that followed were busy and exciting ones to all directly concerned with the much-heralded race. Following the big surprise dealt by Cartwright, Broadwinder threw himself into the task of preparing for more than just another voyage. Every rope, plank, and inch of canvas required inspection by experienced eyes. A seaman did not look at a frayed line or sail edge with happy weather in mind, but with memories of angry seas, hellish winds, and the ice of the antitrades, those fierce westerlies of oceans far down under. Nor did he impatiently sign on a crew of untried adventurers; instead, he selected hardened men who cursed Cape Horn weather even as they signed their names to the articles. Captain Broadwinder held the advantage, since sailors loved a race and a winner. A salt's stock soared in the taverns along the water front with the statement, "I'm sailin' aboard of Broadwinder."

Jenny regularly accompanied Philip to East Boston where the *Calcutta Eagle* sat lifelessly at a fitting-out berth. Under her eyes the vessel seemed to sleep while carpenters, calkers, and riggers busied themselves with necessary surgery. Artisans all, they knew their business. Aft, painters spread gleaming new coats on her deck stanchions and rail, while across her stern smaller brushes in skilled hands gilded the steamer above the Bengal tiger. Occasionally the artists smothered oaths and raised the decks in protest of the jarring operations amidships. There a crew was taking in a main lower mast, shortening the purchase as the mast upended. If all went well, the great spar would soon be stepped and dropped to keelson. Philip waited. The riggers waited. Jenny watched intently. Men sweated and tensed all over as the man in charge cried orders from the foretop. It was a very important mast, though for that matter, Jenny admitted, so were the fore and mizzen. To a ship, each of the three masts was as essential as faith, hope, and charity to a mortal's soul.

Then they stepped it and the tension eased, and Philip surveyed the work forward and abaft the main with approval everywhere. The *Eagle* was home to both captain and his lady, and he, smiling spontaneously, escorted her below to uncork a bottle. Although the roomy cabin was becomingly salted down to sea and sail by charts, sextant, and the maze of ship's and mariner's personal effects, the touch of feminine hands was in evidence. Bunk bed, exquisitely carved desk, chests, hanging bookshelves, chairs, polished mahogany walls, all reflected something of Jenny. As now, a sewing bag with crochet needles protruding almost covered the captain's prize telescope.

As Philip hummed a ditty while opening the locker, Jenny seated herself at the table and winced at every sound of the falling hammer on deck directly overhead.

"It's more peaceful at sea," she almost shouted.

"Eh?"

"Particularly when you send the whole shipyard crew home on wobbly legs every night."

"Eh, Mistress Jenny?"

She resorted to a shout: "Why humor them with whisky every evening?"

"Because I'm not Captain Tom, Dick, or Harry," he cried. "I'm Broadwinder!" he yelled back at her.

So he was. With ebullient expression devilishly at work to save him from the crime of braggadocio, his energy amazing after a most trying day, he remained typically Broadwinder. So he was, she reflected. Where other captains groused and swore at workmen, delay, and their own frayed nerves, Philip made a game of inconveniences, gave the workers to know they were welcome aboard, and went so far as to spoil them for the next captain. There was the difference.

The hammering above ceased abruptly. Jenny rose. "I'll wait alongside, lest I cramp their style," she said wearily.

"Aye," he replied, hugging three bottles which would soon go on deck. "It's a shame you had to be a woman, Jenny."

She paused near the door. "Is it now? Would you have it otherwise?"

Before he could shape a reply, Jenny slipped outside and closed the door. She moved unhurriedly to decks and soon departed the ship. On the portside platform she waited some distance from the copper-petticoated clipper ship, her roving glance taking in the *Calcutta Eagle*, bows to stern. She was a long vessel of deep brown hull with white stripes twice around. Tall-masted, each tapering spar angling rakishly aft in true clipper fashion, she was further typed by a most distinguished bow. They had built grace into her fore. Long bowsprit and jib boom pointed a finger at destinations, as though they were endowed with absolute confidence touched by just a degree of haughtiness. They had built spirit into her lifting fore. It was in evidence now, in the set of her dolphin striker, the knife of her cutwater, the flaring sweep of the cathead, not to mention the fluid scrolls of white and gold bordering the figurehead.

Jenny gazed at the goddess in flowing white robes. The figurehead represented something more than a lovely, determined woman flying forward with eyes peering eternally over the waves. She was a replica of a woman, with her big breasts, thighs, and waist, but it did not end there. In her face were a woman's emotions. She led men on, sent them to new adventures. In her face one saw the wife or sweetheart left behind to wait and watch and grieve; and in another of her expressions one saw something of a dream, of things a mortal would forever wish for and never quite grasp. And again like a woman in real life, the goddess would never stop staring into the future.

Someone at Jenny's side said, "A salty woman, that figgerhead."

Jenny turned quickly to see her husband's second mate, Mr. Winston. He was a short, stocky man in his early thirties, with a shock of flaming red hair and a white skin that defied seas and winds to color it. His narrow blue eyes twinkled, and his perpetual sidewise grin was in evidence. His expression seldom changed, though with it he conveyed humor, respect for the quarter-deck, and menace to any sailor who "showed stubborn." He had been a long time under Broadwinder and Mr. Fortune and he knew his business.

"The captain, ma'am, sent me to stand anchor watch wi' ye while the boys take their fill o' grog. And the owner boarded us just as I left the weather deck. That's him standin' by the main fife rail. Said he to old Samuel in earshot o' me, 'Sometimes I'm inclined to wonder, like Captains LePage and Maxwell, how Broadwinder can be the jolly good fellow and still keep discipline at sea.' He said that, and old Samuel, bless 'im, speaks right out, sayin', 'Maybe that's why Maxwell and Le-

Page ain't Broadwinder.' Could be. I never thought of it that way," he concluded reflectively.

Jenny smiled. "You know Mr. Cartwright is sailing with us, of course."

"Aye, not that any sane seaman approves," came the dismal reply. "But he brought news. Said the Hull Signal Station telegraphed Cap'n Keys blowin' into harbor on the sunset. Could be he's lively for a conn o' the way Cap'n Keys cockbills his yards before bettin' from his deep pockets. He's a bit cautious, y' know."

Jenny stifled a reply of "Yes, I know," and said, "So Captain Keys is making port."

As she turned her head toward the sea, Mr. Winston laughed with enjoyment. "Aye, and about as wise to the skipper's merry challenge as a petrel roostin' atop his mizzen royal. I'd like to scan his count'nance when he hears."

"Yes, Mr. Winston, so would I."

Jenny soon learned that the men aboard ship were of the same mind. Their voices rang loud and clear and, to her genuine astonishment, George Cartwright was raising a cup with the harbor workers to his captain's success. Mr. Winston's statement, "Blows a new wind, s' help me!" just about expressed her feeling of the moment.

Less than an hour later, Jenny, in the company of Philip and Cartwright, joined a considerable throng at the foot of State Street to watch Mayo Keys bring his famous ship *Emperor* into port. A sleek vessel of the clipper class, ebony black hull dulled gray by salt, she opened the harbor under great clouds of canvas; but all higher sail was coming in, fluttering as her host of topmen clewed in and harbor-stowed. A glint of late-afternoon sunshine mellowed her driving sails and before she took a pilot aboard, ship, rime, and big-yarded masts were painted in orange fast shading toward sunset red. She came on, slowly, warily, her lights showing long before she worked into her moorings.

The *Emperor* had no Broadwinder aboard. The fact was made evident by the run of conversations on every side: Broadwinder would have had her moored before darkness set in; Broadwinder would have spanked her in heeling on the wind; Keys hadn't the cut of Broadwinder's jib; and so on. But Keys had his defenders. They declared he could, did, and would fling sail to a wind where it counted, out in the deep.

Philip grinned. "You can't argue that," he said. "Mayo's that kind of a sailor."

Cartwright crooked a forefinger at the cleft of his chin. "Granting as much, how does the *Emperor* compare with the *Eagle*, Captain?"

"She's a thoroughbred from trucks to keelson. But I'll match her wind for wind any old day."

"Of course. Of course," the shipowner replied meditatively. "But given the same wind and an equal disposition to use, could Keys match your speed?"

Jenny listened avidly. Cartwright was probing cautiously, seeking answers to questions far ahead of the time when they could be answered by deeds, and Philip was replying with a truthful recklessness that made her uneasy.

"Could he?" Philip boomed forth. "He did once. Might do it again." As she despaired of his open frankness, he went on to say, "But on a long stretch, Mr. Cartwright, I can show him my heels again."

"Again?" The shipowner darted him a quick glance.

"Aye. Don't ask me how, and I'll not tell you whether it's merit on my part or a failing on his. But it is definitely the little things that make a difference. Don't you think so, sir?"

There! Jenny sighed with relief and pressed his arm gently with her fingers. No matter how off guard her man appeared, he kept his wits sharpened.

Further conversation was cut short when Captain Keys and the pilot suddenly emerged from the shadowy stern into the full yellow light of deck. The pilot moved on to the gangway, leaving the *Emperor*'s master at the poop rail near the starboard companion. Jenny had known Mayo Keys several years, had met the man in various ports, with no particular awareness of any disparity between him and the usual run of sea captains. Certainly she had never for a moment considered him Philip's equal. But now she studied him closely, with a discomforting realization that she was shaping fresh estimates. His appearance, which was singular, had nothing to do with it. He was very tall and thin, with big bones and a long, pointed nose; a shock of black hair hid the back of his neck. It was his full mouth, looking as if it were carved out of marble to represent grim determination, together with his agate-hard gray eyes, that caused Jenny to credit him with great strength and unleashed driving power. The thought was vaguely troubling. He stood there, with hollow, sea-reddened cheeks painted in orange, taking in every movement aboard. Not once did he issue an order, and his silence seemed a virtue.

Jenny looked at Philip's averted face and instantly felt better. Philip was equally as strong, not at all sullen, and one felt his affability quickly and knew it to be genuine.

At that moment the crowd opened a way for a small, paunchy man with thin white hair. He walked with a stoop to the deck and on to where Mayo Keys stood. Everyone knew him to be Oliver Barking, head of the firm of Barking & Pevy, owners of the *Emperor*. Following a brief handclasp between merchant and captain, Barking talked and Keys listened without any change of expression. When the former produced newspapers Jenny knew that the forthcoming race was the topic of conversation.

She watched the captain's face, as did Philip, Cartwright, and the people all about them. What she expected of him she did not know, though the set repose of his face was in a measure disappointing. A man should rise to such a challenge.

Jenny's brows lifted. Pursing her lips, she studied the new man she had discovered in Captain Keys. Since the race ahead would be a contest between men rather than ships, what lay in and behind a man's eyes was far more important than sails on tall masts. Mayo Keys revealed nothing, and therefore much. He became more a threat, a worthy competitor, with each passing second.

Now he and Barking were moving down the starboard companion. A meeting between the new arrival and the challenger was inevitable; the newspapermen would see to that. However, Jenny was more concerned with her own feelings of the moment, for she was acutely aware of her response to the challenge provoked by careful study of Mayo Keys.

Curious, she watched the Boston newspapermen steer Captain Keys in their direction. She wondered what the rival captains would say to one another, whether Keys would talk to the crowd, as Philip surely would, or remain his aloof self.

Soon both captains and the pair of shipowners were standing a few feet apart on the pier, Jenny with a hand at her husband's arm, the crowd encircling them. Since Barking was by nature reserved and Cartwright seldom made a public statement without careful preparation, all attention was turned on the more prominent figures of the race. Thus far Keys had said nothing and Broadwinder, grinning expansively, had finally forced the other's handclasp. Jenny eyed both men closely, a speculative light in her eyes, though she tensed inwardly when a reporter asked Philip why he had singled out Mayo Keys among the famous clipper captains for a race.

Broadwinder did not hesitate in his reply. "Because he's a fast sailor and the ship he commands is far from being a harbor scow."

"Then you think he's a better man than Captain LePage? Or Maxwell, Langmuir, or perhaps Knowles?"

Philip's engaging smile preceded an answer likely to offend no one. "I? Who am I to judge the best seamen of our time? But you omitted Creesy, David E. Mayo, Briard, Devens, and a dozen other crack-on men. Now as to how fast Mayo can drive his *Emperor*, I'll guarantee I've bounced along in his wake."

A Boston *Journal* man asked about the incident, drawing from Broadwinder a statement charged with humor that appealed to the crowd: "Look, Charlie lad, I'm here to praise myself, not Captain Keys."

Turning to big, loose-jointed Keys, the *Journal* man said: "Were you surprised to sail in and learn of Captain Broadwinder's challenge?"

A moment silent, another with piercing eyes on Broadwinder, Keys stretched his mouth into a semblance of a grin. "Indeed I was," he replied sharply.

Jenny was not only wondering why Philip evaded the truth, that the idea of the race had originated in the mind of Keys, but was thinking this was the time and place to reveal the fact. No doubt Keys felt strongly that Philip had capitalized on his remark in his absence. But a reporter was saying:

"Do you feel honored that you were challenged by Captain Broadwinder?"

"No comment." The reply was so matter-of-fact that it hinted of contained belligerence.

"Now, Captain Keys, isn't it gratifying to know that your challenger shrewdly planned this race, as it says here in my paper, 'so that it in no way interferes with cargoes, full holds, and dollar interests,' and because it ends in Boston?"

"No comment."

Mayo Keys listened to the next sentences in the paragraph: " 'For publicity this race has no precedent. Captain Broadwinder's star shines as never before, for he, the central figure in a voyage commercially profitable to mankind now being turned into a world-famous sporting event, proves not only the business acumen of American sea captains but the justified leadership of Yankee sailing ships in world commerce. Our clippers have commanded the attention of envious nations across the Atlantic since the California boom began, and now, thanks to our enterprising Captain Broadwinder, they will be given an added boost.' How does this strike you, Captain Keys?"

"Damned eloquent, I'd say."

Somewhat taken aback, the exasperated reporter asked the *Emperor's* master if he harbored a grudge or in any way resented Broadwinder or the challenge. Meeting with no reply, he asked Keys to make a statement for the press.

"I'll save that for the day Broadwinder embarks."

The newspapermen looked at one another, then turned to Oliver Barking with an appeal that he induce his captain to say something. Up to now, they declared, neither captain had shown at this meeting any spark of rivalry to indicate a lively race; which was very unusual and disappointing.

Jenny nudged Philip, whispered, "They're right. Perhaps you should say something to keep the story from being a very dull one."

Barking spoke up then, saying with spirit: "Captain Keys will make up at sea all he has left unsaid today. He's no braggart. He's a man who can and will throw enough sail in the wind to give Broadwinder a lesson in driving a ship."

"Now," Jenny said, pressing fingers against Philip's arm.

Broadwinder was reminded that he was Broadwinder. He laughed. One felt at once his infinite vivacity and, no matter where one's sympathies lay, secretly cheered him. Jenny could detect it in the faces of the people now, as she had on other occasions, and she knew that Philip would save the situation and further endear himself to the press. It was good business.

Sensing a statement worthy of repeating to their readers, the reporters turned to Broadwinder, who mixed a feigned yawn with laughter and said:

"After all, gentlemen, this interview as it stands is likely to bore the people of Boston. If Captain Keys and I sail like we've talked, our unborn children will be grown before we return to Boston. And since this is to be a race, I'll speak up and say I'm going to win it. That I am. To borrow words from a poem, I'm going to sail my ship so fast that a man on deck can't catch the mast, and a dolphin trying to get ahead will get run over and killed stone dead.

"And another thing. If you boys see me opening Boston harbor stern first, you'll know I'm sailing backward trying to give the *Emperor* a chance to catch up."

The crowd buzzed with this. The racing spirit was emerging at last. Jenny saw Cartwright's eyes twinkle, caught a flicker of retaliation in the narrowing gray eyes of Mayo Keys.

"What's more," Broadwinder added, "I'll help Mayo get his anchor up before I leave Melbourne."

When laughter subsided, one reporter asked Broadwinder if he wished to forecast the end of the race by days. "I mean, by how many days will you beat Captain Keys to this port?"

"I'll put it this way. If for every day out of Melbourne that Mayo looks at the *Calcutta Eagle's* stern he'll toss a button overboard, I'll guarantee that by the time he reaches Boston the coat and pants of every officer and sailor aboard of him will be tied with string."

Jenny tugged at his arm. "Enough, Philip," she said in low voice.

Broadwinder turned his good humor on Mayo Keys. "Come along, Captain, and we'll raise a toast to the better man. It could be you, you know."

It did not matter to Jenny that Keys and Barking moved on after the briefest refusal, or that Philip later sat in sober thought while she made herself ready for bed, she was quite pleased with the gain of the encounter. Captain Broadwinder had, by giving his public the bluff talk it desired in a racing man, sustained his popularity in excellent fashion, even as her own Philip had, without any mention of it to her, shaped a new and respectful opinion of the man he had to beat.

She continued to brush her hair slowly and glance at Philip through the mirror. When he rubbed his jaw with his palm and turned his troubled face in her direction she continued to groom her long hair as though nothing else mattered.

5

☐ Early next day Samuel entered George Cartwright's office with a scowl on his face and a package under his arm. Looking up from papers on his desk, Cartwright waited for the other to speak.

"Sailing cards," Samuel said tersely. "Seems somebody lacks imagination." With this, he turned on his heel, moved to the door, and paused. "Read it, sir, and you'll wonder if all the talk about a race is a cat's-paw wind out of the doldrums belt."

Cartwright suppressed a smile. "Sailing cards should announce only a business venture, Samuel."

"That being true, this one is nothing short of perfect, sir."

Alone, Cartwright picked up a small card printed in three colors, with a picture of a ship under full sail on the open sea just beneath the house flag. Printed below was the announcement:

THE INDIA COMMERCIAL LINE
BOSTON FOR CALIFORNIA!
FROM COMMERCIAL WHARF
As Well as Ports of the Orient and Melbourne, Australia, to Sail Positively on Advertised Date.
THE GREAT A-1 COPPERED EXTREME CLIPPER
CALCUTTA EAGLE
PHILIP BROADWINDER, COMMANDER
Is in berth receiving her cargo, all of which is engaged for San Francisco and Orient. For passenger rates, apply to firm's office on Merchants Row, where wagers will be accepted on the return voyage.

J. E. DON PERSONS, Agent
24 Commercial Wharf
or
JOHN BROWN & SON
58 South Street, Corner Wall, New York

Trite, scarcely different from a dozen other cards, Cartwright admitted. Like a ship's log, in which disaster and death were often chronicled with almost callous brevity, as: *Ship dismasted. Two men lost.* But a merchant vessel was a business proposition, nothing else. Adventure was secondary. One deducted the cost of operating a vessel from freight and passenger revenues and determined whether a captain had made a good or bad voyage. Seas, elements, mutinies and hardships were not written into the final figures placed on Cartwright's desk. This was the countinghouse.

He knew the sea was something else. Nevertheless, from where he sat there could never be any change. Rapport between trials aboard ship and the profit statements would forever be unattainable. Odd, he thought, staring at an oil of the *Calcutta Eagle* in a squall, that he should soon board that very clipper with adventure in one hand and ledgers in the other. And how he would carry the two at once would be interesting to see.

It was but a passing thought, a fancy, and he smiled it off. He was a practical man, not a dreamer, and a sense of guilt assailed him because he had for a moment stepped out of character; as on that day when Jenny Broadwinder arrived in port. For days after that he had silently scolded himself. She had opened up a world he was unsuited for. He was content here. He told himself these things and he argued that his boarding the ship for a long voyage would be a serious mistake. And just when he seemed convinced, what should happen but that he was thrown with the Broadwinders again.

Last evening, it was. He had missed little of the play between Jenny and Philip. She had directed the whole thing, within a foot of him, first by telling Broadwinder to speak up in order to save the occasion, and next by reminding him that he had said enough. A remarkable woman, a remarkable team; he in the spotlight, she prompting from the wings. She re-aroused his curiosity.

His brows rose slowly. She stirred up more than just curiosity: doubt of Philip, mystery of the woman behind the composed face of Jenny Broadwinder.

Drumming the desk top with fingers, he looked at the ship in the wide gilt frame without seeing it. Then he stood and walked aimlessly the length of his office.

"She might forever remain a mystery," he said silently. Next he encompassed all in a few words spoken perhaps by every man since the beginning of the human race: "Because she is woman." He smiled in self-reproach as he said this. How very trite those words; yet, no matter how ancient the observation, it was startlingly new to every man. As new as Jenny to him.

At his desk again he eyed the sailing card and admitted that he should have printed life into it. But it was what it was and there was not enough time remaining to print another. So he gathered up some fifty of the cards and picked up his hat. A little later he crossed over to East Boston.

George Cartwright did not board the *Calcutta Eagle* at once, but stood some distance off, intently appraising the vessel. Something he had never seen in her held his attention. It was not her fresh copper, paint, new masts, and cordage; nor was it figurehead, bows, or lines; rather, it was the unseen but felt spirit of a clipper ship. Another of those attributes one did not write into a profit sheet. Of course the staggering repair bill would be itemized and totaled to cause him frowns of disapproval and unkind imprecations directed in silence at his demanding Captain Broadwinder, though against his discovery of life in a ship itself it mattered little. She was a handsome thing, and he could not recall the time since his boyhood when he had praised a ship for anything other than her cargo space.

On deck, he looked toward the break of the poop for either Philip or Jenny. Mr. Winston greeted him and advised that the captain and his lady had just gone below, were probably in the saloon with Mr. Fortune.

"Thank you, Mr. Winston. Here, the new sailing cards are just off the press." So saying, he presented the second with one and awaited his reaction.

The mate read it, glanced up once, twice, then read again. "So," he said. "So. She sounds damn lively, sir. Makes me wonder if we're runnin' a cattle boat to Melbourne and back."

Cartwright eyed the second a moment before deciding to accept the rebuke in silence. The bucko mates these days were impertinent. Meeting Peretta, the steward, Cartwright extended the card and once again paused. The Italians appreciated beauty, he realized. Peretta proved this with all sorts of praise and gestures before shaking his head sadly.

"But, signor, where's a da race?" He turned the card over. "Mother Maria, she's a not here!"

"Fetch me brandy, steward," Cartwright snapped, entering the ship's saloon where the first person to catch his eye was the chief mate.

Ephraim Fortune was Cartwright's favorite ship's officer, the pattern by which all mates should be cut. Were he not so much a part of the *Eagle*, so loyal to Broadwinder, he could now be in command of the India Line's clipper *Express*. A tall man of forty-five with graying hair and light blue eyes, always smiling, he possessed the diplomacy and poise of British luxury-ship captains. Though a native of Maine, he looked and sounded English, and had served as first officer aboard a three-skysail-yarder out of Liverpool.

The mate rose and warmly greeted the shipowner with, "It's a pleasure to see you, sir, on the very first day we have no riggers and carpenters aboard. In fact, we're ready for sea, except for taking on a crew, water, and provisions. And I'm eager for the deep stream, sir. Eh?" he said, accepting a sailing card, eying it closely, "Our card? Indeed, a handsome one." His smile vanished a mere instant. "As usual, a most dignified one."

Cartwright looked curious. Was the man honest? There was no way of knowing, so he said, "I was told the captain was here."

"He and Mrs. Broadwinder will return shortly. Left for their quarters to look for charts. The Melbourne seas, sir." He laughed. "We're opening the race."

Cartwright said lightly, "Then Captain Keys would scarcely be welcome here."

"Keys? Oh no, sir, not with what we're planning. A way to lose good company at sea, you know."

The steward arrived with Cartwright's brandy just as the Broadwinders entered the saloon with charts of Port Phillip Bay and Bass Strait. They talked excitedly until they became aware of Cartwright's presence. Jenny's start of surprise and Philip's sudden silence irritated Cartwright, if only because they made it plain that he was an alien aboard his own ship. But, as was his habit, he hid his feelings and waited for the break to heal. It did soon, for Broadwinder became his usual self and invited the guest, or intruder, to pore over the maps with them.

"Aye. Leave the *Emperor* here," he said, striking Cartwright's shoulder with a palm, "and she's left behind for good."

"Unless Captain Keys refuses to be outwitted there," the shipowner replied, smiling at Jenny.

"The idea, sir," Mr. Fortune ventured amiably, "is to draw Captain Keys north of the Furneaux Islands while we run under them and roar sou'east for The Snares and the winds of the fifties."

Jenny's eyes danced. "Ship for ship, we'll hold the advantage gained."

Cartwright's humor improved. Chuckling, he said, "It was Sir Walter Scott, I believe, who wrote these lines—'Oh, what a tangled web we weave, When first we practice to deceive!'"

Jenny's stance and expression, alive with a certain grace and vivacity one would not soon forget, appealed to Cartwright as she said, "Never doubt, sir, that the ocean is a web to untangle. And Shakespeare, in *King Henry VIII*, said something about throwing away ambition, that it is a sin which fells angels. I can't recall the exact lines, but the thought serves."

Cartwright knew the lines, though he was wise enough not to quote them. It was better to watch her and ponder her spirit; to revel in the unknown. He began to wonder if he made it appear obvious when she eyed him strangely.

"I'm beginning to see what you mean," he said suddenly.

"And once at sea you'll feel it," Jenny replied, shifting her glance to the card Mr. Fortune was turning over in his hand.

When the chief mate handed it to her she looked rather puzzled. "Philip, our sailing card," she said.

Broadwinder showed interest. Turning from a large map of Tasmania, he accepted the card and eyed it closely. A frown crossed his face, eased away, and he looked at Cartwright, who began to brace himself inwardly for what he felt sure would follow.

"'For passenger rates, apply to firm's office on Merchants Row.'" Philip read aloud, "'*Where wagers will be accepted on the return voyage.*' By thunder, this is perfect!"

"Perfect?" Jenny looked astonished, and Cartwright, suspecting trickery, stiffened perceptibly.

"Sure it is," Philip replied, tapping the card with finger tips. "By all it doesn't say, it's eloquent with challenge, Jenny. At first you don't get it, then you do—all business, right down to the part about accepting wagers. Subtle threat!" Looking at Cartwright, he extended his hand. "Anything else said would be too much, sir. It's a masterpiece, and you can lay to that."

Cartwright searched his captain's face for any sign that might betray his honesty. He was aware that Jenny was doing the same. Then Broadwinder was saying:

"Mr. Cartwright, I'm hoping the big posters are identical and that you plaster them from here to Philadelphia."

An hour later George Cartwright left the ship with a sense of well-being. The more he thought about the sailing announcement, the better it sounded. He had actually created a gem of brevity when he unwittingly inserted defiance between the lines. "Eloquent with challenge," Broadwinder had said. Philip was a most discerning man; beyond his other profitable attributes, this captain showed amazing perspicacity. Perhaps he had underrated Broadwinder. On the other hand, was it possible that Philip had resorted to flattery in order to further the demands spoken by Jenny for a greater interest in the ship? It was possible, though not probable. In any case, he, the shipowner, would gamble more than he had originally intended on the success of his asset, the Prince of Sea Captains, over Mayo Keys.

Aboard the *Calcutta Eagle*, Jenny waited until Mr. Fortune left the saloon before tossing the card to a map under Philip's eyes.

"Look me straight in the eye, Captain Broadwinder," she demanded. When he did so she said, "Now tell me the truth, do you believe what you told Mr. Cartwright about the sailing card?"

Under her keen scrutiny he felt that anything short of the truth would be of no avail.

"Yes and no," he replied. "I was at first rather disappointed. Then I felt the force of all the unsaid in those two words: 'Wagers accepted.'"

Her brow lifted, though her gaze remained fixed on him. "I'm still disappointed. Aren't you?"

"Well, frankly, I expected more than just a hint of the race, Jenny. However——"

"Then you were not totally honest with him, were you, Philip?"

"Totally honest?" His lips spread and his face was suddenly animated. "Look here, Mistress Jenny, nobody is ever totally honest. Suppose we spoke our every thought. Lord ha' mercy, this old world would be one dog-and-cat fight, one helluva place to live in!"

Jenny considered this. Then she was thinking of the secret

bid she had made for a greater interest in the ship. Though it was for Philip, she would not dare tell him she had taken the initiative. She looked out the stern window then and said:

"Perhaps you're right, Philip dear."

6

☐ The *Calcutta Eagle* moved to her pier and began taking on cargo. As the long, dull process of loading continued under Mr. Winston's supervision, with crates and boxes of American goods for San Francisco, Hong Kong, and Singapore swinging aboard, Mr. Fortune very carefully selected the crew. Old hands and loyal were augmented by lads with youth and vigor. Experience, willingness, and stamina were on a par. A man should come alive, jump to an order, know what to do and how to do it quickly, from windlass to wheel, royal yard to bilge. Often the safety of all aboard depended on the quick dispatch of a single order, and a race called for constant alertness on the part of a crew. The "All hands!" meant that the off-watch crew should empty out of the forecastle on the double. "Take in or let fly the main to'gannels'ls" was a demand to lay aloft and furl or loose topgallant sails; for a reason. The officers desired no sailor who would "work Tom Cox's traverse," a term denoting skillful loafing on the job, but demanded sailors eager to win the race and who would give their all in order to bring it about.

In East Boston the *Emperor* was taking on a new foremast, Manila, sheets of copper on her hull, and paint from stem to stern. Crews of artisans worked on her round the clock in order to put her to sea soon after the *Eagle* departed; by arrangement between the owners in order that neither vessel would be forced to sit in wait for the other in Melbourne.

Even as water-front laborers sweated and cursed the eternal stowing of goods in the *Eagle's* holds, as well as Mr. Winston for his extreme precaution against shifting cargoes in rough weather ahead, and more wagons rolled to the wharf and unloaded, and Peretta provisioned the ship and pocketed the customary steward's cut on purchases of everything from ship's biscuits, salt horse, to wines for the captain's table, and George Cartwright passed out sailing cards with the exalted pride of a perfectionist by day and argued evenings with his sister Julia over wardrobe and the maze of items necessary to his comfort aboard ship, the newspapers kept alive the public's interest in the forthcoming race with drawings and biographical sketches of the rival captains and ships both in Boston and New York.

There was no escape for Captain Broadwinder. The final responsibility of ship, cargo, provisions, crew, and voyage was his. A natural position, which he did not mind in the least, even though he seemed a slave to his ship from dawn to nightfall. In the limelight as never before, he felt it his duty to attend this affair and that of evenings, many of which were staged in his honor. Often he resorted to drink in order to sustain the Broadwinder legend, and as often returned to his hotel tired and listless. Both he and Jenny counted the days remaining until embarkation.

On the night before the scheduled departure Jenny waited up for Philip until two in the morning. He entered, slumped into a chair, and stared tiredly at her before saying:

"Thank the Lord for forty fathoms of water under me this time tomorrow, Jenny girl."

Drawing a silken robe about her, she stood a moment in sharp study of him. "Mr. Fortune came at ten last evening with the papers. Mr. Winston sent a sonnywhack with a message that he is restowing the forward hold tonight, and Mr. Cartwright sent a messenger with an urgent request that you find room for a pianoforte to San Francisco. Also, the last ton of fresh water had salt in it, so the tanks are being cleaned. I went to the ship myself at around eleven. Now what happened to you tonight?"

He raised a hand wearily. "Nothing counts now but the racing spirit."

"Which you gave freely of, I suppose."

"It's expected of me."

It was, she agreed in silence, her attention full upon him. He had given of himself until he wore a strained look even mornings of late, poor boy, and she was wondering what he would have left for the swarm of people who would be on hand within a few hours to see the "Prince" embark.

"My shadow is a better man than I am, Jenny. It seems I'm

the sucker. Mayo Keys has forced me to carry the whole show. And tomorrow——"

She placed a finger to his lips. "Is a few hours in the future, darling. You need rest, and that's what you're going to get. And besides, I'm sleepy."

"I'm taut as a towing hawser. Any brandy left?" When she reluctantly handed him the decanter, he poured and said, "Today Mayo will break his silence. So I hear. Wonder what he'll have to say?"

"Whatever it is, he'll catch you between wind and water from lack of sleep."

Philip laughed, drew her roughly into his lap, and studied her face until the scolding expression vanished before a smile she could not suppress. "Who wants to sleep? Many's the time I've stood the deck for thirty-six hours, and you know it, Mistress Jenny. So!"

She knew that when a sailor said "So!" he meant belay, or enough. "So," she said, if only to get in the last word, and placed her head on his shoulder. But only for a minute.

"Philip, I have just one thing more to say. Please remember when you board the ship that tiredness and whisky don't mix."

Again she placed a finger to his lips, though he snapped at it playfully, causing her a start of surprise. Grinning broadly, he took her chin between thumb and forefinger and drew her face to within an inch of his.

"And don't you forget it," she said, meeting his gaze. Then, "Philip Broadwinder! Whatever is on your mind?"

Jenny averted her face and tried to rise, but he held her tightly. Then he brought her mouth up to his and kissed her until she ceased to struggle.

"Still sleepy?" he said, openly exulting in her response.

She did not look at him then but placed an arm about his neck, thinking as she did so that he belonged to her now. Soon cheering people, a ship, embarkation, and waiting seas would claim him. But these things did not make up the present. Only Philip counted, despite the fact that he chose the strangest times to play the merry devil with her emotions.

It seemed to Jenny they had scarcely fallen asleep when the unmistakable rapping of a seaman caused them to sit up in bed. She looked into Philip's haggard face and cried, "On deck, sir! Squally weather ahead."

Philip struggled up and made his weary way to the door,

and soon Jenny heard Samuel's voice among what seemed a
dozen others. The ship was ready, they told him, and a sizable
crowd was already on hand; also, the captain looked as if he
had stood the deck through a four-day hurricane and emerged
a scarecrow. Where was the Broadwinder they knew? Philip
responded with hearty laughter and told them right off that
Broadwinder was and had been too long in the clutches
of ruthless landlubbers. He dressed and went along with
them to a victory breakfast, after telling Jenny he would join
her aboard ship within an hour at most.

As the door closed behind him, Jenny's brow knit. A feeling
of uneasiness would not go away; it kept her company even
as she selected her finest dress for the occasion and tried to
think of nothing but her carefully groomed self on the quarter-
deck. She wanted Philip proud of her on this occasion as much
as she wished to be proud of him. But Philip was actually too
spent to be his real self at a time when his every word and
gesture counted most.

Then Julia and George Cartwright arrived to escort her to
Commercial Wharf. While Jenny was grateful to the shipowner
for the courtesy, she resented his attitude of indifference
where Philip was concerned. It seemed that he had surren-
dered his captain to the shore wolves.

Julia was a kind and genuine person underneath the long-
inculcated Boston crust. A large woman, several years younger
than her brother, she was a spinster endowed with a certain
vivacity and hidden sense of humor. But she could not quite
drop out of the upper stratum of society to which she was
accustomed, a fact she inadvertently made known to Jenny
while they waited for the ship's hands to convey the Broadwinder trunks to the *Calcutta Eagle*. How George could desert
his club, civic duties, and the gay social life of the fall season
ahead for a long, boring cruise, she simply could not understand.

"And you," she said to Jenny, "give up everything a woman
should rightfully possess for the sea."

"Not everything," Jenny replied. "If I didn't go to sea I
might be doing just that."

"Oh, the captain." Julia laughed. "I suppose it is not unnatural for me to overlook the importance of men." She appeared to enjoy her brother's cold stare.

The sailors came for the baggage, and soon Cartwright
handed the ladies into a carriage. By the time they reached

the wharf it seemed that all of Boston had turned out to watch the clipper depart. The tall masts with new white sails and the long decks never looked so good to Jenny. She was anxious to put water between gleaming hull and land. She yearned for the comparative peace of the sea, the deep stream, where her husband's whereabouts and behavior were confined to ship. And at the moment, as the people grudgingly moved aside to allow the carriage passageway, she was hoping above all else that Philip was aboard.

Craning her neck, she searched the poop in the distance. Mr. Fortune stood with the pilot. Philip could be below. The horses moved at a slow walk, stopping often as uniformed police opened up a way. She looked at the great banner stretched between the *Eagle*'s fore and mainmast, topgallant high, and read:

FOR CALIFORNIA, THE ORIENT AND MELBOURNE, THIS A-1 CLIPPER WILL RACE FOR BOSTON AND WIN OVER SEAS, ICE, AND ANY AMBITIOUS MORTAL, GOD WILLING.
PHILIP BROADWINDER, COMMANDER

"And who is responsible for that?" Jenny asked, glancing at Cartwright.

He looked away, said quietly, "Rather, who will get credit for it?"

"Thank you for keeping it Philip's show," Jenny said sincerely.

Cartwright laughed. "By heaven, it is his show."

Jenny saw Mayo Keys then. His grin was broad and his glance was full upon her. He bowed to her, not once releasing her eyes. She nodded graciously, then proceeded to ignore him.

"Make way for the captain's wife!" cried one of the sailors Mr. Winston had sent to aid the police.

The people took notice. One man waved his hands aloft and yelled at the top of his voice. "Three rousing cheers for Broadwinder's wife!"

The noise was deafening. Jenny raised a hand and smiled at them. They pressed close to the carriage, crying: "Tell the cap'n I bet me last penny on him! Make him win the race for us, Mrs. Broadwinder! Keep the Prince sail-minded, ma'am!" There seemed no end of enthusiastic greetings. They kept it up all the way to the ship, where two rows of sailors stood smartly at attention near the gangway.

Excitement got the better of her as they alighted and moved to the ship's waist. Mr. Fortune had descended from the poop. Now he tucked her arm in his and led her to the starboard companion as though she were a queen. Twice she bit her lip to suppress questions about Philip, and only when she stood just abaft the mizzenmast did she speak casually, saying:

"I suppose Captain Broadwinder will soon break away from his friends."

She awaited the chief mate's reply with contained anxiety, but when his "I suppose so" reached her ears she felt a small catch of fear and turned her face toward the harbor. Recovering, she chatted with the Cartwrights about this and that, with no outward sign of anxiety. While searching beyond the sea of faces for any approaching carriage that might bring Philip, she spoke of the comforting sounds and smells aboard ship. Cargo odors escaped the hatches, some pungent, a few thoroughly offensive, though a person on deck soon savored the blend of commerce on the wing with the tar of deck, frolicking waves, and a sea wind. Likewise, the creaking of blocks, flapping of sails, the rush of water down the ship's sides, and the striking of the bell were audibly delightful. All were companions of movement, of progress, and together they created a sense of motion and peace that one could not find on land.

Suddenly aware that all this might strike Julia's ears as more poetic than real, Jenny laughed lightly. "One born to the sea is naturally prejudiced." Then, because she could pretend no longer, she said:

"I do wonder what is detaining Captain Broadwinder."

Cartwright looked at his watch, and Julia asked if Jenny addressed her husband as Captain Broadwinder in private. Hungry gulls circled the upper yards and one of them paused for rest on the shining mizzen truck. Sailors moved leisurely about forward of the mainmast, though the receiving crew stood relaxed at both ends of the gangplank awaiting the captain's arrival. Mr. Fortune joined Mr. Winston on the weather deck for inspection of lines, windlass, boat lashings, cable, and the maze of running gear. The pilot checked the time and darted impatient glances at the people. Several carriages approached the street leading to the pier, only to be turned back. Peretta brought deck chairs and asked if he could serve tea or champagne to the Cartwrights and Jenny.

Another quarter hour went by. The crowd wanted Broadwinder. Where was he? People pressed closer to the ship's sides, calling out to sailors lining the rails, asking for souvenirs from the *Calcutta Eagle*. Mr. Fortune, just under the break of the poop, took out his watch, eyed it, then studied the large gathering of Bostonians.

Jenny was becoming nervous. To allay her feelings she voiced admiration of Julia's gown and hat, evoking more talk which she was forced to bear with becoming face even as she watched closely while Mr. Fortune cut short lengths of Manila and tossed them ashore to souvenir hunters. A splendid idea, she thought, shaping an attentive "To be sure" for Julia's ears. Steam tugs waiting expensively to tow the ship from the wharf drew her attention, and George Cartwright raised his brows as the mind behind them counted, she was sure, the extra dollars Prince Philip was costing him. Exasperated to no end, Jenny behind her calm exterior silently threatened Philip with all sorts of reprisals if he did not soon make his appearance.

Now Oliver Barking, Captain Keys, and the latter's coterie of stanch supporters were moving to a halt near the gangplank.

"Another glass of champagne," Jenny said to the steward when a host of newspapermen arrived. She desired a third bracer upon witnessing the mayor's party behind a police escort. There would follow the delay of speeches. But she could endure that. If only Philip would come.

Suddenly the steady drone of the throng lifted in a new note of excitement. Every eye was turned on a huge wagon drawn by four mules. Atop it, perched on barrels, were at least one dozen men. In the distance, the cry of "Broadwinder" rose above the bedlam.

Jenny stared at the wagon. Turning to the steward, she said, "I'll thank you for the master's spyglass. And show lively," she added, unthinking, coloring slightly.

"But surely that isn't Captain Broadwinder atop—of all things—a brewery wagon!" Julia said.

It was, however. The moment Jenny lifted the spyglass Philip seemed to leap into the circular rim of her vision and, though expecting it, she could not at once adjust what she saw in her own mind. There he stood, supported on one side by banker Bronson, on the other by the cordage manufacturer Cottingham. Atop barrels! And there were old Angus McGovern and Samuel and others, all singing now:

> "Now let us sing—Long live the King,
>   And Broadwinder long live he——"

Hundreds of voices joined in, even the sailors aboard the *Eagle*:

> "And when he next doth ride abroad,
>   May I be there to see!"

In the moment's pause between stanzas, Mr. Fortune said, "He could ride a goat and the people would still cheer."

Jenny pondered this with some misgiving. Whether Philip was well along in his cups or putting on a show, it was all the same in the public eye, she realized. He appeared wobbly on his legs, though the effect could be produced by his companions. As though the opinions of the Cartwrights mattered in the least, she glanced at their grave faces and felt something of their embarrassment rising inside her. Never had she been ashamed of Philip, and she was praying that she would be spared now. Then a flood of resentment stirred in her breast. It was not directed at Philip but at the aloof Cartwrights. It was a rallying of herself in defense of her husband.

She began to sing with crowd and crew. A moment later Julia cast dignity to the winds and raised her deep-throated voice in praise of Philip. Her astonished brother then felt it incumbent on him to support his captain.

Though the wagon somehow threaded the crowd and reached the ship, the noise increased until men were forced to hold the frightened mules by bridle bits lest they stampede in the crowd. But Jenny saw only Philip. She studied his face and legs for tell-tale signs and cringed inwardly when he leaped from a barrel to the wagon floor. As he reached the ground apparently in command of his senses, she breathed a sigh of relief. He was not allowed to walk aboard ship, he was carried on the shoulders of his friends, past Mayo Keys and the mayor and other dignitaries, to the poop, where they put him down near the rail facing the crowd. As a band hidden by the ship's side forward began to play, streamers of red, white, and blue bunting fluttered down the mizzen ratlines. The band marched up the gangway and took its position on the weather deck, a signal to the mayor's party to come aboard.

It was all rather vague to Jenny, who stood at Philip's side trying to place an estimate on his condition without making it appear obvious. Aware of her searching glances, Philip bent to her and said:

"Belay, Jenny girl. I'm half-seas under but I've got the conn of the weather."

"Mermaids and dragons all?" she said sharply. He laughed openly, laughed when the occasion demanded the opposite, and she felt the color rising from her neck. She should have known better than to provoke him, though her polite error in no way excused his impoliteness. Then the mayor was lauding the people of Boston for their maritime spirit, their ships, and their famous men who took them to sea. By his eloquence one might have thought this a vote-getting rally. In his favor, however, was his regard for brevity. In conclusion, he requested Captain Keys to come aboard and when the rival captains stood on either side of him he shook their hands and trumpeted to the crowd: "Two great seamen. May the best man win!"

Cheers and "Who are you betting on, Mr. Mayor?" greeted him. Striking an attitude of amiable tolerance, he waited until his upheld hand commanded silence before nodding briefly to Broadwinder. The crowd responded.

"Speech! Speech! Give us a speech, Captain Broadwinder! Tell us how many days you'll wait for Mayo in Boston after you've won the race."

"Captain Keys is my guest," Broadwinder managed, rather thick-tongued.

"Aye!" Keys boomed forth. "Thanks for that courtesy, Captain Broadwinder." He addressed the people below him, with emphasis on the word "that." Then he said, "I scarcely expected as much from you." A pause. "Especially after I entered Boston harbor to find myself on the acceptance or refusal end of *my own challenge*, delivered to you in Singapore—to race you to any place at any time. Do you deny this, Mr. Prince of Sea Captains?"

With all eyes on him, Jenny's included, Philip Broadwinder seemed for once at a loss for words. Jenny saw his bewildered expression and knew that his mind was dulled by exhaustion and drink.

"Philip!" she said just above a whisper. "If you ever laughed, do so now! And ask him—to the crowd—how it feels to let a better sailor catch him in stays."

Philip appeared a little dazed, though he spread a grin over his face and burst into laughter. It was something he could do well, and it was infectious. The crowd laughed with him and then he put Jenny's question squarely up to Mayo Keys in a voice to the people, swayed a little now, and braced himself against the rail, the silly grin still dominating his countenance.

"Aye. Now answer that one, friend Mayo," he demanded, with surprising control of his speech. "If you sail that way, I'll beat you here by a fortnight."

Drunk or sober, he had a way with people, and it was made evident by the reaction of the big audience. Minutes passed before tall, gangling, big-boned Keys could restore silence. When he did, he cried, and to his credit, without loss of the mocking air he began with:

"Sure I'll answer you, Broadwinder. With a fact. Since you twisted my challenge into your own, you'll swallow it harder." He reached into his pocket and produced a roll of currency. "Five hundred American says I'll open Boston harbor with your fancy *Calcutta Eagle* a full day under my stern."

"Belay, Mayo. I'm bled dry of wager money," Philip protested.

Jenny saw and felt the scales of opinion tipping in favor of the *Emperor's* captain. Philip's reply, though in low voice, rippled from the ship's side deep into the throng. Like wildfire. It would never do. She opened her reticule and extracted a little more than one fifth the amount, then turned an urgent face upon Cartwright at her side.

"Sir, we're desperately in need of the difference."

The shipowner understood. He obliged her quickly and she slipped the full amount of the wager into Philip's hand. "Call him, Philip. At once!" she commanded.

Captain Broadwinder did just that, but in a manner to further appeal to the massed audience. He cried, "So ho!" threw back his head and roared, and once his mirth subsided, he held the sum before Keys, saying, "Mayo, if you beat me by the length of your long nose, I'll give an equal amount to charity."

Captain Keys would not admit defeat; the crowd did it for him, however, and he soon departed. The ceremony, if one could call it that, ended. The band struck up a lively tune and people cheered. It had been a good show. Mr. Fortune gave the tugs the signal and soon the *Calcutta Eagle* eased away from Commercial Wharf. Julia waved from the shore and Cartwright blew her a farewell kiss just as Mr. Fortune cried to the topmen now scrambling aloft:

"Cut away the banner between the masts!"

A minute later Jenny disappeared from deck, flushed of face though otherwise as calm as one could expect of a woman who steered her famous husband below decks.

7

☐ George Cartwright's gaze dwelled on the spot where Jenny was last seen, before sweeping ashore to the people awaiting the Broadwinder touch in romping out to sea. Even Cartwright admitted that Philip had taken the triteness out of sail and replaced it with a spirit that quickened the romantic pulse of men. A showman, he gave sail the spice it needed. So much for the Prince, who had on this day been caught aback only to be rescued not once but twice, by Jenny.

Fresh in his memory was her whispered command: "Philip! If you ever laughed, do so now!" Atop this, he would never forget the determined set of her face, softened somewhat by the deep appeal in her eyes as she turned to him with, "Sir, we're desperately in need of the difference."

He was wondering just how many times in the past Jenny had saved face for Philip when she appeared on deck again.

She moved unhurriedly to Mr. Fortune's side, paused there and lifted her eyes to the pennant whipping in the wind atop the mainmast. Cartwright watched closely as she looked into the wind; he listened as she addressed the chief mate, saying:

"Mr. Fortune, Captain Broadwinder judged the wind correctly, two points north of east, and wishes me to advise putting the ship in the wind's eye for a tack south'ard, all points under east the harbor allows, all sail blowing."

Cartwright said under his breath, "In Broadwinder style." This would be interesting to see from the deck.

Mr. Fortune spoke the tug through his trumpet. The ship was soon on a course that blew the pennant flat aft. The quarter-deck then cried, "Hands about ship! All hands!" The below watch jumped at the order. "Ready! Ready!" The words were scarcely spoken before the hands were throwing down the gear of the main and crossjack, clear for running. Here was quite a show, Cartwright observed, trying his best to follow every movement aboard. An interval of gaining position followed, every man alert and waiting for the ship to put more harbor in her wake, to drop the pilot and cut loose from the tug as she cascaded sail in great white blossoms from yards close-hauled on the port tack. Ashore, Boston waited for Broadwinder to shake out canvas. Aboard ship it was the same.

Up came the trumpet in Mr. Fortune's hand. The ship spouted sail after sail, running lively into the eye of the wind, white cotton shaking, now flattening against masts. "Spanker boom amidships! Ease the helm!" Then, "Rise tacks and sheets!" The ship was a beehive of men leaping to orders, grinning as though each fancied himself a Broadwinder as he hauled, swayed up on the courses, pawed at pins, and lifted. Surely each was a reflection of the master, an integral part of a smart show. But the ship! Her pennant eased around the gleaming ball topping her main, and the wind found a new weather bow and began to fill her sails. Now she would fall off, lose a little of her headway, for she was swinging fast. But no! The order, "Right the helm!" seemed timed to the second and the *Calcutta Eagle* came around, barely taking the wind on her beam before righting herself and blowing hard for the open sea.

The tug and pilot were falling away and the order aboard was, "Let go and haul!" soon followed by, "Watch below!"

If Mr. Fortune was all for ship at the time, it was to his credit. He had neither missed stays nor miscalculated in his timing. But he had overlooked one detail, and Jenny reminded him of it without any trace of reprimand in her voice:

"Mr. Fortune, the captain will never forgive us if we forget to dip the colors."

Under the daring press of canvas, the *Eagle* dipped her ensign, once to tug, once to all ships, and once to Boston, typical of the man who commanded her, then tore on, rising and plunging and heeling as she spread her great wake under the eyes of Boston and roared on for the deep stream.

It was done. The big job was complete in every detail. For once George Cartwright had witnessed the Broadwinder style of embarkation at its source. He saw in memory the spectacle from shore, recalled the thrill he had experienced, and thought it nothing to compare with the on-deck scene. The skill and dexterity, the beauty of co-ordination of command and smart crew, the clipped orders, all blending with snaking ropes, swift, sure hands, falling snow-white canvas, and an acceleration of movement through the water until now his ship, which he had until recently admired only through a profit statement, raced along with the speed of an express —these things did more than just impress him, they aroused something in him. Under the spell of it he seemed more alive and unchained than ever before in his entire life. He knew a compelling desire to tell someone just how he felt, though he put it down and turned his glance inboard where it fell directly on Jenny.

He saw her draw in a deep breath and exhale, then touch her cheek with a finger as active eyes darted from bows into the rigging and back to deck with inspection everywhere. A slight nod of her head, as though she were satisfied with all she saw, preceded the smile she bestowed on Mr. Fortune.

"My compliments," she said. "Captain Broadwinder will be pleased to learn that he embarked in the usual manner without the slightest deviation from his orders."

Cartwright's expression sharpened. His hand lifted to his face and a thumbnail moved slowly back and forth between mouth and cleft of chin. The picture of Broadwinder in her hands as he departed from deck, legs wobbly, eyes glazed over, was scarcely that of a man capable of giving such orders. However, Broadwinder remained a puzzle. Perhaps the behavior of his ship before a shore crowd was an obsession with him. Perhaps. On the other hand, his ability to think clearly seemed unlikely, and that being true, only Jenny remained to issue the command. Who could be the wiser, unless it was one who had nothing to do but observe? There was no proof either way. None was needed. And yet—little things mounted until they were big things, such as her attention to wind direction before she voluntarily informed Mr. Fortune that her husband had judged the wind correctly. Had he? Could he have done so? It was possible, yes, but of one thing Cartwright was sure, and that was Jenny's ability to do so.

A transient bit of thinking, all of it, Cartwright admitted. There was no reason why he should concern himself with the puzzles of their married life. The Broadwinder legend had been upheld, the ship was reaching in long, safe strides for distant horizons. She was in good hands.

PART TWO

8

☐ On her tenth day out of New York the *Calcutta Eagle* ran with some seas on, tossing from side to side and throwing her mast tips in wide arcs. Under no great press of canvas, she used the quartering wind to lift the bows by her foresail and plowed the tops of racing waves with the knife of her cutwater. The sky from horizon to horizon was thick with heavy dark clouds piled up by the freshening wind.

Captain Broadwinder on the poop eyed the weather, sent his gaze aloft in swift inspection of the top hamper, then studied the lifting, plunging jib boom a minute or so before ordering the upper main topsail set. When the sail bellied full in the breeze the bows were pushed a trifle downward and the ship ceased her efforts to fly off into space.

George Cartwright studied cause, remedy, and effect, as he did everything else aboard, and decided that the captain had struck just the proper balance of sail. Were the wind on the beam, he knew that some after sail would be necessary since a sailing ship pivoted at a point near her mainmast. Balance was a law of ship and sail. The helm demanded it, the same as the steersman of one's voyage through life demanded balance of mind and spirit. Forward of the main stood the forecastle, representing the brawn of the vessel, while aft stood the poop, a ship's brain. The muscle responded to the mind's impulses. Again, here was balance.

On the lee side of the quarter-deck Jenny sat with book in hand, her glance fixed on a boy who, judging by his facial expression, wished to be elsewhere. However, a cabin boy's education was important and he seemed half resigned to the suffering required of a young aspiring sailor.

"Ten times ten is how much?" Jenny was asking. "No, Tobias, save your fingers for ship's duty."

Jenny looked into his round face, where a labored expression tended to make his small blue eyes smaller. Tobias had cottony hair, freckles, and an upturned nose that shone like a polished button and seemed to draw his upper lip out of reach of the lower.

"Comes to a hunnerd, ma'am," he said.

"Hundred, not hunnerd. Then one hundred divided by ten is——"

The boy screwed up his face. "They is some connection, all right, but lessen the answer is ten, damn'd if I know."

"Tobias Dunlap! Such language for a lad of ten! Don't ever use that word. It in no way makes a good seaman or gentleman of one. Did Captain Broadwinder become a famous mariner by the use of such language? Did Mr. Cartwright over there come by so many fine ships with foul words?"

Tobias frowned sheepishly. "Maybe not. But I've heard the cap'n say the word, and he added a lot more fore and aft o' it. Course, the owner is just a landlubber."

"So!" Jenny looked shocked. "I shall speak to Captain Broadwinder."

Cartwright met her surprised glance at that moment. His brows raised, as did the corners of his mouth, and she smiled with him despite an effort to keep a straight face.

"That's all for this morning, Tobias. But tomorrow when I ask you where Paris and Shanghai are I don't expect to hear you say California and Italy."

As the lad scampered away, Cartwright moved to the lee rail near Jenny, thinking as he surveyed her in crisp white dress that she completed the balance of both the ship and the team of husband and wife. Certainly her shipboard influence was felt from forecastle to staterooms.

"Rather amazing," she was saying, "how the rough and tumble sea life appeals to a boy. Tobias had rather listen to fo'c's'le yarns than learn where he has been or is going. I suppose it's a part of growing up. But do boys ever grow up?"

She raised her glance from knitting needles before he could reply. "The dashing widow who boarded the ship in New York seems to be absent from decks again today. I must look in on her."

Cartwright felt sure she spoke tentatively. Mrs. Littlefield, who could not endure a tossing deck, had shown considerable interest in him, and Jenny knew it. He also suspected Jenny of entertaining ideas of building a romance between himself, the bachelor, and the widow; if only to spice the voyage. Or she could be aware that Mrs. Littlefield was young and pretty and spent a little of each day on the captain's side of the deck, her six-year-old daughter the decoy.

Cartwright took a chair facing Jenny. "I noticed our young lawyer who plans to hang a shingle in San Francisco seemed to be rather impatient this morning."

"Mr. Fulton?" Jenny looked up, smiling speculatively. "Oh, has he—do you think—any romantic notions regarding Florence Littlefield? But of course you men seldom see what's going on."

"No," he replied. "Seems we have to be told."

Cocking her head, she studied him with open amusement. Aware that he could be bluntly reprimanding her for mentioning the widow, or looking back to the day she entered his office and spoke her piece about an added interest in the vessel, she said the opposite of what she was thinking:

"I simply refuse to believe you are fishing, sir."

He laughed with enjoyment. She sparred nicely, he admitted. Almost, she tried to convey the idea that she had nothing better to do than engage one in idle repartee. But he knew better. In fact, he would gamble that were the helmsman pinching the ship too close to the wind, she would be among the first to notice it. Therefore, she was, for some unearthly reason, merely trying to draw him out.

Broadwinder removed hands from hips and walked to the wheel. "Strike the bell six, Barnaby," he said.

With the last stroke of eleven o'clock, he gave the helmsman the "Steady as she goes, sailor," and moved unhurriedly toward Jenny and the shipowner. "All's well," he said, darting a glance into the rigging. "Driving long at a steady eleven, and not a passenger on deck."

"I'm curious," Cartwright said. "Why just eleven knots?"

"A good question." Philip's face lit up. "She's newly sparred and rigged and fresh cotton is in the wind. She'll do more. So why eleven?" He never took his eyes off the ship as he spoke. "I could blow sail and rake the sticks out of her before we hit the doldrums, work all hands watch and watch and clip off sixteen. But I'm saving speed for the time when I need it, testing as I go."

Squinting an eye on Cartwright, he laughed. "Don't look so surprised, sir. I'm a prudent man until the occasion demands the opposite. I'm also a man who calculates not only risk but the value of speed. By way of explanation, suppose I ran to

San Francisco in eighty-eight days, one under Creesy's *Flying Cloud*, wore out crew and ship and then lost the homeward run to Keys, would I be hailed for setting a new record to 'Frisco town?"

"I see," Cartwright replied, showing pleased surprise. "Excellent reasoning, Captain. Speed governed by purpose."

Jenny glanced mischievously from Philip to Cartwright. "Or it could be the captain's way of trying to impress the shipowner."

"Ha! Don't I own a quarter of her, Mistress Jenny?"

"Sure," she came back at him. "But he owns three quarters." Dropping her eyes to her knitting, she said, "Now suppose you owned half, would you have made such a long speech, Captain Broadwinder?"

"Save your arithmetic for Tobias," he retorted merrily. "Aye, for you have to go higher than calculus to figure out a way to part a closefisted shipowner from his shares.

"Correct, sir?" Tapping Cartwright's shoulder with the back of his fingers, he moved on to the weather side with a warning of worsening weather ahead.

A strained silence followed his departure. Jenny was aware that Cartwright knew she had intentionally seized upon the opportunity to mention again the disparity of ownership. She knew he was thinking of it now, realized that he knew the matter remained uppermost in her thoughts.

"Would you care for tea?" she asked, meeting his gaze squarely.

"Not now, thank you," he replied, looking level with her.

A moment later she bent to her knitting. If her lingering smile seemed touched with a measure of defiance mixed with faint amusement, it was because she realized suddenly that in the brief encounter they had flung the gauntlet, the issue that extra quarter interest in the ship which Philip surely deserved and which George Cartwright would never give up without a struggle. She had not the slightest notion of how she would go about getting it; she knew only that the voyage would be a long one and that Cartwright's definition of Philip's calculated prudence—speed governed by purpose—was appealing enough to form the key to her strategy.

Peretta appeared on deck. She ordered tea, adding, "Will you inquire about the ill sailor in the fo'c's'le and report his condition?"

As the steward bowed away, she said blithely, "Too bad

the physician engaged for the voyage could not board us in New York, Mr. Cartwright. I'm at a loss to know whether the sailor has ordinary fever or some contagious disease. I've looked in on him twice and——"

"You?" he said. "You should not take such risks."

"Why not? I'm mother to ship's cat, cabin boy, apprentices, and all. Now could I rest leaving a sick man to old Lowery, the sailmaker? A callous and primitive sort of man, he'd have the patient walking the deck under a hot sun to relieve fever."

As she talked on about this and that, the lurching of the ship seemed to increase. A look over the side at charging waves and deepening troughs verified Captain Broadwinder's prediction of worsening weather. Spray flew high as seas hammered at the stern and starboard quarter and fell back for repeated onslaughts. Bad weather and rough going for passengers, it was nothing out of the ordinary to the captain, whose experienced legs gave to the scend of deck as he continued to eye sails and pennant. He knew the fickle sea wind. It could shift and throw cross seas at a ship, fall away and come on with devilish glee from another direction, the same as running seas could pile up ahead and sneak a dirty blow at the bows.

He had moved to the wheel for a conn of the binnacle when the *Eagle* buried her nose to the gammoning in a heavy sea. She staggered an instant, in which everything loose aboard was thrown forward, including captain, crew, and all. As she lifted and tossed from side to side, Cartwright helped Jenny to her feet and supported her with one hand as he clung to the lee braces with the other. Broadwinder somehow maintained his footing, though the steward sprawled flat of belly in spilled tea while the saucer rolled away from broken cup in crazy circles toward the rail.

"My tea, Captain Broadwinder!" Jenny cried. "Seems you could replace the upper tops'l with the lower and strike a proper lift."

The captain had no sooner obliged her by shouting the order than Cartwright said, somewhat surprised by her ready solution of the problem, "I thought he had found the perfect balance of sail."

"But not with weather," she replied directly. "Weather changes." She added, "Changes all things with it."

She continued to amaze him with her candid expressions, many of which carried a double meaning and suggested in most significant manner observations one made in the voyage of life. But he was unaware that he still held her arm, until her hand briefly touched his. Releasing her quickly, he saw that her attention was directed at the topsails and took it as a matter of course that she had unconsciously freed herself.

Jenny, however, was conscious of her doing. Her pretense had been deliberate, a means of forestalling embarrassment on his part; for the sake of politeness, nothing more. As his hand fell away, she turned slowly, gave him a gracious smile, and extended her hand.

"Thanks for rescuing a poor sailor from the deck, sir."

He accepted her hand for the brief moment she gave it and said with a twinkle in his eye something about a land-lubber's heroism in saving Neptune's daughter from a perilous sea. Then he watched her move across deck to Philip. The touch of her hand had rather excited him, he realized, as had her penetrating glance and smile. She could be very close, almost revealing, one moment, and very distant the next.

Seldom did George Cartwright indulge in what he termed pure nonsensical thinking. Even now, as he turned his gaze from Jenny to the running sea, he sternly reproached himself for trying to solve the eternal mystery to man, woman. Like her husband, whom he was inclined to believe overrated at times and again entirely deserving of heaped praise, she kept him guessing. Even so, he was sure of a number of things:

The Broadwinders constituted, singly and as a team, a triple puzzle. The voyage ahead would make demands on husband and wife and team, and serve to uncover much. As the race would surely put the vaunted Broadwinder to a test that would eliminate all doubt, it could scarcely fail to present the true Jenny. All things considered, this sailing adventure aboard his own vessel promised more than just a race between two ships.

The seas charged in stronger, slapping harder at the sides. Broadwinder stood alone, oblivious to flying spray now dripping from his nose and soaking his blue coat. A shift in the wind, ever so slight, sent his gaze alternately aloft and a-weather, as though his sensitive mind felt and regulated the pulse of ship and elements. He spoke an order and men leaped to obey it. He was adding sail, cautiously jockeying for balance and speed. Testing. The current gave him push and the forward surge of the *Eagle* increased as the wind slanted more to starboard and met canvas ready to belly taut.

Cartwright watched as a student might a master, realizing as he did so that Broadwinder had stolen the jump on the weather. Though it was nothing to be amazed about, it was nevertheless an impressive show, one man calling for yards hauled and sails loosed one by one to capture expertly every breath of wind in its gradual shift.

The warning of the change of watch sounded, then the ship's bell struck the hour of twelve. Mr. Fortune appeared on deck, and the steward announced the noonday meal.

Captain Broadwinder took a last look at top hamper and seas. The ship rocked and roared along on a strong beam wind. He seemed pleased with her behavior, and the "All's well" look in his eye as he gave the ship to his chief mate was replaced by a friendly grin and:

"She's logging a good thirteen, Mr. Fortune. Care to try for fifteen?"

Cartwright looked up suddenly. "A question, Captain. Just a little while ago you said something about saving speed for a time when you needed it. So why a reach for fifteen knots?"

Broadwinder replied in preoccupied manner, "Just limbering her up." Suddenly aware that the answer failed to satisfy the other, he said, "Mr. Fortune and I alternate four hours on and off, sir. Since the race won't entirely change that, I'm getting my first officer used to taking advantage of every breath of wind. Just testing."

Cartwright understood then. What had appeared to be a contradiction was nothing short of a captain's constant awareness of the big challenge ahead.

9

□ The *Calcutta Eagle* continued to spread her wings on the path of the great semicircle deep into mid-ocean. She ran her latitude down through the variable winds, and blew on with the lusty northeast trades on her port beam through every kind of weather other than icy gales and hurricanes in a swift reach for the tropics and the belt of calms along the equator.

On southward she tore, straining at her boltropes, knifing the seas, spreading foam down her sides, her log line trailing in her long white wake. Good running weather, good dispositions aboard. Squalls roared in, dumped their watery ballast aboard, and hissed on, leaving decks wet, sails and cordage dripping. Slowly the winds backed, came on again, weaker than before. Captain and crew knew they were running out of the trades, entering that stretch of weather called the doldrums. Then, of a sudden, so it seemed, the *Eagle* folded her wings and sat right in the middle of a still, breathless sea. However, it had not been sudden. The quarter-deck had recorded for three successive days the diminishing speed and progress. At the end of the third day Broadwinder entered into the logbook the date, ship's position by latitude and longitude, and:

Scarcely a breath of wind. Made only three miles today.

Dawn on the following day threw colors high into the cloudless dome of heavens. It came up mightily out of the sea, rimming the line of horizon with first the pearl and pink of a sea shell. The glassy sea reflected from its depths the changing tints, and the limp hanging sails of the stilled clipper seemed painted by the brush of morning. Swiftly, almost in a sudden burst of violence, orange and flame touched the ocean's rim, leaped up into the green-hot sky, and heralded the sun.

Hanging in the humid, transparent sky, a lone gull flashed white and circled and disappeared. It caught the captain's eye a moment before the Southern sea, a vast motionless mirror stretching off into eternity, drew his attention.

"We'll stew in our shadows today, Mr. Winston," he said, conning the uppers.

"You said it, sir," the mate replied, glancing up at the poop. "The figgerhead'll be squintin' and sweatin' before the hands soojie-moojie the decks." Casting an eye aloft, he stroked his red hair. "Seems we're snugged down for a heathenish hell, wi' the old air risin' hotter'n a brass furnace."

A faint cat's-paw animated the canvas and moved on, stirring up a narrow breeze lane across the water.

"Smoke and oakum! A rotten teaser, sir."

Broadwinder had had his rightful share of calms in both the Atlantic and Pacific. He recalled one voyage in which he gained not a mile in eight days. The inactivity of the sea could be monotonous and maddening to all aboard ship. Day after day under a burning sun with scarcely a stirring of the clammy air, with the same glassy seas for company, a mischievous wind suddenly rattling the top hamper and building hopes that vanished as suddenly when all canvas hung limp again. After a time tempers flared. Only strict shipboard discipline eased the tension. Four hours on duty, hands scraping the cable, mending sail, splicing, scrubbing and tarring, manning stations as if under full sail, these things kept the crew busy and made for a happy ship.

Down on the weather deck, big Norwich, a good sailor and somewhat of a bully, was saying to his companion in mopping, "I 'member the time when we come through the doldrums wi' never the loss o' wind. I was sailin' on the old blackballer *Chester Barnaby*. We had a cook nobody wanted and we was plannin' to feed him to the finned monsters once we was calmed. But the wind kept us busy." He added rather mournfully, "So we was stuck wi' the Celestial and his chow all the way to Shanghai."

The other, Stokes, was a wiry lad with close-set eyes in a round face. "Buster," he said, looking at Norwich, "maybe it's the heat and maybe it's I'm tired listening to a slack-jaw who's always talking about doing a human being dirt. So belay."

Norwich eyed the other with the kind of a threat in his expression that bespoke action. Then he looked up cautiously and, seeing the captain's attention full upon him, fell to his task at once, saying for the ears of the master, "I never done a man harm, friend Stokes. Never a man."

Broadwinder knew them as he knew the seas. They were like children, living from one day to the next with their small hopes and desires and memories. At sea they longed for the land and on shore for the deep water. They nursed grievances, drank to excess at every opportunity, spent their pay freely on women, then cursed the memory of them. But they knew their business.

Old Lowery, the sailmaker, emerged from the sail locker with sharp gray eyes peering out of deep sockets and a hard scowl on his leathery face. "Damned wet decks!" he growled. "Always when a sail is ready to be laid and cut it's holystone the decks or it's pitch bubblin' out o' the seams. Dockins!" he cried to the sluggish boy who had signed on as sailmaker's mate. "Show lively here!"

Rubbing the growth of white stubble on his cheeks, he studied sky and sea with open disapproval. "This is a Paddy's hurricane, all right, sir." The term meant a calm. "And it'll last through this day."

That was the verdict. Broadwinder had never found his prophecy in error.

The bosun, Draper, knocked the ashes from his morning pipe and blew out fat cheeks. Turning to Chips, the name bestowed on the ship's carpenter, he said, "For once I'd give me right eye to catch old Sails wrong on the weather."

O'Hara, the carpenter, was a gangling man with a big Adam's apple and a shock of coal-black hair. Taller than any aboard, he seemed all bones and scant flesh. But he had a sense of humor. He laughed and his voice carried like chain plunging through the hawsehole.. "That's his joy. Ever the time comes old Sails misses the weather he'll pine hisself to Fiddler's Green."

"Go to hell, Chips," Lowery said without zeal. "If I sewed a boltrope like you saw a line, we'd have to shape yards like a new moon."

"Ho!" Chips's big mouth flew open. "Recall once you cut a jibs'l for a spanker in the Chiny Sea. Come from mixin' rice wine and samshu, didn't it?"

The bosun chuckled. "Had we of bent it on, Chips, we'd be gathering sternway yet."

"A man makes mistakes, all right, all right," Lowery said wearily. "Once I knew a carpenter with more brains than Chips O'Hara. He sawed his thumb half off before he caught on. But as I said, he had brains. Chips has sawdust in his top hamper, and one fine day the plug'll slip and he'll choke to death before a friend like me can cut his throat."

Broadwinder stood with eyes twinkling merrily as he listened. The older the sailor, the sharper his imagination and wit, the more fluent his curses. The long verbal duel between Sails and Chips was as much a part of the Calcutta Eagle as wheel and compass. And whenever Norwich ceased to bully a new hand or the bosun failed to kindle an argument the ship, as much as these men, would appear entirely out of character.

Cartwright came on deck in the company of Mrs. Littlefield and her six-year-old daughter Madeline, nodding his head and hiding a wince as the widow talked a blue streak. Then her large expressive eyes lifted to the captain. She smiled.

"My dear Captain Broadwinder," she said. "Had I known

we were to drop anchor in this hot sea I do believe I'd have booked passage on another ship. Just how long will this awful calm last?"

Broadwinder bowed, spread his best face, and made a reply in jest. Scooping Madeline up, he asked how she was enjoying the voyage, only to be told that he certainly went to extremes with his weather. "First great big waves and now none at all, sir. Why, when Mother says you're the King of ship and sea? And since you are, why don't you have a prince or princess?"

"A great idea," Broadwinder said. "I hereby proclaim Madeline of the house of Littlefield Princess of the Sea."

Neither Broadwinder nor Cartwright was blind to the intent gleam of interest in the widow's eyes. They dwelled on the captain, and they seemed sharpened somewhat by the firm set of her pretty mouth as the smile vanished. She had the smooth, delicate white skin and healthy color of a girl in her teens. Her oval face was small-boned and seemed as youthful as that of a sixteen-year-old, though further examination revealed a woman in full maturity. Where her blossomed youth of line and detail had gone of a sudden one did not know; or care, for in its place was something of experience and life, things that indicated vitality and challenged a man to put his finger on them. Cartwright did not think her behavior studied; she appeared too changeable and spontaneous for him to reach any such conclusion. And yet there was something about her that he could not quite trust.

And Philip? Cartwright looked at him and wondered at his strength or weakness under circumstances he had heard about —two mortals thrown together in the narrow confines of a ship. Many a captain who had successfully defied the seas had been caught up by a chance relationship that cost him his ticket. However, Broadwinder had Jenny, which should serve to keep the cats at bay.

A trivial, negligent thought. Cartwright dismissed it. "Mrs. Littlefield"—he smiled—"perhaps this is just the kind of weather you need. You were seldom on deck when the going was rough."

Her brows arched and she gave the shipowner an engaging sidewise smile. "Now that I'm discovered, what do you suggest for entertainment?"

"Cards, books—the ship's library seems to be an excellent one, or there's fishing from the rail in perfectly still water."

She appeared to consider his suggestions before once again

turning on Broadwinder. "Sounds rather dull. Books and magazines are printed to read only when one can do nothing else. And fishing—what would I do with a fish? Perhaps you have a suggestion, Captain."

"I've heard you play the piano."

She showed her disappointment in him by a glance. "Somehow, that doesn't sound at all exciting."

"So it's excitement you want." Broadwinder laughed. "Then suppose you lead the ship in a song to whistle up a wind, and if that's not enough, climb the futtock shrouds to the royals."

After a moment's careful study of him, her face lit up in a smile. "And after that, sir, I suppose I could swim out a ways."

"Indeed, Mrs. Littlefield. Now, if you'll pardon me, I'll serve Mrs. Broadwinder her morning coffee."

As the widow's eyes widened and clung to his departing figure, Cartwright silently applauded his captain. Then, not wishing to become her audience again, he hailed the second mate and descended the companion. When she turned her glance he was already on the weather deck asking questions about fishing gear.

Young Jeremiah Fulton had no sooner showed himself on deck than the widow drew him to her side. Tall, broad-shouldered and erect, he struck Cartwright as a man of immense energy and ambition, the kind that belongs only to youth. The furnace of experience had not yet burned these appealing qualities out of his fine angular face. In his bright blue eyes his growing interest in Florence Littlefield shone for all to see. Honesty and forthrightness, mused Cartwright, who was thinking it would be quite interesting to meet the lawyer ten years in the future.

When the widow's discerning eye appeared to be taking Fulton apart Cartwright felt instinctively that the young man was tottering on the brink of some undisclosed misfortune. But Mr. Winston was saying:

"The bigger the hook and bait, sir, the bigger the fish, I alluz sez."

"Of course. Of course." Cartwright eyed the gear and suppressed a statement about not wishing to angle for a whale. He paid little or no attention to the widow's daughter Madeline, who stared curiously from big hook to sea and back at him. Then the baited hook was cast over the side with a splash. When scarcely three fathoms under, the line jerked taut and George Cartwright braced himself against the rail and threw a neat loop over a pin to slow the burning line. A moment later the surface of the quiet sea seemed to explode in silver and sapphire as a large marlin cleared the water and remained for a photographic second suspended in air. He rainbowed in a frenzy to dislodge the hook then fell with a resounding pop and thrashed the sea into foam.

With advice from every side, "Give him line! Pay out, sir!" Cartwright realized that he had to land this fish. The on-watch crew raised their voices and the below watch were fast crowding the rail. The quarter-deck seemed a beehive of passengers. Failure meant loss of face.

He was no fisherman, and he knew they were versed in this sort of thing, so he tried to forget his own blistered hands as he flipped the cord from anchored pin. The monster of the deep fairly flew with it. The line seemed to smoke as it tore through his hands and wriggled like a snake afire over the rail. He dropped it and saw it pay out fast, too fast, the coil diminishing so rapidly it would soon be gone unless something was done to stop it. There was little time to think and smaller reason to do so, he admitted, for his work was cut out for him. Either he would fight that searing line or he would not. It was a matter of determination and grit, of the qualities that made a man versus the prudence of his years. He knew he would be burned, probably jerked over the rail a bruised and battered old man who had tackled a sport belonging to youth. They would laugh, of course.

The bosun cried almost in his ear, "Want me to take it, sir?" And the sailor called Norwich was saying, "Let me at 'im, sir!"

Something seemed to snap inside Cartwright; a chain, he thought, one that bound him in all dignity to prudent behavior. A little fire sprang up inside him and he was suddenly angry; at the fish, at himself.

He caught the line with both hands and tried to pit his weight against it. It was like a long hot coal in his hands, a thing of motion and power that jerked him off his feet and propelled him toward the rail. But his eyes were glued to the pins and, as he struck the rail with shoulders and head, he threw the line around a pin and circled it again and again. It jerked taut with a sound like that of a bowstring loosing an arrow. It held, and he, with the last yard of line in his hand, hung on as though his very safety depended on it.

He did not see the marlin leap out of the water some distance away, but he knew from the yells about him that he still had his fish. He felt a moment of amazement at his own doing. It was followed by an awareness of pain. The palms of his hands burned unbearably and his head and shoulders ached as never before. And he was breathing hard. Sweat ran down his face. He thought of Julia and, despite the pain, smiled at the picture of his horrified sister.

"That's playing it mighty close," the bosun said excitedly. "Down to the last few feet."

"Aye!" Chips cried. "By damn, I thought that fin was on his way to Africa! But he ain't landed yet."

Young Fulton struck Cartwright on the sore shoulder. "Sir, you're a better fisherman than I'll ever be. I thought for a minute you were afraid of that line."

Cartwright stared at him. "By God, I was!" he exclaimed, to the delight of all.

The marlin kept him busy. All the while the sun lifted higher and blazed down without mercy. The unruffled sea threw the heat back and aboard ship until George Cartwright felt himself broiling in his clothing. The palms and fingers of his hands were raw before he finally worked the spent fish to the port beam, where the happy crew gaffed and heaved it aboard.

As he looked up at his catch swinging from the end of the main yard, he pondered the gain. Certainly he had no use for the fish. Throbbing pain made him feel a little foolish. But there was a reward. He was a new man, and he felt now as he had when boyhood discoveries of his strength and the will to win pleasantly astonished him.

He was not aware that Jenny was anywhere near until she surprised him with: "So you caught a fish, Mr. Cartwright."

His head turned quickly. "Yes," he said, wondering if she had read his thoughts. Evidently she had, for her half-amused glance was steady and rather disconcerting.

"We watched you," she went on in a matter-of-fact voice. "Saw you wince often and blow to cool your hands." She paused a moment. "We were divided on the outcome. Some said you would quit, others believed you'd stay with it."

He considered this in the brief silence between them. "And which side did you take?" he said finally.

"Oh, I was merely hoping, sir." Her glance fell to his

hands. She took one of them in hers and turned the palm up. "Heavens alive, another patient aboard!"

Cartwright did not move, but waited for her to look up. When she did he asked, "Just what were you hoping?"

"It doesn't matter really." She smiled. "However, I thought you more stubborn than wise, just hanging on to something that would benefit you more had you let it go."

The way she put it coupled with something lurking behind her eyes caused him to think of the extra shares in the ship. He was almost sure she had that very thing in mind until she sighed wearily and said in gentle scolding tones:

"A look at your hands proves it."

Even then he could not wholly dispel doubt.

10

☐ The *Calcutta Eagle* sat out that day and the next with no motion whatever in her sails and hull. The very air was dead and there was no roll to the sea. Not a block creaked. Heat waves danced over the water and up into the still rigging. The burning sky met the blistered mirror of the sea far away on every horizon; like a line drawn in a vast circle to disgorge heat and smother all inside it. The sun dropped atop the water on the second day and seemed to shoot bolts of fire across the sea with a vengeance. It reddened and went under swiftly, almost violently. Then the quick night of the tropics panted in and tiny and great stars popped out in the heavens. The sea reflected them and, with the seam of sky and ocean swallowed up by night, the ship seemed to be floating in a breathless universe with stars above, below, and on every side.

As night closed in, passengers and crew hoped for some relief from the oppressive air of day. Exchanging remarks about the weather, stateroom voyagers moved down the companionways for strolls to the bows and back. With nothing better to do, they paused often at the rail to follow the silver streaks of flying fish or leaping porpoises that animated the evening sea; or a star that blazed a line of white down the sky, reflecting upward in the water until a meeting in the opaque distance put out the light. Soon the surface of the water was streaked with moving shapes of luminescence, and often splashes told of the eternal battle among the carnivorous fish.

Sheet lightning trembled faintly across the far northeastern horizon. Playing restlessly upon sky and water, it seemed to dance about as though to entertain the gods of the doldrum seas.

Forward of the mainmast members of the crew gathered. Sounds of a violin being tuned were interlarded by laughter and jest. Old Lowery said nothing as he tightened catgut to his satisfaction, then began sewing away. The tune evoked words from his rasping throat and he was soon joined by his companions.

> "Did somebody say she's a clipper queen;
>   Pull, me bully boys, pull!
> Wi' a ringtail spanker and Jamie Green;
>   Pull, me bully boys, pull!"

A string snapped with a "ping" and the sailmaker instantly spiced the chantey with a muffled oath and a remark about a "fiddle as far off its true course as the cook's recipe for apple grunt."

With a hand tucked at Philip's sleeve, Jenny smiled. "Captain Broadwinder, you should either demand that fiddle go by the board or find evening chores for Sails."

There was no reply. Philip, she observed, was more interested in the play of lightning; as though he were whistling for a wind. "Tobias named the continents today," she said. "Before the voyage ends I'll have him versed in geography and—— Philip Broadwinder, you're not hearing a word I say."

"Every word, girl. Now there could be a wind from that direction," he replied, steering her toward the stern rail.

"So you said off the coast of Borneo last voyage. As I recall it came from the opposite corner."

"Changing monsoons."

"Look, Philip! The widow has Mr. Cartwright in tow."

"And he's suffering from worse than raw hands." He added with a note of interest in his voice. "Or is he?"

"Why did you ask that? Does it mean you'd enjoy a stroll with her?"

Broadwinder grinned at Jenny. "Perhaps. If she didn't rattle like an anchor cable, she might be good company. I often wonder if she talked her husband into a grave."

Jenny looked up at him, starlight flashing in her eyes. "Just the same, you're very attentive to her. And only yesterday I noticed that exploring look in your eye."

They paused at the taffrail near the wheel and under the spanker boom.

"So Mistress Jenny is jealous of a passenger! Now if I was turned that way, I'd be thinking of tossing Cartwright over the side. Why, you've practically spoon-fed him since he played hero to the crew and got burned for his trouble."

"Have I now?" she flared. "And so you think he was playing hero. Perhaps he was, but not to the crew, or anyone other than himself."

Broadwinder eyed her a moment, then shifted his glance to the lightning waves and on to Cartwright and Mrs. Little-field at the port companion. "You should know," he said blithely. "The widow is more interesting, however. She has a darn good figure. Clipper-built and——"

"Captain Broadwinder, I'm wondering if you would like to see lightning strike here and now!"

He laughed with enjoyment. "If there' a wind in it, yes." Then he took in decks and top hamper and said, "She really doesn't interest me, Jenny girl; rather, she's more a curiosity. Makes a man wonder."

"Wonder? About what?" Jenny demanded.

"Oh, whether she's like this weather or a gale of wind."

"Philip!" she cried, shocked, whirling to leave him.

"There she is, Captain!" she flung hotly. "Go find out whether she blows a gale or not!"

She had taken no more than two hurried steps when she felt herself being swept dizzily up into his arms. He held her close, until the stubble of his chin scratched her cheek and ear.

"A spirited little cat, aren't you, Mistress Jenny?" he said in low voice.

With that, he roughly turned her face to his and kissed her on the mouth.

"You took that kiss," she declared. "I didn't give it."

"Well, well," he said with mock concern. "You're a most

unreasonable woman. The very idea of a wife objecting to
her spouse's interest in another pretty face and ankle! Shame
on you, Jenny girl! Now apologize while I'm master of my temper."

"If I should be ashamed?" she asked incredulously. "I
should apologize? Have you lost your senses, Philip Broadwinder?"

A brief mocking laugh escaped her. Then the situation
struck her as being so ludicrous it was actually funny. As she
began to laugh with enjoyment, her jealousy appeared as
silly as unwarranted.

"All right, Philip darling," she managed between outbrusts,
"I apologize." Soon a contented sigh escaped her. "Put me
down, Philip."

Instead, he spoke something in her ear.

"I'll do no such thing!" she told him, then touched her lips
to his in a brief peck that refuted her statement.

Jenny went below. Although not a breath of air stirred, she
did not think of heat and weather as she obeyed his order,
then gazed critically at the flowing gown of pale blue silk in
the mirror. Philip had bought it from a French merchant in
the East. A lovely garment despite its filminess that revealed
more of her figure than her sense of modesty condoned.
Rather discomforting, that nagging awareness of exposure,
even with Philip. A look at her face caused her color to rise,
for the mirror reflected excitement.

She turned her glance at once, though not soon enough to
put down a small catch of resentment. It was not directed at
Philip or anything she could put a finger on; rather, it was
more like an abrasive touching her pride. Perhaps she was, as
Philip once said, too stubbornly proud and entirely too self-
sufficient. Or it could be that she resented these planned meetings, preferring to be caught up blessedly natural and un-
awares. She didn't know.

A sound above caused her to look up quickly. Philip perhaps. She glanced at the door, instinctively drawing the gown
tight about her neck as she did so. Philip did not come.

"The devil with him," she muttered, moving to a chair and
reaching for a brush. Always while grooming her hair she
lost herself in reflection of this and that. After minutes of failure to think of the past, she moved to a port for a breath of
air.

A long red lane lay over the water, stretching endlessly off into space, it seemed. It ended on the line of horizon where a late moon showed half its crimson face. Suddenly a fish broke the moon lane, hung reddened a moment, then thwacked itself down. Then the sea healed over except for wide diminishing ripples.

She and Philip had seen many moons come up like this one. Moons in every kind of sea. She turned away, put out the light in the cabin, and returned to the open port in time to hear a voice directly above.

"What a thrilling, romantic sight, Captain. Something in a moon over the sea engulfs one in a strange spell."

"Quite true, Mrs. Littlefield. I recall my wife's saying almost those very words on our first voyage together."

The widow laughed lightly. "My dear Captain, must you always be so formal? To my friends I'm Florence."

Sol Jenny bit her lower lip. So he was more interested in that designing widow than in his blue-gowned wife! And just what would he say in reply? She listened with bated breath.

"Thank you. I am pleased to be called a friend. However, a captain must remember his office, Mrs. Littlefield. He neither addresses a man before the mast as Mister nor ever fails to honor his officers with the form of address."

"How very silly, sir! I suppose if you were making love to a passenger—say me, for example—you'd still call me Mrs. Littlefield."

Philip's chuckle was audible to Jenny. "On deck, yes."

"Now I've caught you, Captain," she retorted merrily. "Not a half hour ago I could not help but hear you call Mrs. Broadwinder Jenny."

"So I did, madam. I shall try to be more careful in the future. Now if you'll excuse me, I must take a turn about the ship before going below."

Jenny smiled. Philip had put ice in his farewell. It both pleased her and stirred warmth in her mind and heart. She gave the rising moon a bright look of thanks, put her back to the port, and gazed at the door through which Philip would soon appear.

Her eyes danced with anticipation of his coming. She knew what she would do first, repeat the conversation she had heard with no shame for eavesdropping. Then Philip would tell her he had been aware of her ear at the port directly under his position at the rail, and he would of course

say that he had forced a parting with the lovely widow lest
he succumb to the charms of "dear Florence."

All the while his arms would be about her yielding waist.
Then warm lips would press against warm lips and he would
lift her, more gently than on deck this night.

Minutes later, the door opened and Philip paused to stare
at her neck and shoulders bathed in moonlight streaming
through the round port. A touch of blue and wide eyes smiling held him rooted there.

"Do come in," she said in stilted tones. "My dear Captain,
must you always be so formal? To my friends I'm Jenny."

"Now are you, madam?" he replied, moving to her. "However pleased I am to be called your friend, a captain must remember his office, Mrs. Broadwinder."

Standing before her, he tilted her chin upward with one
hand and drew her close with the other. "So! Sits the wind
in that direction? Sure, I knew you were listening to every
word between us."

"How very silly, sir! Now if you were making love—to me,
for example—would you still call me Mrs. Broadwinder?"

There was no reply. His hands were now at her waist.
Jenny smiled contentedly. Everything seemed to be going
exactly as she had predicted.

11

□ At four bells on the grave-eye watch, two o'clock in the
quiet of morning, a breeze rattled the sails of the sleeping *Calcutta Eagle*.

Captain Broadwinder fairly leaped out of bed. With a sensitive ear he tried to determine whether he had a cat's-paw
or driving wind. It seemed to be constant, though a man could
never be sure in this fickle belt. Then he listened for sounds
of activity on deck. Satisfied that the crew had not been
caught napping, he whistled a tune and began to dress. Mr.
Fortune had a gauge of the weather, all right. He was calling

for yards braced around and the spanker boom shifted. A pat-
ter of feet followed the clipped orders.

Ah! This was good. A fine breeze blew in the ports and the
old girl, the *Calcutta Eagle*, was gathering headway. Good
ship, good crew. He was half a mind to catch a few more
winks of sleep. It would never do, however; a master hit the
deck at a time like this, if only to make his bow to the wind
god. "Thank you, sir. Thank you from the bottom of our
hearts." Then, "An extra ration of rum for the crew, steward.
All hands waiting, so show lively."

She moved along now at four-five knot pace, shuddering
ever so slightly as she waited impatiently for the proper trim
of sails. Mr. Fortune should have called "All hands" to hasten
her departure; indeed, for one had to gamble that this was
another teaser and race ahead for a wind with marrow in its
bones, one that would kick up seas and exercise a man's sea
legs.

Putting down an urge to nudge Jenny awake, he went
straightway to deck and stood at Mr. Fortune's side. The wind
came over the port quarter, seemingly constant. It had left
them days back on the port beam.

"We're milking the northeast trade dry," he said to the
chief mate.

"Aye, sir, but any's a favoring wind."

"And we could fling more sail to it. Eh, Mr. Fortune? Say
all the way, royals high."

"As you say, sir." In the next breath he cried the decks
with, "Break out the main and fore to'gannels'ls, and let fly
the main royal!"

In due time the sails filled from "clew to earing," and
Broadwinder stood under bright moon and deck lights hanging on to his wind. He had the knack of sail, the chief mate admitted in silence, down to the last line and halyard. As wind
began to haul abaft the quarter at around six bells that same
watch, he shifted the helm to hold it to the set of yards and
canvas, and when it settled down squarely out of the north,
he hauled up sail aft, squared the after yards, then the foreyards, took in fore-and-aft sails and put the helm amidships,
taking his wind right over the stern. The *Eagle* fairly leaped
ahead.

Mr. Fortune read the log line. "In the mathematics of sail,
sir, you play it down to the last fraction."

Broadwinder squinted an eye aloft. "It'll take that and the luck of a lord to beat Mayo Keys, Mr. Fortune. And don't you ever forget it."

The chief mate considered this in respectful silence, thinking as he did so the captain guilty of, perhaps, an overstatement. Somehow, he was unable to swallow all the talk about Keys's giving Broadwinder trouble. He was biased, naturally, but for good reason. He knew of no man who handled a ship better or who, with the possible exception of Creesy of the *Flying Cloud,* drove a ship faster. Therefore, he thought the captain was playing a game with his officers and crew. A gullible lot at best, they would in due time come to believe such remarks as this last one and respond by doing their utmost to outsail the *Emperor.* Well, it wasn't bad logic, come to think of it.

He gave the captain a wise smile and said, "Yes, sir."

Broadwinder eyed him narrowly. "Mr. Fortune, your tone of voice was quite natural, but your expression seemed rather dubious."

"Yes, sir." The mate scanned the forward deck. "However, sir, I'll support your statement at every opportunity. In the right places, of course."

"Of course." Broadwinder's eyes twinkled.

Jenny appeared suddenly on deck in wrap and bonnet. "And just who or what are you two conspiring against?"

"Weather and men, what else?" Broadwinder replied pleasantly. "And why aren't you sleeping?"

"Have I ever failed to help celebrate a wind in the doldrums, Captain Broadwinder?"

She glanced from one to the other, rather mischievously, then took in the rigging and decks in businesslike manner. Wetting a finger, she felt of the wind and raised her brows. "According to Sir Polaris in the after sky, we're on a north wind. It won't last. What do you think, Mr. Fortune?"

"You're probably right, but we're using it to pick up one that will."

She eyed the sail flying. "I might lend you my petticoats for spirits'ls, Mr. Fortune. That is, of course, if you wish to reach for a wind while this one blows."

She saw a sharpening and thinning intensity come into Philip's eyes, and the brisk motion of excitement playing in Mr. Fortune's. Their glances met and both smiled. The mate said, "Shall we run them out, sir?" and the captain replied, "Why not?"

Mr. Fortune cupped his hands and cried: "Boom out stun's'ls on the main!"

Maintaining a discreet silence, Jenny watched topmen scramble aloft in the shadowy light and work themselves out to the yardarms. Moonlight played on the varnished booms that soon reached from each end of the yards out over the sea. Then sails dropped from the spars and lines were hauled taut. The supplementary sails, like wings on a bird, snared the wind and gave the *Eagle* extra speed. As the sailors said, she "boomed along."

Jenny went below. Now that Philip had his wind, all care and worry seemed to depart. She shut out of her mind all sounds of ship and crew and water and was soon fast asleep.

When she opened her eyes Philip lay beside her. Bright morning light flooded the cabin and the ship rose, fell, and heeled under the press of a good wind. Forward, sounding as distant as Philip's endearing words of the night, the crew sang an old sea chantey. But Philip's watch had begun at four in the morning. So it was well past eight now. Perhaps past nine. Tobias would be waiting for his tutoring, though he was probably hoping she would sleep round the clock. And George Cartwright! Poor man, his hands should have been dressed an hour earlier. And the apprentice in the forecastle suffered a shoulder cut from a fall. If it wasn't one thing it was another; always illness or injury.

She sat up in bed, breathed a sigh, and threw back the coverlet. She was soon holding a summer dress at arm's length and asking, "Now when did I last wear green?"

Her gaze left the dress and fell on Philip. He lay still, eyes anchored down. A smile, reflective, tender and mischievous, formed on her face and lingered a minute. Philip liked blue. So she would wear a ruffled dress of azure blue. And when he appeared on deck at the change of watch his expression should be worth seeing.

She dressed with all the care time would allow. Although punctuality aboard ship was expected of even the captain's wife, already tardy on deck, she used up long minutes before the mirror, and more in admiring study of her sleeping husband. She touched a finger to his hair almost wonderingly before kissing his forehead lightly. Then she left him and moved unhurriedly to deck, where sunlight painted her dress the color of morning sky and highlighted the maze of ruffles blowing in the wind.

With eyes squinted against the sudden glare, Jenny quickly took in the scenes of deck, top hamper, and ocean. Tobias sat in a deck chair talking to Cartwright, whose hands dangled awkwardly. The young lawyer and the widow—Jenny thought her somewhat overdressed—were engaged in conversation with the quiet elderly couple from Albany; Mr. Fulton and the Sherwoods doing the listening, of course. But the set of the yards and sails! The wind blew in over the portside just abaft the beam, proving they had lost the north wind and picked up an easterly while she slept. However, she would not appear curious. The ship bowled along fast and merrily and the weather seemed pleasantly cool for equatorial seas.

The tall, gray-mustached Georgia planter with his diminutive wife at his side bowed low and greeted her with a "most pleasant good mawnin', ma'am."

"Thank you, Mr. Mason. And the same to both of you. Isn't it nice to be moving again?"

The St. Louis merchant and trader, Big Jim Allison, as he liked to be called, came up with Prince Thomas, the ship's yellow cat, a wide grin on his huge face. "Like a wind off the Rockies, Mrs. Broadwinder."

She joined shipowner and cabin boy with a cordial greeting and, "Tobias, fetch the medicines and I'll hold school while dressing Mr. Cartwright's hand." She turned her face. "Good morning, Mr. and Mrs. Sherwood. Yes, I'm tardy, but we had to trap this wind in the night. Isn't it wonderful? And Mr. Fulton, a good morning to you, sir. I trust the fine blow didn't disturb your sleep. Hello, Mrs. Littlefield. What a pretty dress!"

With the return of Tobias, the passengers respectfully moved on. Jenny opened the medicine chest, sent a critical glance at the departing widow, then looked up at the shipowner.

"I do declare," she said with a gentle scolding on her lips, "I'll never understand why grown men do such things." Then, "Tobias, have you studied the map of oceans and continents?"

After attending to Cartwright's hands, Jenny devoted a half hour to the cabin boy's schooling and sent him on his way with all sorts of assignments. Watching him go, she said suddenly:

"I'm famished. Not a bite of breakfast!" A heavy sigh was

followed by a flashing smile. "Ship's chores, Mr. Cartwright. And now, would you care to join me for a daily visit to the fo'c's'le?"

Cartwright said he would. His brows rose at the thought of a gentlewoman's invasion of the crew's quarters. Sailors were at best a rough lot and he could not understand why Broadwinder allowed her to mix with them. However, he soon learned that her safety was well ensured. The second mate announced her coming and gave the hands time to "show presentable." Upon her entrance, the respect and adoration in the faces of the men further assured him. She was not aloof, but friendly, and her interest in their welfare evoked unmistakable signs of appreciation as well as tender memories of mothers or sweethearts. But they were not entirely honest with her, and she seemed wise to their ways when, after the sick had been treated, this one or that in a bid for attention presented a "most painful" scratch or bruise.

"Well, Jamie Stokes, I think you'll survive that cut," she would say, or, "Now, Dockins, as long as you follow Lowery with palm-and-needle, you're bound to miss the sailcloth every now and then. But we'll put something on the wound."

A sailor snickered. "Now ain't he in bad shape! Think he'll slip his cable, ma'am?"

"Oh, he'll live. I doubt if a Cape Horn snorter could do him in," Jenny replied.

The bell sounded the warning of the change of watch as they left the forecastle. It reminded Jenny that Philip would soon appear on deck, so with eyes alert she took a position where she might covertly witness his first reaction upon seeing her in blue. Thinking he had already partaken of his noonday meal, she was hoping he would seat her at the captain's table before relieving Mr. Fortune. She could endure inattention when the ship really needed him, though she doubted if she could ever become used to it.

And now Cartwright was talking of one thing and studying her strangely, as though he were thinking of another. Perhaps after the forecastle visit he was forming new estimates of the captain's wife. However, he could scarcely suspect after this full morning that she was primarily a selfish woman with designs on an extra quarter interest in his ship.

Then Philip came on deck and drew her darting glance. She eyed him surreptitiously as he took in ship and sail in the usual perfunctory manner before looking at her with a sudden

sharpness of expression. With surprise, excitement, and amusement all vying for control of his face, he came up to them,
doffed his cap, and held her attention with a pair of devilish
eyes.

"My favorite color, Mrs. Broadwinder." That was the extent
of his remark. But he had a faculty of packing his words to
her with a wealth of things left unsaid, none of which escaped
her.

She met his gaze directly and they said to each other in silence a thousand things, all in a stirring moment. "Thank you,
Captain Broadwinder."

Flashing a smile at Cartwright, she said, "A most dutiful
husband, sir, is one who might wreck the ship but never fails
to compliment his wife.

"But I'm hungry. Now will one or both of you lead me to
the captain's table without further ado?"

Philip had eaten, so he gave her to the shipowner with a
sailor's expression, "Mr. Cartwright has his stun's'ls set,"
meaning he had a woman on his arm.

"So he has," she replied. As an idea popped into her mind,
she told Philip not to bother to seat them.

Jenny was secretly pleased to be rid of Philip at this time.
His absence at the table presented an excellent opportunity
to push her conquest of George Cartwright's business mind.
For the occasion she had already decided on a subject inspired by the color of her dress. Although her wearing of blue
suggested to Philip an intimacy of love that caused her to
blush even now, blue stood for loyalty, the same as red stood
for courage and white for purity. Loyalty, such as Philip's
to ship and owner, and as constant as night and day, was a virtue upon which confidence was built. She would not preach,
heavens no; it was better to plant the seed among the many
she had sown and watch it grow.

She looked over her shoulder at Philip, now a man all for
ship and weather, bless his heart, then turned her head and
gave her escort a smile, one meant to convey her thoughts of
the moment, that life aboard a clipper ship was anything but
dull.

12

☐ Dawn broke next day with the captain on deck, lost in deep study of the elements. He paced back and forth, darting concerned glances from rigging to horizons on either side before resuming thoughtful study of the Southern sky. Down there dark boiling clouds rose up out of the sea, slowly but with ominous warning.

At the break of the poop Mr. Winston surveyed the banking sky over the bows, felt of the wind, glared aloft, and said, "Sir, I smell dirty weather o' the damnedest sort."

No doubt existed in Broadwinder's mind. The color and behavior of the clouds verified the barometric forecast of hours earlier.

And now he was debating, back and forth, in an effort to reach a decision. With the glass dropping steadily, a sure indication of rough weather, he could shape a course to the southeast or southwest in an endeavor to escape the full force of the blow. Experience cautioned him, however. Better to determine the storm's direction before doing so. Often the weather veered the same way and caught a vessel up in the very thing she sought to escape. It had happened to him, once off the coast of Brazil, again in the South Pacific. It could happen again.

Not even Jenny knew his fear of storms. Winds and seas of the roaring forties, wild and unrestrained as they were, were more often steady. But not so a storm of hurricane intensity. He did not tremble under snow squalls far below Cape Horn, frozen sails and rigging, or fog on a land approach. He had won over these things, won in himself and over himself. He ran with confidence through moderate gales and fresh gales when winds blew at forty-five miles an hour. Strong gales and whole gales and storms, with waves from thirty to forty feet high, the very air filled with foam and spray and lightning, these things threatened to unnerve him. Once a master lost his nerve, he was through; even if he survived he was finished.

Captain Broadwinder knew this, for he had seen it happen to one great seaman, a grand old man they called Captain Contestable. Back in forty-four, a few years after Philip Broadwinder, fresh out of school, sailed as apprentice aboard the *Osprey*.

A long time ago, he reflected.

He found it difficult now to recapture in memory any feeling of poor health. But he had signed aboard the *Osprey* for that very reason and sailed under the old salt to the tea and jute of the Far East, to the ivory of Africa, the olives of Spain, and the wines of France, and found in the sea that unknown remedy and cure. He became a man of muscle and bone and endurance. After several years before the mast the crew elected him to the office of second mate. He was then Mr. Broadwinder to the hands and Mr. Broadwinder to his superiors. Captain Contestable liked him and shared with him a vast knowledge of ships, men, seas, ports, and cargoes; shared with him secrets of the trade: how to steal a wind right out of a rival captain's hands; the running of narrow channels; and the manipulation of sail. They became great friends. On sea and shore the young mate and the Old Man imparted, each to the opposite, the spirit of youth and the wisdom of age.

He would never forget that morning when the heavy-jowled captain appeared on deck, with gravy spots on his coat, a gnarled finger at his big blue nose, and eyes squinted almost shut in study of long rolling swells and the peculiar yellow cast of sky over the China Sea. He knew what lay ahead, though he spoke of a capful of wind instead of a typhoon and calmly shaped a course to the east. So did the storm. The meeting on the following day did little to upset the gray-haired old sea dog who thought he was outsmarting the elements by riding the fringe of the storm. It was when seas almost swamped the ship and he thought the hatches would go that he realized the full storm was upon him. Keeping the *Osprey's* nose to the wind seemed impossible. Storm sail blew in that terrible wind and waves towered fifty feet high. The *Osprey* was a tremendous heavy-sparred three-sticker and not a member of the crew could imagine her standing bows nearly straight up; that is, until they saw it. Then the deep troughs reversed her position and she seemed to be sliding on a greased track fast for the bottommost pits of the sea. She struggled, groaned, and twisted for a day and night. She sprang leaks and felt her boats being smashed into kindling wood. As the gale howled and screeched, the ship required four men at the wheel to hold her head to wind and seas. She lurched, bows under, stern swinging wildly, not enough steadying sail on her to aid the helm in holding her nose to the weather. As she hung there perilously between destruction by capsizing and a miracle that would save her, Philip witnessed what long hours of worry and fear could do to a man. Despair gripped Captain Contestable. Panic seized him, silenced his voice, and paralyzed his muscles. He could neither cry an order to the steersmen nor move so much as a finger to stay the hand of fate. Somehow, the masts snapped back upright when she seemed doomed to lie on her beam ends; somehow, they flung her bows into the teeth of the hurricane and she lay to trembling. She came out of it. The Old Man however, was through and he knew it. But he commanded the *Osprey* for another year, sailed her because young Broadwinder would not let him quit. In heavy seas the young seaman, then chief mate, took over.

And now Philip admitted that his own terror had equaled that of the master. Only his regard for Captain Contestable saved him from his own finish on the high seas. A strange thing, he reflected, though it was as true as it was mysterious. And ever since that mad typhoon of the China Sea he had not once battled a storm with confidence he could call his own; rather, he seemed to borrow that something which the old veteran of the seas had lost in peril. It was as though the other had lovingly bestowed upon him his very all.

Captain Broadwinder felt the wind back and come on again in gusts. He held his course and when an hour later the ugly bank of clouds ahead still hung directly over the ship's bow, he changed his course from south to southeast.

It was a guess, only that, though he hoped it was a good one.

All that day he kept an alert eye on sea, sky, and barometer. Long swells heaved and humped up like giant porpoises, overlapping in watery hillocks of blue and green until the sky slipped a murky veil over the sun. The wind freshened, but without any direction chopped up the water, fell off suddenly, and blew in again as though exploring the compass. The ship met the night with falling glass, moderate rolling sea, dry decks, and thick pall overhead. As the running lights punctured the starless gloom with red and green fingers dancing atop the close seas, the *Eagle* ran on southeast under topgallant sails.

Captain Broadwinder left the deck only once between the dogwatch and midnight. His distrust of weather kept him noticeably quiet and inattentive to the passengers. The widow gave up her conquest, or attempt at being just friendly, after several minutes, and Mr. Fulton in talkative mood retired to the saloon. Cartwright observed the change in his captain with a rising curiosity that held him on deck when all but Jenny had gone below. They talked of this and that, though she appeared more interested in Philip's various expressions, the increasing roll of the ship and howling of the now steady wind in the rigging.

The captain, Cartwright noted, kept the crew jumping with orders to trim sail and haul yards around. He read the log line often and, unsatisfied with a speed of eleven, twelve, then fourteen knots, crowded on more canvas, as though he were running away from something that only he could see. A natural threat, weather, Cartwright thought, still baffled by Philip's lengthened concern. To further confound him, Broadwinder had to his knowledge stood the deck for more than fifteen hours.

The captain at last spoke a word to Mr. Fortune and strode across deck. Smiling wanly at Jenny, he said, "Shall I see you below?" Her silence and inquisitive glance evoked more. "All's well, Mrs. Broadwinder."

Cartwright did not miss the look between them. He was wondering if Philip's accent on the word "well" signified more than he said. He was sure they were exchanging signals when she replied:

"Then well it is, Captain Broadwinder. But if you don't catch your wink you may blow right out endways."

His "Aye" and nod following her nautical expression "blow right out endways," meaning winds of hurricane force, was not lost on Cartwright. Clever people these. They had considered him incapable of landing the marlin. And now they thought to talk around the landsman merchant in the vernacular of the sea.

He recalled an expression used by the bosun during the calm. Since oars were made of white ash, any air stirred up by rowing a boat was named after the wood. So he said with devilish intent:

"A wind or two now, Captain, might help you in a reach for a white-ash breeze."

He took a great delight in their surprised exchange of glances. Then, before either could reply, he voiced a courteous good night and strode off feeling as though he had caught another marlin.

Cartwright slept little that night. He was not alone, however. The ship tossed and rolled to the discomfort of all passengers. Seas mounted and winds tore in stronger. Below, one could hear great waves striking hard at the ship, leaping on decks, and snarling out the scuppers.

At around three in the morning Jenny went on deck. Stinging drops of rain and spray pelleted her oilskins and the wind over the quarter threatened to carry her to the lee side. By clinging to rail and after shrouds she reached Philip and raised her voice with a question regarding their course. His cry against the wind, "East-sou'east!" was barely audible. He repeated it, and Jenny studied the water streaming down his face.

East-southeast meant that he was sailing six points of the compass north of his true course. Why? She did not voice the question. The sea was rough, though the wind was blowing no more than a moderate gale, and waves reached no higher than twenty feet, proving it. Then she carefully studied the press of canvas on the yards. Small wonder the ship pitched like a mad stallion.

Lowering her gaze, she examined Philip's face again. Under the lights, he seemed bathed in oil, though the observation was a detached one, for her mind dwelled on the puzzle he created. If prudence sent him so far off his course, why did he imprudently fling so much sail to the wind?

Captain Broadwinder stood like a statue as the wind came on without appreciable change. The waves continued to break and smash over the decks at the waist and bows. Eight bells, four o'clock, sounded. The watch changed. The *Eagle* heeled in the wind, rolled back, heeled again, lifted at the bows, dipped; on and on into the first edge of breaking day, port light red, starboard green, each playing as before on cresting waves and streaks of flying foam.

Jenny had just turned her gaze over the quarter when a faint light burst and flashed an instant in the western sky. Perhaps she had imagined it. It could have been lightning. Curious, she stared into the pall. It came again. When she told Philip about it he eyed her tolerantly a moment, as if to say she had been at sea long enough to contain any hallucinations. Often sailors saw land where only a cloud bank existed. They had a name for it: Cape Flyaway.

Then he saw it.

Eyes slitted, mouth tight, he stood out seconds of waiting. Jenny saw his hand lift trembling to his face. He seemed to shudder. In another moment he cupped his hands and cried at the top of his voice:

"All hands!" Twice he repeated it before whirling. "Helm hard down!" he cried.

As the forecastle disgorged the below watch, the ship began her slow curve into the wind with a clatter of gear in her uppers and a sweep of her stern to port amid a swish of lee seas. Broadwinder's voice rose in competition with orders to brace up the after yards, set the spanker, boom it out over the port quarter. Lively! Lively now! Let fly the crossjack and mizzentop sails for the starboard tack! Three men fought the wheel, and the thump of feet on decks, drowned by wind and continued shouts, ended with men leaping like soaked monkeys up into the shrouds as others on decks hauled away to bring the spanker boom, the main and mizzen yards around.

Jenny listened, watched and waited. With sail aft set, the push of wind behind the ship's center would aid the helm in giving her a turn on her pivot. Only this could overcome the piled-up seas at the starboard bow and the forced lee seas on the port quarter. The ship would point more to west then, and when her foreyards, now squared, began to lift, they would be braced up on the starboard tack for westing.

The wet gray day was breaking when the last maneuver sent the *Eagle* bowling along toward the distress flares of some unfortunate vessel. Lookouts were stationed in the fore and mizzen and on the bows and answering flares were sent up at regular intervals. Rain came down in torrents and the wild sea continued to run. Locating a ship in such weather was no easy task. The *Eagle* might suddenly run right to her, or into her, or spend hours finding her, and more hours in working in close enough to effect a rescue.

As it happened, the latter held true. For four hours the *Eagle* probed her way toward the flares. When at last the lookout in the mizzen cried the deck, saying he had sighted wreckage alee, Captain Broadwinder, now twenty-eight hours on deck, doubled the fore lookouts and took in sail as a precaution against collision. There followed an interval of figuring wind and seas to determine the drift of floating spars, another hour of tacking into the wind before he and all on deck sighted for a brief moment in rising and falling seas to windward the long hull of a half-submerged mastless ship.

A glance through the telescope when she again rose in the distance told a story of tragedy at sea. Her masts had been cut away, proving she had been thrown over on her beam ends, masts flat on the water, unable to lift and spring back under the weight of sodden sails and rigging. And now she looked to be sinking, her head down. She had taken on water before severed masts allowed her to right herself.

The *Eagle* crept cautiously forward, working, working, for a position neither to windward nor alee of the wreck but trying to parallel her drift. It soon became evident that the vessel in distress was minus even helm. At the mercy of the seas, she swung her beam into the wind. Upon closer inspection they saw that her boats had been smashed. And aft, passengers were huddled and the crew, or what was left of her complement of hands, were engaged in building a raft. Nor did the work stop after the *Eagle* was sighted. The bearded captain was taking no chances.

"I don't blame him," Broadwinder said, glass at his eye. "She could dive for Davy Jones's locker any minute."

George Cartwright nodded gravely, glanced at Jenny who was eying him as though she realized he was taking a ship-owner's view of the tragedy, then murmured a reply.

A moment later he frowned up at the captain. "You're not going to lower boats in these seas, are you?"

"As soon as I ease more to windward of her, I am. With oil bags fore and aft." Turning abruptly, he grinned. "Care to go along?"

Cartwright made a grimace at the ugly gray waves and remained silent. As orders to the crew began to fly right and left and Broadwinder took the wheel in hand, he studied the vessel in distress. Her main deck was awash now and she rolled sluggishly. Boats approaching her would be in danger, once because of her roll, again since she might go under and swamp them with her suction. Then the helm was shifted and the *Eagle* lurched into the wind's eye. As sails slatted against masts, the crew lowered a boat on the portside. Manned with men of muscle who fell to the sweeps with practiced skill, the boat angled out with Mr. Winston at the stern sheets. She rose to the very crest of a wave, then rode it downhill to the bottom of a trough. Up she came like a bobbing cork to the top of another wave. When the boat somehow made headway, another splashed under the bow.

Captain Broadwinder swung down from the bowsprit shrouds and unhooked after ordering his chief mate to wear ship and move downwind from the wreck where he should heave to and await the rescue boats.

Jenny and Cartwright looked on as the captain's boat soared to wave crests and plunged into sleeked chasms, one of two frail craft on a perilous crossing. When Broadwinder had put a safe distance between him and the *Eagle*, Mr. Fortune ordered the mizzen staysail hauled down. Jenny seemed to forget Philip. Ship and maneuver claimed her full attention when the steersman responded to the next order of "Helm up, not over." As the vessel began to pay off, the hands worked furiously to square the after yards by the time the wind struck from astern. They succeeded, and Jenny gazed intently at the foreyard as it was being hauled around and all was made ready forward. Her glance shifted suddenly and fell on Mr. Fortune. It was up to him now. He was the sole judge of the situation, wind, sails, helm, and the completion of wearing ship around. At just the precise moment, when the opportunity favored him, he should order the yards braced up and to bring her to.

"Now!" Jenny cried.

As suddenly as she had spoken, Jenny clapped a hand over her mouth. She stood crimson of face until Mr. Fortune completed the job and turned his smiling eyes on her.

"I'm sorry, sir. I suppose I was just obeying an impulse to think out loud. Do forgive me."

Mr. Fortune chuckled. "A most timely impulse. My compliments, ma'am."

Cartwright had watched her from the beginning, had followed her alert, critical glances and studied the various expressions that crossed her face; as a student of something or other might do, he told himself. And now he was more curious than before. He was lost in deep study of her when she scattered his thoughts to the winds with a sudden cry of fright.

George Cartwright and all aboard the *Eagle* stared across the water. The dismasted ship was lifting her stern into the air for a final plunge into the deep. And there at her side, in dire peril of being sucked under, lay the last rescue boat.

Jenny's voice rose in a frantic cry: "Philip!"

Then she turned her back to the rail and covered her face with trembling hands.

13

☐ Both first officer and shipowner rushed to Jenney's side. As she seemed ready to faint away, all the stiffness gone out of her knees and back, Mr. Fortune asked Cartwright and Mrs. Littlefield to help her below at once.

Jenny raised her head then and stared beyond them with unseeing eyes. Her hand lifted and trembling fingers smoothed her brow until, with a violent toss of her head, she rallied and pushed them away.

"No!" she said in protest. Then, "Mr. Fortune, what are you waiting for? Take this ship to Philip!"

Cartwright's head jerked around in time for him to see the sternmost part of the doomed ship sliding into the sea. The terrified screams of those who had waited to be taken aboard the *Eagle*'s boats came on the wind, as did a gurgle and vomit of air from the once proud clipper. She was now on her way to a watery grave, and the confused, boiling seas marking briefly her departure from this world made up her final wake. In that mighty boil of water, the raft stood on end one moment and dived under the next. All aboard it were sucked under. The raft went just so far, then shot upward and fell flat on the surface. A few heads bobbed up.

Captain Broadwinder had literally snatched a woman and her baby from the ship's rail before shoving off with an order. "Row for your lives, lads!" The upended stern of the ship seemed to hang still at its zenith above his boat like a grinning death's-head. It scarcely moved as the oarsmen fell to with all the strength in them. Then the descent of the big ship began. At first slow, then faster, until the rudder seemed to leap downward under the weight of the counter. By that time the suction had commenced. Mad, unnatural currents seized Philip's boat and, as though a giant hand out of the deep had fastened upon them, drew it relentlessly toward the maelstrom.

The *Eagle's* boat was being swept along toward the wreck. All aboard the frail craft stared in horrified fascination as the last part of the ship slid under. Then it was gone and every sensation of shock and tragedy in a mind seemed manifested by the sea. There was no time for realization of these things; the small world about them was all movement, the grim, unleashed motion of destruction. Atop a mighty swirl of water, the boat changed ends, stood high a moment, listed until the thwarts were perpendicular to the sea, then plunged into the outer rim of the suction hole so rapidly it took one's breath away. An oar flew high and a sailor somersaulted, his arms and legs flailing the air before the boiling water claimed him.

Aboard the *Calcutta Eagle* an hour later Broadwinder lay in his bed comparing his thoughts at the time the boat and crew sped through the water toward certain doom to all he was thinking now. In summation, he felt a little foolish.

He looked at Jenny, who sat near him. "No, I wasn't aware of any fear. It went beyond that. Even as the boat was sucked under and I felt myself being swept down and down, all I realized was a sense of guilt. A panic gripped me, Jenny, when I seemed to know all of us would die."

He said nothing for a long minute in which he seemed caught fast in the memory of near death.

"Well, it was I who sent them to Davy Jones. I was responsible." He frowned at the bulkhead and port. "Sheer damn folly. Whatever possessed me to hang on for more of them when the stern stood high I'll never know. Maybe it was the look on that mother's face or the appeal in the eyes of the little fellow I fished off a wave. Why didn't those crazy men launch the raft earlier?"

"Why didn't a lot of things happen?" Jenny said tiredly.

He grimaced. "I could have sailed a little faster. But I didn't. Had to creep in. Prudent Broadwinder. Hang on when I got there for a ticket to Fiddler's Green. Imprudent Broadwinder."

She studied him a minute. "Drink some more tea."

"I've swallowed enough ocean to sprout gills." Taking the cup, he said, "Well, why don't you tell me, Jenny? I know a few of my lads were lost, but how many are alive?"

"I suppose I've been too busy thanking the Lord for spar-ing you, Philip. It was a close call." She paused. "All survived but Norwich."

"Norwich," he said quietly. "I saw him dive headfirst. The boat struck him. Was there a woman with a baby in her arms?"

She was a long time silent, hands folded in her lap. Broadwinder put the cup down, touched the cut on his forehead tenderly. A small price for his folly. Norwich and the mother and baby constituted the heavy loss. Until this voyage he had been able to boast of never having lost a man.

He looked at Jenny. "You're mighty quiet," he said. "What was the mate's name again?"

"Sanderson."

"What's his story?"

"The *Fawn* out of New York was on her return voyage heavy with sugar. They sighted the storm two days back and Captain O'Lee decided to skirt it on the west. When it struck in full force, the cargo shifted and his main hatch went. Listing heavily, she was no match for the weather. On her beam ends, they cut away the masts and let go by the board. You know the rest."

Yes, he knew the rest of it, but he was thinking of the cause, that one fateful decision, a guess on the part of Captain O'Lee.

"He sailed west to skirt the storm," Philip said, his unfocused eyes on the ceiling. "A man and a ship, Jenny."

He had never questioned the accepted fact that a captain was master of his ship. Nor had he ever argued that a man was not the master of his destiny. But now he wasn't so sure. Norwich had placed his life in his captain's hands, the same as the *Fawn*'s crew had entrusted their all to Captain O'Lee. Two commanders guilty of errors in judgment. Surely a greater hand shaped destinies on land and sea. And when all was said and done a captain was not the real master of his ship. O'Lee proved this true, as thousands of seamen had done before him. By one mistake, he placed fate in command of the clipper *Fawn*. He sailed west to avoid the storm.

"Jenny," he said, still pondering it all, "it causes you to wonder why one man's error is so costly and another's so light by comparison. But it goes further. What unseen power caused O'Lee to sail west and me to turn east?"

Slowly Jenny's large eyes came around to him. "Maybe we aren't supposed to know, Philip," she said at last. "So we must be satisfied with just being thankful that you were sent east.

But we do have an expression—we say we'll do something, God willing. Did you say, 'I'll sail away from that storm, *God willing*'?"

There was no reply, just a deep look of wonderment in Philip's face that told her he was staring at things no mortal could see. It was enough for Jenny, who realized that the search for them proved a man was not too far off a proper course in life.

14

☐ With many refugees aboard, Broadwinder searched the Southern seas for a homeward-bound ship and, finding none, ran on southwest, from between the crown of South America and the western bulge of Africa to Rio de Janeiro. There the *Fawn*'s passengers and most of the crew departed the *Eagle*. After taking on fresh fruits and vegetables Broadwinder crossed the Tropic of Capricorn and began the second lap of the voyage down the tapering coast of the continent, down to the worst weather on earth, to a gamble with Cape Horn seas and winds for a rounding into the Pacific. Down to the winter of the Southern Hemisphere.

Officers and crew knew by past experience what to expect in the roaring forties and merciless fifties. The passengers thought only of the present as the hands busied themselves in the belt of variable winds, removing all light canvas from the yards and bending on heavy-weather sails.

The transition of weather was slow. Warm days and nights under a big Southern moon gradually gave way to cool days and chilly nights. The dreaded pamperos, hard tempests that swept cold off the Argentine pampas and raced out to sea, failed to strike the *Eagle*. Good sailing weather continued on down past forty degrees south, where gusts of cold air and chilling rains warned of their approach to winter and the big westerlies.

"Slow comin'," Sails said. "Worse when they hit. May hold

us weather-bound at the Mare." He referred to Strait de la Maire, where the continent's stinger tail opened up a passage. Beyond, a hundred miles southwest, cold, ominous, silent Cape Horn dared a ship to chance a passing. Nearly all accepted the challenge. Not all made it.

Late one afternoon the northern mouth of the strait came into view. Broadwinder studied the heavy pall of sky and gray seas ahead. The wind blew strong out of the southwest. A cold, damp wind that chilled a man to the marrow of his bones. Skuas, snow petrels, pitpits, and mottled cape pigeons flew about as though unconcerned. Down near the smear of land that was Isla de los Estados a single mast lifted up out of the sea in grim warning. A hundred more failed to show, Broadwinder realized, peering into the lively races of the strait.

He could not beat to windward in the dark, so he gave the order to heave ship to and sit out the night.

"This is it," he said to Cartwright and Jenny. "The Cape Horn approach. And I'm wondering if ever a captain sat here with no thought of the Horn jinx."

Cartwright rubbed a cheek to warm it. "Captain, isn't it common practice to send down royal yards in these latitudes?"

"It is, sir."

"Well," he put it bluntly, "you still carry them."

"I may need them. Comes a favoring wind out of the east, I'll fly everything on her to make westing."

Cartwright said grudgingly, "I see." Lowering his gaze from the masts, he spoke of the captain of his ship *Valiant*. "Rodney sat out twelve days waiting for an easterly, Captain Broadwinder."

"I sat out fifteen on my first trip as commander. But a whole gale was blowing. When I went through I met another. We were forty-six days rounding from fifty to fifty."

"Under royals, I suppose," Cartwright said, not cracking a smile.

"Not on your life." Broadwinder laughed. "I sent down even my to'gannels'ls long before I reached the westerlies. I was an old woman in those days."

Jenny looked intently from one to the other, from Philip who waited for some reply, to Cartwright, unsatisfied and busy shaping one. The silence was broken by a question—

how long would the captain wait for an east wind on this voyage?

Broadwinder looked out over the sea toward the dim coast line marking Cape San Diego. "Perhaps I can answer that one tomorrow," he said.

It so happened that he did. Morning brought clearing skies and continuing hard winds out of the southwest. Visibility good, Broadwinder took in the snow-covered coast of Tierra del Fuego and wind-swept seas that opened the mouth of the strait. Experience in getting a ship through here, coupled with warnings from reliable sailing directions, the weather at hand, and a balance of all in his mind prompted a decision:

He would avoid the violent tidal race extending some five miles off Cape San Diego and wait one hour after high water before splitting the seventeen-mile-wide strait on the full and by, closehauled on the starboard tack. The ebb of the tidal current to southward should assist the *Eagle* in her passage.

Broadwinder waited, though not with patience. A perilous channel was one to put behind a ship, certainly nothing to relish while waiting for the ebb. All hands were called out, and he sent Tobias with a message to Cartwright of his intention to run the strait. To himself, he said:

"For better or for worse."

The wind shifted a point nearer west, a boon now, a devil's capful that would force him to seek deep southing later. Still he waited, all hands at their stations. Then sail was set to the wind. The ship heeled and gear clattered as she ran for the center of the strait, disaster to windward, disaster alee. Aboard the vessel walking down the safety line between tidal races and rocks assailed by wind-hounded combers no face appeared more calm than that of the captain. He wore a mask, for he could not scan the shore indented with bays and studded with rocky cliffs without cringing inwardly. It was less fear and more a seaman's craving for room. Several long, weary hours of it, with mind constantly alert, body tense, eyes roving up, down, right, left, all over again and again until even the muscles of squinting eyelids ached. And always an eye for the helm, to be sure from one minute to the next that the lubber's line remained on the prescribed course. He blew warm breath into his numb hands. This passage was different from any other, for a man sailed on to meet what he knew lay ahead, a region of everlasting storms, truly called Horn hell.

Then he was through the strait. He breathed a heavy sigh

and, after warning Mr. Fortune to sail as close to the prevailing wind as possible, "And steer clear of old Cabo de Hornas," he relieved the below watch of duty and took a turn of the forward decks. Every line, pin, stanchion, plank, and sail held his critical eye as he moved toward the bows, even the live pigs, cows, and chickens at the break of the forecastlehead. Jibs and sheets and bowsprit held his attention. Then he returned to the foredeck, examined the hatch coaming, moved aft to the boats, from there to the main hatch, fife rail, and on to the poop, carefully inspecting the portside life line on the way. Pausing at the port ladder, he gazed over the side at animated seas of deep blue, marbled with skirling foam.

He looked up to see Jenny and Cartwright regarding him thoughtfully. In her hand was a pannikin of steaming coffee. He could drink it scalding hot, and he was hoping she had poured a full ounce of fiery liquor into it.

"All's well," she said, though her expression intoned a question; as if she knew all he was thinking.

"All's well," he replied, thinking she had read his cautious sailing mind down to its last petty fear. Covering his annoyance with a slight grimace, he accepted the coffee and tasted it. Ah, she had laced it, all right, proving she also read his mind in other matters. "Aye," he said, a cheery note in his voice as he repeated, "All's well."

To the voiced disappointment of Mrs. Littlefield and other passengers who had made known a desire to view the terrible broad black cape, Captain Broadwinder sailed southsouthwest on the west wind without any explanation to anyone. Mrs. Littlefield pouted, said the captain had deliberately refused to show them Cape Horn, preferring instead to expose all of them to the core of winter under South America.

Unaware of any grousing among the paying voyagers, Jenny appeared on deck late that same afternoon and heard the widow say to George Cartwright: "Pray tell us, sir, where is the dashing Captain Broadwinder, or is the toast of New York and Boston a myth you have contrived to lure passengers aboard your ship?"

Jenny stood still. Suddenly tense, and more curious than offended, she fixed her gaze on Cartwright and waited.

The shipowner laughed. "My dear Mrs. Littlefield," he said, "Captain Broadwinder is no myth. Now if you will join me in the chartroom, I'll prove to your satisfaction that concern for your safety is uppermost in his mind."

Well, well! Jenny thought, with a lift of her brow. Such defense from an unexpected source was at least enlightening, despite the fact that Cartwright as shipowner could not do otherwise.

An hour later, when dark cold night fell over the ship and snow flurries drove all but the on-watch crew from decks, Jenny entered the saloon almost on Cartwright's heels. Mrs. Littlefield at the piano played for Mr. Fulton's ear, it seemed, while other passengers listened and sipped coffee. As Peretta served them Jenny said, taking Cartwright by surprise:

"Well, did you convince Mrs. Littlefield?"

"Eh? So you heard her."

"As well as you, sir, though I stepped back out of sight, once I learned that Captain Broadwinder had a champion."

Cartwright sipped coffee in thoughtful silence before replying to her specific question with, "Yes, I think I convinced her."

Something in his tone of voice prompted her to say, "But without conviction on your part."

"I didn't say that," he protested.

"No, you didn't." She smiled.

He saw in her face a womanly wisdom in the shape of judgment. It oddly bedeviled him. He felt trapped into an explanation. "However, since you broached the subject, I'll say to you what I told Captain Broadwinder—that he could have very easily placated the passengers with a few brief words regarding his decision not to sail for the Cape."

Jenny's face brightened with interest. "So you told him that," she said, lowering her cup. "And just what did Captain Broadwinder say in reply?"

Cartwright hesitated. "He's rather unreasonable at times."

"He is?" Jenny laughed lightly. "Now didn't he tell you he felt no obligation to explain any decision pertaining to course or maneuver to either passenger or crew; that any mention of safety at sea to uninformed parties had a tendency to provoke all sorts of fears?"

He gave her an incredulous look. "Why—yes. He said all that. And then he told me, in the pink of courtesy, mind you, that he was captain of the ship, not I."

"Excellent!"

"What do you mean, Jenny? I have never once tried to presume on my position aboard this ship."

"Naturally, sir. I was merely voicing delight upon learning

that Captain Broadwinder is in fine fettle after a most trying day."

Cartwright's glance challenged her prior to his next statement. "I thought him exceedingly cautious and on edge."

"How very inconsistent you are, sir. Only yesterday you seemed rather concerned because Captain Broadwinder had not sent down his royal yards."

She smiled, though her eyes were sober. "And now, after he boldly ran the strait instead of sitting out days for an east wind, you find him exceedingly cautious."

She stood to leave him, thought better of it, and sat down. He seemed properly rebuked, though still uncertain, with eyes on the floor, hand at chin.

"You witnessed the fate of Captain O'Lee's *Fawn*, sir. You recall the course Captain Broadwinder sailed, almost due east. A guess, you might say, but a good one. However, there is more to it than that. According to the mate, Mr. Sanderson, the *Fawn*'s cargo shifted. After questioning him, I firmly believe the cargo was improperly stowed. Also, the hatches were neglected. Combined, they spelled the ship's doom. She sank. And Captain O'Lee, God rest his soul, went down. The will of God. Perhaps. Or could it be that the captain by his inattention to little things helped shape his destiny?"

Cartwright listened with unguarded interest. His eyes upon her, he was again watching Philip's examination of fife rail, hatches, and life line. The little things. Then she was rising again, compelling him to get on his feet also.

"Be thankful Captain Broadwinder is cautious, sir. Indeed, for caution on land or sea is a virtue that sustains a man's boldness."

With that she left him and braved the snow squall now blowing across decks in a banshee's wail. Wind-driven waves hammered hard at the ship's sides, pushing up seas aweather and alee. The elements were one thing, human nature another. Her face was hot with rising anger directed at a man who seemed diligently in search of reasons for withholding from Philip shares justly due him. The very idea of his approaching Philip with the widow's complaint! Thank heavens Philip had told him which way the wind blew. But how on earth could George Cartwright entertain doubt of Philip, even in his small, land-warped mind? But he did, and she doubted if she had convinced him of anything.

"But I will." She spoke into the teeth of the wind. "You just wait and see, Mr. Cartwright. From now on, sir, I'll give you no quarter."

15

☐ Morning ushered in heavier weather that worsened during the day. Snow squalls came on the near gale and rain froze on sails, spars and cordage.

As the westerly continued to howl in stronger that night and next day, Broadwinder sent down his royal and topgallant yards to relieve the masts. For every inch of westing gained he had been forced to run a foot south. The weather was a devil. To outwit it was his business, and he set about to do just that.

The seas and winds were equally determined; they countered him at every turn. He saw men chop ice from the shrouds, tear fingernails off while fighting frozen canvas, slip from icy footropes only to be saved by alert hands on either side. He felt the incessant winds beat cold at his cheeks and eyes until the chill seemed driven deep into the flesh. He drank coffee, scalded his lips and tongue with it, ordered extra rations of rum to the crew, warmed his hands over the forecastle stove as an excuse to see if the firebox was properly braced for the heavy weather at hand. He thawed his cheeks by rubbing them with snow scooped from a drift piled up at the skylight aft, shortened the on-deck watch from four to two hours, ordered the helmsmen on one-hour duty, cursed the sleet squall that drove ice pellets at his face, and gave the ship to Mr. Fortune. He holed up one hour, no more. Begrudging the lost westing, he went on deck to try again. The great winds held him as before. Unable to carry sail, he had no choice other than riding out the weather.

Cartwright watched his weather-manacled ship, said little or nothing to his stern-faced captain, and soon began to wonder if the Eagle would ever make the rounding. The wind, already a full-grown monster, thought the shipowner, began to roar louder. It came on in deafening, fiendish blasts. Clinging to the weather braces, he darted concerned glances at Broadwinder until a smother of sleet and spindrift drove him groping frantically for the safety of below decks.

He could leave the weather. Broadwinder could not. As he entered the saloon he felt a twinge of guilt.

On deck Broadwinder felt himself, beaten as he was, responding to the situation. The *Eagle* slogged into the gale, shivered all over and met the teeth of the blow under storm canvas, her lower main topsail goosewinged, main trysail reefed, oil bags slung from weather bow and main channels, all preventer gear taut, relieving tackles on the helm, and more. He had done everything he knew to do, little and big. He knew what was coming, and he was suddenly afraid.

The wind screeched through the rigging as only a growing gale can. Hail began to pelt the rigging as night and the whip of the storm bore down on the ship.

The fore lifted, and the charge of mad seas under the ship was felt as on it came, rolling under the hull aft in a racing sweep for the stern. The quarter-deck shot upward under Broadwinder's feet with a push at his knees and stomach, held high as the bows wallowed from port to starboard in the dim light, jerking the heavy masts with savage intent to spring them, then fell with a suddenness that took his breath away. Lord, how she rolled and pitched! Mast tips spun in arcs and on every line, brace, and sheet the strain seemed unendurable.

All the while, the sea lifted higher, sent graybeards of mammoth size at the *Eagle*. They struck and, smashing hard, shot upward into the rigging and seemed to explode in foam and spray before crashing down in hammering fury on decks. Spume froze solid where it fell and under the constant bite of the wind added layer after layer of ice aboard.

The gray light of morning revealed Captain Broadwinder gripping the weather companion railing, back hunched, staring out of red-rimmed, glassy eyes. Forward, O'Hara clung to the port life line while checking the damage aboard, which was plenty. He jumped aft as a wave crashed, leaped over the rail, spilling tons of gray-green water across the deck. And the second. At any other time Mr. Winston with coattail frozen stiffly out behind him, his flaming red hair bleached with salt and his sleeves white-streaked, cap askew and dripping, would look comical. But not now. He reflected the beating taken by all who had handled ship for hours on end. He looked pitifully done in, though now he was putting life and order into the scene of storm-lashed decks, and a warmth that was hope, as he exhorted the haggard men to follow him aloft. And well they should, bruised and cut and weary as they were, for the ice-coated *Calcutta Eagle* wallowed with scarcely a rag of sail on her. An awful sight, empty boltropes, frayed canvas whipping hard to leeward.

Broadwinder's gaze fell slowly to deck, lifted again, and he was thinking of his proud entries into harbors, the glory of ships under sail, the popularity of clipper captains who consistently sped cargoes to destinations. The sight he was now viewing was a part of it. Honor was due any master who survived, but survival was not enough.

Suddenly he forgot all but the present. His eyes were glued to Chips, who was plumbing the bilge with sounding rod. Tense, mouth hanging open, he said in silence, "Lord, don't let him say she's sprung a leak." He knew what long days of backbreaking labor at the pumps, or hated "brakes" as sailors said it, did to a good crew. Aboard the *Osprey* once, the hands had endured three months of it. Now Chips was through with it. There was no leak, thank God.

Broadwinder broke the grim repose of his face with almost a grin, the first pleased expression to cross his face in days.

Jenny saw it. She had battled her way forward to his position with oilskins flattened against her body one minute, ballooning the next. Reaching Philip, she clutched his arm and snuggled close on his lee side, and there she studied his face anxiously. His semblance of a smile held. It was a good omen, for in his expression was thanks and the philosophy of a sound captain who could look at the storm damage with a realization that it could have been much worse.

By late afternoon, when sail was finally bent on and the ship was patched, the gale had backed considerably. The cold wind still blew in strong. Seas were more than rough. But a change was felt by crew and officers. It was not so much in the elements; rather, in the captain's expression. Something was in the wind. The bosun said as much to Chips and Sails. Mr. Winston looked from the trio to the quarter-deck, screwed up his face, and waited expectantly. Cartwright on the poop turned his collar up and narrowed his gaze on Jenny, whose unguarded expression of excitement sharpened his curiosity. Since her full attention was on her husband, Cartwright began to wonder if the suspenseful air hanging over the ship would be broken by Philip. Probably, he thought, but how? What could he say or do to change the heavy weather?

All hands were called. Extra rum rations warmed their stomachs and spirits. Broadwinder did not keep them waiting long. With hands cupped at his mouth, he cried:

"We're down in the sixties, lads."

Mr. Winston relayed the message forward.

"The wind is backing around to south!" Broadwinder yelled. "We're going to run—for the fifties and westing!" A moment of silence, except for screeching wind and the continuous pounding of running seas, was followed by, "Haul the yards around for the port tack! Lively!"

Every crewman knew what lay ahead. They leaped to their stations. The ship would make a short round to, and in doing so would pivot on her stern under headsails, pile up great lee seas on her starboard. She had to get lift forward; she had to answer the turn of ship's head with helm at the very precise moment; she had to get a push aft at just the right time, when the helm was shifted to send her forward; she had to lay oil from her bows and above all, before the order to fill headsails, wait for a smooth.

Else she would find herself in peril.

Any inattention to steering would place her at the mercy of wind and seas. So the captain took over the helm. It was touch and go.

Alerted faces everywhere he looked, the flurry of action, the waiting, all combined to tauten every muscle in George Cartwright's body. He felt the waiting painful. Something had to happen. Something did. A moment's lull in the sea roused the ship. A hand, the captain's, shot upward from aft. Cries forward rang on the wind. Came a shift of the helm and jib sails and forestaysail rose, cracked in the wind, ballooned, and, with the forward gang playing tug of war on the sheets, the mighty foresail, reefed, catching a fill of wind and buoying up the fore, the *Eagle* began to swing. She buried her nose to the gammoning in oncoming seas and pushed up more starboard. As they poured across decks, Cartwright knew why chickens and livestock had been moved aft. The *Eagle* came on around in a boil of water and foam, her portside exposed to the full force of wind and waves. She shook all over, heeled dangerously over in the vise of windward and lee seas, rocking and unsure of herself. Then the helm shifted. To cries aft and forward, the headsails spilled their wind as the after gang brought sail to bear. Foresail was set and, on the fore and main, yards readied on the port tack sprouted sail. The helm met the press of canvas. The *Eagle* groaned, trembled, heeled, and shot forward, her bows pointing northwest.

It had been done, smartly done, Cartwright admitted. The happy look on Jenny's face proved it.

The *Eagle* ran under prudent hands that night. She roared on, but at a pace she might have doubled. The backing wind bore in more out of the south, as Philip had predicted, and the eastward set of the seas caused by the gale continued to run a little contrary to the prevailing wind, stirring up cross seas.

Morning brought abated weather. The wind blew from south-southwest, continuing strong, over a more obedient ocean. Captain Broadwinder set more sail, ran a little faster. He was making westing now. He climbed the latitudes that day and the next and, feeling the gradual shift of weather back to the westerlies and rougher sailing, he crowded on all canvas she would carry. He wanted good westing when the gales struck again.

He played the game with Cape Horn weather from hour to hour. He found by observation that he had placed the Horn four hundred miles due east of him. Excellent. But gales out of the northwest could head him, force him back. The wind was on the climb, from south to west. Another day would see it worsen. He needed that one day, needed it enough to gamble against the dangers of the ragged curve of the southwestern coast of Chile for a madcap's run due north. If the gales came, there would be small room for retreat. But that was the gamble.

He decided in the night to take it.

All hands hit the deck and fell to in lively fashion when he ordered the topgallant and royal yards sent aloft. For long hours they labored.

To catch a beam wind. That was the order of the day. Under royals high, the *Calcutta Eagle* split the waves. Something of the excitement of risk, always appealing, caught up passengers as well as crew that day. A blown royal sail connonaded in the wind. The men scrambled upstairs. Another split. They ran on, repairing, bending on more sail, all eyes on deck watching, listening for the next reading of the log line. Fifteen knots. Sixteen! She was flying now.

The wind was a jealous competitor. By six bells on the afternoon watch, 3 P.M., it moved up a point forward of the beam to force the captain either to increase his risk by putting the ship's head nearer the Chile coast or to give up and sail southwest by south.

Broadwinder debated his course. He was placed on the ragged edge of decision, afraid to try for the coveted prize of escape from Horn hell, afraid to turn back. Prudence cried in a loud voice, "Go south! Keep off the land!" The wind would head him if he ran on north, trap him between gale seas and rocks below the western mouth of Magellan Strait. Wind was King. Man was slave.

Jenny, mate, second mate, bosun, Chips and Sails held their breath almost. Each realized his state of mind, each knew that in weather such as they had endured he might not "fetch by the land," weather a shore, if he ran on. But southing now was a hated word. They waited for a decision. As the ship ran on, something in Broadwinder's face told them he had made up his mind to gamble it.

Bosun Draper sucked at his pipe, eyed O'Hara sharply. "Old Cap'n Burnett o' the bark *Fish* tried it once above here and wrecked on Desolation Island."

Sails's eyes peered out of deep sockets. "Happy damn soul, our friend the bosun. Eh, Chips? Or be ye o' the same trim?"

"Me? Well, since the Old Man don't risk unless it's calc'-lated I'll abide, belay, and show happy. Course now, if the bosun wants to sail south, I'll fashion him a raft o' sorts."

"A good be damned to you," Draper growled, moving off.

From aloft the cry, "Sail ho!" was heard.

The lookout had scarcely given the direction when all on deck saw tall white sails, royals high, lifting above the rolling horizon ahead. A square-rigger with the wind on her quarter, heeling, rising and plunging, her hull coming up fast under a press of canvas equal to the *Eagle's*, presented an exciting reflection of their own ship and speed; furthermore, whoever she was, she shipped a crack-on driver as captain. Broadwinder ordered the ensign run up the monkey gaff even as he eyed her through the glass. On she came, colors whipping forward, her pennant at the main red with two chevrons, blue central, the yellow snapping out her swallowtail. The house flag of Grinnell, Minturn & Campany of New York.

Broadwinder cried, "She's the *Flying Cloud!*"

Every eye clung to her. The *Flying Cloud!* The very name

stirred one. It explained also her daring press of sail. Her captain had no peer as a driver, and one might readily believe that he had taken command of the ship with a single purpose in mind, to make her live up to her ringing name. Perhaps. In any case, one could scarcely imagine Josiah Perkins Creesy aboard a ship with a less romantic name.

Bigger now, she swept closer and dipped her colors in return to Broadwinder's salute. She split the waves in half, throwing up fans of green and white with her sharp cutwater, dipped her nose deep, lifted again, and amid cheers from both ships raced on southwest, cutting for that curve of the Chile coast on a favoring wind, the same wind that threatened to head the *Calcutta Eagle*. She sank rapidly under the horizon, leaving only a long boil of white atop the sea.

The thrilling passing of ships in the deep stream atop the excitement of a day in which captain and weather raced against each other left the passengers restless and in no humor to welcome a dull evening aboard. Jenny felt the pulse beat and, although the battle between ship and the winds had by no means ended, she approached Philip with a suggestion that they break out champagne and delicacies in lavish entertainment of the paying voyagers. At first astonished that she of all people should try to lure him off the deck at a crucial time, he finally gave in to her.

"Good," she said. "Now wear your finest coat and smile, Philip. If only to convince them that you can be the Broadwinder they read about on land."

"Eh? You mean there's any doubt in their minds?"

"Any doubt! Why, they think you're a salt-crusted ogre."

He watched her go. "An ogre, am I?" he said to himself. He was half a mind to prove to them he was. A little later, he gave the ship to Mr. Fortune and went below. At the proper time he appeared in the saloon clad in brand-new blue with buttons gleaming like gold, a big-bowed tie of lighter blue, and wearing the famous Broadwinder grin.

He thought Jenny, in autumn-brown velvet, hair shining, eyes bright, positively ravishing. He complimented Peretta and his staff on the excellent tidbits and he held Mrs. Littlefield's hand an extra moment while remarking on her amazing ability to appear so cheerful on a rough voyage. He kept Mr. Fulton laughing as he tapped his store of courtroom jokes. The Sherwoods enjoyed most his comical poems dealing with sailors before the mast, and all laughed with him when he recited one called *A Salt's Opinion of a Shipowner*, for the benefit of George Cartwright:

> "He sends us to sea on weevily bread,
>   On stale salt horse and never a duff;
> To haul his cranky old ship around
>   For pay that's never enough.
> He dreams o' the day we'll all work free,
>   And train ourselves not to eat;
> When we pay for every sail that blows
>   And catch our wink whilst on our feet."

He held their rapt attention with a suspenseful parlor version of his mermaid story, which kept Jenny in a fidget wondering just which climax he would come up with. When he had finished, Mrs. Littlefield asked, to the delight of all, if the story was based on fact. She seemed rather disappointed when someone told her it was not.

Every quarter hour Mr. Fortune sent Tobias in with a report on the weather. The wind direction remained the same. Broadwinder frowned each time.

He had shown them his gay, convivial side, had presented the Broadwinder they associated with the "Prince of Sea Captains." It had been an ordeal, however, with his mind on ship, shore, and weather. He sobered and glanced anxiously at Jenny, as though seeking escape to deck. She rebuked him with her eyes just as the planter from Georgia asked a question about the forthcoming race with the *Emperor*.

"The race? Oh yes." Broadwinder seemed to enter a distant world. "In my battle with the elements I almost forgot mortals."

The reminder served to put him in his place. He, too, was nothing more than a mortal who, in a race for position against a stout westerly, seemed to have forgotten that he was inadvertently courting disaster.

He arose and walked straightway to deck, where, after verifying the wind's direction, he gave the order to turn the ship's head from east of north, away from the Chile coast, to almost southwest and running room.

Although officers and crew seemed to stare at a quitter, he did not mind. The wind had won over him. He admitted this without any of the bitterness that ordinarily accompanied defeat. He was trading risk for prudence, uncertainty for peace of mind.

And now he felt better. He would join the party again and this time the real Broadwinder, unencumbered by worry or vain, false hopes, would entertain them as never before. Let them talk of Mayo Keys and a race.

A broad grin played across his face. He looked at the mate and said cheerily, "Steady as she goes, Mr. Fortune."

16

□ The shop made considerable westing that night, though before day broke she was hove to under storm canvas with oil bags at her bows.

As the gale screeched louder, Captain Broadwinder joined passengers and Jenny at breakfast with red face almost frozen. For several minutes he sat in silence staring thoughtfully at his plate.

Mrs. Littlefield eyed him curiously. "Captain, if you had continued north we might have missed this terrible cold wind."

"Perhaps," he replied, not looking up.

Jenny glanced from Philip to the widow and on to Cartwright, who studied Mrs. Littlefield strangely before saying:

"Captain, suppose we had continued north?"

Broadwinder shuddered. "I hate to think of it, sir. We're being driven east here. Up there—well, there's only a rocky coast to the east."

"So Mr. Fortune tells me. The crew is talking about it also. But I'm as curious as they, Captain. What caused you to suddenly turn cold sober last night, go on deck, and change your course?"

Jenny lowered her fork slowly. She had placed the same question to Philip several times during the night to no avail. Now she watched him closely.

"Didn't the crew tell you they thought I had made a coward's decision?" he said to Cartwright.

"Something was said about extreme prudence."

Broadwinder made a wry smile. "It's all the same. But the truth is, I was afraid. I like room, Mr. Cartwright, lots of room."

The widow appeared more astonished by the moment. "You mean we are better off here?"

"Considerably," Cartwright said sharply, not shifting his glance from Broadwinder. "Well, Captain, call it what you will, but I'm content to thank the Lord you did it."

Jenny drew in her nether lip and gazed at the shipowner contemplatively. Twice, she was thinking, he had seen Philip turn the ship from the road leading to disaster. Once was enough to convince any man other than George Cartwright of a captain's worth. And last night's decision had drawn the owner of the India Commercial Line into the open. But how far would he go beyond spoken words of praise? She said:

"Yesterday bold, last night cautious. The latter sustained the former again."

Cartwright had not forgotten her use of almost those very words after the *Fawn* went down. He looked up to see her glance full upon him.

"So we should be thankful again," she said.

He could not argue this. However, he said no more in Broadwinder's favor, for he felt that she was enlarging upon a point he had already made, as though she found it useful in making a bid for something or other. Then he knew what it was.

In a voice that declared he wished to dismiss the subject, he said, "Every captain, of course, feels a responsibility for his ship and all lives aboard. And he must therefore act accordingly."

Cartwright did not waver under her glance, which seemed to say, in warning, he had not heard the last of this. Instead, he lifted the honey crock and extended it to her in all courtesy.

Broadwinder and the others missed the byplay. They saw only veiled glances and felt little or nothing of the undercurrent flowing all about them. Only Mrs. Littlefield eyed each of them intently.

Jenny avoided Cartwright all that day and most of the next. All the while, the ship lay to the rough seas under storm canvas. Toward nightfall of the second day the winds backed and the alert master put sail on the yards and began his northward run. At dinner that evening Jenny took her place across the table from the shipowner and smiled at him, saying:

"Captain Broadwinder believes he has a wind he can cling to. If such is the case, we should within a few days sight the Point of Angels marking the entrance to Valparaiso."

The prediction proved true. The *Calcutta Eagle* tore her way up to fifty south, ran on under good canvas with scarcely a change of tack through the forties, and began her gradual deep-water curve for the big seaport of Chile. Although the ship did not outdistance winter, weather in the thirties was not severe enough to make decks untenable. Through the stretch of thawing climate Jenny once again completely disarmed Cartwright. He looked forward to their meetings on deck by day, her various humors and gentle scoldings to the brood she mothered, and her laughter in the saloon evenings. She continued to amaze him with her intuitiveness, loyalty to her convictions, and thorough awareness of everything aboard from the cabin boy's sniffles to the set of the topgallant yard, but most of all by her very silence on the subject of extra shares for Philip. As day after day passed with never a reference by speech or look to the one item of disagreement between them, he began to wonder if the challenge she had extended him was forgotten or had died for want of grounds for fulfillment. Perhaps he had called her bluff. In any case, he liked to think this true.

By the time the *Eagle* opened the harbor of Valparaiso he had come to believe it. It was quite a victory, he decided; one to compare with if not excel his tussle with the huge marlin. He felt a little cunning and mean as he thought of her in defeat, though he was nonetheless quite happy about it.

During their few days in the lively port, crew, shipowner, passengers, and the captain's wife were once more reminded of Broadwinder's popularity. It began when pilot-boat crews hailed, "Señor el Capitan Broadwinder! *El príncipe de los Marineros!*" and all other ships had to wait until he was attended to. Port and government officials as well as British, Chilean, and American friends welcomed him with open arms and flowing champagne. They had heard of the big race ahead with Captain Keys. And should he win, which he of course would, they would greet his next entry into the harbor with a proper salute of cannon and a dipping of colors.

On the day of departure Broadwinder was rowed out to his ship by his friends. The flotilla of small craft came on to the ship's side where gifts to the "Prince," cases of fine wines, hampers of onions, garlic, pears and apples, large lobsters, and melons for his table and boxes galore were hoisted aboard. As crew and passengers assembled on decks to witness the scene over the side, an obese, long-mustached Chilean in uniform rivaling in color and gold braid that of an admiral recited a speech in his native tongue. Amid cheers that floated over the harbor, Broadwinder shook hands and boarded his ship.

Since Jenny stood near Mrs. Littlefield, she could not help hearing her say to a lady, "Never have I seen a more popular man than our captain. Nor a more charming one."

Jenny's eyebrows lifted. She continued to eye the widow who down under the Horn had asked, "Where is the dashing Captain Broadwinder?" A vacillating woman, the widow, Jenny admitted, one who bent to the prevailing winds of opinion as easily as the pennant on the main whipped before a breeze. But the adoration in her voice and gaze was something else, and San Francisco was a long way off. The widow would bear watching.

Soon the *Eagle* began working her way out of the crescent-shaped harbor for the open sea. As they let sail go and dipped once again to Valparaiso, Jenny sighed with relief. The land always took Philip from her. The sea would give him back. And the sea was coming on, sunny and wave-capped. The Point of Angels seemed to dip in gracious farewell, and on the deck Philip's voice rose with an order to let fly the fore and main topgallants. The broad blue Pacific lay ahead, and Jenny looked far into its horizon, like the Queen she felt herself then, and picked up the weave of things aboard ship where she had left off a few days earlier.

A maze of threads, loose ends, she realized. Ship, husband, cabin boy, sick and injured sailors, the balance of stateroom personalities necessary to a happy ship, the quiet little running duel with the widow and, last but not least, the contest with the shipowner for equal interest in the ship.

She looked at Cartwright and, finding his attention full upon her, crossed the deck to where he stood. There she fired the opening gun of renewed hostilities with smiling eyes and a remark designed to please the catcher of marlin.

As the *Eagle* reached far out from the land and up for the

Tropic of Capricorn and the southeast trade winds, Jenny continued to bait her hook with honey. The weather warmed and heavy canvas was replaced with light sails. Ragged gusts came on, as did squalls and calms of short duration. Then the first breath of lively trades was felt. Clear days and balmy nights followed. Everyone appeared on deck of evenings when myriad Southern stars seemed to dangle from the velvety blue of tropic heavens down to the network of rigging. The on-deck crew lazed and the below watch gathered at the hatch coamings or rail to sing of sweethearts and home.

On the day the *Eagle* crossed the imaginary line of twenty degrees south, the setting sun burned on the level of the water at the far end of a flaming crimson sea. With a steady wind aft, the ship scudded along with her booms run out, studding sails set under the reaches of her big canvas and her foresail passareed. The crew waited for the sunset squall to hiss in. It came as the sun dropped under, a short deluge that sped on, leaving the ship glistening.

From the forward deck a sailor cried, "I baptize thee daily." A laugh followed. Then a concertina sounded faintly against the wind and ushered in the quick night of the tropics.

Jenny appeared on deck alone. Philip stood forward in conversation with Mr. Fortune and the second. She stood at the rail a long time, watching the thinnest slice of moon hanging in a silver crescent above the sharp edge of the western horizon, before she became aware that she was not alone.

"Pretty, isn't it?" Cartwright said.

"And promising," she replied softly, not looking at him. "Bigger and higher each night, until it floods the sea with light to fulfill its promise."

His silence seemed thoughtful, though he knew better. The spell of sun, sea air, and tropics was upon him. Jenny and her dreamy observation only heightened it, turned the night into a romantic stage. Now she was saying pensively:

"I've almost forgotten what moonlight on land looks like."

Cartwright made no reply. Only the swish of the sea down the sides and the crush of wind on sails and rigging made any sound until she spoke again.

"Here at sea the moon and stars make water jewels. When you reach for one it is gone. Another lies ahead; a million always just out of reach. Empty. Like dreams."

"But pretty just the same," he ventured, exploring her mood.

"Yes." Then she said, "Pretty things often vanish like an illusion."

The soft breeze eddying down the cavities of sail above their bare heads stirred her hair. He was thinking how lovely evening painted a beautiful woman, and that she had not once turned her face to him when she said, "You know——" and paused.

"You know," she said again, "it's like a ship encircled by sea and sky. She lies to under storm sails in heavy weather and runs with bonnets in the trades. They wet down her canvas in the doldrums. But always she moves, on and on to another horizon, to the unattainable. And the circle of sky and sea moves with her. It may change in color and humor but it always moves with the ship."

"Horizons are like water jewels."

"A poetic thought," he said at last. "Almost, you paint a picture of life. But you sound rather moody. Or lonely."

"Oh no! Not at all." She looked at him then, her serious eyes reflecting star points. "At least I did not mean to sound so. However——" She faced the silver slice of moon now reddening down into the sea. "Perhaps it is a picture of life."

She laughed lightly. "Life aboard ship."

"You seem to thrive on it," he said tentatively, gazing at the Southern Cross.

"I'm married to it."

She moved slowly aft a few steps and he followed leisurely. At the mizzen shrouds, she paused, as though the shooting star she watched an instant brought her to a halt. "In fact," she said, smiling ever so briefly, "I'm married to a horizon. Don't you agree?"

Cartwright indulged in a chuckle. "The way you put it, yes. Only there are a thousand horizons."

"And I'm married to all of them? Heavens! Seems I'm surpassing life. Or is it your desire, sir, to suppress my poetic thoughts on such a lovely night?"

She was more the steady, gay, shipboard Jenny now, and he was quick to declare that he thought the evening and poetry were synonymous. "I'll add another ingredient and make it perfect—you, Jenny."

Her eyes widened and searched deep into his. "You flatter

me, sir. Now whatever prompted you to put me on a par
with all this?"

"The stars, maybe. The night, the tropic sea, or all of
them. Perhaps horizons and the little evasive jewels have
something to do with it."

"So!" she said in a voice of discovery. "It's you who's lonely
and moody." Her eyes twinkled as she placed a hand on his
arm. "Saying such things now! Why, you should have spoken
that way to some pretty lady years ago, sir."

"I wanted to do just that several years back. In Medford."

"Medford?" she asked.

"Yes. But while I waited someone else stepped in."

"In Medford," she said curiously. "Perhaps I know her, Mr.
Cartwright."

"Perhaps. But let us say you knew her. She has married
since and everything has changed but my regard for her."
He added hastily, "That and an undeniable fact, I find her
more charming now."

Jenny saw a tautness come into his face. Even in the faint
light cast by deck lamps there was no mistaking it. He seemed
to hold his rigid glance over the dark starlit sea with an iron
will. As she began to wonder, a catch of alertness stirred her
mind and pulse. He was boldly scudding before the wind,
rather dangerously, she thought, that is if what she suspected
were true. She could be content with what he had said, secretly flattered and a little afraid, or she could draw him out
in obedience to the little imps clamoring inside her. She pondered the gain, realizing that the latter course could hardly
serve her since it would at best create an awkward situation.
So she said cheerily:

"And now she's just a water jewel."

The remark, the fact, jerked his glance around to her. She
saw the muscles of his jaw and mouth tighten, then slowly relax. The spell was broken and she breathed a sigh of relief.

Later, as Cartwright in his stateroom frowned contritely and
stared at nothing but a memory of his rash behavior on deck,
Jenny sat before her mirror with eyes unfocused and brush
in still hand at her hair. Philip eyed her a full minute from
the bed before asking what occupied her mind and closed her
eyes with her reply of, "Oh, nothing much."

Jenny shuddered at the thought of what Philip would say
or do if he knew all she was thinking. Why, he would come
up like a harpooned whale thrashing his flukes. But Philip did

not know that she was secretly at work planning her next move. He would never know.

She would use the gain of this night, which was a great deal. Cartwright had revealed much. Indeed, for she had never so much as suspected that he had noticed her back in Medford. And that had been several years in the past. And to think that he had singled her out with admiring eyes and thoughts of courtship! Hmm—she might be a shipowner's instead of a captain's wife now. Utterly absurd, of course, loving Philip as she did, but the possibility could not be denied any more than his continued regard.

In any case, George Cartwright had shown his hand, had made a grave mistake, and in doing so he had rescued her from uncertainty and put her on a true course. A wave of elation swept over her, only to be suddenly driven out by a twinge of conscience that brought her eyes into sharp focus. She was blushing with shame, and asking if she were actually capable of such deception. Toying with a man's emotions for gain was nothing short of a crime. Could she do it and be able to live with herself?

For Philip she could, and would.

Resolved, she considered the dangers ahead. The slightest error in speech or glance could open Cartwright's eyes to her scheme or draw her into deep water fraught with unforeseen perils. But seldom was anything worth while won without risk. Risk with caution at the helm, the way Philip sailed. He gambled topmasts against a wind for speed, but he knew when to take in sail. So did she.

Jenny glanced up at her face in the mirror. She was suddenly surprised at the intensity of her thoughts, for all she was thinking seemed to surface in a thin smile and in the pinpoints of her eyes. Meeting her own glance was then difficult. She did so, however, excusing herself by a simple admission:

She knew what she wanted, a prize her husband had long since won but had not collected, and she felt entirely justified in playing a harmless game to win it.

"A perfectly harmless game," she told herself while slowly brushing her hair.

17

☐ From twenty degrees south to almost the limit of the southeast trades above the equator George Cartwright avoided any meeting with Jenny under the stars and growing moon. He felt considerably ill at ease in her presence, for he was definitely sure that she had known his mind that night and had saved him from making a complete fool of himself. So, rather chagrined and amazed at the thought of sober George Cartwright's show of temerity—it was that, pure and simple foolhardiness—he made a solemn vow that he would never through any fault of his own be caught in such an embarrassing position again.

He thought it strange in the days that followed that Jenny appeared to retain no memory of his folly. She invited him to sit with her on deck as usual, to visit the sick in the forecastle, and, on one occasion, to drill the ship's boy in arithmetic while she administered to an apprentice who had fallen from the crossjack yard. She talked of Captain Broadwinder's speed—he had logged well over three hundred miles a day for four days running—of the bazaars in Singapore, of books, art, cargoes, ships, slavery in the South, politics, and no end of things. With never a mention of Medford.

He was beginning to think she had missed his meaning entirely when one morning she lowered a piece she was crocheting to her lap and said with startling suddenness, "I watched them build this ship on the bank of the Mystic River. But I don't recall seeing you there until the day they launched her."

Before he could reply, she was telling of a humorous incident involving two shipwrights at work on the unborn vessel. As she talked on, saying nothing more about his visit to Medford, he wondered why she had touched on the subject only to hurriedly run off and leave it. It was like the flick of a whip. Gently uncoiled and gently retrieved, its sting was nevertheless felt. And she merely smiled and talked of other things while he jumped back and forth in an effort to avoid the lash.

Now in the doldrums, the *Calcutta Eagle* spent days creeping along on capricious winds and more days sitting as still as a rock in the Pacific. Position approximately 10 degrees North, 120 degrees West; a breeze stirring out of the west, then out of the east, and then, no breeze at all.

Broadwinder began to look anxiously at the calendar and Jenny told Cartwright on deck one morning that unless they caught a wind soon an overdue notice might be posted against Captain Broadwinder in San Francisco.

"Which," she said, staring over the still north ocean, "would be something new for him."

"He would then join the ranks of the great majority of sea captains," Cartwright said with noticeable unconcern.

Jenny cocked her head inquisitively. "I should think that would rob you of something you can now point to with pride among shippers."

"True," he replied, stroking the gray hair at his temple. "But it might also give Captain Broadwinder a certain deep-stream maturity in their eyes." Under her close scrutiny, he added, "Something to convince the maritime world that he does not sail in just luck alone. Understand what I mean?"

"No." She eyed him narrowly. "Nor was I aware that such an opinion existed, sir."

"You would be the last to learn of it, naturally. Sorry I mentioned it."

About to launch in to a strong defense of Philip's record, she checked herself and with quick discernment assessed the stubborn set of his jaw and the touch of belligerence behind his blue-gray eyes as a bid for the initiative he had lost under the stars. She knew how necessary it was to a man, and she decided to let him regain it, if only to disarm him.

"I didn't know," she said, suddenly meek.

Jenny found it very difficult to sustain the look of troubled wonderment as she saw him taking her in with subdued pleasure. Frowning, she lowered her eyes lest by the merest change in her expression she give herself away.

The northeast trade wind blew in that night and sent the ship happily on her way. Jenny was aware of more than just a change in weather. George Cartwright wore the face of the man who had caught a marlin and his reserve thawed into geniality. Secretly amused, she watched and listened, realizing that with his confidence restored she must perforce act the part of a woman whose loss of sureness was proportionate to his gain. So she began to brood in his presence. She talked in a detached voice and assumed troubled expressions wholly unlike the Jenny of the quarter-deck and watched and waited.

At first Cartwright seemed to view the change in her with taciturn satisfaction. Gradually, she noticed, his smug manner gave way to puzzlement, then uncertainty. He tried to cheer her and, failing, studied her curiously, as though it had begun to dawn on him that he had been a little cruel perhaps. Wanting him contrite, she prolonged the act for several days. Then late one afternoon something happened to convince her that the time had come for what she had in mind.

The pleasant tropic day was running out on the ship. Bowling along with almost perfect running weather at his command, decks dry but for flying spray and a steady wind blowing across the reaches of the sea, Captain Broadwinder was trying to make up time lost in the doldrums. He had just spoken his desire to Jenny for a wee bit more life in the wind when Cartwright appeared on deck. As he said something about the excellent weather to Philip, Jenny turned her attention on the western sky where the dying day marshaled clouds of every shape, piling them up in overlapping layers and deploying streamers to the north and south for a brilliant parade. Philip spoke to her and she made no reply, causing him to ask what had come over her lately.

"Cheer up," he said. "The Lord willing, we'll reach San Francisco well ahead of our due date. Now that should put a smile on your face."

"Yes, I suppose it should." She met Cartwright's glance and, observing his quick frown, almost forgot to end her statement with a wan futile smile. It was forthcoming however, and her listlessness belied the exultant feeling that leaped up inside her with the sudden realization that the look on the shipowner's face was the one she had patiently sought.

Alert in herself and thinking competently, Jenny said something about the view of the sunset from the lee deck and excused herself. As she had anticipated, Cartwright soon broke off his conversation with Philip and joined her with an odd look of sympathy in his eyes.

She wore a low-necked dress that half exposed a white shoulder and she noticed that he missed nothing of her appearance, from small corseted waist to hair tumbling in the wind; all of which served to predispose him into a silence that often precedes some momentous decision.

She had welcomed him with an expression like a smile in her eyes, one that scarcely altered the composed fullness of her lips, before looking at the sunset clouds again. Now she waited.

"I've been thinking," Cartwright began rather hesitantly, as though groping for just the proper words. Moments later he blurted forth, "It was damned unsporting of me—that remark I made the other day, about the maritime world's opinion that Philip sailed in luck alone. I hope you'll forgive me."

"Is there anything to forgive?" she asked in a calm voice. Watching the clouds' tinting of reds and golds, she said, "I've thought a great deal about it, of course. And I've wondered about many things."

He met her long pause with a curious, "Yes?"

"I suppose Captain Broadwinder's personality has much to do with it. Were he older and more reserved and, as you implied, seasoned with reverses, smart sailing would not appear to be just luck."

Knowing he could only agree, and not wishing to defeat her purpose by justifying his opinion, she did not allow him a reply, but went on to say, "However, Captain Broadwinder is not older and he is not the quiet type of commander ashore, and he continues to sail with a wisdom and dispatch that even his worst enemy, if he had one, could only praise. So——" She broke off suddenly with a deep breath. When she continued a hopeless note entered her voice. "So that's the way the wind blows."

The remark left him with nothing to say. He could only regard her silently, which he did with firm attention made up of concern, curiosity, and sympathy. She had spoken in an unstirred voice, though he was aware that an emotion strongly worked inside her. It left its impression upon her face.

"However unfair it seems," she was saying, "there is little to do about it other than wait for those inevitable reverses. They will come, no doubt about it. The sea will attend to that—one way or another. Storm, reef, a slight miscalculation, and Captain Broadwinder is suddenly mature—if he survives."

Vivid colors in the far-flung western sky deepened as the sun slid under. Clouds quickly spilled their rich purples, pinks, and crimsons until only ashes remained against the backdrop of searing light from under the sea. As suddenly, swift night charged in from the east.

Jenny's eyes dwelled pensively on the horizon as she said, "And I'll go on as before. Living in a house that moves from one horizon to another. Envying often, I'm sure, a fisher's wife in a hut anchored to a rock. Wondering what it would be like to have a home and children, and the things a woman expects of her marriage."

Cartwright considered all she had said in thoughtful silence. The disparity between the things a woman expected of marriage and her life aboard a ship was great. He saw his ace captain's wife sacrificing her good years by sailing on and on, the narrow confines of a working ship her home. But worse, she sailed from day to day with always that fear of the future to keep her company, a firm conviction that somewhere a reef was waiting for Philip Broadwinder. Even now the history of ships seemed to unfold in her twilight gaze over the sea.

Why had she revealed herself to him? It didn't matter, really. The things she had brought into sharp focus were all that mattered, for they created a true picture of her life, evoked into being a strong compassion and a sense of responsibility he had never before experienced where she was concerned. But what was the answer to her problem?

"I understand," he said quietly. "But is there any remedy? You'd worry every bit as much in a house on land every time Captain Broadwinder went to sea."

Jenny drew her glance in from the water and turned it on him, thinking as she did so that he was fast taking the wind out of her sails. George Cartwright was a worthy competitor, and she should not forget it.

"You're so right," she said. "However, Captain Broadwinder could not afford a house like that. If he could, I'd more than likely send him off to sea while I caught up with the life ashore. For a few years at least."

He had forced her to tell that lie. Any shame she felt was displaced by a surge of anger she found hard to put down. Composing herself, she sighed heavily and said with seeming constraint:

"But that is beside the point, sir. We haven't the money to do it. The only solution, as I see it, is to capitalize on Captain Broadwinder's skill and popularity while it is up for public notice. And winning the race with Mayo Keys is therefore of utmost importance."

He fished then, as she thought he would. "What do you mean?" he asked in puzzled tones.

"A strange question," she replied. "You know what victory over Captain Keys will mean to my husband."

"Of course. But you spoke of capitalizing on his popularity. I don't quite follow you."

"Well, you should, Mr. Cartwright. You know as well as anyone that on the day Captain Broadwinder enters Boston harbor in the lead of the *Emperor* he can write his own ticket aboard any ship afloat or under construction. Do you agree?"

"I'm afraid I must, Jenny," he replied grudgingly. A hollow laugh escaped him. "It seems I planned a race to lose a captain. Now that thought did not once enter my mind."

"Nor ours, sir. Captain Broadwinder's loyalty to you cannot be questioned."

"How about your loyalty?" he asked pointedly.

"Mine? My first obligation is to my husband. His welfare. His present and future. I have shared his loyalty to you. But now that I've learned he will not reach his maturity in the trade until he meets with reverses at sea, I am going to do my utmost to see that he makes his fortune before these things happen."

After a lapse of seconds, he asked, "For what purpose?" When she stared as though in despair of his sanity, he said, "I don't see how that would solve your problem."

"You jest, surely. Captain Broadwinder could then build me a great house on land."

"And he probably would," Cartwright said. "And after that?"

"Why, he would quit the sea, of course."

Cartwright laughed. "He would? You could change the color of your eyes quicker than you could turn Broadwinder into a landsman. And you know it's the truth. So what would you gain, actually? Nothing but a house to be miserable in, or one to board up while at sea."

Jenny tensed and stood speechless, unable to believe she had been neatly trapped. It left her cold, her mind racing for a means of escape even as she bit her lip and tried to put down recurrent waves of anger directed at both herself and the cunning shipowner. She could argue that Philip would listen to her and leave the sea, as she was sorely tempted to do, despite the fact that she knew it would avail her nothing to speak without any semblance of conviction. The alternative was silence and she clung to it as a refuge.

18

□ Several days later the lookout cried the land and the *Calcutta Eagle* opened the Golden Gate and San Francisco harbor in true Broadwinder fashion. Dipping his colors to the maze of ships and the sprawling city two full days ahead of schedule, Broadwinder ran on to anchorage with a land-hungry look in his eyes. He caused quite a stir in the harbor and along the water front, and before the maze of duties that befall a captain on port entry were half attended to, a welcoming committee steamed out to claim him.

As the boat came alongside and voices lifted with "And Broadwinder long live he," Cartwright looked from his popular captain to Jenny. Her expression was the same as he had noted when the anchor splashed in Valparaiso. How well she masked her disapproval, he thought. On second glance, he wondered if she covered her feeling of loss at all but merely retained her composure in absolute resignation to something she could not hope to alter.

Then Broadwinder, suddenly the Prince, claimed the shipowner's attention. As the business at hand was quickly delegated to his subordinates, Cartwright asked himself if his captain were guilty of betraying his duty to ship. But as Messrs. Fortune and Winston accepted the responsibilities, thoughts of betrayal vanished under a grudging admiration for a man capable of surrounding himself with trusted, competent officers.

The passengers' effects were no sooner piled near the gangway than a passing lighter's crew hailed the ship with, "Broadwinder, ho! How many days you going to beat the *Emperor?*" The reply, "By as many barnacles as you ship on your bottom," sent them merrily on their way to repeat ashore the Prince of Sea Captains' boast.

Mr. Fulton shook hands around, complimented the captain and his lady for a most enjoyable voyage, then gave Mrs. Littlefield a look that spoke of wedding bells. The Sherwoods, the Masons of Georgia, the St. Louis merchant, and other stateroom guests said farewells and moved to the gangway ladder. Mrs. Sherwood wiped her eyes as she kissed Jenny's cheek and the planter's wife departed with a "God bless you and take care of you, dear girl." Still the widow hung back, her eyes dancing nervously from Jenny to Philip, back and forth. Although Jenny's eyes were misty—partings did that to her —she was aware of Mrs. Littlefield's play for the captain's undivided attention. She saw Philip lift her daughter Madeline and hold her in his arms.

"Sail with me again, little miss," he said. "And next time don't try to climb the ratlines."

"Yes, sir, Captain, 'cause my mother thinks you're the mostest adorable man."

"Madeline!" The widow colored.

"So ho!" Broadwinder laughed. "Well, that's quite the impression I like to make with pretty ladies."

He extended a hand to the widow, who chose to take it in both of hers. Then, to the surprised horror of young Fulton, she tilted her head up to the captain in a manner he could not mistake. Sweeping Jenny with a glance, Philip rose to the occasion by giving his lips to Mrs. Littlefield a little longer than Jenny thought necessary. When minutes later the passengers waved from the ship's boat, Jenny asked Philip what the bold woman had said to him after their touching embrace.

"That she's stopping at the Parker House."

"An invitation, I suppose," she said frostily.

Broadwinder grinned. "I certainly hope so, Mistress Jenny." As she put her back to him, he said, "Now if you'll oblige me by seeing to the invoices, bills of lading, and so forth, I'll not keep my friends waiting any longer."

So saying, he turned to Cartwright with a request to see Mrs. Broadwinder ashore.

"Where are we stopping?" Jenny asked.

"The Parker House, of course," he replied.

She eyed him severely, tempted to say, "Rather convenient, isn't it, sir?" though she did no such thing, for she knew his reply would be, "Couldn't be better, Mrs. Broadwinder," or words to that effect.

Jenny watched him scramble down to the steam craft and his friends, merchants, sea captains, a banker, a Maine Yankee whose profitable business was mules and wagons, a colonel of the Army who had fought his way overland to the gold regions and the German Jew who had traded his holdings in Connecticut for a shipload of picks, shovels, and Irish whisky bound for California. They would wine and dine Philip. There was no doubt on that score. Perhaps she would see him before dawn of the next day. Perhaps not. In the meantime she would be a widow, like Mrs. Littlefield, she admitted, except she would have no daughter to keep her company.

Sighing wearily, Jenny swept the harbor with its forest of tall masts and brought her gaze to bear on the hills and, closer, the myriad buildings that constituted the hellhole of the booming West.

"Always the land," she said in silence. Always ports and loneliness. At sea a braving of all sorts of weather with sails set and striving for the shores that never failed to separate husband and wife.

The monotony and the injustice of it assailed her and aroused something akin to rebellion inside her. With nothing to combat the encroachment, it warmed into a small fire. She would not sit alone waiting, waiting, for Philip. Instead, she would demand something more of this port she despised among others.

Feeling a little reckless, and liking it, Jenny encompassed the entire voyage in a single memory, Cartwright's spoken regard for the woman in Medford, herself. The thought was freighted with a certain appeal. All women liked attention, all enjoyed a harmless adventure. Just to wet a foot in the hungry current, no more. She told herself these things even as she whirled and trained her gaze on George Cartwright.

There was a speculative light in her eyes as he looked around at her. Then their glances met and she saw only a tight-fisted shipowner who had parried her every thrust in a battle for shares in the ship. In the instant, hatred of ports, Philip's neglect of her and loneliness were forgotten, and surging in to fill the sudden vacancy and sustain the spirit of conquest and adventure was an implacable desire to wrest from him all he denied Philip.

And now that a worth-while purpose excused her indiscretions of moments before, she felt better; but with no loss of the excitement that stirred her into this undertaking.

When everything was attended to and Tobias was placed in the custody of Mr. Fortune, she made the crossing from ship to shore with Cartwright, who handed her into a carriage and down at the entrance of the San Francisco palace built by Boston's Robert A. Parker. It was a long building with pillars supporting a gallery for the second-floor guests and a protected loitering place for the assorted citizenry milling about underneath. Eight large dormer windows lent further colonial charm to the place. The Parker House boasted of the most magnificent ballroom in the country, a room for billiards, a famous dining hall noted for fine dishes from all over the world, the most spacious and elite gambling hall in the West and a respectable address for particular people. To Jenny it suggested once again a jewel in a pigsty, an echo of the famed Parker House of Boston. Although the streets of San Francisco had improved since 1849, mushroomed huts, stacks of lumber, and piles of merchandise from a dozen lands were still in evidence to remind visitors in the fifties of what travelers once called the most "jackassable" streets in America.

Cartwright escorted the captain's wife through the door under the eyes of gamblers, miners and men in the uniform of the Army and Navy, and on to the suite reserved for the Broadwinders. They had talked of this and that, the ship, the reported dangers of the Oregon Trail, though mostly about the growth of San Francisco. While in the carriage, he had mentioned a thirst and a desire to accustom himself to the roll of land gradually, preferably under the influence of chilled Spanish wine. Following his invitation to partake of a glass, she had replied, "At dinner perhaps, if you'll be so kind as to escort a widow of the evening to the dining hall."

And now, standing at the door, she extended a hand and thanked him for his attention. As he accepted it, she recalled his expressions of pleasure and anticipation of the evening ahead and felt a devilish desire to give him something more to think about. Obeying an impulse of the moment, she suddenly applied a gentle pressure of her fingers to his. It was ever so slight, to be sure, and as harmless as it was confounding.

As quickly as it was done, she withdrew her hand and turned to her parlor.

George Cartwright stood tense and silent, unable to take his eyes off her until the door closed between them. He could believe she had done this subconsciously, in a gesture of innocent friendliness, or he could believe she had acted deliberately. He knew how she attracted, excited, and irritated him, how by virtue of simply being the woman he admired above all others she served violently to inflame him. Her touch lingered like an electric charge, and it upset the stern realist in him and left him a tumult of unanswered questions and strange emotions.

Downstairs he claimed his effects, had them sent to his room, and, mopping his brow despite the chill hanging over the town, decided that he could do with a touch of wine, perhaps a glass of the fiery whisky favored by sailors and miners. He drank brandy instead and, his composure restored once again, reserved a table in the dining hall and ordered lobsters and chilled wine for eight o'clock that evening. Retiring to his room, he sat down and applied reason to the puzzle of Jenny Broadwinder. He was somewhat disappointed when in final judgment he could find Jenny guilty of nothing more than extending a friendly gesture. She was a lonely woman. The fault was Broadwinder's, and the captain was a fool to think he could go on neglecting a pretty wife for friends who would drop him in a minute should Mayo Keys win the race. But the devil with Philip, whom he envied. The admission of this fact evoked a frown, for he had refused to face the truth up to this day. Then he put the thought out of mind. The disturbing beauty of Jenny was far better company.

Alone in a bedroom that seemed a bit of New England transplanted in the far West, Jenny sat before a long mirror framed in massive gilt scrolls, brushing her hair. For nearly an hour she had done this, slowly, lazily, thoughtfully. She felt no guilt for her first and only flirtatious act since her marriage. Although resentment at being left alone had set the whole thing in motion, the deed itself had followed her decision to obtain for Philip something he deserved. So it had been a sacrifice on her part, nothing more.

Dressed in next to nothing, she studied the oval of her face and contours of her figure. The late-afternoon sun flooding through a window highlighted her burnished hair and painted her skin a tawny gold. Vaguely at first she connected the intimate nature of the picture she created to the word she pondered. Sacrifice. She was asking herself just how far she was prepared to go after the shares in the *Calcutta Eagle* when the mind and eye suddenly were one. The effect caused her to start. Frowning curiously, she shuddered a moment, as if afraid of her own stubborn resolve, then arose and covered herself to the neck in a robe.

Not quite so sure of herself now, she tried to place a value on the prize she coveted. The real worth of the shares seemed reduced to ashes in her hands as she thought of what she had already done.

"Jenny Broadwinder," she said to her image, "you should be ashamed."

She was ashamed. The admission stirred up a flurry of anger at herself, then at Cartwright, who had brought it all about by tightfistedly refusing Philip his just reward. Why did he do this to her? Because he was stingy, because he, lacking in foresight, wanted to exploit Philip for all he was worth. Then, if and when Philip lost popularity or failed to fill his coffers like a money mill or met with disaster at sea, rich George Cartwright would follow the pattern drawn by shipowners and find himself another golden goose. So the devil with him. He deserved all she had given him and more.

She laughed but without humor, and saw in the eyes staring back at her from the mirror no sign of mercy. She was no longer ashamed; rather, she was eager to continue the attack along the lines she had planned.

Jenny dressed for George Cartwright that evening. He came for her at eight and seemed unable to remove his eyes from the striking woman in dark green velvet. Her smile full upon him, her eyes deep and searching across the small table, she seemed to compliment the luxurious dining hall by her very presence. He had never seen her more beautiful. When she raised a tall-stemmed glass brimming with champagne and said, "To the health of my handsome escort," instead of the toast he expected, to victory over the *Emperor*, or some such remark having to do with ships or Philip, he felt a pleasant quickening of his pulses.

She found him easy to draw out of his shell. With little prompting on her part, that and a show of genuine interest, she launched him into accounts of his youth, and then into rather lengthy and meticulous recitations of his attitude concerning this and that. Jenny sipped champagne sparingly and listened as though every word that fell from his tongue was a gem. The wine was chilled to perfection, the lobster was as delicious as she had ever tasted, and George Cartwright seemed cosily at ease, fascinated and unsuspecting. She was thinking the time had come for her to find a means of broaching the subject uppermost in her mind.

As she looked about for an opening, she realized that it was up to her to create one. She heard him out, then lifted a finger to a dimple in her cheek. Her eyes were shining as they dropped from a chandelier to favor him with a deep, admiring glance. She said:

"I find it difficult to believe my companion of the evening is the same man I delivered the ship's papers to in Boston."

"Perhaps I'm not," he replied directly, his gaze level with hers.

She felt the challenge he extended and lowered her gaze an instant. "I suppose I have misjudged you." She raised the glass to her lips, watching him all the while. "And now I am trying to adjust both of you into one man. It is not easy, I assure you."

"Then why try it? The businessman is not here."

"No?" Her smile mocked him. "Care to place a wager on it, sir?"

"Naturally." He frowned curiously. "I seem to remember your saying something of the sort to me in Boston? But this is not as ambiguous as that wager, whatever it was."

"Whatever it was! You mean you don't remember?" She laughed.

Her good humor disarmed him. "Vaguely. And I'll confess to something. I couldn't exactly put my finger on it a minute after you named it."

"Why, how could you?" she demanded with mock asperity. "Shame on you for taking a serious woman so lightly. Now, if you'll kindly refill my glass, I'll acquaint you with our *honorable* wager, sir."

"Gladly. But wait. Before I forget the wager we have just made, I am saying the businessman is not here tonight and you are saying he is. Correct?"

"Correct." Flashing a smile, she said, "I hope you win. But you won't."

"Go on. We'll see," he said, with a dare in his voice.

"You will recall I told you that day in your office the road to the East was strewn with wrecks, that the threat went with ship and master, and that it was too bad Philip didn't own half of the ship then, while God favored him. And then I said it could not last forever. You——"

"And I said he sailed in luck and skill," he interrupted.

"Excellent! For a man who can't remember. You said also you had the utmost faith in Philip, that with another man you might wonder if his popularity loomed as a threat to his vigilance as a sailing man." He nodded, pushing back a frown, as she went on, saying, "And I replied to you in these words: 'Only a Yankee shipowner could so discount an asset.' Then, later, I was looking at a painting of the *Bengal Runner*. I said, 'Struck a reef. See what I mean?' and you said, 'Which I refuse to admit.' It was then I asked if you cared to place a wager on it. When you told me to name it, I did—the sum that separated Captain Broadwinder from a half interest in the *Calcutta Eagle*."

"I remember, all right, Jenny. But just what exactly were we betting on?"

"I was betting you would admit that I had grounds for my fears regarding Philip's extended good luck."

"Umm." He glanced at his plate. "Right you are. But how did we get off on this subject?"

"You mentioned it, not I," she replied cheerily. "But now that we're into it, may I ask if after witnessing the fate of the *Fawn* and the terrible seas under the Horn, you still refuse to admit it?"

"I do. And if the way Broadwinder handled the ship on this voyage is a sample of his skill, I'll not likely change my mind."

She studied him almost incredulously. "I hope you are being honest, sir," she said in low voice. Dropping her glance to the rim of crystal, she continued barely above a whisper, "Thinking as much of you as I do, I'd rather see you honest than blind."

Caught aback by her unexpected compliment and the emotion in her voice, he could only regard her in silence.

Jenny lifted her face and looked into his eyes a long serious moment. "You have won the wager we made tonight. The businessman is not here." She waited for an inquisitive expression to form in his face, then placed a hand over his. "I said I hoped you won. Now I'm not so sure. But you have, and the proof is conclusive, for if the shipowner George Cartwright were here tonight he would realize that on this lap of the voyage to the big race some public honor to his captain was overdue on his part."

She did not remove her hand from his, nor take her appealing eyes off him. Aware that her last remark had not been lost on him, that under her touch the arguments of a stubborn shipowner had been silenced, she decided to deliver the *coup de grâce*. A cruel stroke, to be sure, and one demanding all her courage and guile.

Gazing at a sapphire of light on the glass before her, she said quietly, "Perhaps you have won the first wager also. I don't know. But"—she faltered—"it seems that Captain Broadwinder is confronted by more than the threat of seas and weather."

She lifted her hand from his then and, avoiding his glance, forced herself to play the final trump. "Perhaps it would be better if you returned to Boston, Mr. Cartwright."

The words seemed to fall from her lips like lead. Afraid now, she found it unnecessary to pretend as she rose nervously and hurried away from him.

19

☐ Jenny fairly flew to the refuge of her room. Once inside, she closed the door and leaned against it for support. Across the room a mirror drew her attention and she stared at a woman she had never seen before. It was not a pretty picture. She dropped her head to shut out the sight, knowing as she did so that the memory of what she had done on this night would forever remain a part of her. As she had joined Cartwright irrevocably committed to this deception, so must she live with it.

She raised her face. "I did it for Philip," she said with a trace of defiance in her voice.

Yet what actually had she done for Philip, other than cheapen herself? Oh, she had spun quite a web, no doubting the fact, but it could not be as bad as all that. After all, what she had done had been for her husband. Regardless of consequences, no one could change that. Not even Philip.

"Philip?" she said, sinking into a chair.

She was suddenly weak all over. The thought of Philip in judgment of her evoked a shudder. She drove it out of her mind, only to pick up an equally frightening thread. Forgetting the marital side, if she could, the damage she had inflicted on Philip's business career was enough to bring his full wrath down upon her. Though she had not thought of this, the fact exposed in no way lessened the effect. The situation seemed fraught with enough unpleasantness without that; the event clearly dramatized the tragedy of her own thoughts and actions, for she knew in her heart that deception was betrayal and betrayal was the worst attack one partner in marriage could make on the other. But the relationship of captain and shipowner was something else. It demanded something of her, and she thought about it for some time before reaching a decision.

Although writing a full confession to George Cartwright was a terrible blow to her pride, she managed to complete it. Ashamed to think of what she had done, much less put it down in words, she paused often. Philip seemed to push her on until it was all there. Then she read what she had written. Her face burned. It was like the confession of a dockside hussy, she admitted. Minus the will to deliver it, realizing that she could never face Cartwright again after it reached him, and suddenly afraid that the letter might jeopardize Philip's captaincy, and more afraid that it might reach Philip, she burned it.

She stared out of troubled eyes until the paper was a char. Disposing of it, she felt as though she had destroyed evidence that would have ruined her. It belonged to her again, only her. Slowly she undressed, then sat before her mirror and brushed her hair, thinking, wondering, waiting.

George Cartwright watched Jenny go. When she disappeared from view he poured another glass of champagne and drank it down. Once in his room, he paced back and forth, one moment jubilant, another apprehensive. Her every glance on the ship had stirred the intense longing in him. And now he felt the return of his youth. The cocks of conquest crowed inside him as he reviewed her declaration of the night and tried to reconcile it in his dazed mind. She had said Broadwinder was confronted by more than the threat of seas and weather —even then he had not guessed at her meaning; then she had told him that perhaps it would be better if he returned to

Boston—it had taken his breath away. His heart still pounded like a kettledrum. Imagine him, George Cartwright, threatening the Prince of Sea Captains by stealing the heart of his Jenny! How invincible was the great captain?

That was one side of his mind. The other half pushed itself forward, slowly, inexorably, until it dominated his thoughts. Gradually the tinsel vanished and Jenny in green velvet changed from an object of conquest into another man's wife. As suddenly as the transformation came into view, he felt the change in his role. His regard for Jenny had fed on his daily meetings with her until it had reached the state of unbridled covetousness. Once he had almost blurted forth his feeling for her. Perhaps he had, though the present and not the past was up for inspection.

He sat down, drew his brows together, and studied the ten fingertips touching and separating over and over. The crowing cocks had vanished. In their place a pointing finger persisted. An annoying thing, a feeling of even small guilt. But how small or large was it? *Perhaps it would be better if you returned to Boston, Mr. Cartwright.* Her voice seemed to lift with it again, though up out of his conscience this time to remind him that marriage was a sacred thing.

Somehow, somewhere along the voyage he had forgotten a great deal.

He got up, put on his hat and went down and out into the night. Walking slowly, he looked at the many lights on masts in the harbor, and moved on, realizing now that he was trying to reach some rapport with his conscience.

Was he, he asked himself, bereft of all honor? Where was the family pride; what had happened to those precepts of integrity that a gentleman could countenance? In reply, Jenny's face loomed up desirably. It was one or the other, the woman he wanted most versus what was right and honorable.

He could not have both. He must choose between them tonight.

He did.

Aware then that for his own peace of mind he must make amends for his blunder and guilt, not tomorrow but this very night, he hastened his walk.

Jenny opened her eyes after a brief troubled sleep to see the pale light of dawn creeping through the window. A sound at the door jerked her eyes around. "Philip!" she cried, leaping out of bed and rushing to his arms.

"Philip, I have something to tell you!" she burst forth.

Tilting her chin with a finger, he grinned and arched his brows. "So? Well, it's about time, Mistress Jenny. And what a salt-water man we'll make of our son!"

"But, Philip! You——"

"Enough!" he cried, sweeping her off her feet. "It comes at a proper time, let me tell you that, for I have good news too, girl. Now listen to this and don't faint away. George Cartwright came to the party and made a public announcement, one, said he, that was overdue. Guess what?"

Jenny waited, her eyes wide.

"He declared me half owner of the *Calcutta Eagle*."

Jenny slowly dropped her eyes and rubbed her forehead with a trembling hand. As in a trance, she pushed him away, moved to a chair, and sank weakly into it.

Broadwinder laughed. "I knew it would be a shock. It almost broached me to."

Jenny scarcely heard him. To herself she said, "So it worked!" Then she was asking in silence, "Why? Is this a proper reward, or is the devil at work?" But something was expected of her, a reply or smile, not just a lifeless stare. She tried to muster her wits and a semblance of calm, though she failed. Cause and effect were too closely knit and all she could see was the reward for her folly.

"Philip." Her voice trembled despite her every effort to calm herself. "Philip, we can't accept it. Not yet."

The room rang with his laughter. "Can't, the woman says! And I thought I was tipsy."

She got up and put her back to him lest the growing panic she felt break through her eyes and voice. "No, we cannot. I feel a strong warning against it." She whirled to face him. "Until we earn it, until we win the race. Tell him that, Philip."

"I? I tell a closefisted shipowner that?"

Slowly all merriment faded from his face before a look of disbelief that turned into frowning wonderment. He rubbed his jaw, squinting his eyes almost shut as he surveyed her despairingly.

"What the devil has come over you, Jenny? Have you forgotten the past? Haven't I gambled sail and hull through storms, seas, and weather year after year for this very thing?"

"Of course. We both know that. It is deserved but——"

"But what?" he demanded, throwing off his cap.

"I have a strong feeling against it, that's all."

"A feeling? You amaze me. A feeling! Just like that. So did Cartwright nurse a feeling against it for years. And I wasn't one to ask him for what I'd worked for. I made no promises, but sailed to fulfill more than I would have promised. He said as much to the gathering. So if he feels that way and we know he's giving us nothing unearned, how can you all of a sudden stir up a feeling against it? Now shift your helm amidships and answer me that."

She drew in her lower lip and looked absent. "I can't answer it, Philip. How can one make sense out of a feeling. But does it alter the fact that one does experience a sense of warning?"

"Maybe not, but I'd be the biggest fool under the flag if I refused. So I'm not refusing good fortune."

"You're not?" She looked up suddenly, her eyes and mouth firmly set.

He removed his coat and tie in silence, flung them across the room, and grumbled something about a man rushing home proud and elated only to have the wind spilled out of his sails.

"Did you say *rush home?*" she said crisply. "All you ever do in port is rush from me. I'm beginning to hate the sight of land." When he paused to dart her a hard glance, she said, "I mean it."

"And the albatross said to the seal?" he replied.

"You're not funny. Perhaps to your rum-guzzling friends of the night, but not to me. Even send me ashore by the chief mate, second, shipowner, or whoever is handy. Pretty soon I'll be lucky to rate the company of the ship's boy."

He could arrange that, he said, and she told him to do so, that even young Tobias possessed a sense of loyalty missing in him. One word led to another, until angered exchanges drew them deeper into the first serious quarrel of their married life. No match for her, and knowing it, he reached for his tie, coat, and cap and said he would go to the ship where a man could find a little peace.

"There's the door, Captain Broadwinder." She flicked him by tone and glance. Watching him stalk in that direction, his eyes still blazing wrath, she said with startling calm, "Philip, you have never disregarded my premonitions. Do so now and I shall return to Boston."

He whirled about and stood motionless, his large figure stamped with a kind of ruthless dignity. "Very well, Jenny," he retorted grimly, "I'll ask Cartwright to book passage for you aboard the ship he's taking home."

With that, he stalked to the door, flung it open, and slammed it after him.

Jenny simply stared at the space Philip had vacated. Stunned by what he had revealed, she seemed unaware of the finality of his statement to her. So Cartwright was going home! The shocking news crowded all else out of her mind. Going home. Why? Because she had suggested it, the same as she had sent him to Philip with a handful of shares.

She dropped her head into her open hands and shook all over. What a mess she had made of everything, her marriage, her love; all because she had placed a higher value on something that was now valueless. A hard sob racked her and she threw herself on the bed, wondering in her flood of tears why, how, she could have ever conceived this ill-starred play for the shipowner's affections. But worse than a memory of her deliberate doing was the harvest.

Her plans had met with success, though success itself had amazingly backfired and brought about her separation from Philip. Then, as if this was not enough to bear, Cartwright, by his intention to return to Boston, gave positive proof of his regard for the type of woman she had pretended to be.

20

☐ Jenny waited for Philip to break the silence between them, and Philip did the same. Day after day went by without any word from one to the other. As Jenny kept mostly to the suite of rooms, visiting with friends who had come west from Medford and Boston only when loneliness seemed unbearable, Philip worked days in readying the ship for her run to the China coast and spent his evenings in the company of admiring San Franciscans. Each experienced anxiety and unhappiness, stronger with each passing day, though longing did nothing toward breaking the stubborn resolve of either.

Happily, Jenny had not seen Cartwright since the night she left him in the dining hall. She supposed he had moved to another hotel or to the house of his California office manager. She remained prepared, however, determined to either pass him by or to speak briefly and go her way.

Unhappily, she saw Philip only once. It gave her a start that morning of the seventh day in San Francisco to look out the window of her parlor and see him standing across the street gazing up at the hotel. Her pulse beat leaped up and her blood raced warm as she gazed down upon him. The desire to cry out to him was strong, though her independence was stronger. Hastily she put on a hat and with a quick glance at herself in the mirror went downstairs. Upon reaching the street she caught a fleeting glimpse of him walking away. When she turned, Mrs. Littlefield hurried past her in Philip's direction.

Jenny followed the widow. Growing angrier by the moment, she imagined their meeting clandestinely, his arms about the gushing Mrs. Littlefield in lieu of his estranged wife, then that Philip had not come out of loneliness for her but to meet the widow. And woe unto both of them if what she suspected were true. But the widow did not meet with Philip. Satisfied and repentant, Jenny returned to the hotel and found a letter under her door.

"Philip!" she cried joyously. "That's why you came, to send a boy up with it."

Suddenly she wilted. It was addressed to Miss Jenny Cornish. She had used her maiden name in booking passage aboard the extreme clipper ship *Grace Darling*. Crestfallen, she opened the letter and learned that the vessel would sail for Boston two days hence. It was not from Philip.

She felt a catch of fear. Time was growing short and they were no nearer any reconciliation than on this day a week past. "Two days remaining," she said to herself, moving toward a window overlooking a jumble of housetops between her and the harbor. A fog was rolling in, smothering in a pall of gray everything in its path. She watched, thinking it a bad omen, then feeling with alarm that it was a forerunner of the gloom and misery she would know in a life without Philip.

"No!" she said in a voice close to breaking. Then she turned suddenly, determined to save her marriage. "I'll write to Philip and tell him he has won."

She sat down and penned eagerly, "My darling Philip," studied the paper, and began anew with, "Dear Philip." Pausing with index finger at the cleft of her chin, she gazed thoughtfully at the ceiling a long minute before writing on another sheet, "Captain Broadwinder."

An hour later a messenger from shore approached the *Calcutta Eagle* and hailed the deck. The activity aboard drowned his repeated cries and he growled his displeasure before pulling at the oars to send the boat alongside at the ship's waist. Once on the deck, he was told to wait until the captain completed inspection of the extra spars coming aboard.

Forward, Broadwinder, carpenter, sailmaker, second mate, and crewmen were lashing topmasts to decks. Cartwright watched the work, thinking of cargo discharged and cargo to be stowed for China. Sperm oil, crockery, hardware and navy soap, together with the chief cargo cotton, as well as molasses and candles reshipped from his clipper *Angel* now in port would fill the *Eagle's* holds. Profitably, he mused. He had planned well in advance. The race, which occupied Broadwinder's sailing mind, as perhaps it should, would complete a voyage with ship laden. Too bad, however, that he would be unable to witness the contest of sail between Broadwinder and Keys. Jenny entered his thoughts again and once more he drove her out of mind.

"Odd though," he said to himself. "Philip staying on the ship, Jenny in the city."

Broadwinder came to a halt at his side then. Breathing hard from exertion, he said, "That timber could mean the difference in the race." He grinned devilishly at Cartwright. "I'll lose a few topmasts, all right, and every time I do it'll be dollars by the board. Sure you won't change your mind and go along?"

"I'm sure of it, Captain. And now that you mention dollars over the side, I'm surer. It so happens my purse is the tenderest part of my anatomy."

Broadwinder threw a grimace toward the land. "I wish to hell that was my sensitive spot." He looked at Cartwright. "I might as well tell you something, sir. Jenny and I are at odds over the extra interest in the ship you presented to me."

Cartwright looked gravely curious.

"You know, she has a crazy idea that we should wait until the race is won. A feeling, she says, a strong warning against accepting it now."

Cartwright's heart skipped a beat. He thought he knew why, and his sympathy went out to a repentant woman. It was a matter of honor with her, and he was glad. But Philip awaited a reply.

"Whatever you say, Captain."

"I'm no fool."

The shipowner wanted to say, "I'm not so sure," though he held to silence. He was somewhat relieved when a messenger appeared with a letter for the captain.

Broadwinder appeared most anxious as he broke the seal. Then his face assumed a ravaged expression. As though he had forgotten he was not alone, he read in low voice:

Captain Broadwinder,

Since you did not book passage for me as promised, I am sailing for Boston on the day after next aboard the Grace Darling.

Jenny Broadwinder

George Cartwright turned away, leaving his captain with crumpled note in hand staring hopelessly into the wall of fog.

Cartwright moved to the fife rail, his mind in a whirl of confusion. Surprise, concern for both, coupled with an awareness of his inability to do anything toward settling their differences were freighted with a sense of personal guilt. He was responsible for all that had happened. And beyond this sad fact, he felt a responsibility for future happenings. Broadwinder would drive his ship like a madman. He might wreck the *Eagle*, lose the race, and with it perhaps his life.

Suddenly Broadwinder's voice lifted in a roar that scattered the harmony of decks: "Fall to the cargo, every mother's son of you, and show lively! This is not a damn shore picnic!" Turning to the messenger, he said, "What the hell are you waiting for?"

"A return message, sir."

"There is none. Now make for the land."

Broadwinder turned on his heel and stalked aft. In his cabin he glared at a cabinet, flung it open, and jerked a bottle forth. After downing a couple of fiery draughts, he sat down and placed tightly knotted fists atop the table. Everywhere he looked were reminders of Jenny.

"Peretta!" he yelled. When after repeated calls the steward came running, he said, "Look, Peretta, I hired you to bounce in on the first cry, so you'll look alive and show willing or find yourself shoring on the docks." With the other's meek "Aye, sor," he said, "Now I want everything that belongs to Mrs. Broadwinder properly stowed and shipped to her at the Parker House within the hour."

As the steward stood out a moment of curious silence, Broadwinder said, "What do you damned Italians do with stubborn women?"

A twisted, knowing smile crossed the steward's face. "Signor, she's a most simple thing. First we lose the temper. Next thing, we talk big with the threat. Mother Maria, we just ready to cut her throat! Then, when that's a no good, we smile nice, sor, and maybe slap her real gentle across the bottom." He made a shrug. "So she's a happy!"

Broadwinder nodded. "Seems things are pretty much the same the world over."

Peretta turned up his palms. "The same." Then he said, "Sor, maybe you wait, no? Maybe you——"

The captain cut him short with a fist laid hard to the table and a crisp order to proceed as directed.

Jenny waited impatiently for a reply. With her ear trained to the slightest sound at the door, she sat with lacework in hand and fingers busy. An hour passed and still another. She got up often, walked back and forth, all the while making excuses to appease her growing anxiety. The fog delayed the messenger; perhaps Philip was not aboard ship; or he might have decided to deliver his reply in person. Imagining his standing in the door now, she thought of her face. She looked a little tired and wan. Sleepless nights did that to one. Presently she returned from retouching her face and debated on her behavior when he arrived. Should she meet him with open arms or simply bid him enter as though he were a stranger to her?

A hard rap sounded at the door. Holding her breath, she took time to compose herself before moving with measured steps across the room. It was Philip's rap, of course, and she must meet him as he met her, although it would be wise to hold her emotions in check until everything was settled. He must agree with her regarding any gift from George Cartwright at this time. And since he had walked out of their marriage, he should be the one to seek reinstatement. Such were her thoughts as she opened the door.

Jenny was never more unprepared for what met her gaze. Wide-eyed astonishment gripped her as she looked from the ship's steward and helpers to boxes piled high.

"The captain's compliments, signora," Peretta said, motioning his crew to work. When all her effects were inside he ordered his men out and shook his head sadly. "I'm a much a worry. The captain is like a bear in a trap. Signora, maybe you should do something. Like perhaps in sunny Italia where a wife she see this thing and pour him wine real nice and smile just so, and tell him who's a boss but him! You the boss, he the boss, what's the difference if he think he's a that boss, no?"

Jenny laughed. "Why, Peretta, you amaze me. Captain Broadwinder is always the master. Now I thank you for bringing my things. And I wish you a good voyage."

"You mean—you no go too?"

"To Boston," she replied, moving to the door. "So you take good care of Captain Broadwinder."

The door had scarcely closed on the bewildered steward than Jenny burst into tears. This was Philip's answer. It was so final. All that had been was gone, and only memories remained. But it had come all too suddenly, like a wicked squall in the night. Given time she would recover from the blow, but for the present she could do nothing but wring out her heart.

On the morning of embarkation for Boston, Jenny carried aboard the *Grace Darling* all the conflicting emotions that had assailed her during the last two days. They kept her company as she stood on deck scanning the shore for Philip. The pain of parting was sharp, though the hurt was offset by resentment. Philip had been stubborn, callous, and unjust, and as much as she wanted him she told herself she could never forgive him. Just the same, she found herself praying that the ship would not soon depart.

She swept the decks with anxious glances as the pilot came aboard and she thought in detachment of the English heroine of 1838 after whom this fine new clipper was named. Grace's father William Darling had been keeper of the Longstone lighthouse in the Farne Islands off the coast of England when the *Forfarshire* struck in heavy weather, losing forty-three of the sixty-three aboard. Grace and her father had taken a boat out and rescued, by sheer bravery and skill, four lives. And the Briggses of Boston had named this ship, now on her maiden voyage, after the brave girl and had placed a woman in white dress at the bows for a figurehead.

Jenny did not feel nearly so brave as Grace Darling when the ship's crew were ordered to look alive. From the quarter-deck commands familiar to Jenny rivaled the yells of men and sounds of iron on iron as the hands ran round the capstan to haul up the anchor cable. She sent a frantic look to the land, as though her last hope went with it, then jerked her head around as bewhiskered Captain Doane cried to his first officer:

"Look, will you, there opening the harbor!" Lowering his glass, he said, "She's the *Emperor!*" As Jenny stared at the great ship coming on, Captain Doane laughed. "Aye. 'Tis Mayo Keys, who's likely to show Broadwinder how to sail a ship."

Defiance crept into Jenny's face and it was all she could do to suppress a retort in defense of Philip. But she was not aboard as Mrs. Broadwinder. She was Jenny Cornish. The thought caused her a catch of fear, which she fought down as the *Emperor* slid gracefully nearer. She seemed to hear a clamor inside her, voices crying, "Philip needs you! Philip needs you!" Over and over.

Ready to cry, "Put me ashore!" she drew her mouth into a tight line and tried to slow her fast heartbeat. The *Emperor's* figurehead seemed to squint at her over the harbor chop as the ship eased in on her idling wake. Again, she noted, Keys made no Broadwinder approach, but entered with sails in prosaic harbor stow. There were times to fling sail and times to furl, she admitted reflectively. Of late she had done both, though as matters now stood it seemed she had flung when she should have furled. And now?

The clanking of chain through the hawsehole brought the present and her panic into sharper focus. She closed her eyes and sent with all her heart and soul a plea to the land:

"Philip, don't let me go!"

Her eyes opened on the distant shore. A steam craft was putting out, her stub bow pointing straight for the *Grace Darling.* No feeling of elation came over her, for she dared not hope now. The *Grace Darling*'s breast anchor was in and she was swinging her nose around toward the Golden Gate, headsails up and signals flying as she called for the road to the open sea. A tug snorted and the pilot at the wheel stared from helm to traffic and on to the body of water marking the exit to the sunlit Pacific. The rules of the road would be observed and in short time the harbor would lie astern, quiet and peaceful under the maze of hulls and masts.

Sutter's Mill, picks and pans, the City of Gold, as they called bustling, wicked San Francisco, would soon be far astern. Jenny had felt the call of gold that encircled the globe, its romantic lure that inspired songs and drove people over the plains and around the Horn, drew them onward as a magnet pulls iron filings, had responded to "Blow, boys, blow, for Californi-o!" and she had seen what a gold strike had done to lift sail out of the doldrums into its glory. But gone was the thrill she had known when bands marched down Boston's State Street with embarking adventurers to the tune of "Susannah, Don't You Cry." The City of Gold had brought her nothing but misery.

The steam craft was cutting the water, coming fast now. Perhaps Philip was aboard after all. But the ship under her feet was also gathering headway, outward bound. Once clear of traffic, Captain Doane would cascade sail, drop his pilot, and proceed at a fast clip.

At her request, the steward brought a spyglass. As she brought it to bear, Philip leaped into the circle. A great wave of gladness flooded her and she was crying in her heart, "Hurry! Hurry! Hurry!" A closer look caused her to say aloud:

"My, the wrath on Philip's face!"

He was shouting now, his booming voice drowned by distance and the inboard noise on the *Grace Darling*. So Philip was angry! She smiled and turned her back on him. Philip had been as stubborn as she, thinking to bluff her into submission. But she had won. However, the ship was now holding her own with the chasing craft. Perhaps she should notify the captain that a boat aft was hailing him. Or should she? No, she would do nothing of the kind. She would not give up one inch of ground to the arrogant man who had walked away from her, who had sent her baggage ashore.

"Let go the fores'l! Lively now! Swing the spanker boom around!"

Jenny swallowed hard as the orders rang in her ears. Now

the cry sounded for topsails and topgallants. The wind was brisk. Soon the yards spouted sails and the ship lurched ahead. Jenny whirled to see Philip, plainly now, waving and shouting and striking fists to palms in his frustration. And all the while the *Grace Darling* was pulling away from him.

Jenny was suddenly afraid. Once out to sea, Philip would never catch the clipper, unless he boarded the *Eagle* in chase. The song went out of her heart as she felt not only victory but a dearer thing, Philip, slipping away from her. She ran to the captain then, only to meet with a gruff reminder that it was no time to converse with passengers.

"But, sir, a boat aft is——"

Captain Doane's voice drowned her frantic reply with a shout aloft, and she turned her gaze hopelessly astern in time to see Philip boarding the pilot's boat. Weak with relief, she sank to a deck chair and silently gave thanks. He would reach her now, and nothing else mattered.

After an eternity the ship slowed and the pilot boat moved alongside. Captain Doane gave a start as he looked down. "As I live and breathe, it's Captain Broadwinder!" he cried. Rushing to the side, he greeted Philip with, "Welcome, sir. To what do I owe this pleasure?"

"My wife, sir," Philip replied, his angered gaze fixed on Jenny. Amid the rippling of the word "Broadwinder!" across decks and up into the rigging, he walked straightway to Jenny and roughly lifted her into his arms.

Glaring into her big curious eyes, he said, undeterred by the ship's company, "I ought to spank hell out of you. I may do it yet."

Clinging to him, joy flooding her, she replied, "You may, darling, if you have done as I wished."

"You tell me that? Stow your tongue. Can't you see I'm mad enough already?"

Every man aboard was watching intently the unexpected drama. Jenny saw out of the corner of an eye Captain Doane nudge his grinning chief mate as she said, "Then you'd better put me down, Philip. I'm serious and I'll go to Boston unless you promise to do it my way." She met his glance unwaveringly.

"And you'd better hurry. The pilot boat is waiting to take either one or both of us ashore."

His reply was a deafening, "All right!" He carried her to the ship's waist and lowered her to the pilot's deck with all the gentleness he might accord a bale of jute. With hands on hips, he cried for her baggage, then looked down at her.

"Get below!"

"Yes, Philip," she said smiling.

"And stay below!"

"Yes, Philip," she replied again, joy and triumph shining through her meekness. The expression held even when Captain Doane's voice reached her ears with:

"Broadwinder, I've changed my mind. Any man who can set his old woman on the proper course can show Mayo Keys his heels."

21

☐ To Jenny Broadwinder every plank, spar, and rope of the *Calcutta Eagle* was an old friend welcoming her home. She touched the rail and felt a warm handclasp as her eyes swept the decks and top hamper. Although Philip, who had just helped her aboard, had spoken scarcely a word since placing her on the pilot boat, the deadlock had been broken. She was home, the hands looked pleased, Peretta grinned, and Mr. Fortune appeared to be every bit as delighted as young Tobias, who was saying:

"Ma'am, seems you've been gone a hunnerd years."

Jenny knelt and looked into his freckled face. "Have they been giving you trouble?" she asked, brushing the hair off his forehead with a hand.

"Aye. And ye can lay to that. The Old Man, I mean the cap'n, ma'am, has been growlin' like a bitch wolf with spotted pups."

"Tobias!"

"Chips said it, not me."

Jenny left the boy with a gentle scolding and instructed Peretta to send her things below. Entering the cabin, she paused and closed her eyes in a brief prayer of thanks. She had no sooner opened them again than Philip entered, sat down, and eyed her as though he didn't quite know what to make of her. She waited in silence, wondering which side of him would emerge.

"Jenny," he said at last, "just what the devil can I tell Cartwright without appearing to have lost my sanity?"

"Why, Philip dear," she said, laying a finger to her cheek, "since when does Captain Broadwinder need advice on how to express himself? And isn't that beside the point at a time like this? Since I have just returned, I think some kind of welcome on the part of my husband would be proper."

"You do? After all the embarrassment you caused me, I'm not so sure you're welcome."

Jenny pretended to inspect the cabin. "Just when do we embark, and how could this place be so untidy?"

Turning to him, she added, "And the way the crew's washing blows in the breeze one might readily believe the vessel is a flagship. Oh, incidentally, when does Mr. Cartwright sail?"

"We embark Thursday, three days off, and this cabin looks all right to me, and the crew can hang their shirts royals-high if they want to. Furthermore, Cartwright doesn't have to answer to me."

"My goodness, Captain Broadwinder. Perhaps it's time the steward served your raw meat. Does he put it in a bowl or hand it to you on a long spar?"

Broadwinder glanced at his watch. "I'm due on deck, where half the cotton from the South is coming aboard."

Alone, Jenny sat down and said, "What a welcome!" He had not taken her in his arms, spoken a single endearing word, or appeared in any way glad to see her aboard ship. Yet he had raced after her, had brought her back. Aware that the *Grace Darling* was now at sea, she decided Philip had done enough for her on this day.

She fell to work tidying their quarters with a song on her lips. The captain did not seek her company at the noonday meal, though she continued to sing. At round three she dressed and went on deck, where, shortly after her appearance, the crew in a body, Chips O'Hara their spokesman, moved to the break of the poop and welcomed her aboard with a large bouquet of flowers. With Philip a short distance away and showing surprise, O'Hara said, Adam's apple bobbing:

"Me, the bosun and Sails has a conference with the other lads after ye boarded this mornin' and decides, ma'am, to present ye with this here nosegay. Whilst most of us older Jacks has seen the day we wouldn't sign on of a vessel ship-pin' a female, we recalls how ye was a mother to us when we was sick, and how ye treated us for years like we was men and not the dregs o' creation. So with all respect to the cap'n, despite his crankiness of late, ma'am, we say this would be one hell of a ship without ye."

Jenny had not expected this tribute. A little overcome by their sincere regard for her, she accepted the flowers and told them she had never received a gift she appreciated more. "And I love every one of you."

She stole a glance at Philip. He stood still, expressionless. When the feeling that some token of her appreciation was due these loyal men and boys, she looked at Philip again, wondering this time why he did not rise to the occasion with perhaps an extra ration of rum around. But stubborn Philip looked as if he might have in mind poison instead.

"Captain Broadwinder," she said, "may I take the liberty of asking for a serving of rum to my friends?"

"You may," he replied crisply. "However, I refuse."

In the embarrassed silence that fell over the ship, Jenny witnessed the hurt in the faces of the sailors, felt it herself. But worse was his cruel betrayal of her, his wife, before these men. Now they were turning slowly to go forward of the deck. Suddenly Philip stopped them with a curt order to remain where they were. Then he said:

"Rum, no. For these stanch lads it's the finest whisky from the captain's locker."

Jenny went weak all over. Philip's laughter rang across the decks to revive her. The hands exchanged looks of surprise and delight, and Chips roared, saying he knew it all the time, and old Lowery eyed him and said, "Not that I doubt yer veracity, Chips, but you was caught twixt wind and water same as us, so you lie." Perhaps, Chips admitted, but for the "privilege o' tappin' the cap'n" Sails should forgive him.

When the ceremony ended Jenny hurried below. Wanting at once to give thanks and cry, she composed herself and waited for Philip, who had shocked her to the core before showing gratitude to the men who had honored his wife. They were wonderful men despite their roughness. Grateful for every little kindness, they put their trust in the captain, worked oblivious to danger, shared common dreams in a common life, gave their dead to the sea with nothing more than a transient wave for a marker, and sailed on into other horizons.

The door opened to scatter her thoughts. Philip entered with her flowers. "Forget them, Mistress Jenny?"

She nodded, studying him curiously.

"Well," he said, "they turned pockets inside out to raise the money for them. So I'm sending all but the briefest anchor watch ashore for a night of it." A smile lit up his face. "And since a fling is what I need, I'm going ashore for the night also."

Jenny acknowledged his remark with another nod. Feeling her heart slowly sinking, she dropped her glance and turned away.

"So show lively, madam!" His near shout jerked her face around to him. "Since I'm taking the prettiest woman in America to the Parker House, I'll have her looking her very best. Now get busy."

He closed the distance between them and took her in his arms. "You do beat all, Jenny Broadwinder. You know, I'm hoping Mayo Keys doesn't sail a ship like you think. If he does, I'll be staring into his wake all the way from the Tasman Sea to Boston Light."

Jenny laughed. Touching his cheeks with the fingers of both hands, she said, "And then you wouldn't be able to claim the extra interest in the ship."

He made a wry face. "You would have to bring that up. Well, it will be settled tonight. I sent Cartwright an invitation to join us at dinner."

Jenny started. "You didn't! Now I don't think I'm going to enjoy the evening, Philip. Perhaps you'd better go without me."

"It's all your idea, refusing the shares," he said, stern of face. "So you're going to sit through it."

If a meeting with George Cartwright was the last thing Jenny desired, the setting for it caused her a shudder. Philip had unwittingly—she hoped it was that—arranged to bring them together in the Parker House dining hall, the scene of her great error. It was as though by some strange twist of fate she was being forced to meet a just reward.

All the joy of a reunion with Philip departed. She dressed with a noticeable lack of zeal, all the while looking for some means of escape from the ordeal ahead. But there was no escape. She had forced the issue, the refusal of the shares, the same as she had labored to secure them. And now she was caught fast in a trap of her own making.

A few hours later Cartwright joined them under the very lights that had betrayed her. She felt the crimson rising from her neck to diffuse her face and, in a gesture of defense, she drained a glass of champagne. Knowing she could not hope to avoid his glance the entire evening, she mustered all her courage and raised her eyes. The look between them was unlike anything Jenny had ever before experienced. It was like the clash of steel on steel, searching, challenging, all in an instant's meeting. The softness and the inquiry she had seen in Cartwright's glance in no way relieved the accusation of self strong inside her, and she hated him in that moment; hated him because he knew what she had done. But Philip was talking. Slowly the shock passed away. The rent healed and she took hope now that the worst part of it was behind her.

Philip was saying exactly the things she wished to hear, that they had decided not to accept his generous offer until the race ended in Boston, even as she, with gaze fixed on the stem of her glass, was thinking of how she had schemed to obtain the very thing she was so anxious to return now.

"So that's the way the wind blows," Philip said in conclusion.

"As you wish," Cartwright said contemplatively. "You have your reasons, I'm sure." He did not look at Jenny, though he was thinking how lovely she was this evening. How lively and fiery that look in her eyes had been, despite the little-girl contriteness that vaguely stirred behind them. Beyond these things, he felt a little elation at having for once put the eternal businesswoman in her proper place.

"Of course," he said, "there is no reason to make your decision public."

Philip had no sooner admitted that this was so than Jenny said, "Aren't you overlooking something? It seems that Captain Broadwinder's refusal of the shares, until he wins over Mayo Keys, would be a choice morsel to feed the race-minded public."

Cartwright was discerning. He saw her, the meddling woman, striving to completely erase the transaction that had caused her grief and a feeling of guilt. He admired her even as he marveled at a woman's odd sense of reason. He said:

"Not a bad idea."

Broadwinder gave Jenny a smile. "A stroke of genius," he said to Cartwright, filling all glasses. "It might do much to off-set the fact that you're deserting the ship before the race. And, come to think of it, you never did explain to my satisfaction just why you're not going on with us." He scoffed when Cartwright murmured something about the demands of business. "Business! What business is bigger than the race ahead?"

Jenny bit her lip. Aware of Philip's persuasiveness and her inability to check him, she resorted to silence and a hope that Cartwright would remain determined.

"Captain, I could hardly aid you in winning. Besides, I've probably worn out my welcome aboard of you."

"No such thing. Hell, sir, we're just getting used to shipping the owner aboard. Aren't we, Jenny?"

She made the only reply possible: "Of course."

Cartwright touched his chin thoughtfully. "Well, there's nothing I'd enjoy more than watching you match sails and winds with Oliver Barking's man. You know, I really want to beat that old rascal. Probably as badly as you'd like to beat Mayo Keys."

"So!" Broadwinder said in almost a shout. "Since we're both of the same mind and on the same wind and course, we'll drink to victory together."

Something of Philip's enthusiasm overflowed into Jenny. She saw it manifest itself in George Cartwright and, despite her disappointment at his decision to complete the voyage and race, she touched glasses with him and came very close to forgetting the unpleasant memories he evoked.

PART THREE

22

Never had the winds blown so fair on the *Calcutta Eagle* as on the crossing from San Francisco to the China coast. Following tack and tack for good westing, she caught the lively northeast trades on her starboard quarter and fairly boomed along for Honolulu and tropic seas. A charmed ship, she continued her westward course between ten and twenty degrees north without encountering more than light squalls. Old Sails remarked often that the weather was "too damned good to last," but as it continued past one hundred and seventy degrees east of Greenwich he added the word "forever" in order to sustain his reputation for predicting rightly. No buffeting her way to windward here, but a sense of motion under full sails blowing and a ship frothing the limitless sea ahead of a white wake pointing always eastward. There was a steady bracing lift in the trades over the sea and on balmy evenings stars in the velvety-blue heavens seemed to lace themselves to the rigging. Flying fish shot like silver out of the morning sea and far off, on the edge of the horizon, funnels of water raced across the boundless ocean. Then came nights when the moon was an enormous ball that paled the sky and sea and threw moving shadows sharp in outline down to the decks. At such times the ship seemed a repository for memories, so silent she was but for the harping of the rigging aloft and the swish of water down her sides. Jenny was no exception to the others; she stood with Philip's hand in hers on deck, her head on his arm in the privacy of the cabin.

On the first leg of the crossing both she and Cartwright maintained an almost stiff reserve. She knew that she was determined to avoid further entanglement and she seemed to know that he felt the same. Not once did she invite him to accompany her on those daily visits to the forecastle and seldom did she sit near him while tutoring the ship's boy. She had had her lesson and he had the look of a man who had emerged from an experience far wiser because of it. But at times she felt a little sorry for him, even as he admitted to himself no change in his fond regard of her.

The ship drove on, east to west, day after day, passing an Indiaman under full sail one morning, meeting another homeward bound in the sunset. Broadwinder on deck dipped his colors and, like the goddess under the bowsprit, stared ahead into the sea. Then he began to look at the calendar with an eye that was curiously alert. Having eaten up the seas on this run, he became conscious of the existing record in running time between California and the port of Hong Kong. With a little extra push from aloft, he was thinking, he might cut a day off the record and give the clipper captains a new mark to shoot at. The sun burned hot, however, and he wet down canvas to get an extra knot or two, only to feel the trade wind backing. There was sport in trying, regardless, and he kept on day and night.

Then one morning a batwinged junk appeared up out of the western sea, her course bent for the Philippines to the southwest. She lumbered on under lateen sails and was soon hull under horizon. The China Sea lay ahead, and half a thousand or more nautical miles west lay the thriving free port of Hong Kong.

"There blows the Chink!" cried a sailor. "And I smell a thousand more."

Pirate or fisherman, one could never tell.

Next day junks were sighted almost every hour. Night running was slowed as a precaution against collision, though when a fleet of them fired on the ship and tried to match speed with her for boarding shortly after midnight Broadwinder ordered more sail on the yards and the single cannon aboard readied for use.

Jenny eyed the Hong Kong roadstead with small concern for pirates. The land, Philip's many friends and Philip, himself, occupied her mind. Would Philip run true to form and spend his first night at one of the English clubs, or would a memory of the San Francisco experience change that? She would soon know, for the lookouts were crying the land lifting blue against the sky and marking the entrance to Tathong Channel. Far ahead, coastwise junks, barks, schooners and square-riggers moved up and down the Kowloon-Swatow-Amoy-Shanghai track and farther to the south tiny dots on the flat edge of the sea represented the traffic from Canton and Macao.

Pilot boats waited for ships far out from shore. Soon a dozen were clamoring for the Yankee. Farther on, bumboats appeared, each lined with Orientals or whites trying to sell their wares. Sampans, like floating wooden shoes, were everywhere once the pass opened and drew the *Eagle* into the blue strait separating the towering hills of Hong Kong Island from the Kowloon Peninsula. The commerce of the East had prevented the usual Broadwinder approach and now the *Calcutta Eagle* crept in to anchorage as unostentatiously as any other vessel. She had completed her run to the China coast with oil and cotton. The cable rattled through the hawsehole and suddenly the hook touched bottom.

"Thirty-five days!" Broadwinder cried. "Lads, it's a voyage only twice beaten."

Jenny remained quiet, her sober eyes on the English craft moving out to the ship. The men aboard were friends of the Prince of Sea Captains. She looked at Philip and then she intercepted the curious glance of George Cartwright, and thought that he, too, was wondering if the captain would join his friends or remain with his wife.

Philip walked up to her, his face beaming. "You know, Jenny girl, the land smells good. Now I'm wondering if you would help Mr. Fortune with the papers while I——"

"Smell the land," she said, cutting him short. "Of course! don't I always respond to the training you gave me, Captain Broadwinder?"

"Sure. That you do, sweetheart. Tonight is ours, and I'll be back by sundown." Turning to Cartwright, he said, "Now, sir, if you'll oblige me by seeing my wife to our hotel——"

Again Jenny stopped him in midsentence. "The captain will be eternally grateful." Walking to the rail, she said, "However, that won't be necessary. I'm staying here."

A half hour later Captain Broadwinder left the ship. Mr. Fortune busied himself with duties attending port entry. Lighters came alongside, and a junk with one sail up, like a bamboo-studded fan, slid by with every slant-eyed occupant aboard silently taking in the big Yankee merchantman. Then the beggars arrived in sampans and poled their cups up to the rail as they wailed forth in Cantonese for alms. Across deck from Jenny, George Cartwright, for some reason or other, looked at his watch. Jenny wondered why. For a minute or two she gazed at the flag of Britain waving serenely above a government building, then studied in detachment a British man-of-war at anchor and a big three-skysail-yarder taking on a human cargo, coolies for the gold fields of either California or Australia.

Frowning, she drew in her gaze and darted a glance at Cartwright. He was at least company, relief from boredom. But did she wish company? She breathed a sigh and looked up at the streets of Victoria that climbed the hillsides like ladders. The town seemed to stand on end, lifting from the water with warehouses, business establishments, narrow Chinese streets and brothels, to barracks and governmental houses, to cricket clubs and racecourses and houses where fashionable teas were perhaps now in progress. She could enter the latter circle of society as she had done on her first call here. The captain's wife was welcome. She could dress for an elegant lawn and dinner party this very evening if she chose. The British honored the Prince and his lady. It was not that she was an unsociable woman; rather, it was because Philip preferred to storm a port in male company, that and her natural aversion to ports of call.

The smells here were fishy and offensive and a view of junks and sampans by the hundreds was rather monotonous. Once again she looked across deck at the shipowner. Seized with a sudden impulse to go ashore, she lifted her voice.

"Mr. Cartwright, have you any idea of all that goes on in this city?" He had not, he replied, moving toward her with the eager look of a lonely man who suddenly finds someone interested in his company.

For the next several hours Jenny seemed to forget Philip and her dislike of ports. Cartwright saw her gay, curious, carefree as a child, and again shocked by this or that. Beyond the wharves and banking houses lay the narrow streets where everything on earth was sold in the open under vertical banners lettered in Chinese characters. She admired a bird in a bamboo cage and he hastened to buy it for her, then to lug it for hours. But he had failed to bargain with the seller and as a penalty he was besieged by sellers of pigs and chickens in baskets, dealers in fish, opium, and, once, by a man who rented girls. Jenny looked horrified at a sidewalk dentist who used horse sweat as a painkiller and next a doctor's display of prescriptions which included trays of dried toads, centipedes, and cockroaches. Live serpents were sold for cures as well as food, and the sight of them even before she learned this caused Jenny to clutch at Cartwright's sleeve and go pale. Moments later, he saw her stir with excitement when an old saffron-colored violinmaker sold a Chinese fiddle to him for one dollar.

"Yours," Cartwright said to her.

He said the same at a silk bazaar and at a counter where perfume was marketed. He studied her out of a corner of an eye as they sat in a Chinese theater watching the stilted antics of performers in some melodrama or comedy. Her mouth parted and assumed all sorts of expressions; wonder, awe, delight, bewilderment and more, all good to look at, he admitted in proper silence. He bought a Chinese doll because she cried, "How beautiful!" and he paid two coolies the handsome sum of a few American pennies for a ride in a sedan chair to an English club where they sipped brandies and laughed at their adventures of the afternoon.

Minutes passed before Jenny looked at a clock and said they should return to the ship. Giving him a spontaneous smile, she took his hand in hers. "You've shown me a wonderful time, sir. I shall never forget it."

"Nor I."

Something in his expression or voice, or both, caused her to look deep into his eyes. A hint of regret that it had ended, she thought.

Slowly she looked away. "I'm sorry, sir, about—about what happened in San Francisco."

"I understand," he replied after a strained silence. "You're a brave girl, Jenny. Brave and wonderful."

"I?" Her glance lifted an instant, then fell to the table. "I'm neither," she said. Rising, she brightened. "Now I'll carry the doll and fiddle. And don't you dare forget my bird, for I'm going to name him George, even if he never sings a note."

They returned to the ship and on deck saw the sun go down behind Kowloon in a blaze of color. A squall hissed in, departed, and the lamps of Hong Kong shone as stars in the evening. Still Philip did not come. Mr. Fortune, Jenny, and Cartwright played cards in the saloon until the hot night drove them on deck. There talk of ships, cargoes, and the race occupied them until close to midnight when the captain, well along in his cups and apologetic, arrived with silks, a carving of ivory, and numerous potted flowers and shrubs for Jenny.

"I tried," he said. "Tried like the very devil to get here on time, but they just wouldn't hear of it until I met the governor and his staff and told the mermaid story over a couple

—or was it a dozen?—whiskies. But look, Jenny darlin', I brought you a few trinkets."

Despite her pique, Jenny smiled. He was like a tardy schoolboy, guilty but disarming.

It was the same in Singapore two thousand miles south. As the *Calcutta Eagle* entered the strait between Singapore Island and the Riouw Archipelago under a blazing equatorial sun, Jenny knew what to expect. Only here at the crossroads of the East the word of Broadwinder's coming had been sent ahead, and even the curious public could be expected to be on hand to greet the famous captain about to embark on a world-heralded race. The governor of Singapore with his colorful troops complete with bagpipes would perhaps be waiting on the bund.

True to her prediction, the teeming city with its English population greatly outnumbered by the Chinese, Malays, Siamese, Hindus, Borneans, Javanese, and Africans lined the water front to greet the American merchant captain. English-women prevailed upon Jenny to stay a few days at a luxurious countryseat. Not having seen Philip since their arrival, Jenny and Cartwright returned to the ship. There cargo was being discharged into lighters under the direction of the mates in order to take on India rubber, guttapercha, Japanese lacquer ware and raw silks, Philippine sugar and spices, mats from Borneo and gums from Siam. They learned that Mayo Keys was due in port soon for a mixed cargo of tin ore and Sumatra pepper, that he would not long rest on his anchors here.

Once more Jenny and Cartwright roamed strange, quaint streets together, visited the mosques, Chinese and Hindu temples, theaters, and English social clubs. They saw fire-walkers emerge barefooted from a bed of glowing coals, apparently none the worse because of the experience. They sniffed the enticing aromas from island ships laden with spices, watched coolies straining at ropes attached to heavy frieght wagons, counted the flags of nations over the ships at anchor, timidly sampled the tropical custard apple, mangosteen and other fruits, sat down to the Dutch dinner of numerous courses called *rijkstafel* in the Singapore house of a wealthy East Indies merchant, and purchased gifts for friends in America from Chinese shops dealing in hand-carved ivory, sandalwood, teak-wood, as well as jade and rare procelain. The past and future seemed forgotten by both as their daylong pursuits led them with each new sun into still more interesting sections of the city. To Jenny, Cartwright was faithful friend and escort; to Cartwright, she was Jenny the woman unfolding before his eyes qualities heretofore imagined but scarcely met until now. His regard for her increased until at times he felt overpowering desires to give it expression.

It was on an evening two days before the *Emperor* dropped anchor in the roads that Cartwright paused at Jenny's insistence before a silversmith's shop. A necklace of exquisite filigree had caught her eye. Its tassels in a trellis of finely plaited design together with pendant flowers set with rubies declared it the work of an artist and therefore an expensive piece. When he saw her fascinated by its beauty, Cartwright entered the shop and asked the price. The sum named held him speechless. He tried to bargain, though the seller smiled and lifted palms in refusal. Finally an old Burmese emerged from a rear curtain and advised in broken English that in his native Burma the use of silver and gold for ceremonial worship and domestic purposes was prohibited, that only persons of royal blood might obtain the metals. Yet he had smuggled and stored silver enough to create the necklace, only to be found out and punished, then exiled. His blood and his uprooting were graven into the piece. He had refused great sums, but now he was in need of money in order to purchase emeralds from India.

Cartwright departed without the necklace. After boarding the ship, he walked the decks a while before hailing a sampan. From the bund he took a ricksha to the silversmith's shop, where he haggled for more than an hour in good Yankee fashion, which seemed to please the seller. They partook of tea and began anew. Shortly after midnight Cartwright returned to the ship in bad humor. Twice next day he visited the shop and twice left without the necklace. When he arrived that evening prepared to argue through the night if necessary, the Burmese greeted him as friend and worthy competitor. They talked of ships and trade over tea, with never a word about the item in contest. The old man from Rangoon placed a hundred questions about the world of the West and the shipowner answered them with a shrewd awareness that under the cover of conversation as idle as talk about cabbages and kings he was making progress. The personal freedom enjoyed by Americans appealed to the silversmith as much as their prosperity. He had heard of the gold strike. Finally he spoke of San Francisco as a place in which to pursue his trade and explored the possibilities with oriental patience. Soon it dawned on Cartwright that the owner of the necklace had been leading up to this all along. Feeling a trade in the making, he made the other fish for what he might otherwise offer forthwith in order to close the transaction. At midnight, tea, eternal tea, was brewed again. The old craftsman arose, parted a curtain of beads, and soon returned with the necklace on a pillow of black velvet. A silence that lengthened into minutes was broken by the Burmese, who said:

"You have not told me why you desire the labor of my years.

"A gift," Cartwright replied. "For a dear friend."

"The lady whose eyes could see nothing else?"

Cartwright nodded. "She is the wife of the captain of my ship *Calcutta Eagle*."

"The ship that will race another soon? Of course. Of course." The old man contemplated this for a time. "The captain's wife, friend, is a lovely creature. Indeed, and I am wondering if the great achievement of my life could be an agent of unhappiness. It must not be, for the object of one's life on this earth is to do good in order to prepare for the next reincarnation. I promised Buddha of the great Shwe Dagon pagoda of Rangoon that I would look deep lest my artistry do evil."

"Evil? Do evil?" Cartwright began. "Now you look here——"

He got no further. The other raised a hand and said, "If honor exceeds all else in you, we can trade. But honor is not a virtue when one argues that he is possessor of it. So I place you at a disadvantage, for which I beg a thousand pardons even as I await some word from you."

Under the scrutiny of the wise old eyes, Cartwright looked at the pale silver necklace and examined his motive anew. Suddenly the stern realist, aware that the old pagan had neatly cornered him as far as a reply was concerned, and vexed at the terms exacted, he said with marked asperity:

"My regard for the captain's wife exceeds friendship, if it's any of your business. However, I am not trying to buy her. She's above being bought."

"Then you are honest. We shall begin trading."

At two in the morning Cartwright boarded the ship with the neckalce. Although he had effected a substantial saving over the original price, he was not sure that he had not been trapped by the terms of the sale—honor exceeding all else. True, Jenny could not be bought. But she could be influenced by such a gift. However, he did not entertain any notion of drawing her away from Philip. All he desired was to contribute to her happiness. Or so he told himself.

Next day Mayo Keys was accorded a reception rivaling that given Broadwinder. With both captains in port, betting on the outcome of the race began. British currency joined American, Dutch, Peruvian, and Spanish money as wagers were placed. But again Mayo Keys wrapped himself in noticeable silence and became a favorite of many people because of it. Jenny felt again a twinge of fear and she detected undue thoughtfulness in Cartwright when the two captains were mentioned.

Sailing day arrived and Broadwinder dipped his colors to Singapore and set sail for Sunda Strait and the Indian Ocean. The monsoon blew favorably for the southern passage and he ran the *Eagle* southeast to the Java Sea, then southwest for the strait separating Sumatra and Java. Several days later he caught good water, slipped through, and began the long stand down the western coast of Australia. From down under the continent's corner the winds of the forties would blow him east to Melbourne at a fast clip; the same great westerlies that would bowl him along in a contest of sail to Cape Horn.

As the clipper ran her latitude down on the northwest monsoon to the southeast trades, she met severe weather and heavy seas. Days of beating for every inch of southing were followed by calms and long uneasy swells, then squalls one after another. Then the trade winds seemed as erratic as the monsoon and the handling of running gear kept the crew too busy for bending on heavy Cape Horn canvas. The big winds due at around thirty-five degrees south reached up to thirty and caught Broadwinder unprepared. Forced to put the ship about, he encountered heavy seas and lost several days in near-gale weather before braving the wild winds. Once the lower capes of the continent were rounded, he put the west wind astern and scudded for Melbourne. The *Eagle* fairly flew under the Great Australian Bight, her jib boom dancing ahead of her cutwater, sails bellying full on the strong following wind. She ate up the sea in long reaches. Now she felt free, she seemed to say, an eagle of the main testing her wings for the long race ahead.

All the while, George Cartwright kept the necklace a secret. It was better that way, better to wait for a most propitious moment for presenting it to Jenny. And besides, the waiting was freighted with a great deal of fond anticipation.

23

☐ The lookouts at the Heads opening Port Phillip Bay scanned the tall ship taking on a pilot and, after adjusting the C of her pennant and the American flag to the cut of her bows, telegraphed Melbourne some thirty-five miles inside the pass of the arrival of the famous clipper *Calcutta Eagle*. As they watched, she braced her yards and slid forward into "The Rip," a two-mile opening chopped up by tides, winds, and the currents of the Yarra Yarra River and other streams. Bouncing through, she cascaded sail in the manner they had heard was typical of Broadwinder and heeled on the wind. Within the hour she was a white blur fast hulling under the northern horizon for Melbourne.

Aboard ship, Broadwinder conned decks and water, paced the quarter-deck with an occasional glance at his watch, another up into the rigging, as though awaiting something. Then it came, the muffled roar of cannon, the salute of a city to a racing ship and captain.

Broadwinder smiled. "All hands, Mr. Fortune."

The below watch turned out and the deck watch moved abaft the mainmast for the captain's brief speech.

"Lads, what you just heard was Melbourne firing us a greeting. Now I want to sail from the city welcome to come again, so remember you're not just an ordinary crew aboard an ordinary merchantman and behave in port accordingly. Now to your stations and below. Come out showing presentable and relieve the on-watch for the same. Lively now."

Jenny left Cartwright's side. "Captain Broadwinder, I'll have you show presentable yourself," she said in low tones. "In new tie and coat if you please."

"Aye, Mistress Jenny. And might I expect your assistance below?"

"As quick as the ship's cat, sir." She curtsied and fell in step at his side. "And I'm hoping you'll find life in port without me quite miserable," she added, with a flippant toss of her head.

"Without you! Do I ever splash the hook without you, girl?"

"No, but you make yourself scarce until the time comes for catting the anchor and away."

His arm went about her as they descended the after companion. "Ho! A man has business in port that doesn't concern his old woman."

"I know. Whisky and awful stories. But why should I complain? I'm your water petrel. Remind me to call your admiring attention to my webfeet."

Laughing together, they entered the cabin where she placed her shoulders against the door and eyed him as he threw off his coat and shirt and demanded fresh linen. "In keeping with a man the Australians salute, Mistress Jenny. You may not realize it, but damn few merchant commanders rate that."

"Sure. Just you and Mayo Keys," she scoffed pleasantly, moving to his chest. "But how will the pair of you leave Port Phillip Bay? I'll tell you, sir. Captain Mayo as sober as he came in, and Prince Philip nursing a head and wondering in his dull mind how he can show the *Emperor* his heels."

Broadwinder sat half dressed on the bed grinning at her. "Mayo is too serious. That's his trouble. And the more I show merry the more he tightens up inside. Why, come to think of it, I might succeed in laughing him into my wake before the race begins."

"Tell him your mermaid story." She did not turn to him but on her knees tossed a shirt over her head. "There now. And while you dress I'll cozen dear George so I won't be alone a fortnight."

"You'll come here," he replied. "Now!" he added with mock severity.

She had no sooner approached to within arm's length of him than he reached out and drew her down to his side. Her scolding "Philip!" repeated twice did nothing to stop him.

"Philip, you're due in port—soon! Now let me go!"

"To dear Goerge? Oh no! Maybe I should be jealous of him—spending all his time in Hong Kong and Singapore with my Jenny. And gifts! Lord he's anything but stingy where you're concerned!"

His good humor held her as defenseless as his tight clasp about her waist and shoulders. She ceased to struggle and, unable to suppress a light laugh, she pulled at his ear and said, "Philip Broadwinder, you don't know the half of it. George Cartwright would propose marriage to me in a minute if you were out of the way. Why, he almost bought a very expensive necklace just because I fell in love with it."

"Almost?" he teased, falling back on the bed and taking her with him. "Almost, the woman says. Well, that proves it. He's the spendthrift."

"Let me go, Philip! It's—it's uncomfortable." As he clung to her, a devilish look in his eye, she said, "I'd still love to have that necklace—and I suppose you realize you're holding me against my will."

"Aye. Broadwinder at the helm, girl. And maybe I'll buy the necklace for you one fine day."

"You! You couldn't afford it, and if you could I doubt if your Singapore friends could spare you long enough to look at it."

All of a sudden his expression underwent a change. Looking deep behind her wide, curious eyes, he brought her face close to his. "Do you actually think I neglect you in port, Jenny?"

Her glance reproved him. "For a moment I thought you were serious, Philip. And then you ask a question like that."

"I don't mean to neglect you," he said soberly. "You know that. It's just that—well, suppose I didn't join the fellows for a reunion, where would that put me?"

"With me, where you belong. At least once in a while. Look at it my way for a minute and tell me how you'd enjoy being a widower every time we touch the land. You wouldn't. But in Singapore—we were at anchor there all of three weeks—you spent four evenings with me."

"Five," he corrected, his muscular mouth lifting at the corners. "But looking at you now, Jenny, I wonder how the devil I could let the business of sustaining my popularity keep me away from you. By the deep six, I don't."

Jenny read his uncovered thought. "Philip Broadwinder! you're not two hours from port and there's much to do before——"

The crush of his mouth to hers put an end to useless words.

Her lips remained firm and resisting an instant and then all firmness dissolved before a bottomless softness and a fire burning against her. She struggled a little to free herself from his consuming love; why, she didn't know, unless it was an instinctive gesture born to woman. But as her lips slid aside, she murmured:

"My darling Philip! My sweetheart!"

Her eyes met his and the look that passed between them was one of startled, eager devotion. Then her fingers touched his shoulders and clung to his neck as she placed her mouth to his. He held her close for some time, as defenseless as she. Then the last reserve melted, and he removed the fastenings that separated them from a free and unhindered love. They were one in the extremity of passion and when it was over they remained one in their hearts, their heated bodies forgotten as soft words of endearment were spoken. Then he arose and laughed at her lying there with her head framed by a wealth of madly tousled hair.

He had sponged and dressed himself but for his tie and coat, when she turned her head to him. "Philip," she said.

He looked at her in the mirror, then back at the flaring bow of dark blue silk. "Yes, Jenny girl."

"You know something?" He said nothing and she continued. "I'm a very foolish woman."

"Agreed."

Ignoring his reply, she said, "I should have remained on deck if only to keep you waiting. Now you'll probably desert me for those horrible friends on shore."

"Well now, madam, seems you have an uncanny knack of figuring a course." There was mischief in his eye and smile. "But remind me to return by dawn."

So saying, he flung on his coat and reached for his cap. She seemed too quiet and he darted her a glance just in time to see a pillow sailing straight toward his head. As he stepped gingerly aside and blew her a kiss from the door, she cried:

"Philip Broadwinder, you're a devil!"

Then he was gone. She lay back, stretched the muscles of arms and body luxuriously and added, "A dear, wonderful devil."

Smiling, she closed her eyes and felt as though her whirling mind of minutes before were groping again for the present and realities. And it seemed that she was finding them even as she floated blissfully in a dream that was slowly cushioning her down to earth with a promise to remain alive and glorious. It was a good and natural state of being, she admitted; it was love; it was born of love and its untrammeled manifestation in marriage.

A sudden forward lurch of the ship scattered her thoughts like autumn leaves before a wind. She sat up, now aware that Philip was restoring to the usual burst of speed, the trademark of the Prince of Sea Captains, on port entry. Conscious of time now, she leaped from bed and hurriedly fell to the task of preparing herself for deck. The shore was never far off when he boomed out the studding sails for the benefit of admiring landsmen. Within short minutes he would cry for a lively stowing of sails in harbor furl, and all sail on Broadwinder's yards would come in fast. Then, with motion slowed, the ship would slide in for anchorage. Philip had the show timed to perfection. And while pilots often felt uncomfortable on the Broadwinder approach, almost without exception they seemed to feel obliged to honor a legend and thereby become a part of it.

Jenny appeared on deck in blue and ruffles, bonnet framing her oval face. With head high, she walked to the rail and watched Philip out of a corner of an eye until he raised his brows in surprised wonder and walked to her.

"Glory be the dazzling woman!" he exclaimed, eying her from bonnet lace to hem. "Is this a lure to strap me to your side while in port?"

The lookout forward cried the harbor. "She opens, sir! Melbourne on the port bow!"

The *Eagle* ran on with wings spread until the line of shore rose distinctly in the sunlight, with its rows of buildings in orderly pattern. Before them on the hilly northern bank of the Yarra Yarra stretched a young city which in 1834, like Manhattan much earlier, had been purchased for a few trinkets from a wandering tribe of blacks and, like San Francisco, had grown with the discovery of gold at Castlemaine, Ballarat, and Bendigo into a thriving city after the English pattern with its gardens, churches, cricket clubs, racecourse, beaches, and its social life. Although gold beckoned to rough adventurers, the British way of life prevailed.

Jenny spoke of these things in reply to Cartwright's questions as the ship blew on into the broad mouth of the Yarra Yarra. "The climate here is very changeable," she said, with a feeling that he was paying more attention to her than to what she was saying. "It can rain here with slightest provocation, almost out of a clear sky. Certainly it cannot be compared to the more equable climate of the eastern coast."

She placed both hands on the rail and looked ahead. "But it's summer in February here and the smells of flowers in blossom and ferns and trees are invigorating. Don't you agree?"

He did, putting the necklace out of mind in a hurry as she smiled up at him.

"I shall never forget the first time we put in here. I was sea-weary and Philip was, as usual, carried away by his friends. A Mrs. Gordon-Cummings, from Edinburgh, rescued me and——" She broke off and looked up into the towers of sail, then sent Philip a look of concern.

"Captain Broadwinder!" she said, lifting her voice. "Surely you aren't bent on winging in at this clip." With his show of surprise, she asked, "Or shall I in company of the ship's sonnywhack lay aloft and furl?" She added, "After I dip the colors, sir."

When Broadwinder shouted a command that sent topmen scurrying upward, Jenny turned to Cartwright. "Now what was I saying? Oh yes, dear Mrs. Gordon-Cummings entertained me at her countryseat. I shall never forget the fragrant hawthorn hedges and graceful willows in the December moonlight. She promised me potted plants on my next visit."

Her hand fell to his arm and her eyes danced with sudden brightness. "Would you take me there one day soon?"

George Cartwright was caught aback, though he rallied and forced into his reply all the reserve of a man making an ordinary business appointment: "Of course."

He kept the promise four days after the tumultuous welcome Melbourne gave the Broadwinders. On the morning he called for her at Scott's, a leading hotel, and handed her into an open conveyance, she still talked of the reception that commenced actually the moment the *Eagle's* anchor rattled into Hobson's Bay.

"You recall how these fine people lionized us," she said, once they had talked around to the subject. A little later she laughed. "I thought Captain Broadwinder would fall when everyone stood—after his sixth or seventh whisky, I'm sure—and drank a toast to the Queen. He almost did. And before so many social leaders out in full force at the Melbourne Club with their fashion, sobriety, decorum, and British dignity! But at the ball, a few of the honored gentlemen dropped some of their dignity. As the one you rescued me from. I thank you again, sir."

She talked on. Philip had taken her by train to Ballarat to a dinner in his honor. This Cartwright knew, though he enjoyed her candid and refreshing account of the affair as much as the various expressions parading her face in the telling.

Cartwright thought of the necklace. It was with him now, and Jenny's pretty neck seemed to await its complimenting beauty. But he continued to wait, as he had done since Singapore, and he did not know why.

They were soon in the open country beyond the city, where smells of flower, shrub, and tree in late-summer maturity were matched by welcome views of colors flecked against verdant green and the blue haze of rising hills in the distance. To rovers of the deep ocean the quiet Australian landscape seemed a never-ending paradise. Ahead the giant gums, eucalyptus trees, lifted their heads two or three hundred feet in the air above forests of fern. Evergreens, they shed their bark but retained their leaves. Here Jenny and Cartwright left the conveyance and walked into the forest.

Here he decided to give her the necklace, to place it about her neck. Jenny was standing before a great tree of wide girth, her head back as she stared up into its branches. Watching her, he placed a hand in his coat pocket to withdraw the piece. Again some inner caution stayed him. Perhaps the setting had something to do with it, they were so alone, or it could be fear, he thought, fear of completely exposing his heart or fear of what he might say now and regret later.

"Oh, I wish Philip could see this," she was saying. "But I wonder if"—she laughed—"if he would see magnificent trees or masts for a ship." Looking at Cartwright then, she asked, "What do you see?"

Somewhat tense and crestfallen, he looked up and about him to regain composure. Then he said, rather disconsolately, "Something to admire, but always beyond one's reach."

She placed a finger at the cleft of her chin and proceeded to study him closely. "A most equivocal answer, I must say. Unless I am to believe you find it difficult to admire something without wishing to own it."

With nothing left to say, he remained silent.

"But you do own what you admire," she went on. "Even the legal owner of this forest could admire and enjoy the beauty of it no more than I. One does not have to touch this tree and say, 'You're mine.' Ownership is a relative thing, don't you agree?"

He met her glance and withstood it. "Speaking of a tree, yes."

For an instant she eyed him so intently that he felt no doubt of her complete understanding. Nor did the sudden drop of her eyelids change this opinion in the least, any more than what she said next:

"We should be on our way, sir."

"Yes." He took her arm as they stepped over logs and uneven ground. "I could disprove all you said about admiring something without wishing to own it," he said tentatively, drawing a quick frowning glance from her.

"Rather an anticlimax after your last remark, isn't it?" she said sharply proving she had not missed his meaning.

"Hardly," he replied evenly. Smiling, he challenged her first with his eyes then with a question: "Or shall we say no more about it?"

"As you like. But you have convinced me of nothing."

He stopped still, and as she paused to eye him curiously, he said: "Perhaps I have just the item that will convince you, Jenny."

So saying, he removed a long envelope from his inner coat pocket and tore the edge. Her eyes were round with wonder before he extracted the contents. Then he held the silver filigreed necklace between the thumbs and forefingers of each hand and watched closely as her eyes grew wide and her mouth parted. She stood speechless, a hand pressed against the cleft of her bosom for long seconds in which she seemed unable to remove her fascinated gaze from the jeweled piece, and he said after a minute of silence:

"Can you touch it as you did the tree without wishing to own it?"

Her glance lifted briefly to him and slid away. "I'm afraid you're right," she said at last.

She brightened suddenly and gave him an accusing smile. "But you went to a great deal of trouble and expense to prove it." Her expression underwent another change as she looked at the necklace. "May I touch it?"

"You may. But then you'd wish to own it."

"I already wish that. And you know it, Mr. Cartwright! But

the very idea of your—your doing this! Why, I thought——"
She broke off, her face clouded as she looked at him and bit
her lip. "Why did you do it?"

"Because I decided that you are the only person in the
world who could do it justice."

Her eyes were deep and questioning as she pondered this.
Trembling fingers touched her cheek in a face drained of color
one moment and flooding pink the next.

"Thank you." She could say no more.

"But you haven't even touched it," he said in an attempt
to lift her out of a sober trance.

"I—I don't dare," she said. "I want it so much, but I can't
accept it."

"Sit down, Jenny. Over here." He indicated a large log.

He told her of his many visits to the silversmith and the
terms of the purchase, honor exceeding all else, of his reply
—that his regard for her exceeded friendship, that he was not
trying to buy her, that she was above being bought.

"So the old man said to me, 'Then you are honest.' Perhaps I
am. And I would not have presented the necklace to you here
had you not so skillfully, and unwittingly, put the idea in my
head with your talk of trees and ownership. I apologize,
Jenny, for that, for not giving it to you in the presence of
Philip."

Jenny nodded slowly. She had listened with unfocused gaze
on the giant ferns almost enclosing them. A silence, except for
the wind and rustling leaves, lengthened.

"It is strange," she said finally, "that you should think of
me as you do."

"Is it, Jenny?"

"Yes. You know of my devotion to Philip. And you know
that nothing could change that. And"—she raised her glance
to him—"you know that you would never try to come between us, even if you thought you could."

"Yes. I'm aware of all that. And I thank you for finding a
virtue among my many faults. But to me, Jenny, you're the
tree. It tells my story, even to disproving all I thought to
prove. I don't have to touch you and say, 'You're mine,' even
though I must admit I'd like nothing better."

She gave him a kind look and smile.

"But the necklace," he said, as though to dismiss a subject
that had come at last into the open, "is yours. However, I
shall give it to you in Philip's presence."

She continued to look at him. "It would be better that way." A pause followed. "Then I could thank the honorable man who gave it to me with a great big hug and kiss."

His glance dwelled on her as he tried desperately to solve the puzzle of woman. At first gay, then thoughtful, next moody and very sober, she had accepted the gift on terms she had forced him to propose, and with a promise on her lips augmented by a twinkle in her eye. He could only admit that if, long ago, he had thought the intricacies of business were mere child's play as compared to the strange machinations of a woman's mind, Jenny Broadwinder had on this day proved conclusively that it was so.

24

☐ Two days later Mayo Keys blew in on a wet wind. His arrival was telegraphed from the Heads and, despite the weather, he was greeted by a fleet of small boats at anchorage.

In the days that followed, the *Emperor*'s master was accorded every honor Melbourne could bestow on a merchant captain. As Broadwinder, he was made an honorary member of the Melbourne Club, lionized at every turn, and hailed as a paragon of sail in the great American tradition. Soon, however, the people learned they were hosting a man rather difficult to entertain. He neither drank nor indulged in idle talk. Certainly he was no Broadwinder. To counter his fast-ebbing popularity, a group of racing enthusiasts became his champions and proclaimed him a man of action rather than words; a sailing man who cracked on canvas at sea instead of in a drawing room. And because he looked the part, long, bony, firm-lipped, and determined of eye, opinion shifted once more in his favor. If Broadwinder represented dash and geniality, Keys bespoke the type of seaman who would "hang on to a halyard til hell froze over."

While Broadwinder's host of friends showed Keys every courtesy, they placed their money on the Prince of Sea Captains to win. Two days before embarkation Broadwinder was a two-to-one favorite. The betting odds on his reaching Boston two full days ahead of the *Emperor* rose from even money to seven to five.

Neither captain was content to rely on public opinion, however. From the hour of anchorage, both ships had turned into beehives of activity in final preparation for the stiff winds and seas ahead. New suits of heavy-weather sails were augmented by every precaution known to seamen. Head spars were given extra lashings, all preventer gear was checked, all rolling tackle inspected, and cargoes trimmed and stowed with less regard for convenient discharge in Boston and more for the effect on helm and speed. More dunnage and shifting boards were used to secure cargoes against the heaviest weather.

During the final week in Melbourne, Jenny in the company of both mates carefully made the rounds of deck with an even more critical eye. She made observations while talking of this and that to disguise her purpose. She mentioned extra cases of ale, porter, delicacies, and medicines as her sharp eye detected infinitesimal things that had escaped notice. Perhaps it was her sense of order, of neatness—she wasn't sure—but the boat lashings, the fastenings on the forecastle door, a frayed strand in the flying-jib sheet, iron rust on the cap which joined bowsprit and jib boom, these things and more arrested her, all very important things in running. Cartwright, who had accompanied her in the rounds of decks, was not surprised when Broadwinder ordered a new cap on the bowsprit, the forecastle door rehinged, and other repairs. Cartwright smiled. Jenny possessed an uncanny knowledge of ships and the faculty of hiding it from even Philip. He recalled that she had more than once with ostensibly idle remarks caused canvas to be flown or taken in at the proper time. She was clever and tactful, and she seemed to fool all aboard with the possible exception of Mr. Fortune.

Such were Cartwright's observations as the day of embarkation drew closer. As always, with each new discovery of Jenny's wisdom and secret concern for the ship, his admiration for her increased. And now, he remembered again that he was the possessor of a rare necklace designed for her white neck.

It was late afternoon of the last day in port that he did something about it. Philip and Jenny met him on deck dressed for the farewell banquet Melbourne was giving for the departing captains. He had never seen Jenny more lovely. She wore a gown the color of ashes of roses, with tiny pale-green leaves embroidered at the hem. It was low-necked and more Southern, such as he had seen in Mobile the year before. With hair combed back and falling to her bosom in a long curl over her left shoulder, a fan in her slender fingers, she could in Cartwright's adoring eyes be waiting to command a carriage in the deep South instead of a ship's boat to put her ashore in Australia. All that separated her from perfection, he decided, was the silver necklace. He thought about it while watching her at the stern sheets of the boat, and again in the carriage transporting them to the Melbourne Club. The necklace demanded her this evening or it could be the other way about. In any case, he realized she must wear it.

Just as they reached their destination Cartwright produced the necklace. A laugh, a shrug and, "No use waiting until Boston to present this," he said. "She's made for finery tonight, Captain."

Jenny's feigned surprise did not compare to Philip's genuine amazement. He held the jeweled piece, uttered an exclamation as nautical as unexpected before handing it back to Cartwright in silence. So, he was thinking, this is the expensive gift she spoke about. Was Cartwright insane, in love with her, or what? He recalled with startling clarity her statement: "George Cartwright would propose to me in a minute if you were out of the way." Perhaps he was doing just that now. If so, the look in her eyes denoted acceptance. Philip Broadwinder felt himself caught aback in those moments before he rallied with memories of Jenny's love, honesty, and loyalty. She was not one who could be influenced by gifts. So he was thinking when Cartwright placed the necklace about her throat.

"Why, George Cartwright," she cried excitedly, "I could kiss you! And I shall!"

She did, full upon the lips.

Broadwinder started. Cartwright felt recurrent charges of electricity running through him. Jenny experienced an odd sense of fulfilling a promise. It ended there, outwardly, and both men listened to Jenny's exclamations of delight.

"But, sir, you shouldn't have! It's so very costly!"

Broadwinder's hand fell over hers. "Why not? Cartwright's a spendthrift with good judgment. Now who could wear it better than the Queen of the *Calcutta Eagle*?"

"Then you don't mind, Philip—if I accept it?"

"I? Mind? Ho, Jenny! It's well timed to the race, isn't it? We'll call it a good-luck charm."

He frowned, nevertheless.

The lavish party continued until past midnight. Jenny twice reminded Philip of the demands the day ahead would make on him. Mayo Keys had long since departed, as had all but the hosts, one a leading underwriter and the other publisher of the *Daily Herald*. Philip Broadwinder remained, with glass in hand and another enchanting yarn on his lips. Meeting Jenny's stern glance, and finding it most disconcerting and unwelcome, he said to Cartwright:

"See her to the ship, George, old fellow." Then he addressed Jenny with, "I'll be along shortly. And don't you worry. This time tomorrow I'll be staring aft at Mayo—over a horizon."

As she reluctantly turned to go, he said, "And watch after that beautiful necklace."

Jenny remained silent all the way to the ship. At her cabin door she thanked Cartwright for his courtesy, then removed the necklace, and, to his astonishment, placed it in his hands.

"It won't do, sir. I'm sorry, but that's the way it must be."

She left him standing there. Alone, he looked at the gift returned and then at the closed door. He had seen the disappointment in her face when Philip sent her away, the hurt filling her eyes after the shock of that last remark fell away. His anger at Philip Broadwinder increased by the moment. It was, he realized, a helpless anger, though the fact did nothing to slow his resentment. Broadwinder was a fool, a blind fool. He owned a jewel and didn't know it. He thought himself the greater of the pair, the celebrity his friends made of him. His popularity was more important to him than Jenny.

His greatest desire was to wait up and confront his vain captain with these facts and more. But he knew he could not. He had no right to interfere. Jenny was Philip's wife. Now and always.

His troubled eyes fell again to the necklace. He saw in it his own foolish behavior. The piece of silver had lured him on, had brought his secret thoughts and desires into the open. Then, as though it were a tool of the devil, it had caused him to bring hurt into the life of the woman he loved.

For long seconds he considered the advisability of tossing what appeared to be a bad omen over the side, then placed it in his pocket. In his stateroom he realized that only his Yankee sense of thrift had stayed him. His sister Julia could wear the necklace without inviting harm. No entanglements there, none whatever.

25

☐ Although Captain Broadwinder had returned to the ship a mere hour before the break of dawn, he met the crowds putting out in small craft that morning in fine fettle. The crew lined the rails and yards of the *Eagle,* and a few ship lengths away the *Emperor's* hands waited with the same feeling of excitement the order to bring in anchors.

On deck after a sleepless night, Jenny smiled at the well-wishers crowding the ship's side and listened to a band playing an American air from the deck of a yacht now working alongside. Her tired eyes lifted and fell on Mayo Keys's long, graceful ship. The Blue Peter still flew, a signal for all hands to come aboard, and as she watched, a flag calling for a pilot fluttered in the wind.

The weather could not be better. A stiff breeze blew out of the southwest, chopping up the broad expanse of sunlit harbor. The sky gave no indication of any change, though once outside placid Port Phillip Bay, the weather might follow the pattern of seasonal change with anything from dead calms to driving squalls.

She drew her gaze inboard. Cartwright stood across deck, for which she was thankful. After last night's embarrassing events, she found herself wishing he were sailing aboard the *Emperor.* Philip had been purposely cruel. There was no excuse for his behavior and he offered none. Jealousy was one thing, one's manifestation of it another. She had never given him cause for turning green-eyed. She had said as much to him in the hour before dawn when he held her in his arms and told her she could have accepted the gift without giving her lips to Cartwright, that by the devil and the deep it had better not happen again. When he learned that she had returned the necklace, he appeared somewhat contrite, though more pleased than he let on. He relaxed and by-passed all apologies due with love-making, and he seemed at a loss to understand her when she could not be aroused. And like an overgrown boy used to having his way, he continued to pout. It served him right, she admitted, flicking him with a glance.

Now for the first time she seemed conscious of the fanfare about her. It burst into reality, as though out of her dreams along the way, pictures she had created of the joy and excitement incident to departure from Melbourne. Yet here in the midst of it she was unhappy. The realization cut like a knife. She and Philip, one, partners in the biggest sailing event of their lives, were at odds. It was a bad omen, one she felt compelled to banish before the ship moved a single inch. She considered ways and means of going about it before deciding to approach Philip. At his side, she drew his attention to her, smiled up at him, and said:

"Captain Broadwinder, I wish you every success in the race ahead."

Surprised, he eyed her for sincerity and, finding it, placed an arm about her waist. "May the good Lord bless you, Mrs. Broadwinder!" he cried. In a whisper, he added, "Despite your stubbornness, girl."

She chose to ignore the last. A happy beginning was imperative. "Now, sir," she said, as though all was settled between them, "are you going to signal for a pilot?"

"At the proper time. I want it said that Broadwinder gave Keys first run through the Heads. Eh, Mr. Fortune?"

The blue eyes of Ephraim Fortune twinkled. "Indeed, sir. Most generous of you, sir. However, I predict an abrupt end to your generosity once we bounce into the open sea."

Broadwinder's answer was cut short by cries over the harbor. Sailors were pointing toward the *Emperor*, now creeping out into Port Phillip Bay in a beginning of motion that would continue through thousands of miles of ocean. She slid like a swan, a picture of line and symmetry and grace upon the water, her wings unfolded as yet, her tread gentle.

Tobias returned from the standard of the wheel with telescopes for the captain and his lady. Jenny raised the glass and brought the rival captain into the circle of sight. Mayo Keys stared straight ahead, his long, bony face and steel-gray eyes chiseled into a study of grim determination. Watching him as the black-hulled clipper eased on, with Keys looking neither to right nor left in response to the cheers of Melbourne, she recalled his correct social deportment of last evening. He had been seated next to her, oddly enough, and before she realized it she had reshaped former opinions of the man to a surprising degree. Reticent but attentive and very alert to topical discussions, he had replied to questions directed at him with astonishing ease and knowledge. Astonishing because of its unexpectedness; as when a scholarly Englishman brought desultory literary talk to an end with, *"Books! 'tis a dull and endless strife,"* and, unable to recall who authored the line or find the answer among those about him, turned to Keys, who said, as though giving the time of day, "William Wordsworth."

He was therefore a man to bear watching, not because of his acquaintance with poetry or drawing-room manners, but because of his unplumbed depth and bearing. He would not be easily outsailed, Jenny thought. He knew his business. It was said he was an officer "come in through the hawsehole," meaning he had risen from the ranks; which, if true, meant he knew how to sweat gear for the last burst of speed in a ship.

The *Emperor* moved on into the hazy union of sky and sea in Port Phillip Bay under sail lazily flung to the wind. Keys seemed in no hurry whatever. Nor did Broadwinder, who continued to wait with pilot aboard until the *Emperor* was all but sail under horizon. The band continued to play and the small boats sent up more cheers. Then Broadwinder ordered the men to their stations. The cable was hauled noisily in and as the anchors dripped, topmen went aloft. A movement was felt, a first trembling at the bows, as triangles of white ran up and filled. The ship swung her nose to the south and met the wind with yards close-hauled. The *Calcutta Eagle* slid forward, knifing the water even as she heeled mightily. Then she was off in a commencement of another Broadwinder show.

The race had begun.

Jenny could not put down the increasing feeling of exhilaration evoked into being by Philip's tremendous burst of speed. He made the ship cavort and prance like a stallion freed of bit. He dipped his colors. Jenny saw the thrill of it surface in Cartwright's expression as well as the pilot's. Perhaps it was the suddenness of change, from stillness to fast motion with all the accompanying inertia of a ship flying her canvas full and high.

Old Sails and Chips and the bosun looked on with eyes

dancing brightly. "She blows!" they seemed to say. "In Broadwinder fashion!" Melbourne lay tiny over the white turmoil of water from the ship's stern, now stretching far aft into the sunny chops of the bay. Then the city bounced gradually under the seam of sky and water, and the Heads began to show like blue smears on a seascape. Ahead, now in full view lay the *Emperor,* working her slow way to the sea. Fast overtaken. Some sail was forced off the *Eagle* now in order to allow the other ship to clear the Heads. Keys took his time in opening the pass, and when he was through and piling on sail in earnest, Broadwinder said it was time for the *Eagle* to go through.

In short time the *Eagle* ran the Heads and came to a stop with her sails still set to disembark the pilot. As the pilot struck palms with Broadwinder, the latter presented him with a gold watch and thereby carved another niche in his tablet of fame.

"Next time, Jerry, time me from Hobson's to the Heads."

"Already have, Cap'n, for a record in the bay. I'll telegraph it in and—may ye blow into Boston town a week and a dolphin's leap in the lead."

Miles ahead the *Emperor,* a leaning tower of white canvas, was winging east and down for South East Point, apparently intent on reaching for southing through Bass Strait north of the Furneaux Group. Here was a time for figuring the best sailing route to the big winds that would push one steadily for Cape Horn. Bass Strait was full of islands and shallows, a squally area and ordinarily treacherous. The safest and longest passage was down the western coast of Tasmania, though the wind could head a ship this time of year. Tacking and tacking down past King Island to the west for southing was not to Broadwinder's liking, not now when the wind was fair to Bass Strait. But there was still another and shorter route. Instead of topping the Furneaux Group, many a gold-carrier and clipper ship romped southeast to the narrow channel of Banks Strait, which separated Tasmania and the Furneaux Islands. Broadwinder defined it accurately as he studied the *Emperor:*

"Shorter if the wind is with you."

Mr. Fortune called the captain's attention to the winds one could expect at this time: "Out of the south from one direction or another in these latitudes. A sou'easter would head us, sir."

He was right, and Broadwinder knew it. But to run Banks Strait on a good wind would place him far in the lead of Mayo Keys, that is if Keys was really driving east. And since east appeared to be the better course, he believed Mayo would take it.

"Do you agree, Jenny?"

"I agree to nothing, Captain Broadwinder, for to support either or both of you"—she glanced from Philip to the mate —"is to put us on the defensive at the outset. May I suggest we run our own race and let our competitor do the wondering and worrying."

Cartwright heard. He knew instantly she had scored a point and formulated a policy. Success, the very ring of it, was in her voice and suggestion. She flung tall sails into one's imagination and she banished doubt with spirit and decisiveness. Broadwinder's and Fortune's faces proved it.

"Aye," Broadwinder said. The mate echoed him.

"Then we'll drive south, Mr. Fortune. And for a while we'll show our port quarter to Mr. Keys. Let him think we're standing down for the west coast of Tasmania. When he's sails under we'll swing her and drive fast for Banks."

Then Jenny stayed in character, superbly so, Cartwright admitted, when she turned suddenly into a woman with curiosity in her eye and a note of concern in her voice. "Odd, I haven't seen the ship's cat since we left Melbourne. Do you suppose Prince Thomas deserted us?"

So saying, she left them, her mission accomplished, with none the wiser. Or so it seemed. But George Cartwright behind his sober expression was cheering the wisest person aboard. The captain's lady was Athena with a trident in her hand. And watching her as she went through with it, a thorough search for the big yellow cat, he wondered just how much of her one could ever hope to see.

The racing *Eagle* ran a false course until the sea burned with sunset colors. Then the ship was placed on another tack. The beam wind struck and sail after sail piled high, filled, and sent the ship bowling over the seas toward Banks Strait.

"A rare and beautiful sea tonight," she said to Cartwright when moonlight painted sails and sea. "Perhaps because we are at last fulfilling our purpose." She paused. "Purpose, whether it's racing or grinding corn in a mill, enriches one's life. Immeasurably. It is less the touch of a star and more the reaching for it that keeps the flame alight in our eyes. Look at the hands tonight. No below watch, but every man handy and handling, of his own volition, to beat the *Emperor*."

She looked into his eyes then.

"You are to be congratulated, sir, if only for lighting that candle in the hearts of these men."

"I'm reaching too, Jenny," he said, after absorbing her unexpected kindness as best he could. "I thought I had touched the star, as you said. Life became a little dull until I found another to reach for."

She did not reply to this. He sounded a note she remembered all too well, an echo from the eucalyptus forest.

"I know what you are thinking," he said slowly. "But you are wrong. It is another kind of an adventure, Jenny. Call it observation, a witnessing of the adventures of people with a purpose. You, Philip, Mayo Keys, the old man who sold me the necklace, Mrs. Littlefield, Mr. Fulton, for once people other than myself. A never-ending puzzle, but an interesting one. For example——"

He hushed suddenly and gave an embarrassed laugh. "Excuse me. I was going strong, wasn't I?"

"Don't quit now," she implored, smiling at his modesty. "Just when for the first time you break through your shell to reveal something of yourself and of your thinking!"

"Other than the penny-pinching businessman?"

"I recall a necklace," she countered, lifting a brow.

"That, my dear, was a weakness for beauty. But I haggled like a true Chinese or Yankee."

Diagonally across deck, a voice, Philip's, sounded over the wind in the rigging: "Run out the stun's'l booms!" Like a song came the rest, "Fore and main!"

"But you enjoyed that kind of bargaining," she said.

"The same as I'm enjoying the myriad and various things that go into a race between ships, Philip's order just now. I doubt if I've thought once today of the freight value of the cargo we're carrying—close to a hundred thousand dollars."

"Begging your pardon, sir, one hundred and eleven thousand, nine hundred and seven dollars and forty-eight cents."

He simply stared at her. Recovering, he said, "You figured it while crocheting, I suppose."

"Something like that. You forget little, sir."

"And remember more. All I see and learn about some of the people I mentioned a few minutes back."

Jenny flashed him a disarming smile. "Mrs. Littlefield, I presume—Mrs. Fulton now."

"And Mrs. Broadwinder," he answered readily. "Was our cat ever located?"

"In the chartroom, curled up on a map of Sunda Strait, his tail touching Java Head."

"Excellent. And thanks to Prince Thomas, the captain took the initiative in this race."

She knew what he was getting at, though she said, "I don't quite follow you. Thomas had nothing to do with the course we're on."

He pretended to meditate. "Perhaps no, perhaps yes. But you're beginning to understand the adventure of an observer of adventure, I'm sure. You see, Jenny, I'm wiser and you're wiser."

She bit her lip and said nothing, for there was little to say unless she chose to deny a fact, that he was wise to her methods of playing guardian to ship and all aboard. For a moment she resented his intrusion on her secrets, then she was aware that he had carried off the moment admirably.

As though by common consent, they spoke of other and lighter things. The lookout's cry of breakers dead ahead, the shouted orders and activity aboard a ship awake to sudden danger put an end to further conversation. It was just as well, Jenny decided. He had given her enough to think about for one evening.

No sooner had she arrived at this conclusion than Philip drew her attention He was ordering the studding booms relieved of sail. A rather wise decision, she thought. There were times to run and times to creep; in sail and in life.

They ran only forty miles by the log on the eight-to-twelve night watch. The exhilaration that came with greater speed fell away when the foam rushing down the sides and the big roar of wind in the rigging diminished. The ship ran on through the night as though racing interested the captain not in the least. Day broke with backing winds and overcast sky. By noon, to the disgust of all, the *Eagle* crept along, lucky to eke out two or three knots an hour. That evening Broadwinder wrote into the ship's log:

MAR. 3, SECOND DAY OUT: *Calms. Ran less than fifty miles in twelve hours. Rain and flat sea.*

With morning, Jenny looked into the long faces of officers and crew. Silence was a companion of the decks. "Captain Broadwinder," she said, sending her voice down to the dispirited crew, "you can cut the gloom aboard with a knife." Every eye below the break of the poop lifted to her and slid dolefully past. "A fine lot of sailors, acting as though we had never been to sea, never experienced delay before. As for myself, I'm going to coax a wind through the eye of a needle as I darn the captain's socks."

The carpenter thought this funny. He grinned, and old Sails laughed. The bosun, undecided, took one look at the sailmaker and cackled. Soon every person on board seemed to have gone crazy.

"Us!" O'Hara said between outbursts. "If somebody had of said yesterday we'd be sittin' out a Irish hurricane and splittin' our sides laughin', I'd a swore he was balmy as a forktailed petrel in the Sahary Desert."

"Aye!" Stokes the sailor agreed.

Tobias stuck his head out the forecastle door. "What's so all-fired funny out there?"

"Now there's a stout lad for ye. The boy asks a question, Chips."

"Which has a answer, sonnywhack," O'Hara said, peering out of one eye at the ship's boy. "The Old Man's wife is goin' to darn socks so fast the air through the eye of her needle will whistle up a wind."

The eyes of Tobias widened and his mouth hung open. A moment perplexed, he said, "It ain't possible!"

There was no sign of gloom aboard the *Eagle* for the remainder of that long, dreary day. Tobias Dunlap's reply went the rounds; from galley to lookout's perch to the captain's cabin, it put a laugh in the throats of all.

The wind struck like a devil out of the deep at around nightfall. A southwester, it blew in with a chill in its teeth and kicked up rough seas that slapped hard at the sides. This was more like it, a push in the sails, colder weather, but dry. The sky was swept clear and under the big moon they ran under topgallants until eight bells midnight when a topgallant sail split as cleanly as though slashed with a knife. Topsails then, with the mighty foresail reefed. Morning of the fourth day out showed a night's run of close to one hundred miles. The wind continued strong and Broadwinder looked pleased.

He would try to run Banks Strait on this day. An ambitious thought, Jenny observed, calling his attention to shallow water, islands, and hazards of night and channel.

"I've got to do it, girl!" What he said next was something she was trying to get accustomed to: "I wonder where the devil Mayo is."

Jenny wondered also, with more concern than he knew, and she realized that all aboard would no doubt ponder the whereabouts of the rival captain often during the weeks and months ahead. It was a part of a race, a companion to tension, fear, worry, and trouble. Things truly a part of every worthwhile endeavor, as were hope, skill, and the God-given will to win.

26

☐ Late in the afternoon of the fourth day out of Melbourne, Captain Broadwinder felt the wind backing just when Tasmania's blue heights lifted over the starboard bow and Flinders Island and Cape Barren rose to port ahead. In the middle lay Banks Strait.

Although Mayo Keys was unaware of it, he held the advantage. Having reached the Tasman Sea after calms and adverse winds, he was standing down the east coast of the Furneaux Group in a reach for the southeast. But now the wind was panting out in the *Emperor*'s canvas also. The boil of her wake lessened and she slatted her sails as if gasping for air. Even so, Keys remained his inscrutable self as he stood with a pannikin of coffee in one hand, telescope up in the other, scanning the horizon for any cloud that might bear a wind.

At the same time, Broadwinder on the other and wrong side of the Furneaux Group was likewise engaged, though unlike Keys he fretted openly. He had taken this clipper road to Cape Horn to steal a march on Keys, only to trap himself in light airs with the strait in sight. He stared into it a long time before raising his glance to the pennant atop the main. It hung limp, then lifted weakly, enough to evoke alarm in his face. As he watched, hoping, praying, for a wind from any direction but southeast, a gust in the upper air curled the swallow-tail out from the main truck—straight northwest. He cursed, for he knew that the breeze blowing in would head him.

As the wind came on from the direction he wished to steer the ship, and since he could not point closer than six points of the compass to it, he had but one choice beyond waiting for a slant to get through and that was to tack for it. He did this, sailing zigzag courses east-northeast and south-southwest, back and forth, swinging the yards, determined to beat through the strait even if he exhausted the crew in gaining a passage. He almost did the latter, and when darkness fell, not a man before the mast waited to get his "tuck."

The ship sat it out close to the entrance of the strait, neither inside nor through.

The night brought rain and thunderstorms. As lightning darted out of the night, Broadwinder stood, with water streaming his oilskins, testing the wind direction. Due east now, which would turn him on his heel. The shift continued. Praise God, north! It was north. Morning broke clear and the *Calcutta Eagle* rejoicing in her freedom ran the strait and saw land widen and open up. The broad Tasman Sea beckoned and the hands began to sing a chantey of their own composition, about the *Eagle*'s voyage "from Melbourne down, to Boston town."

On the poop Broadwinder scanned horizons for a sail before turning on his first officer. "Scarcely four hundred sea miles from Melbourne, Mr. Fortune. In four and one half days! Why, we've logged almost that in a single day."

Mr. Fortune turned this over in his mind. The captain was a hard man to please, which, he decided, was the way it should be. So he said, "Well, sir, we can only hope and try for many such days between here and the Cape."

"Cape Horn," Broadwinder meditated aloud. "Over six thousand long, hard miles."

He was thinking of his route, of taking his southing while running his easting down, of the dip under New Zealand, all the while still reaching deep for fifty degrees south, fifty-five, sixty—even lower, if that was where the big winds roared—of the ice drift up into his path at this time of year, of all these things and more, when the mizzen lookout cried a sail.

"Where away?" Broadwinder sang out, suddenly restored to the present.

"Port quarter, hull under but coming up fast, royals high, sir!"

Broadwinder's eyes wrinkled shut as a wide grin of pleasure spread his face. "It could be, Mr. Fortune. It could just be Mayo Keys! If it is, we've jockeyed him into our wake."

Several minutes earlier the *Emperor's* forward lookout had cried the deck. Mayo Keys soon joined the lad and sent his telescope in a rake of the curvature of ocean ahead. Probably Broadwinder, he thought, fresh out of Banks Strait and doing his utmost to make up for lost time. They were of one mind on that score, both on the same course, both taking full advantage of the light wind. Simple facts. Keys added another, the Prince had won the jump on him, however slight. But the real race would not begin until they reached the west winds farther south. So, voicing no order to alter course or sail, he returned to deck and sent a sharp eye over every yard and line. Perhaps he could take the slack out of this rope and that, brace the yards a trifle more, even fling out studding sails or wet down the driving sails, though he took little stock in the latter methods. He had his own rules and a code of his own, and he meant to beat Broadwinder without changing them.

He harbored no real dislike for Broadwinder. They had once been on good speaking terms, affable racing terms when the occasion presented itself. Often commanders of ships found themselves on identical courses and crowded on sail for the sheer sport of it. So had he and Broadwinder, once on the way to Hong Kong, another time on the Valparaiso road. Every man of the sea had a good word for Broadwinder back in those early years of the gold rush. He was a man's man, deserving of welcome in every port. Soon the bigwigs, merchants, bankers, owners, and shippers became aware of his flair for entertainment and, coupling this asset with his reputation for making speedy and profitable voyages, they virtually declared a monopoly on his time in ports. Then, following one voyage in which he, almost in the pattern of Josiah Creesy, turned trouble into profit, a group of underwriters gave a dinner in his honor in New York. They could well afford it, since he had saved them thousands of dollars by delivering the full cargo undamaged. The newspapers found him then. He made good copy. They wrote of him as the "Prince of Sea Captains," hailed his challenge to the British as a symbolic awakening in America to the glory of her merchant marine, and so played up his victory over the clipper *Panther* to San Francisco that he was soon generally accepted as the fastest sailing man of the time. Perhaps he was.

In any case, Keys began to wonder where fact left off and fiction began. Upon learning what few men believed, that George Cartwright and not Broadwinder had inaugurated the popular policy of sailing at a specified time instead of when laden, he became possessed with the idea of settling in his own mind Broadwinder's ability or inability to outdistance all other clipper captains. He continued to think about it. Then in Singapore he met Broadwinder and challenged him to a race. It was Broadwinder's unethical manner of twisting the challenge about for the purpose of enlarging his fame, so Keys thought, that aroused his anger. It also fanned his determination.

And now Broadwinder's mighty sails were in plain foretop view, despite the shortcut the Prince had taken. Which hewed the celebrity of the day down to size.

Mayo Keys continued his study of the blue horizon with his mind on the race. Like most seamen, he had a great respect for luck. He could cope with skill and match wits with most men, but the luck of Broadwinder was something else. It made itself felt in even his thinking. As now, when he stood debating a southeast plunge under New Zealand against a drive south to pick up the roaring forties in advance of Broadwinder. The mathematics of the problem consisted of guesswork as to how deep he would have to reach for the west wind versus Broadwinder's luck in catching the big blow on a southeast course. Caution advised him to keep Broadwinder in sight down to the westerlies and from there match him sail for sail. His more aggressive self urged him to drive on south. But this was scarcely the time and place to gamble. On the other hand, the whole thing was nothing short of a gamble.

True enough. But how far down to the great winds? Only the Lord above knew. Which left him with a decision to make, one likely to be as important as any in his endeavor to dethrone Broadwinder.

The lookout reported at intervals on the progress of the ship ahead. By four bells on the first afternoon watch the *Calcutta Eagle* lay all but royals under, proving she worked better in light airs than the *Emperor*. At sunset she was but a speck on the horizon, cause for celebration aboard of her, Keys realized, with no loss of confidence. At nightfall he still held his course, southeast. The moon came up with a watery expression and the fickle wind danced in and out before easing a little west. At midnight the *Emperor* ran "thick o' fog," as the sailors called it, with visibility limited to decks. Morning came and the fog was still with them. It wept out of the canvas and beaded every surface.

At this rate Cape Horn lay more than thirty days east. Keys did not like it. As the ship ran on all that day in the heavy pall of mist, her top speed ten knots, her average eight, he liked it even less. He took the stretch out of his gear, flew all the light sails she carried, even "stun's'ls" beyond the yard-arms later in the day. Midnight found Keys still on deck, fog-soaked, ill-humored. Temptation was strong in him to put the weak wind over his starboard quarter for a southward push—maybe down there he could trade the devil his wind for a better one.

While aboard the *Calcutta Eagle*, Captain Broadwinder stood the deck most of that woolly night. Unmindful of weather, moisture dripping from visor, nose and ears, he kept the on-watch crew jumping about taking slack out of lines, rigging masts above royals, and flying spritsails from the bows. He wanted and got the last stretch of speed out of the following wind. By juggling sail, adding a kite here and there to snag a wind, and tautening his ropes constantly, he eked out and sustained a ten-eleven-knot speed on a wind that would have otherwise given him nine at best. To not a few seamen so much work for so little expected gain might have appeared foolish. Though on board the *Eagle* racing was a serious proposition. Reputations, money, future business, and popularity were at stake, and Cartwright, Broadwinder, and Jenny knew it.

If Jenny in uncomplimentary oilskins remained on deck with Philip most of the night, it was not just because she too realized the importance of holding the initial lead over Mayo Keys. Back in Melbourne, Phillp had in a cosy humor vowed he would not remove his clothes at night until he reached Boston. His words were made public, to be remembered or forgotten. It didn't matter really, for the waiting world was less interested in the long sleepless hours and untold sacrifices aboard an ocean racer and more in the final outcome of the race. Only that would be long remembered. But the race was young yet, opening its sixth day, and Philip was expending energy faster than he could replace it. So she was naturally concerned.

Twice during the night she laced his coffee with whisky and he drank it between shouted orders, hardly aware of the cup in his hand. But the sea was his life, Jenny admitted; all he could coax from her. He gave of himself to compensate for the taking—the sea demanded as much, which was reason enough for men to speak of sea and ocean as "she" and "her," as a woman. Only the strong won her favor. And now she was demanding all of Philip.

When the day came up thick and leaden Jenny put Philip to bed and rubbed his neck, back, and feet until he slept. He was up within the hour, throwing on his clothes and growling his displeasure at the fog shrouding the porthole.

Jenny sat up in bed and regarded him in silence until he demanded to know why she stared at him so.

"Maybe it's because I don't quite understand you," she replied in such matter-of-fact tones that he paused to eye her curiously. "Where's the gain, Philip, if you exhaust yourself and crew before you reach the big westerlies?"

"A fair question, that one," he scoffed. "The idea, my dear Jenny, is to beat Mayo to the big winds." He said, seriously now, "This stretch of light airs may not seem important. Perhaps the promise of the westerlies below us causes you—and, I hope, Mayo—to forget that this race might be won or lost before we reach them."

He left her with that, and she could only admit he spoke the truth. However, truth and strategy did nothing to lessen her concern, or answer the question uppermost in her mind.

Would Philip remain on deck all through the night to come?

Broadwinder slept an hour or two during the forenoon watch and spent the remainder of the day getting the most out of the prevailing breeze. A freshening west wind lifted the fog that afternoon and the sunset played on ragged streamers of mist hazing the surface of the sea. With visibility restored and the ship running at twelve knots on a steady quartering wind, tension seemed to fall away. The hands sang under clearing skies and as their chanteys rolled tunefully over the sea, Jenny and Cartwright roamed the decks watching the play of the aurora australis in the Southern sky and stars peeping out overhead.

Near the lee rail amidships, Lowery or Sails related incidents of other voyages along this clipper road to the Horn. Looking at young Tobias, Sails told of how the old bark *Anderson* under only one sail had run so fast it required thirty minutes for a man to negotiate the distance from poop to bows. And it had been so cold that the figurehead's pulse beat stopped altogether and the galley stove shivered with a full fire going.

Farther aft, Jenny replied to Cartwright's questions concerning Philip's odd passion for speed in light winds of the night before in almost the same words Broadwinder had employed with her.

Appearing somewhat surprised, and next thoughtful, Cartwright admitted to having thought this stage of the race a mere prelude to the real thing. He continued to study Philip as he would a puzzle, which pleased Jenny until he asked with sudden directness if the captain's doing had actually fooled her.

Odd, his asking that, she told him. Of course Philip had fooled her. She observed the doubt in Cartwright's expression, and began to wonder if he credited her with a sailing knowledge equal to Philip's. Perhaps. He thought strangely about many things.

The late moon surged up into the sky and lit up the sea as it paled the stars. Thinking this might be the last romantic night until they moved up into the distant Atlantic, Jenny looked up at the moon, a friend soon to depart, then at Philip. But he was Captain Broadwinder now, and she soon realized that the big moon was to him nothing more than a convenient light to aid the lookouts in their search for a sail in the night.

Cartwright interrupted her trend of thought with an observation which proved he missed little: "I doubt if the captain has absented himself from deck a single full watch since Melbourne." Next he said, "I don't mean to pry or instruct, but don't you think you should do something about it?"

"Sir," Jenny said, surveying him with open amusement, "one doesn't teach an old sea dog new tricks after the curtain goes up on his performance." She took a step toward Philip. "However, one doesn't quit trying."

To her surprise, and Cartwright's, Philip went below with her. He returned to deck an hour later and stood out the remainder of Mr. Fortune's watch and then his own four-hour stretch. Shortly past four in the morning he looked so haggard and heavy-lidded that the chief mate suggested he catch a much needed wink before the day broke. Giving Mr. Fortune a friendly pat on the back, Broadwinder went to his quarters, where he sank into a chair and stared dully at the still coverlet under which Jenny lay.

Twice he jerked himself awake, the last time wondering just before sound sleep claimed him why he did not stir out of his chair and return to deck.

27

□ The great westerly winds came on, gradually increasing in force. On the seventh day out the *Eagle* logged almost three hundred miles. In the next twenty-four hours running she topped this by fifteen nautical miles, each one eighth longer than the land mile. She was flirting with the big winds now, Broadwinder driving, bidding them come on.

At noon of the ninth day Captain Broadwinder shot the sun and figured his position at forty-nine degrees south between The Snares and the Auckland Islands. Although the distance covered gave him small cause for jubilation, he was gathering speed, beginning to sail in the manner of an ocean racer. His expression as he walked the poop on this day seemed surprisingly cheerful, although it by no means reflected contentment. With collar turned up at the neck and hands rammed in coat pockets, he measured the drop in temperature since dawn at fifteen degrees and foresaw the probability of a much lower reading by nightfall.

An albatross flew inquisitively about the ship. The sailors guessed its wingspread to be eleven, then twelve feet as it hovered close portside. The captain gave the hands a surprise when he laughed for the first time in long days and deliberated the possibility of harnessing a few such birds to the ship's head for extra speed. As suddenly as he had thawed, he swept bellying canvas and cordage with sharp, hungry glances. The men were aware that his every look aloft was freighted with a relentless demand for the utmost in driving sail. And always, his eyes dropped from top hamper to the sea, as in silence he made known a wish for that perfect combination, a freshening wind to push him on and not enough sea to check his speed.

The sea continued to rise, however, and the wash of flying water kicked up a froth that indicated a speed greater than the ship was logging. The wind held out of the northwest, right aft, and the *Eagle* scudded along, rolling a little as though in protest of royals and staysails flying in a top gallant-sail breeze. And now the weak sun disappeared and thick clouds astern were gaining on the ship. Cold rain pattered sails and decks an hour or so, moved on.

Broadwinder shook off afternoon fatigue—he had slept four hours of the last thirty-six—rubbed vigorously the stubble of his cheeks, and squinted an eye aloft. His sails were straining hard at sheets and jackstays. With the mainsail furled, so as not to blanket the big foresail, the *Eagle* was running clean, taking her lift at the fore with all the grace built into her fine lines. If she lurched a little now and then, it was her royals. They should come in soon. This was one part of Broadwinder's meditation. The other part had to do with the whereabouts of the *Emperor*, which he had not seen for three days. Keys could be in any of four directions, above, toward The Snares, below, behind or ahead. Fog and wet horizons screened a runner, opened up secret avenues. Mayo was no fool.

Broadwinder turned to the helmsman and ordered the bell eight, shot a glance into the royals and equated balance up there, conned seas, weather and decks and, as the watch changed at four o'clock sharp, asked for a reading of the log. Eighteen knots tied in the log line registered the maximum speed in theory and two or three more knots than were ordinarily needed. Few ships attained the top speed. One or two on rare occasions ran more than the line recorded. But every clipper captain aspired to the big eighteen, Broadwinder no exception. Twice he had touched it briefly. At this time, he knew of course it was impossible, as he knew that in the days ahead there was every probability that he would gain and hold that speed. He had the ship to do it.

He turned to Mr. Fortune. "We're getting a little of the weather we came down for." Accepting the log reading as another perfect guess on his part, he studied the royal sails a moment before saying, "I'm reaching farther south for weather that will drive us along with only storm canvas set."

The remark came as no surprise to the mate. Nor did the one that followed: "Mr. Fortune, since I'll be below a while, you're inheriting fore and main royals in to'gannels'ls weather. I'll thank you to fly them."

Mr. Fortune did so, though with marked discomfort. He expected one or both to go any minute, and the very fact that they held seemed due more to Broadwinder luck than Broadwinder foresight in fiddling masts for just such an occasion.

The *Calcutta Eagle* drove on into murky night and increasing seas. The barometer began to drop slowly. The rain beat at the ship, colder as the night progressed. Broadwinder, absent from deck one hour following the first afternoon watch, weathered the next seven, during which he took in the kites or staysails, and rolled the dice with the wind for his royals. At midnight he still flew them, but perilously. He admitted to Jenny later that he might have taken them in but for some devilish enjoyment he derived from Cartwright's worried glances aloft.

"Shame on you, Philip. Mr. Cartwright has been most——"

A thundering of flapping sail aloft stopped Jenny in midsentence. The main royal had blown.

With amazing unconcern, Philip said he would send up another. Ignoring her protests and suggestion that he wait until daybreak to do so, he went on deck, where he remained until the bell sounded the morning watch. As if to further annoy Jenny and deepen the crease between Cartwright's eyes, Philip did not relieve the fore-royal mast of sail. It continued to hold, though in the forecastle the hands were betting cuts of tobacco and rum rations that it would or would not blow before eight bells noon.

To the sailor, this kind of sailing was a lively game. Though his world was one in which cause and effect were ordinarily accepted with matter-of-fact indifference, the Old Man's game was theirs for sport, regardless of hardship or pain, and they played it with the knowledge that he would "go as the big wind blows." If there was doubt, they had only to look at him on the poop. There he stood, with a tight grin on his face, one that defied the devil, weather, and Mayo Keys. Aye, he was their kind of sailing man.

On the following day they found cause to alter or magnify

their oneness of opinion. The rough seas and squally skies fell away during the night and dawn of the twelfth day broke clear.

The *Eagle* was knifing the seas of the upper fifties, her figurehead staring over the silver tips of the waves in a comparatively easy sea, when the long silence up in the lookout's perch was broken by: "Sail ho!"

"A sail?" Chips wrinkled up his face. "The last damn thing this side of a iceberg we want to see."

Broadwinder's "Where away?" evoked from the lookout, "Breaking horizon over the port quarter!"

Port quarter? Broadwinder's eyes thinned to slits and, even as he turned his head in the given direction, his voice rang out sharply with, "Stand by, forward there!"

The hands tensed and waited. The below watch rolled out of their bunks and Mr. Winston forgot that his hand tugged at his red beard. On the poop Mr. Fortune stood with head cocked in an attitude of inquiry and Cartwright stared over the sea astern. Jenny continued to look aloft.

"What course does she shape?" from the captain.

"Same as we, sir."

"So." It could only be the *Emperor*, for no ship of lesser purpose could pull up over horizon on the *Eagle*. And the very fact that she had not been sighted earlier meant she was gaining. But with what? Sails? And if so, how? So, the captain reflected, it was to be a race after all.

As Broadwinder debated a course due west against the course he steered, Jenny knew intuitively his thinking at the time; his expression showed momentary indecision. She moved unhurriedly to his side.

"Captain Broadwinder," she said impetuously, "I do hope you won't give Mr. Keys the satisfaction of believing for a minute he can alter your course."

As a straw can tip the scales, so can a word break the deadlock of conflicting thoughts. Jenny's statement broke the captain's silence and the suspense of decks within the space of short seconds. Broadwinder ordered all sail on the *Eagle*, emphasis on the word "all."

Under the spell of the action he stirred, Broadwinder cried, "And stretch the leg that stands to port, lads, for she's going to heel on the wind!"

In quick time sails cascaded white in the sunlight and booms swung and sheets and halyards flew white hot from the pins as kites caught a wind and bellied like quartered balloons high above decks. The wheel spun and the *Eagle* tried to yaw as she adjusted the bit from order to canter to full gallop. Broadwinder felt of the helm himself, his sensitive mind reaching for a balance at the ship's pivot near the mainmast. And now, instead of adjusting sails and yards to his course, he did it the other way about, sacrificing a point of the compass from due southeast in order to humor her trim.

The reward was a clipper ship of clean lines heeling in yacht fashion over on her portside in a mighty surge forward. As though giant hands shoved her along, she seemed to skim the surface on the springs of the sea. With decks aslant and a roar in her towering loft, her captain facing forward, legs pumping to the rhythmic list under his feet, the *Calcutta Eagle* rode the tossing waves like a flying fish. Dipping jauntily, rising proudly, her every gesture as graceful as defiant, she raised a voice to those whose ears were in tune with her. "I am the reason the winds blow," she seemed to say.

Her master was her twin. His face reflected the whole adventure. Standing there now, he evoked in George Cartwright a memory of words spoken back in Boston: ". . . Some few men shine as symbols of something infinitely greater than the men themselves." He could not argue that at this moment. "In Captain Broadwinder one sees ships and sails and is aware of some fascinating mystery beyond one's grasp." Cartwright realized that this too had finally pierced the crust of a stanch realist's brain to implant itself as not just something observed but as something felt.

Then Broadwinder broke the spell. As the log line showed a speed of sixteen and one half knots, he appeared displeased. The wind, the sea, the ship added up to the maximum. He was therefore spilling wind somewhere. A look over the sides and at the angle of the pennant to the wake proved he was making too much leeway. Accordingly he braced up the yards and eased off the sheets and hauled the spanker boom. He watched until the luff of the sail he used for a weather clew quivered, then sheeted in until all trembling ceased. The ship's tendency to move sideways ceased and in doing so relieved the pressure from pushed-up lee seas. Within an hour the helmsmen admitted that the balance on her pivot was next to perfect.

"Our speed, Mr. Fortune?" Broadwinder yelled.

He waited, as did all aboard. Then it came. She was touching seventeen. A cheer lifted from the crew and died away when the Old Man failed to respond with more than, "She'll do better."

All the while Jenny stood with back to weather rail, her hair whipping from the edges of her bonnet as she took in every maneuver. Aware that Cartwright was equally attentive and watching her sharply now, she drew in her thoughtfful gaze from the mainsail and moved to Philip's side where she hoped to convey a message in secret. It had to do with the giant foresail, which was double-reefed for the purpose of giving the ship a greater lift at the fore. But since the mainsail blanketed off a portion of the foresail, the lift was in a measure reduced. She was thinking that by furling the mainsail, as always when running with the wind aft, this could be corrected and thereby lessen the resistance of seas at the bows.

Drawing Philip's attention, she held a handkerchief with fingers at the upper corners to the wind and then before her. As her body shielded the cloth and it went limp, Philip's face wrinkled in puzzlement. He bent an ear to her at last and she whispered:

"That's your fores'l, sir!"

His brow arched. "Eh? So it is!" he said, fingering his chin as he gazed straight ahead.

Whatever the play between the captain and his lady, it was forgotten by the crew when Broadwinder prompted the lookout and learned that the *Emperor* continued to rise slowly above the horizon.

That Keys was matching their pace came as a great surprise, but the fact that he was gaining on the *Eagle* seemed incredible. It was not that anyone aboard underestimated the sailing ability of Mayo Keys; rather, the *Eagle*'s officers and crew were asking if it were humanly possible to sail a ship faster than Broadwinder was now driving this one. A few argued that Keys was merely showing a burst of speed, though others countered by asking how, if this were true, did it happen that on this the twelfth day out of Melbourne he was crowding the *Eagle*.

Broadwinder frowned before addressing the second mate: "Mr. Winston, we'll relieve her of mains'l."

With her fore getting a better lift above the seas, the *Eagle* sailed along at a steady eighteen knots. It soon became evident that she was not exceeding this speed and Broadwinder once more began looking about for ways to coax an extra knot out of her. He kept at it, and when the sun slid closer to the edge of the western horizon he continued to jockey sail for a little more push.

Jenny stood by, watchful, and wondering if she could hope to persuade him to quit the deck that night. It was when the sun lay half under the sea and the lookout sounded the last observation of the day that she realized the attempt would be futile, for the *Emperor* continued to hold her own.

28

☐ On the following day the *Calcutta Eagle* logged close to four hundred miles. The next day, her fourteenth day out, she did almost that. Shortly before noon of the fifteenth day, Sunday, March 16, she was bowling along under full sail in unusually clement seas and weather at around 56 degrees South, 172 degrees West. As her captain held his course for the sixties, to ensure continued good winds, he was kept company by a worthy rival with the same purpose in mind. Not five miles of water separated the two ships, and Broadwinder was beginning to agree with Cartwright, however much it hurt to do so, that the *Emperor* was the better ideal-weather ship. In light airs he had outdistanced Mayo Keys. In heavy weather he might run away and leave the Barking clipper. There had been quite a lively discussion about it at the captain's table the evening before. Philip had called Cartwright a pessimist, adding in a heated moment, "And that, sir, is just a step above a jinx."

Standing with Bible in hand, one eye dedicated to the Lord, the other to ship, Broadwinder began the customary Sunday service by removing his cap. His glance paused on Jenny at his right and swept hurriedly past Cartwright lest the resentment he continued to nourish influence his brief sermon. It was enough that he had chosen to read parts of Chapter Thirteen of the Gospel according to Saint John, which dealt with Judas. Beyond the text, he intended to recite in words the crew could understand the meaning of betrayal in a sense of disloyalty among persons associated in any given undertaking.

When he had finished and checked the position of the *Emperor* astern, he escorted Jenny below. Once in the privacy of the cabin, she eyed him with amusement overriding accusation and said, "Philip, you were rather obvious, weren't you? George Cartwright has a right to his opinion, the right to speak it, the same as any man."

"Not when he implies that Keys is a better sailor than I am. And by thunder, he'll think twice before doing it again!"

"I agree," Philip," she said seriously. "He apologized to me for disagreeing with you at a time when the strain of the voyage has your nerves on edge."

"Me? Nerves? Hell!" Philip thundered. "I'll have you both know I'm under no strain and—— Say, just whose side are you on, anyhow?"

"Yours. When you're right. But you're wrong. And unless you get more rest, you'll go on showing your raffish side, Philip." She moved across the cabin and breathed a heavy sigh. "That sermon today. I won't say you were sacrilegious but you were certainly childish."

The thud of his fist into a palm jerked her eyes around. Philip was really angry now. So red of face; and—there, he was taking it out on his cap. She watched it sail across the cabin at a terrific speed. The visor would surely be crushed against the bulkhead.

Instead, the cap flew out the porthole.

She had never seen Philip more surprised. His "Well, I'll be damned!" together with his look of incredulity struck her as funny and she fell weakly into a chair as laughter threatened to consume her.

Then Philip threw back his head and roared.

On deck a little later, Jenny observed the change in Philip. He was once more his cheerful self, even with Cartwright, and Jenny could not help thinking there was nothing wrong with a man who could laugh.

Toward one o'clock thin clouds out of the west overtook the sun. Though riding the upper air they promised a change in the weather, an end to sunny days and easy seas. Sharpening his "weather eye," Broadwinder glanced around the horizon, pausing in study of the *Emperor's* cloud-shadowed sails on the edge of the water, before addressing Cartwright with a prediction of true deep-fifties weather ahead.

"We'll see how well Mr. Barking's lad Mayo sails his *Emperor* in the real dirt."

As something out of their recent clash spawned a camaraderie heretofore missing between shipowner and captain, Jenny drew in her gaze from the sky ahead, now clouding over, and smiled approvingly at the pair. Pleased at the good-fellowship warming the hearts of two men close to her, she was thinking that Cartwright reminded her more of the marlin catcher now than at any time since his singular triumph. Philip was once more the "Prince." And yet, so much separated them, stood between them. Even the race they shared had been conceived by one to test the other. It remained that way, she realized. Nothing had changed.

Philip coughed, and she reminded herself to dose him with soothing syrup again. She gazed into the east and wondered how with the wind out of the west the murk had piled up ahead. Visibility would narrow before nightfall, and the cry of the wind, now with a rainy undertone, promised a nasty evening. What of the wind? Regardless, she must check Philip's cough before it got out of hand.

At four bells, two o'clock, on the afternoon watch, the sea began to run and throw up rollers that raced boiling in white lace toward the ship. A rather confused sea, not knowing quite what to expect from the wind. Monday, Jenny thought, would probably dawn bleak and miserable, colder no doubt. Which reminded her that she had not as yet unpacked Tobias's heavy "Horn woolsies." And she should not forget how he suffered from cold feet, the poor dear. For that matter, the whole lot of men she mothered were like boys, all in need of someone to see that blankets in stow were shaken out before nightfall.

Before the bell sounded the half hour the wind freshened out of the southwest. At three it slanted in with a chill in its teeth. The hands were kept busy hauling yards and taking the slack out of lines until almost four in the afternoon. Aft, a noticeable change in the *Emperor's* canvas was taking place. As the barometer began to drop, Broadwinder talked of the long Horn reach under storm canvas. Such talk! It caused Jenny a shudder.

The ship's bell had just clanged the warning of the change of watch, which made it exactly ten minutes to four, when the lookout in the foretop cried the deck with more than ordinary concern.

"Some shape ahead. Like a mountain, it grows bigger."

Broadwinder said something about a Cape Flyaway, a vision of land where there was no land, and thought no more about it. In the gray pall that hazed the sea a man could see almost anything. A few minutes more and the lookout said he was sure he sighted a peak dead ahead.

"And a burnoose on a India elephant's head," cried a sailor. "It's the air up there, Murphy."

Amid the laughter and ribbing, Broadwinder moved forward of the ship and handily into the foretop. He saw it too but, doubting his own eyes, looked away and suddenly back again. It had not vanished. He tried again, looking aft and over the sides for some time before training his gaze ahead once more. It was there, only closer now. He called the deck for the ship's speed and received shortly:

"A good sixteen, sir."

Broadwinder worked downward until sail no longer hid the *Emperor* from view. She remained a good five miles astern. He gazed ahead, wondering at his vision, at what lay in his path. If real, he should act at once. It could be ice, with nine tenths of the berg under water. If he were seeing things, as seamen often did, a run to the south to avoid an imaginary ice hummock could lose him the lead he now held. He had made all the southing he needed for the present, and more of it now could prove as beneficial to Keys as disastrous to him.

But supposing it was ice.

He paused in his descent to study the *Emperor*. She drove ahead, unsuspecting. Keys would see the *Eagle* turn south. All her attention would be on the *Eagle*. Keys would not slow her. An iceberg threw out a long shelf just under the surface. Broadwinder could not deny that he was tempted. The racing fever. He shuddered. It did that to a man, deadened all else but the desire to win.

He clung to the futtock shrouds as beads of perspiration oozed from his pores. He was afraid of ice, but more of himself, and fear caused an awful emptiness in the pit of his stomach. The deck was far below; the man he had been seemed as distant: the Broadwinder who exemplified fairness and good sportsmanship.

On deck again, his face chalky white and clammy with sweat, he withstood Jenny's inquiring glances and turned to Mr. Fortune. "I saw it too. A Cape Flyaway or ice. Will you take a look?"

The chief mate saw it and Jenny and Cartwright saw it. The law of the sea rang in warning: "Give it a wide berth, sailor!" Prudence won over racing instincts, and the order to run her off was spoken. It was all hands then, a clatter of gear and men jumping to orders, a ship trembling from stem to stern. Expert hands soon had her under control and gathering headway to the south.

All the while the *Emperor* came on, gaining fast until she closed the distance between ships to less than one mile. On the *Eagle*'s decks, a dismal silence told of hard-won miles lost. Fifteen long days of grim fighting every foot of the way had gone for nothing, all in the time it took the captain to order the helm down.

Aboard the *Emperor*, the sight of the sail-laden *Eagle*'s run into the wind was cause for no end of astonishment and wonder. Mayo Keys alerted his brain with a maze of questions. Had Broadwinder lost his mind, or was this some trick to throw off pursuit? The latter thought dominating him, he watched the *Eagle* without once searching the hazy seas ahead for any danger. Nor did any member of his crew. Keys was then asking what Broadwinder hoped to gain. Something, surely, for why else would he give up his lead? He was gambling four miles so he was evidently hoping for forty in return. As the *Emperor* raced on, eating up the distance between the ships, the *Eagle* grew larger. Now she was gathering herself for a southward dash.

A glint of discovery played across Mayo Keys's eyes. "A lure," he said to himself. "The foxy Prince thinks I'll follow and lose miles in the exchange of tacks for southing."

As he studied the *Eagle*, she responded admirably, her sails full and her bows dipping and rising as she split the seas. He saw her ensign and pennant flutter down almost in unison, as though she wished to speak the *Emperor*. A second later the thunder from her rocket gun rolled across the sea, a sure sign she wished to attract his attention. Then she hoisted her flag. A ball followed and snaking up the monkey gaff after it was, no mistaking it, a pennant. The telescope fairly leaped to Keys's eye and he read in the signal:

You are running into danger.

Captain Keys frowned. Ball over pennant was no joking matter but a simple distant signal which not even Broadwinder would dare to employ for an advantage. Mayo Keys came alive then. He cried to the lookout in the foretop, dashing for the main deck as he did so. When, seconds later, the signal was verified as a timely warning, Keys called for a dip of his flag, an answer that he understood, before shouting at the top of his voice:

"Run her off! Hard down the hellum!"

He paused to gaze at the rival vessel at a time when his own ship demanded his all, a moment in which his grim face softened and a message from the heart rose up into his throat:

"Thank you, Broadwinder."

Seconds later, the *Eagle*'s captain dipped his colors and re-hoisted in a signal of farewell.

29

□ On the twentieth day out the elements gave Broadwinder a taste of the weather he had asked for. Dawn broke colorless, promising another wet day like the last four. The sun had disappeared a thousand miles back, and the whole universe of sea had since been coated in drab gray. But today the crashing of seas against ship and on decks thundered in his ears, and the barometer was beginning to drop. The topgallants flying up there would soon join the royals in stow, for there was no doubt in the mind of any experienced sailor aboard that topsails weather lay ahead.

Approximately five miles behind the *Calcutta Eagle*, like the sunsets one knew were there but never saw in this weather, the *Emperor* scudded before the wind under topsails, one topgallant, mizzen poles bare.

Both Broadwinder and Keys knew what to expect. They were aware that boisterous seas lay ahead, that with speed the order of the day, daring, prudence and skill were, like the legs of a tripod, of equal importance. Boldness without restraint could prove as disastrous as clumsiness coupled with fear. Even so, this was a race. The "sailingest" man would reach Cape Horn first, and probably Boston in the lead. Thus, with foresight on a par, the captains had prepared for the worst. They rove preventer braces, sweated up the gear, getting the last inch of stretch out of sails. Rolling tackles were clapped on the heavier yards, relieving tackles were hooked and extra tarpaulins were battened down.

They were ready for big seas and hard winds; as ready as experience and knowledge could make them. They were not kept waiting long, for the day that dawned with a threat ended with constantly increasing winds and mounting seas. As the glass continued to drop, the elements hurled dark squalls of rain and sleet at both ships, swept up seas that gathered momentum, size, and fury before striking bludgeon blows at the sterns. In the absence of wheelhouses, each captain lashed two men to the standard of the wheel. A helmsman's hell began. His duty was clear, his responsibility great. He had a course to steer and his eyes were on the lubber's line as great waves crashed behind and on each side of him. The ship could be thrown to port or starboard, to yaw and veer off her course. The slightest inattention could result in the ship's breaching to. The tons of cold water smashing on board, often atop him, were to be expected and accepted as a part of his job.

All that heavy night Broadwinder remained on duty. He stood swaying with the roll of deck from one foot to the other. In leather sea boots and red wool cap, oilskins over greatcoat, he cut a huge figure under the pale yellow light of deck as he surveyed ship, sail, the cant of his yards, again and again, felt of the weather and helm, ordered the wash ports lashed open, so seas could run freely out the scuppers, and, as every man aboard knew, debated the wisdom of further gambling his topgallants with the wind gods.

The wind screamed louder, almost in gale fury, beating at the rigging and straining canvas, crying threat to the brave topgallant sails that stood like gestures of defiance as Broadwinder refused to strike them. Midnight, and the storm growing into a real monster, and the men of the below watch waiting, waiting for the top-gallant sails to split, dreading the fight to get aloft, wondering at the Old Man's willingness to blow sails he might use tomorrow. One o'clock in the black night —the press of her upper canvas slowing her down to sixteen knots by pressing the bows deeper into higher seas, and the below watch just huddling in their blankets answering to the second's yell of: "Aloft! Secure to'gannels'ls!" The struggle to climb in the teeth of the wind now singing like a demon in the slanting rigging, the pelting of hail against heads and faces as they gained the yards and edged blindly out on the footropes. Seven men to a yard, cold fingers on the iron jack-stay grasping frantically now on the sea gaskets, passing them, catching turns, clawing, smothering the bulk of canvas, praying a gasket would not part. Then triumph. There was no reward, just weariness and cold as they worked into the slings for a climb down, these things and a dull awareness that the master had to their knowledge held to crazy sails longer than any other man before compromising with the wind.

On deck, with hot coffee warming stomachs and spirits, they agreed that the captain was "one more hell of a sailing man."

But these men were not through. Drenched to the skin, it seemed they had no sooner steamed half dry around the forecastle stove and crawled into their bunks than the storm drove in stronger. Out of the unseen black night ragged lightning pronged the seas close to, and hail of size commenced a barrage that threatened to brain a man and perforate sails. On the wind, now howling a true gale, seas of greater height and fury threw giant graybeards against the ship and on decks in a thunder to compete with the heavens after each stab of lightning. The life lines shaped a course on deck, and no man was safe without a hand on the running ropes, for seas crashed inboard armpit high, rushing, tossing, foaming across decks, decks scending to port and back, spilling one sea to make room for another.

In all this, the mate made himself heard. The order was hell itself: "Secure upper tops'ls!"

At four o'clock in the morning, eight bells, the *Calcutta Eagle* ran, or rather, she was tossed like a chip in the rapids, under storm canvas. She shipped less water now and with the lift of her bows drove before seas and winds at a tremendous clip.

As dawn stole wearily up out of the night, the gale showed no sign of blowing itself out, nor did the barometer give any indication of rising as seas continued to pound hard at the ship. At times the *Eagle* swung her stern wildly. She yawed and sent fingers of fear up Broadwinder's spine. Afraid of storms and gales, he felt the tension building inside him, layer atop layer, it seemed, stringing his nerves tighter, like fiddle strings already too taut. The pinpoints of his eyes and the set of his mouth revealed to Jenny more than he knew. Things suspected but never spoken were examined side by side with his determination to drive on, and she could not bring herself to regard him as anything short of brave; for one who kept on fighting when terribly afraid was braver than the man who knew no fear.

Yet even the valiant and strong can endure just so much. Mortal or ship, there is a limit. Toward midafternoon of the twenty-first day of the race, a rain-whipped, hail-lashed Broadwinder stared out of lusterless eyes at men waist-deep in deck seas and on up to canvas and lines taking a severe beating from the storm. The ship plunged and rolled, veering dangerously off as four men at the wheel fought to keep her from running up into the wind. A sudden shift in the wind would spell her doom. The crazy, killing pace could not last, he told himself.

On the other hand, he had a fair wind. Which, then, should prevail, the combination of sickly fear and prudence or the touch-and-go gain of time and miles? Which? He was afraid to drive on, and he fought back at his fears, and in the fight forgot wisdom, telling himself that once he gave in to fear, he was finished.

The grim face of Mr. Fortune turned often on the captain, eyes imploring him to heave her to. Then he was shouting in the wind, pleading with his captain to bring her head into the wind where she would lie safely with weather helm. His voice was lost in the wind, as was the reply. But Broadwinder's determination to carry on was made clear by the sweep of an arm forward.

The fight for longitude continued hour after hour. The ferocity of the storm increased until the air between poop and crossjack yard was thick with flying spray driven horizontally over the stern. Dusk crept in with the gale mounting steadily in force, with every man aboard beaten into that state of apathy wherein the body often responds before the mind. Duty at the helm was reduced to one hour, for a man could stand little more.

And still Broadwinder drove her on. On into peril, it seemed. He stared blankly at things about him, seeming oblivious to danger as the tiredness of body dulled the mind to everything about him. He saw the crowds of distant Boston greeting Broadwinder the winner and their cheers rang in his ears. The applause continued and slowly he became aware that it was not applause but instead the scream of rigging and thunder of seas on a full-gale wind.

It startled him. He was not in command of his senses, of his ship. Fatigued, he could not cope with real danger if it arose. A great fear such as he had never known sickened him. His eyes spread wide and he stared with a vacuity in his gaze. He was in dire peril and he knew it. He had gone too far, and in doing so had lost his nerve. He opened his mouth to cry, "Cut sheets and halyards!" thought better of it and was shaping a "Let go sheets and halyards!" to cover his feeling of panic when great seas leaped aboard from both sides and swept the deck below him. Head high! The hands could do nothing but cling to the safety ropes. Then another great shock of water climbed aboard, this time over the starboard bow.

Dusk was falling when Jenny ventured on deck in a state of alarm. She clung desperately to a spanker vang near the companionway, trying to catch her breath in the terrible blow. Then a towering wave crashed over the stern and slammed her to deck, almost smothering her. When the water sloshed out the scuppers, she saw that she had been torn from the vang and swept to the rail. Her oilskins hung in shreds. Wet through and through, she fought the wind for long minutes before covering the few feet separating her from the spanker sheet. She clung to it with all her strength and frantically surveyed ship, sail, and weather. If it had sounded terrible below it was because it was worse up here. The wind sang in the rigging in high and low notes, depending on her roll to weather and alee. But the demonic screech was too ominous. It seemed, like the terrible seas, to be crying:

Too much sail, too much storm, too much risk; and— probably too late to do anything about it.

She saw Philip, Cartwright, and Mr. Fortune in a huddle, all with oilskins and clothing whipping like ribbons. They clung to the life line stretching from mizzenmast to after shrouds; rather, the force of the wind flattened them against it. Mr. Fortune pointed up at the topsail and Cartwright was waving a finger in Philip's face.

Then a sea sent Jenny tumbling forward. She was swept up off the deck and flung hard against the port after shrouds, where she hung on for dear life, both hands in the ratlines sloping upward over her head. There the ship pitched her forward and back, and the gale pushed her off her feet at times even as the seas swept her up and dropped her again. Any chance to return to the safety of below decks had gone the moment she stepped on the poop.

Now towering seas were arching high from windward and

the gale was blowing the crests off them and hurling them at the ship ahead of hard blows to come.

Jenny had no sooner begun a prayer when a great wave that made all others seem like mere ripples broke over the starboard side and ran the ship's length forward. The *Eagle* went under from poop to bows, tons of water holding her head down as the mighty wind drove on into the sails. Something had to give. Something did. The main topsail blew. As it banged like a cannon in the gale, another great sea tore in from over the portside. Water, foam-flecked and streaked, a veritable rapids, streamed across the decks, burying even the forecastle. The ship was under, forward, sail driving, ocean holding her down. But her stern was up, and up it caught the terrible oncoming waves. All balance was gone. Caught thus, she had to rise up out of it or her stern would swing around. The helmsmen could not stop the turn, for her rudder seemed lifted above the water.

Jenny knew that any order to cut sheets would be like spitting into the gale. It was impossible now. The men were underwater down there, those who found something to stop them from being swept overboard, if any.

"Oh, God!" Jenny cried, holding on. Again she appealed to heaven, for she knew that only God could save them now. Even as she prayed, she stared at Philip, who stood there as though stunned, watching, waiting for the ship to rise. But she could not rise, for the screaming gale threw more giant waves at her, pinning her down from bow to abaft the main-mast.

While the ship struggled there, her bow pushed deeper under by the overpress of sail, the boiling seas climbed aboard from forward and astern. They ran her length, sloshed at the break of the poop, receded as if to allow those from aft to flow like a waterfall off her poop. Then she seemed to go under, all of her.

As the *Calcutta Eagle* strove upward, with only her stern atop the seas, a tremendous wall of water struck at her quarter. It was a mighty blow. It lifted the stern high up out of the water and flung it like a chip to starboard. The press aft sent her charging ahead until it drove her fore deeper under. The helm was of no use then. Canting off, staggering, her wheel spinning, masts heeling far over, she swung her broadside to the seas, her masts on over until half her hull lay up to weather—until she lay on her beam ends.

She had broached to!

She wallowed in the trough at the mercy of the seas. Sail went, thundering in the wind, threatening to dismast her. Clinging to the shrouds, water up to her neck, knowing that to let go would mean her death, Jenny fought for breath and stared up at Cartwright, and Mr. Fortune. Then Philip.

Philip simply stared out of big, unseeing eyes, with no more feel of ship or anything about him than a sleepwalker. She cried out to him. He could not hear her. She cried again.

Cartwright in those long seconds of peril when life seemed very cheap recalled his own estimate of Captain Broadwinder months in the past: *A man who had so long walked arm in arm with luck that his ability to cope with real trouble seemed a virtue untested.*

Then the ship came up in a violent roll that threw her masts over on the other side. The trough held her down, tossed her like a matchstick. She lay helplessly on her side, the weight of her masts threatening to turn her bottom up. With after shrouds under and seas sweeping in, on and over the almost perpendicular deck, Jenny stood high now and the mate, Cartwright, and Philip had somehow managed to lash themselves to line and rail at the break of the poop where they clung to knurled posts.

The *Eagle* tried to right herself, tried desperately. Up a little, then down. No helm, and she seemed to cry for the aid of the helm to get her off.

When the ship settled back for another valiant effort to lift off her beam ends Jenny filled her lungs to bursting. Then in that lull just before the masts began the upward push, she screamed to the top of her voice:

"Helm aweather! Now!"

The helmsmen heard. They put their weight to the wheel. The *Eagle* shuddered, seeming to give her all in an effort to rise. The masts lifted a little, hung there a moment between water and sky, between safety and doom. Then she responded to the helm. Up she came out of the trough, rails awash, masts snapping upright. How she wallowed, reeled, and whipped! Jenny was thinking she would go over, broach to again, perhaps to stay, when she saw Philip come alive and risk his life in a struggle against wind and seas to the wheel. Weak all over, she dropped her head and closed her eyes in a brief prayer of thanks when Philip reached the standard of the wheel safely.

Later, when the ship's head was brought into the wind and she lay easy to the weather riding out the gale, Cartwright watched Jenny leading Philip below. In the saloon for a stiff whisky minutes before, Ephraim Fortune had told Cartwright he had never in all his years at sea witnessed a smarter job of bringing a ship's head to such weather than Broadwinder's performance on this night.

Cartwright thought of the mate's remark now. Staring into the wild night, he could only wonder. In the captain's favor was his heavy burden. But in favor of Broadwinder, ship, and all aboard was his wife.

Out of the storm new estimates were born.

30

☐ All through the howling night the *Eagle* lay like a wounded bird on the surface of the sea, with her bows to the fury of the storm. Although she held herself proudly erect, the foremast was sprung at the hounds and her top was a tangle of lines. But her hatches stood. "Thank the Lord!" The cry from Chips cheered the dull minds of all when toward daybreak he tested coamings and plumbed the bilge. There was no water in the holds.

There was considerable damage, however, and Cartwright's critical eye dwelled on effect with cause in mind. The wreckage here was in his opinion a grim monument to one man's imprudence.

The inventory of damage revealed the best foresail and topsail blown into ragged sheets, three animals and all the chickens at the forecastlehead either drowned or washed overboard, flooded galley, forty feet of rail lost, half the effects of the hands swept out of the forecastle, one boat smashed, and all charts and sailing books damaged. Atop these things, two sailors suffered broken arms, one lay with ribs broken, and three more were temporarily disabled by painful cuts and bruises. As to the latter, Sails summed it up with, "The lot of ye'll do well to show damn happy to be alive."

It did not matter that every person aboard was in rags, even Jenny and the dignified shipowner, thankfulness was due and made evident by all. Jenny's arms were bruised and in the violent motions of the ship in trouble they were nearly jerked out of their sockets. What a haggard, torn, and water-soaked lot they were! But a gladness was upon them—all but the captain.

Even as Jenny and Mr. Winston worked furiously to bandage cuts and set bones in the wreck of the forecastle, and George Cartwright estimated the damage to ship in terms of dollars and cents, Captain Broadwinder eyed the logbook as he had done for some time, gulped his fourth whisky, and shuddered all over. His hand still trembled as he wrote the entry of the day:

Gale winds and terrible seas. Some damage. Am hove tc.

That was the extent of it. Even as he sat there, overturned chairs, his books, and Jenny's sewing basket and chests lay in confusion on the sodden carpets. Salt caked the varnished bulkheads and the door was sprung. These things didn't matter. The routine of log entry was behind him.

Glad it was done with, he snapped the book shut and took a step to the door. He was needed on deck, he realized, despite the fact that his every muscle and bone ached and his mind was still clouded by fatigue. He sat down and reached for the bottle, wondering as he poured if he had lost any men. How much damage had the storm inflicted? He kept on rubbing his forehead with thumb and forefinger in an endeavor to relieve the tightness inside him. It would not go away. Probably never would after the ordeal of broaching to.

He got to his feet to go on deck. Men, yards, spars, sails blown—these things were his responsibility. The light swung in the gimbals, animating the shadow of his hand on the bottle. The sea ran down the ship's sides in a constant roar. There was a tiredness in even sight and sound. If he could only close his eyes and sleep. If only Jenny were here. He slumped into the chair again and braced himself with elbows on table.

A faint ray of cheer stole into his brain and he forced himself up, as if by a reassuring laugh that formed in his throat. "Easy," he said. "Easy as you go, Broadwinder. It happens to every captain. You came out luckier than most. The *Fawn*, remember?"

He remembered. Captain O'Lee. The woman and child. Norwich. He remembered more, the very thing he had pushed back into a cell of his memory since danger made itself a partner on the quarter-deck. He had fought to keep it penned outside the realm of his thoughts. But it was loose now and running berserk, shouting into his mind's ear that immutable prophecy out of the past:

Once a master loses his nerve he is through; even if he survives he is finished.

It threw unwelcome pictures before his eyes, and he was seeing again heavy-jowled Captain Contestable on the *Osprey*'s deck in that awful storm. The ship was about to capsize and the panic-stricken captain could neither move to the helm nor shout any order to save her. A miracle of the sea had saved the *Osprey*. Nothing had saved the grand old captain from the knowledge that he had ridden out his ticket.

Broadwinder's fist struck the table hard. The sound and feeling startled him. Then he was saying hoarsely: "No! Not me!"

He knew he had been found wanting in time of peril. Jenny had voiced the order that should have been his. She had saved the ship, not he. His future then was tied closely to this event. Either he would emerge from it a Contestable or the man he wished to be; rather, the man he had thought he was.

His next clear realization was that of stumbling out of the cabin. He paused at the companionway, wondering if he could climb it to deck, knowing that each step would require a tragic effort of will. He seemed suddenly aware that the human body had certain definite limits. Beyond that one's perceptions were blunted. That had been his trouble. Like discovery, he took hope in a fact—his failure to rally on deck had been due to the dreamlike state of mind brought about by exhaustion.

"Aye!" he mumbled. "Brought it on myself. A little sleep and I'll be as good as ever."

But first he would look after his ship. Then he would sleep, sleep halfway to Cape Horn, regardless of Mayo Keys and his *Emperor*. He took a step and another, groping upward, clinging to the handrail. Somehow he reached deck and stood a minute with both hands on the spanker sheet. Duty impelled him forward as fatigue held him rooted there, as his mind alternately raced and slowed. A fit of coughing racked his body.

He shook his head savagely and walked toward Mr. Fortune.

That was the last he remembered until he opened his eyes as night was closing in. Jenny sat nearby reading. She started when he leaped out of bed and rushed to a port, and eyed him as he gazed at the sea for some time before saying:

"Still hove to." Whirling, he said, "Why?" She did not answer. "Why?" he demanded.

"Repairs, Philip," she replied in a quiet voice.

"The devil! Seems every time I so much as shut an eye we let Mayo Keys gain on us. And just why wasn't I shaken out for the forenoon watch?"

"Because I wouldn't allow it."

"You? Just who is captain of this ship?"

"You. But I happen to know just how much a man can take. You don't, Philip." She closed the book, placed it on a shelf and met his sharp glance. "And just what happened when you sailed under Captain Contestable of the *Osprey*?"

His look of surprise gradually faded into one of bewilderment. "Why do you ask, Jenny?"

"Because you talked to him in your sleep. Even before Sails and the bosun placed you in bed you kept saying, 'All's well, sir. I'll take the *Osprey* in.' "

Broadwinder moved to a chair and sat down. "Sails and the bosun? They put me in bed?"

"You made the rounds of deck, Philip—walking in your sleep. You checked the damage and gave the right orders. You put Sails and a crew to work cutting dry bedding for the hands, had the fo'c's'le stove replaced and the galley made shipshape, a fire going and coffee brewing. It was just after you'd ordered rum for the crew—of the *Osprey*—that you sank to the main deck."

Broadwinder eyed her dubiously a minute, got up and began to dress. He paused often to glance at her, to open his mouth to speak, then to frown in silence. When she said, "You must have thought a great deal of Captain Contestable," he replied, "I did," and proceeded to look more curious than ever.

"What happened between you, Philip?"

"You ask too many questions. Now where the devil is my cap?"

Jenny reached for her sewing basket.

"Probably at Cape Horn by now." As he searched for another cap, she said, "Every man aboard has worked like mad to present you with a repaired ship, Philip. So don't fail to notice it."

"How could I fail to see it, Jenny?" he replied irritably. Coming up with a sea cap, he said, "If only I hadn't lost my only good fores'l."

"And every block and buntline on the fore. Its whipping broke the weather fore ratlines. But everything is ready for you. The sprung spars are fished and the foremast is all wedged and chain-lashed."

He moved to the door, grumbling.

"Philip." She waited for him to turn about. "The *Emperor* hove in sight at around three this afternoon."

"Yes?" He stared intently.

"She sailed on."

Broadwinder slowly lowered his gaze to the floor. After a minute he retraced his steps and sat down heavily at the table. The silence lengthened. He did not get up as Jenny expected him to do. He did not burst out angrily at her for not waking him earlier. In fact, Philip seemed to Jenny a contradiction of himself.

Out of concern, she went to him and placed an arm about his shoulder. He did not look up or move. "Philip," she ventured placatingly, "that does not mean you can't catch the *Emperor.*"

He continued to sit there. The ship's bell sounded the hour and the steward announced dinner. He did not stir. Jenny decided to leave him with his somber thoughts and dressed for deck. She had no sooner left him than an idea formed in her mind, one which she thought might put an end to his brooding. Approaching Mr. Fortune, she said:

"Captain Broadwinder sends his compliments, sir. He asked that you put the ship on her course under upper tops'ls."

The *Eagle* had scarcely come around and gathered headway when Broadwinder came on deck and studied the canvas set. The wind had dropped, though the high seas that followed a storm still ran. But Jenny, standing a little apart from husband and mate, knew it was topgallant-sail weather to Philip and waited for him to order them loosed.

He did no such thing, however, and at midnight the ship drove along under upper topsails.

Morning broke almost clear, the wind west-southwest and

less vicious seas on; position by observation at noon of the twenty-third day out 110.40 degrees West, 55.30 degrees South; the *Emperor* standing on the edge of the eastern horizon. By nightfall the rival ship lay all but under, her gain visible. Concern was voiced on the working decks first by Sails who scratched his head and declared that a look up at "tops'ls in to'gannels'ls" weather all day had caused him to look often at the quarter-deck to see if the Old Man or Tobias was running the ship. "It ain't like the cap'n."

The steward said to the cook, "It's a not like the cap'n," and Mr. Winston said the same to the chief mate, even as George Cartwright over cards looked at Jenny and said, "It isn't like Philip Broadwinder." Shortly after eight that evening, Jenny looked up from her plate and said, "It isn't like you, Philip."

The next day the *Eagle* loafed along under almost the same trim of sail. The *Emperor* lay under the horizon out of sight. The lack of driving sail to match the elements provoked silent examination of the master by every sailor aboard. He had lost his good humor. "And his tongue," O'Hara said. "I was workin' at the skylight this mornin' when the ship runnin' nor'west passed us, and heard Mrs. Broadwinder say to the cap'n, 'You forgot to dip your colors.' And he says not a word. Nor does he dip."

That afternoon Cartwright leaned against the rail, pondering the change in his captain. Until recently Broadwinder had seemed a depository for all the ingredients that constituted a great sailing man. Until the race began, Cartwright reflected. Even at the beginning of the contest he had shown flashes of brilliance. Then fatigue began to build up inside him. It had finally caught up with him. Probing deeper than the physical, Cartwright realized that exhaustion could play havoc with the delicately balanced emotional side of a man. In Philip's case, however, he was of the opinion that emotional strain had both preceded and provoked fatigue.

Turning his coat collar up against the cold wind, Cartwright argued against all he did not wish to believe, that the ordeal of risk and competitive sailing had been too much for Philip; that Philip's inability to relax long enough to sleep proved he had been thrown off balance by the first real test of his colorful career.

And now, watching Broadwinder, a man withdrawn, one so accustomed to leading the way that he seemed unable to reconcile his present position as runner-up, Cartwright was wondering if his popular captain had not already justified the apprehension he had felt back in Boston.

Within the hour Jenny appeared on deck and conversed with Broadwinder in low tones. This was not the first time of late that Jenny had studied the sail set and husband with concern she could not hide. Nor was it Philip's first show of annoyance at whatever she was saying. Cartwright had heard enough to verify all he suspected. Even now Jenny's voice reached him:

"But, Philip! This is sixteen-knot weather!" The rest went unheard, except her last remark: "Philip, you're not an off-and-on sailor."

Something broke inside Broadwinder then. It had the look of anger born of frustration when his tight mouth stretched wide and the muscles of his jaw knotted and rippled. "Very well," he said sharply. Then he gave vent to his feeling with a mighty roar:

"Break out to'gannels'ls and royals on the fore and main!"

With the cry, he felt a small victory. Only he knew of the battle that had raged inside him, a struggle against fear, of being finished as a sailing man. With Jenny's help, he had at last snapped out of indecision. But he knew that victory had not been won. The future and what he did in the days ahead would decide that.

There was another roar left in Philip Broadwinder. He loosed it then: "And run out the studding booms! Lively! Lively!"

31

☐ No person aboard would ever forget the change that came over the captain on that twenty-fourth day of the race. Nor would any one of them ever erase from memory the events that followed the order Jenny nagged out of him.

Throughout the night Broadwinder flew all the canvas the *Eagle* would carry, and he arrived at the maximum by blowing out of the boltropes that overplus of sail. With morning

breaking pink and lavender over the restless ocean, he
pushed on to meet another day of ideal driving weather. He
stood his four hours on, and he took his four hours off only
after reminding Mr. Fortune that no sail should be taken in
without his express order. His succinct log entries told the
story:

MAR. 26, 25TH DAY OF RACE: *371 miles today. Cape Horn
not far off.*

MAR. 27, 26TH DAY: *Running steady 16. Main royal lost.
Sail sighted ahead.*

MAR. 28, 27TH DAY OUT: *Some sea on, wind shifting southerly and cold, snow squalls, glass dropping.*

MAR. 29, 28TH DAY: *Running 14 under topgallants. Rough
seas. Sail ahead closer now. Heavy hail.*

Broadwinder's next entry read: *Heavy gale. Hove to under
Chile coast.*

When Broadwinder wisely chose to lie to the weather under storm rags, George Cartwright's recent judgment of his
captain seemed rather severe. He waited, thinking that, with
the *Emperor* riding out the storm also in full view ahead, it
was reasonable to believe any rashness on the captain's part
was sure to break into the open. Certainly the temptation to
seize the lead was felt by everyone. Broadwinder put prudence over desire, however, and as a result Cartwright began to consider his commander in new light, a man greatly
matured by the near tragedy.

That evening he was further inclined to favor this revision
of his opinion when Broadwinder said at dinner, "I would
have bet my all that we would round Cape Horn in less than
a month."

"You may do it yet," Jenny replied.

"That's not what the lookout told me a few minutes ago."
Meeting the curious glances of shipowner and wife, he said,
"Ice drifts ahead."

Jenny studied her husband closely. Although the racing
man had finally emerged out of the most perilous situation
ever to face him at sea, the ebullient Philip, the Prince, had
not. It worried her more than she cared to admit and, wishing
now to steer him out of a state of chronic depression, she said
cheerily:

"Maybe the ice will go away."

Broadwinder could not quite conceal the gleam of intensity suddenly coming into his eyes, for he was looking about for a chance to redeem himself in his own mind. Jenny thought it bespoke hope; Cartwright made no guess and thought no more of it until morning of the next day.

The day opened slowly with dove-gray clouds racing atop the charging seas. The wind blew a near gale and by the middle of the forenoon watch the sky lifted to reveal the *Emperor* lying with head to wind. Beyond her and stretching on into horizon numerous chunks of white dotted the sea; ice in various sizes from small bergs to islands no wider than a deck, but all dangers a running ship must avoid. It was less what one saw and more the unseen that sent chills up a spine. As the sailmaker was saying, "Takes a hell of a lot of it to float the handful that shows." But it was the next sound aboard that electrified all on decks.

"All hands!" Broadwinder's shout reached forward on the wind. It was followed by orders to bring the ship around stern to weather and break out running sail.

While hands rushed aloft with talk about "the Old Man threadin' a needle he ought to leave be," Cartwright stood out minutes of dismay before deciding to speak his mind. His "My God, Captain, you're not actually thinking of going through that ice!" evoked no reply whatever. When Jenny appeared on deck minutes later Cartwright acquainted her with the situation, saying, "Philip is all risk and no reason!"

Jenny's brows came up and her gaze swept to Philip and on to the lifting and falling ice. "He's also the captain," she said calmly.

Soon the ship came around. Under foresail, "three topsails on a sou'west gale," fore-and-afters down, the *Eagle* took to seas paralleling her course. She ran at a fast clip, sometimes for a great distance in one long streaked trough. The water had the appearance of a plowed field, great furrows straight but changing, tops a marbled-green flecked with frenzied white. She ran on, heeling, dipping, rising, on toward hummocks of solid white, any one of which could grind through her hull and send her to a watery grave.

Sea room is a sailor's must. Lack of it, the land close to, a rock awash, breakers, all are a sailor's living hell. On this day breakers ringed the ice drifts, often far out, though the seas were too lively to give fair warning. In the captain's favor, the ice appeared to be widely separated and driven on a strong sea that did not oppose his own course. In a measure, he ran a calculated risk. Once into it, he intended to pace the drift under shortened sail until it opened wide, then add sail until the time came to snug down again. However, an eye could not penetrate his mind, and had it been possible, the risk would have been too great.

Mayo Keys saw only the rival ship moving up to him. Thinking Broadwinder intended sitting it out once they were matched evenly again, he watched the *Eagle* stand by a mile off his starboard beam and move on with no indication of taking in sail. Odd, he thought. A half hour later he began to wonder. Yet he could not believe even Broadwinder foolish enough to attempt a threading of ice. Not with the wind shifting gradually but surely to southerly and more ice lifting over the southwestern horizon. No, Broadwinder was up to something other than that; he had to be, for no sane man would risk trapping himself between ice out of the south and land to the north. Yet there was little else to believe when the *Eagle* ran on until she was swallowed up in the haze of distance.

"What do you make of it, sir?" the chief mate asked.

"A fool," came the laconic reply a second ahead of an order to take the *Emperor* out of the ice track.

Broadwinder figured the velocity of running seas against ice drift and roughly estimated the force of collision at various speeds. None of the answers invited cheer. Wanting the ship's head up, he double-reefed the foresail, took in down to upper main topsail. He still moved at a fast pace. Sailors were placed at the bows in the chains with hand leads for sounding and Broadwinder took the fore lookout's position after posting men close enough to relay orders against the wind to the helmsman and mates with quick dispatch.

The first ice sped by a half mile off. Though not an acre lay above the surface, it was given a wide berth. More ragged white shapes came on, some pointing skyward like needles, others humpbacked and awkward in appearance, some small, some large. How close; how much running room between them? These were the questions in every mind. How much ice spread out underneath the water? Multiply the visible by ten and double it for safety. Helm up! Helm down! As orders issued from Broadwinder's throat they were swiftly echoed to deck and helm.

A big one lay ahead of the ship now, a small iceberg.

Jenny stood at the port bow. Unable to take her eyes off the large hill of ice scarcely more than a mile away, she watched it grow larger, whiter and longer by the moment. Charging seas dashed against it a clear green and broke mightily in clouds of blue spray. Directly to the north of the small berg a low, whaleback of solid ice blocked passage while to the south of it the running ocean was dotted with countless smaller blocks of white. The floe thickened. Passageway seemed impossible. If this were true, it left Philip a single choice, a run to the north. And unless he accepted that choice soon, he would be unable to effect a turn of the ship. She waited for the order.

It did not come. The *Eagle* slid on. Jenny bit her lip and showed other signs of uneasiness.

Ahead, the confused ice field out of the south was driven on by strong seas until great chunks of ice ground against one another, creating a menacing floeberg. There could be no opening there, Jenny thought. She looked up at Philip high in the fore, lowered her uneasy glance to Cartwright, and suppressed a shudder that seemed long overdue.

Broadwinder broke his silence by calling for a cast of the lead. Finding good fathoms, he ordered headway reduced and the ship's head canted a little to the south. The leadsmen were ordered to cast again and again and, with speed lessened, the *Eagle* continued her wary approach, sounding as she went.

It seemed that the ship herself, a wise old lady of the stream, trembled under the risk. The crew to a man watched and waited with building tension in their somber faces. This thing the captain was doing surpassed unorthodox sailing, exceeded bravery, and fell short of heroism; it was recklessness of the worst kind. Opposing this indictment was their confidence in a captain whose skill and practical seamanship over the years could not be questioned. Thus two admitted facts collided in their minds and left them suspended in a state of strange bewilderment.

All the while, the man who now feared ice as he feared storms studied the ice and seas through telescope from the lookout's perch in the fore. If he felt a burning desire to put ten hours and one hundred miles between him and Mayo Keys, he also realized that he could not fulfill his purpose by wrecking the ship. On the edge of the field of ice entering his path, he could do as Keys had demonstrated, retreat north in all safety. And he intended doing just that and very soon if the one hope he had fed by observation and nursed for verification proved false.

That hope for ample running room between the small berg and the floeberg was less an idle dream and more a possibility born of study of the effect of current on surface ice as against a solid mass. Within thirty minutes he had seen a passage open up from next to nothing into an estimated mile. He wanted over two miles. Once through, the biggest hazard would be behind him if—if he could clear the field before nightfall. To run after Keys would at best entail a loss of the day at hand and night to follow. To go ahead, west—on toward Cape Horn, while Keys sailed up into the Pacific on the wrong side of the continent—and discover an error in his judgment would be to find himself trapped between crushing ice and the rocks of the bottommost Chile coast.

Chill fingers ran his spine. He did not actually know what lay ahead. The very fact that the ice had a day's start on him proved it. The sensations of dread slowly departed as he watched the passage widen. Then he forgot entirely traps of rock and ice and thought of the miles he could put between him and Mayo Keys.

The berg grew larger. The lead continued to splash. Deep water. Good fathoms. The *Eagle* crept on toward it, standing three quarters of a mile off, then a half mile. "No bottom!" the portside leadsman cried.

"Keep the lead going."

Though the sea ran deep, every eye was fixed on the man who swung the lead. Every eye but the captain's. And his, sharp with suspense and freighted with trepidation, darted from berg to floe and back again. Now was the time to break out sail and tear through. The berg held him. It would continue to hold him until he could open the passage around it. Anxious now, he peered at the field of ice at his right, saw it bearing closer on his starboard side; a mere mile off.

The devil and the deep! He was fast running out of room. Trembling, he cried the deck to cant the ship's head two points to starboard, toward the running ice drift. By his next order, he seemed intent on converging with it in a hurry, for he called for driving sail on her yards. "Lively! Lively!"

Before the *Eagle* got a trim to supplement her helm, the peril had changed from berg at left ahead to floe at right.

Then she began to gather speed. This alone was enough to cause a scalp to tingle, though the captain's cry of "Stand by sheets and halyards," to let them go in order to spill all wind out of sails in an emergency, seemed to lend reality to one's fears.

Jenny watched great blocks of ice, white, flat, ragged and broken like the meat of a coconut, charging toward the starboard bow. Up in the loft the cry sounded to make ready for a shifting of the helm by trimming yards fast for a canting of her head to port. The ice was all too close now, and Jenny closed her eyes to shut out the sight.

Broadwinder had himself a crew who could handle smart and lively. The yards were hauled, sails tautened, sheets and halyards secured at the pins, and now the helm was responding. The *Eagle* swung to parallel the ice now no more than five ship lengths off. And in doing so, she jockeyed herself out of the clutches of another hazard. First the berg, next the drift, the former demanding a wide berth, the latter now flanking the ship.

The passage had been gained.

"Set the main to'gannels'll!" Broadwinder's command reached deck and sent topmen aloft. Topgallants would blow, they thought; either that or drive the ship to an inglorious end on the floeberg ahead. The passage had opened, but opened to what? The answer then was: more of the same; the uncertainty that walked hand in hand with recklessness; speed when the road cried for a slow, probing advance; a daring, foolhardy race with the floeberg for a comparatively clear sea that would wait and wait for a wiser man.

The sailors loosed the sail for their captain and moved slowly down to deck, where they stood with grim expressions on their faces before knotting into small groups. Jenny felt a change in them. Mr. Fortune eyed them closely. They hinted of insubordination. Now Mr. Winston was moving slowly among them, a look of sharp alertness in his face. His crisp order, "To your stations, every mother's son of ye," possessed a minatory ring. And at his side to lend a hand were bosun, sailmaker, and carpenter. Then there were words. The men gesticulated, said they would follow the Old Man to hell and back as long as he played his game with safety.

Jenny looked at Cartwright, who saw and understood. A minute of thoughtful silence was broken by her suggestion that they move aft and placate the men. "They are a faithful lot, sir. But they are afraid."

"With justification," Cartwright said, a crispness in his voice. "You know, Jenny, I've been seriously thinking of relieving Philip of his command until we reach safer waters."

Containing the start this gave her as well as incipient anger, she replied with all the calm she could muster, "Let me congratulate you, sir, for not making such a blunder." His incredulous look prompted her to say more: "Beyond the unpleasantness such an order might provoke, you need Captain Broadwinder now as never before—to get you safely through."

Cartwright had little time to ponder her amazing loyalty to Philip or her nicely veiled threat. The drama of a tense sailing situation held him in its grip when it became apparent to all that the captain and the *Eagle* were locked in a win-or-lose race with the ugly floeberg ahead for an opening between huge grinding blocks of ice and the long, whale-backed mass to the left. The distance between the two perils had narrowed the channel of escape from two miles when the ship put the berg on her port beam to a mile wide now.

Up in the fore Broadwinder stared at a gate fast closing on him. He had been unable to foresee this hazard earlier. Cold fear vied for command of his mind and he fought back. He realized with startling clarity the penalty for failure to run through the frozen jaws. Worse than an ice-locked ship, he would be at the mercy of a wicked floeberg climbing his bows and a world of running ice driven madly on by wind and seas to crush his stern and sides. The devil himself could hardly devise a worse trap.

He looked all around him. To the left was ice, behind him lay the silent, creeping berg, farther aft on the starboard side and flanking his right were the tossing heads of floes. There was no way back, and there was no sitting it out. The only road was straight ahead. Time was precious. Speed and only speed would give him a ghost of a show. The gamble was now or never.

Under foresail, topsails, and main topgallant, he was driving at a good clip. But that was not enough. Nothing short of the maximum of sail set to the wind in a hurry would, the Lord willing, give him a chance of beating the floeberg to open water.

His shout for royals was followed by repeated cries for

speed in loosing canvas. "Faster! Faster! For your lives, men!"

The hands needed no prompting now. They knew the danger, the reason for sails that could not withstand the force of the wind, the tragic urgency of the word "Faster!" and they leaped to obey. Never had sail fallen from the yards so fast. Canvas strained at the boltropes and the *Eagle* surged forward.

Two miles ahead the channel continued to narrow perceptibly. Broadwinder worked his hands into and out of fists and stared so intently at the most coveted strait of his entire sailing career that it blurred over. Shaking his head, coaxing with mind, heart, and voice the *Eagle* to give her all, he was not prepared for what came at that moment. The rending of wood and a terrific banging told him that his main royal mast had blown. He gazed fearfully at the fore royal above him. It would go next. But until it did——

The ship plowed deep, lifted, tore ahead. Now less than a half mile to the thin avenue of escape, the floeberg loomed up large and terrifyingly close. Ice blocks stood on end, falling, lifting again, piling atop others, grinding, powdering into ice spray. Seas smashed at the mounting blue-shadowed confusion of the drift, licking high, curling, and falling away to charge again. One giant block seemed to leap straight up out of the sea and fall with a crash that could be heard far to windward. It was anything but a pretty picture, and Broadwinder shut his eyes only to open them in time to see a cake of white bobbing up as if out of nowhere not a hundred feet ahead. Clammy sweat oozed from his pores as he debated on its course. The seas threw it a little to the right and he ran her on.

Broadwinder felt crawling fingers at his spine as the danger flew past. More were forming as he surveyed the narrowing channel. Less than a half mile of water! At the rate of speed it was closing, he would have little more than a quarter mile left by the time he reached it. Could he clear?

"God willing," he said in prayerful tones before voicing an order born of desperation: "Boom out the fore stun's'ls!"

The order reached the deck. Glances exchanged seemed pregnant with the unsaid: Studding booms were like matchsticks flying paper kites! For proof, the fore royal chose that time to go with a cannonading that seemed to vibrate through the ship. Broadwinder countermanded the order for studding sails. He carried the maximum, carried it into the danger that was no longer ahead of him but upon him.

On into the narrow channel the *Eagle* sped, a low hummock on her left, a charging floeberg on her right. Three hundred yards of water on each side of a ship driving beyond the last knot of her log line caused Sails to swallow hard and say: "Nineteen knots to hell!"

Another mile and she would be free. Three minutes. The alternative was eternity. Jenny wondered how fate could measure time in such small and great portions. Life hung in the balance here, and she knew it and all aboard the flying *Eagle* knew it. The ice that sped by a few feet off minutes before was a harbinger of more to come. The floeberg stood as proof, and the shelf of ice under the whaleback either stood in their path or so very close that their approach was nothing short of death-defying. Jenny waited, praying, her every muscle painfully taut, her nerves frayed, like the tag ends of the royal sail still hanging overhead.

Broadwinder stared from sea ahead to peril on one side and then the other, both sides fast closing in on him. His hands went white from gripping the supports.

Dead ahead a great cake of ice shot upward. Broadwinder saw it too late to cry any order to the helm. Then the *Eagle* charged down upon it. She struck with her forward port hull, a glancing blow that but for the grace of God would have been head on at the cutwater. It was bad enough as it was, however; the ship was thrown up and over to starboard. Her masts reeled, and everything shot forward. A grating noise sounded down her side and vibrated the length of the ship. The helm spun and Mr. Fortune ran to the aid of the two men at the wheel in time to jerk her back before the stern swung to seas that would have thrown her broadside to wave and weather.

Thrown clear of his perch, Broadwinder caught at a topgallant shroud and swung into space a minute. As the ship righted herself and tore on, he cried the deck to examine her hull and plumb the bilge. The order was purely mechanical, for his heart stood still with the thought of her side ripped open and of seas gurgling through to sink a mortally wounded ship.

"Oh, God!" he said. He prayed then. He was nearly through the channel, but was he taking a sinking ship through? He offered to compromise with the Lord: "Give me a leaky ship, God, but not a hole in her side."

Even as the captain bargained with the Creator, Mr. Winston was unbattening the forward hatch for a look below and Chips was lowering the sounding rod. All the while the *Eagle* drove on in defiance to seas and ice. To those feeling of her by instinct born of experience, she did not appear to be listing or slowing her pace. But these men knew that a ship's heartthrob lingered after a death stroke. As did her captain, who was chained to the fore by necessity. Soon the verdict came:

She had sprung a leak. She was making water badly, enough to keep the pumps going day and night.

The captain said nothing. The pumps would be manned without his command. The Lord had answered his prayer and the *Eagle* was fast opening up the wide road to Cape Horn. He was thankful; the good Lord knew he was. He had run the closing gap to safety. A look behind him at the passage revealed how narrow his escape had been, for the floeberg was now piling against the whaleback of ice. The awful fear still gripped him, but another feeling warmed his heart. He had won over that fear, had redeemed himself. He was not a Captain Contestable.

A different Broadwinder made his way to deck. Though in command of a leaking ship, he knew he could pump his way to Boston. If it broke the back of every man of the crew, he could do that. He was free again and the ship was free and far in the lead of Mayo Keys. Reaching the quarter-deck, he summed up his feelings in a single sentence:

"Thank the Lord, Mr. Fortune, and keep the pumps going."

32

☐ That evening the sailmaker entered the forecastle and studied the long faces of the men huddled around the stove. Oilskins and boots swung with the roll of the ship and the shadows they cast under the flickering lamp animated strange patterns on bulkheads and chests. Sails watched men and shadows as he held chilled hands over the stove. After enduring minutes of unnatural quiet, he asked who they were sewing in a shroud for commitment to the deep. The answer in no way surprised him:

"We done wrong, Sails," a sailor spoke up.

"Aye, ye done wrong, Barnaby."

"The Old Man figgered every situation, he did, and timed the trim o' sails and yards perfect to ice and seas and weather."

"Aye, he did that," Sails agreed.

"He got us through alive, Sails."

"Aye, he did, Barnaby."

"He's one more hell of a drivin', calculatin,' crack-on, deepwater man, every hair a rope yarn and his heart pumpin' blood o' pure Stockholm tar, Sails."

"Aye, and ye can lay to that," Sails said in response to the greatest compliment one could pay a seaman.

"And us doubtin' him when we got scared. It's ashamed of ourselves we are. I'll go to the pumps willin' and I'll break my unworthy back to prove it, so help me God, Sails."

"Aye, and I'm glad to hear it, Barnaby. The second advises she's makin' ten inches of water an hour and he asks me to tell you lads to lay willin' and able on the pumps."

"Ten inches? That's a hell of a lot o' water!" Barnaby glowered at him. "Means we'll pump her to Rio, maybe to Boston Light. Now, I'm wonderin', I am, why I ever signed aboard o' sich a foolhardy captain. Aye, if it ain't the sail set that which blows, 'tis mast to mast and yard to clew line to downhaul. And now the brakes to stir the sin o' mutiny in a man."

As Sails grinned and walked out of the forecastle with a feeling that all was well aboard his ship, Broadwinder in his cabin scribbled a line in the logbook and sat back wearily in his chair.

The elation he had felt was on the wane. A heavy tiredness seemed to press down upon him. It was as though singlehanded he had pushed the ship through the danger of that terrible day. That was the physical reward. But another weight kept him company, and that was a realization of the risk he had run in order to prove to himself he was no coward. Under the guise of racing, he had recklessly gambled ship and the lives of all aboard. And now he was wondering if the gain was commensurate with his after feeling of guilt.

Jenny got up to put the logbook in its proper place. In doing so, her glance fell on the entry of the day:

Under Cape Horn. Some ice, ship leaking.

Her smile turned accusingly on the author of this prize understatement. "Some ice?" she said. "Hardly enough to cool the captain's Singapore punch."

She laughed and Philip roused himself long enough to shape a feeble grin. With the break of tension inside him, she took her rightful place in his lap and stroked his hair and brow.

"I knew you would get us safely through, Philip," she told him. "I was terribly frightened, enough to pray, but I didn't lose confidence in you."

He eyed her steadily, then smiled. "I don't know what I'd do without you, Jenny," he said with sincerity.

"Neither do I, Philip dear. As now, you need me to tell you to get some sleep. You're a tired sailorman."

"Sleep? But——" He broke off suddenly.

"But what?"

"With the ship making ten inches of water an hour, do you think I can sleep?"

While Jenny stood a little worried, a little vexed, watching Philip drag himself toward the door, George Cartwright accepted his third whisky in a row from the grinning steward and frowned back on events of the day. The saloon was an empty place, causing him a wish in detachment for the company of even Mrs. Littlefield on this evening. It had been a most trying day. His nerves were a million frayed ends, all weaving in and out in an effort to settle into their proper places. The recent storm and a ship on her beam ends seemed small when compared to the ordeal of ice. He knew why: the former had been sudden, the latter slow torture.

"Put some whisky in the next one, Peretta," he said irritably.

"Make it two," a voice at the entrance demanded. "Only I prefer red wine."

Cartwright looked up quickly, then got to his feet. "Jenny! I was never so glad for company."

"Nor I," she said, moving to him and clutching his arm. "I'm all nerves, sir." Her large eyes darted over his face. "And you?"

"I'm not sure." He seated her and, avoiding her intense glance, took a chair. "Perhaps I'm caught between two desires—one to blackball your husband in every port in the world, the other to applaud the greatest sailing feat it has ever been my pain or pleasure to witness or hear about."

"Oh," she said, the brightness going out of her eyes. Soberly she studied him, her head cocked a trifle. "Make up your mind, Mr. Cartwright."

"Eh?" He frowned. "Why?"

"Because I'm in no humor for the doldrums on a night when thanksgiving is due."

Peretta placed glasses before them. With his departure, Cartwright said, "Thanksgiving? Aboard a ship tearing through dark seas at eighteen knots?"

"Twelve, sir. She's down to tops'ls. Captain Broadwinder is a prudent man." She added, significantly, he thought, "Tonight."

"Why did you say 'tonight'?"

She sipped, her gaze meeting his. "Perhaps I should have said that once the threat of ice is gone—well, just hang on for Boston, sir."

Although George Cartwright had only half an ear for predictions at a time when her very presence seemed just the tonic he needed for relaxation, morning aboard a ship heeling strong on a beam wind out of the south refreshed memories of things said.

Cartwright was becoming used to the sight of too much sail on the *Eagle*, so he accepted all that met his eye as he joined Mr. Fortune on deck after breakfast. The new royals bent on during the night were bellying full and the mate was estimating the gain on Mayo Keys at over one hundred miles when a tall ship appeared on the horizon beating her way for southing. She came on; rather the *Eagle* overtook her. As they sped past, Cartwright brought the glass to bear on her deck and saw the captain pointing in amazement at the high sails of the *Eagle*. He knew why, for the other captain had sent down his royal masts.

Aware of the shipowner's concern, Mr. Fortune said: "Captain Broadwinder is racing with the weather now. And well he should, for it's going to be a tight squeeze to make a rounding into the Atlantic before the east wind heads him."

The contest between ship and changing winds lasted all that day and night. Before noon, bleak, silent Cape Horn reared its dim head above the northern horizon. Several clipper ships were seen that day, two loafing along waiting for the east wind to put them around on the California road, others sailing prudently toward the Atlantic on the *Eagle*'s course.

All were left far behind. Dusk brought snow and sleet and all sails driving on a heeling, dipping racer riding out the last breath of the south wind.

Morning and freshening winds slanting out of the southeast did nothing to dampen spirits aboard the *Eagle*, for she had, as Sails put it, made a rounding of the continent "by the thickness of her shadow." Instead of beating close-hauled, she put the weather over her quarter and circled fair up into the south Atlantic for the Falkland Islands.

As one day followed another in the *Calcutta Eagle's* climb of the latitudes, speed and more speed became the order. Philip Broadwinder seemed to think of nothing else. Often he would leap out of bed after a mere wink of sleep and rush to deck. He kept the pumps going round the clock and he flung sail to the blustering winds in a manner that amazed even venerable crack-on clipper captains winging their way south and more of their kind bending on for New York and Boston. Occasionally north-bound captains matched speed with Broadwinder for a time, only to fall astern. The pace was too fast, the sails they blew were too many.

Aboard the clipper *Orion* bound for San Francisco, Captain Underwood wrote into his log one night: "The *Calcutta Eagle* passed me at six bells on the forenoon watch like a comet on a greased wind." Four days later, he wrote: "Met the *Emperor* scudding with topgallants set in weather that saw me hove to under close-reefed main topsail and spencer."

On up beyond the limits of the antitrades Broadwinder tacked ship day and night through the belt of variable winds in an effort to snag the lively southeast trade. He piled more work on the overworked crew. In addition to the pumps, heavy canvas was taken off the yards and light sails were bent on. It was work, work. When confronted by Jenny, more and more often of late, regarding his loss of sleep, Broadwinder either growled and ignored her or spoke irritably of things she already knew, that a day lost in the variables was a day gained by Mayo Keys; that every day the *Eagle* sat it out in the calm belt the *Emperor* on the good winds below the equator would be racing up to sit even with him; that he was driving in order to hold the hard-won lead and to offset these things. Her constant reminders of what exhaustion could do to him went unheeded. He called it nagging. Soon Jenny gave up trying to reason with him and began looking about for some other way to save him from his folly.

The ship continued to make water badly and, although the men despised nothing worse than the "brakes," or pumps, Broadwinder was more concerned with the effect of extra ballast in his holds on the speed of the ship. Aware that he could not repair the hull afloat and unwilling to give up the time for such by touching in at Rio, he approached Cartwright on the advisability of ridding the ship of enough cargo to equalize the weight of unwelcome water. Quite an argument followed and Jenny was forced into the role of peacemaker when Cartwright told Philip he was amazed that his captain's restricted imagination blinded him to the value of goods in the holds. She tried to calm Philip, though he stalked off after declaring that he as captain of the ship carried authority to jettison the "whole damn cargo" if he so decided.

"At your own personal expense," Cartwright said heatedly.

Undeterred, Broadwinder ordered the hatches open and tons of valuable cargo over the side. It was Jenny who finally saved the goods from the deep. She advised Philip of her intention to break even financially by accepting the necklace she had returned to Cartwright. With his angered reversal of the order, she went straightway to Cartwright and slanted the argument around to Philip's unspoken concern for his crew. By ridding the ship of weight, she told him, the hull might lift above the leak, make less water, and thereby relieve the hands of backbreaking work at the pumps. Confronted with a different and reasonable argument, the shipowner reluctantly conceded, but only after telling Jenny he was convinced that sympathy for the crew existed in her mind and not Philip's.

It did not matter to Jenny that she was a nagging wife to one, a meddlesome woman to the other, strained relations between captain and owner were mended and the ship that still leaked sailed happily on her way.

On the afternoon the *Eagle* crossed the Tropic of Capricorn, Mr. Fortune was put to bed with a severe cold, and Broadwinder stood all watches. When Jenny broke the bad news that the mate's cold had developed into pneumonia, he elevated Mr. Winston to the quarter-deck. It was not an ideal arrangement, however, for while the captain had every confidence in his second mate he nevertheless found it hard to sleep with the thought of a racing ship in the hands of a man whose training had been limited to the working deck. Atop this, Mr. Winston was a past master at leading a gang aloft to loose or take in sail. Used to action and unschooled in directing, the mate was the first to admit a noticeable change in the way the yards came around and sail was trimmed. As a result, Broadwinder seldom left the deck days and almost never at night.

When the strain began to show, Jenny took matters in hand. She declared her willingness to lose the race rather than see Philip as he had been before and during the near tragedy in the storm down under. Her demands were insistent and he slept his off watches through for one entire day. Then the barometer began to skid in warning of heavy weather. As the wind freshened and the seas began to rise, Broadwinder refused to leave deck.

For two days the storm-battered *Eagle* slugged it out with the elements. Broadwinder fought two battles during those terrible forty-eight hours, one with mountainous seas and gale winds, the other with his fear of these things. All the while, a third peril was in the making. It was brought to his attention late in the afternoon of the second day of storm. Red-eyed, water-soaked, and weary, he simply stared with unbelief in his expression at the bearer of bad news.

"She's making over a foot of water an hour, sir."

Broadwinder knew what another day of storm would do to the *Eagle*. Heavy seas had already beaten at the hull until she leaked alarmingly. He thought of the reason for her leak; he saw again the mad, tumbling floeberg on his right, the whale-backed danger on his left; he lived again those moments of dread expectancy while watching helplessly the swift approach of disaster.

And now—his reckless threading of the ice had finally caught up with him.

The storm blew itself out and, with pumps working every minute of every hour, the ship moved north on the backing winds until she sat in a glassy sea without a breath of air to stir her sails.

Given an unwanted respite, Broadwinder directed the work of patching the ship's hull and scanned the horizon for the *Emperor*. He knew that unless she had met trouble also she could not be too far behind. The *Eagle* continued to leak. Despite all they could do, water seeped in at the rate of twelve inches an hour. Considerable cargo was thrown overboard, out of necessity now.

Cartwright watched as boxes and goods in bulk splashed into the lifeless sea. He too looked back at the source of this loss and saw a field of ice and thought of the man who had recklessly threaded it. A man who was now gazing strangely at a box from the holds that floated atop the water.

This was Philip Broadwinder, a baffling man whose skill, drive and determination failed to hide his inconsistencies.

His glance swept on to Jenny Broadwinder, a woman fresh from the sickroom where Mr. Fortune lay abed weak and ravaged by long days of illness. In her face Cartwright saw weariness. The burden of the ship seemed to rest on her frail shoulders.

"A race," he said under his breath. As he pondered the whole adventure with growing distaste, a cat's-paw ruffled the sails and water. Hope shone in Broadwinder's eye a moment, then fell away. The bell sounded the change of watch and men relieved of work at the pumps gazed listlessly at those taking their places. The old sea chanteys they had sung on the way down were seldom heard these days.

Now thousands of miles from the cheers of Melbourne, Cartwright realized that they, as he, were witnessing the side of racing the newspapers scarcely mentioned. Here was reality. Instead of joyful anticipation, the heavy adventure of endured trial aboard a tired, wounded ship was etched into every face. In many ways the voyage from Australia, with its merciless demands from hour to hour, day after day, could be compared to the contest of life itself, in which people and events obeyed, however tragically, the immutable law of movement, forward or backward, but moving, because they could never stand still.

There was Philip Broadwinder. Going about like a sleepwalker, but going. He slurred his words with fatigue and he seemed to look twice at any object before bringing it into focus.

Cartwright looked out over the water. Unaware that in times of troubled thought the human mind turns to elemental things for renewed hope, he watched the fall of light on the motionless sea, where shadows of clouds and sky seemed to belittle the problems of man. When he glanced inboard again he could not help thinking that soon a strong wind would send them happily into the last lap of the voyage.

A strong wind blew in during the night. That much and no more of Cartwright's hopeful prediction came true, for the wind was laden with trouble of the worst kind. It struck swiftly in the last minutes of the twelve-to-four watch.

33

□ Unable to sleep, Broadwinder checked the time and found it was ten minutes past three in the morning, fifty minutes until the change of the watch. Twice since one o'clock he had rushed to deck when cat's-paws ruffled canvas and rattled blocks. Twice he had returned to his bed, only to lie there wishing for sleep that would not come. Now aware that something of his own restlessness was causing Jenny to stir in her sleep, he got up and pulled on his trousers and boots.

His head was thick, as though he had had a night of it with friends ashore. He remembered the weather from deck, however, the moon covered by layers of scudding clouds and the sea below as still as a tomb. He sat down, wondering why a wind up there didn't drop down where it could do some good; how long it would take the galley to prepare coffee black as ninety fathoms under; why the desire for sleep was stronger when he stood or sat; how close to his position Keys was at the moment.

Throwing on his coat, he moved straightway to the quarter-deck, where Mr. Winston stood like a statue with hands locked behind him and cap set so low on his forehead he had to hold head high in order to see. The lamps painted decks, lower masts, shrouds and yards in a weak yellow that bled eerily off into the blackness of the rigging. The night was dark and there was no sound other than the eternal creaking of hand pumps.

Broadwinder made the round of decks, looked at his watch, saw it was half past three. At that moment the ship's bell sounded the half hour. The sky kept running. The sea remained still. He looked up at sail set for the northeast trade wind. His ship pointed northwest, and when and if the fickle wind dropped, the *Eagle* would gather headway.

Coffee was served captain and mate on the quarter-deck. Broadwinder almost smiled when advised that the ship's leak had been reduced to nine inches an hour. Then a feeble gust of wind rolled in off the sea and freshened into a small gust before it suddenly fell away. Winston's, "Damn tricky, I calls it," drew a dismal nod from the captain, who said, "I'll go look in on Mr. Fortune."

The chief mate was sleeping soundly. Broadwinder laid a hand gently to his forehead and raised a brow upon finding little or no fever. He returned to deck and said Ephraim Fortune would be good as new before long. "But he'll stand the deck little between here and Boston."

Mr. Winston made a reply, looked at his watch and moved to the bell near the helm. A minute later he sounded the ten-minute warning to the hands below. The dying note of the bell had scarcely quivered off into silence over ship and sea than a rush of air sounded over the starboard beam. It breezed through top hamper and across decks with drops of rain on the wing.

"She smells constant," Broadwinder said. Following the cry to the hands, he moved quickly to the lashed helm, threw the hitch from the wheel and shouted an order to haul the spanker boom around.

Men came on the run, Barnaby to take the wheel, the bosun's mate and others to haul the boom. They had not quite reached the stern when the squall struck with a mighty hiss and roar. It threw the men to deck, Mr. Winston with them, and sent the ship reeling far over on her portside. As she snapped back to windward, the boom tackle parted and the spanker boom went free. Under the drive of the heavy squall wind, it swept madly to leeward, threatening destruction to everything in its path.

Broadwinder heard the tackle go, though when he looked to his right the boom was hard upon him. He felt a sharp stab of pain and a sensation of being lobbed by a giant catapult into swift oblivion. Then all went black.

Mr. Winston saw the boom throw the captain heavily against the wheel and onto the rail, saw him lying in a huddle on deck. For seconds the mate seemed to have lost his voice. The banging of a blown sail aloft restored him. The ship was in danger, and the captain was badly hurt. His cries brought men running to fight the devil of a boom into submission. Then, like the real sailor he was, he ordered canvas taken in and the squall put over the ship's quarter before rushing to the unconscious captain.

As the mate bent over Broadwinder and placed an ear to his heart, Cartwright joined him.

"We'd best get him below," the mate said.

"Take over, Mr. Winston. Sails will help me."

Jenny had been thrown out of bed when the ship rolled under the big gust. Alarmed, she dressed hurriedly and was just leaving for deck when Cartwright, Lowery, and O'Hara appeared at the door with Broadwinder.

She stood still, eyes wide and unbelieving. Her heart seemed to stop beating and then it hammered madly. A cry of "Philip!" formed on her parted lips, but her throat was constricted. Unaware that she was blocking their way, she slowly raised her stunned glance to Cartwright.

The shipowner felt the depth of appeal in her look and said, "The spanker boom hit him, Jenny."

They placed him gently on the bed where Sails and Chips examined him for broken bones and head injuries while Cartwright helped Jenny to a chair and rubbed her hands as he exhorted her in low but firm tones to remain seated until she felt better. Then Sails turned to them.

"Ma'am," he said, swallowing hard, "he's got some ribs busted and his right arm is broke near the shoulder. He'll come out of it, ma'am."

Chips looked around. "Don't you worry none, Mrs. Broadwinder. His noggin is sound and he'll be up in no time."

Jenny stood, pale but in command of herself, and rushed to Philip. On her knees at the bedside, she studied his face intently. He seemed so white, and the skin stretched tightly across his cheeks did nothing to dispel the deathly expression. She cried out to him then frantically. It was only when he stirred that she lowered her head to his and loosed a sob.

Cartwright's heart went out to her, a brave woman.

Slowly she raised her head and placed a hand at Philip's neck. "Sails," she said with amazing composure, "I want you to sew sailcloth tight about his chest. Mr. Cartwright, whisky please. He'll need it any moment now."

Throwing the hair back from her eyes, she faced them, mouth open and heavy. "Chips, fashion splints for his arm, and send Tobias to me. Lively now, all of you."

Broadwinder emitted a groan and opened his eyes. Jenny gave him whisky and talked in his ear. "Easy, easy, Philip. Don't try to move. Philip! Listen to me!"

He stared wildly at her, then obeyed, a bewildered look on his face. A cough racked his body and Jenny wiped his mouth. When he lay still and exhausted, she examined the sputum for signs of blood.

"Thank God," she said in a whisper.

Staring long seconds at the brandy Cartwright proffered, she finally accepted it and drank in detachment. Then she rose to her feet. "Thank you," she said, sinking into a chair. "I suppose, sir, you are wondering who will sail your ship to Boston."

"No, Jenny. I'm wondering what I can do to help you and Philip."

As though she had not heard his reply, she said, "I must say what Captain Broadwinder is unable to say now, Mr. Cartwright. It is this: 'Have Mr. Winston select the best sailor from the crew'—and he would have either Sails or the bosun in mind—'and elevate him to the quarter-deck. Then proceed at all reasonable speed to Boston.' That's what he would say. If you agree to that, sir, I'd be greatly obliged if you would carry the word to deck."

"Gladly, Jenny." Cartwright rose to depart.

"A moment, please." Her fingers moved back and forth across her forehead. "He would also have the crew assembled and let it be known that he expected every man to carry on in an endeavor to win this race."

"But, Jenny!" Cartwright protested. "What comes of racing but tragedy? I don't want any more of it."

"Philip does. Remember that, sir. He's still captain, and you know what it means to him."

Yes, he knew. Resigned to her wishes, he departed for deck.

Jenny had no sooner returned to Philip than he rallied long enough to say, "I heard. You're—you're handy to have——" A violent spell of coughing interrupted him. After minutes of pained silence, he said, "I hurt—like hell. Here."

"Where? Where do you hurt, Philip?"

He did not reply. His eyes were closed in either sleep or unconsciousness. Jenny hoped it was the latter when Chips entered for the bonesetting. Then she braced herself and made ready to do the job.

When it was finally done with she moved to a port and tried to steady her trembling hands and body. Sails arrived with canvas and needle, and she stared at him, feeling suddenly old and worn.

An hour later young Tobias admitted Cartwright, who stood in the door a minute looking first at Jenny, who sat with hands folded primly in her lap and then at the ship's boy. The lad held the cat, Prince Thomas, as he did when trouble or grief boarded the ship. Something to cling to, thought Cartwright, moving inside.

There was a wordless supplication in Jenny's eyes as she looked up at him, and it caused him a feeling of helplessness to be found wanting when she silently begged for comfort. The fates had not been too kind to her, he realized. The jaunty, cocksure Philip and the imprudent, unpredictable sea captain had kept her always on the alert, robbed her of peace of mind. And now an injured Broadwinder, hurt worse than she actually knew, according to Sails and Chips, brought her fresh suffering. He could not censure Philip, for he was what he was, an individual pattern the same as any man. And what had befallen him was unavoidable. No blame, just facts admitted in silence.

He told her that Mr. Winston and the crew had chosen Sails as acting second mate, that the bosun and Chips would stand by to aid them, and that the crew to a man swore they would win the race for the "Old Man."

"How is he, Jenny?"

"I—I don't know," she replied in a voice close to breaking.

Cartwright said nothing. The silence between them lengthened, broken by only the distant roar of wind in the rigging and muted sounds of water at the ship's sides; these things and Philip's labored breathing punctuated by the creaking of the constant pumps. They sat there a long time before Cartwright persuaded her to go on deck, for her own good.

"I'll watch over him, Jenny."

At the door she changed her mind and returned.

The *Eagle* ran under topgallants all that day on a lusty beam wind, though Mr. Winston looked unhappy when he entered the cabin that evening to make the log entry.

"On a sixteen-knot wind, ma'am," he told Jenny, "I couldn't do more'n average thirteen. We're scared we'll lose this race, ma'am." He turned his cap over and over. "One more thing, ma'am, could ye enter the log for me?"

Jenny did so, then asked for the ship's position, which caused the mate to drop his glance and tug at the red beard under his chin. "Ye see, ma'am, I never learnt how to shoot the sun."

Alone with sleeping Philip, she thought of all she had just heard. She was the only person left who knew how to figure position at sea. Navigating was as important as carrying sail. Moreover, the very fact that the mate could get only thirteen out of the ship on the wind Jenny had fathomed by sound and instinct proved conclusively that the *Eagle*'s afterguard was no match for Mayo Keys.

Jenny looked at Philip. Should he wake up one day and learn that the *Emperor* had taken the lead, why there would be no keeping him in bed.

All things considered, she realized that she had a problem on her hands, one she must deal with very soon.

She began to brush her hair, thoughtfully, unhurriedly. Her face in the mirror took on a decisive expression and she was soon dressing for the weather of deck. Tobias was sent after Cartwright, who came quickly. Relieved to learn that Philip was no worse, he readily agreed to sit while Jenny went up for a breath of air.

The moment Jenny reached the quarter-deck she was besieged by questions regarding the captain's condition. Yes, he had slept well. Yes, he had roused frequently, had asked about this and that. Of course, he would be up and about in quick time. Although she enlarged upon the facts, she felt it would do little harm to spread cheer at this time.

Jenny was a close student of shipboard human nature. Years at sea had not lessened her respect for a sailor's keen insight. These men had the faculty of detecting motive a mile off, and although she enjoyed the knowledge that she was necessary to them, she could not afford to underestimate either their quick wit or dislike of taking orders from a woman. So she took her time in conning ship, sail and weather without seeming to do so before venturing a remark in keeping with Philip's character:

"Mr. Winston, Captain Broadwinder said he could judge the wind from his bed, and that he hoped you had the royals set. Of course, I humored him."

The mate squinted an eye aloft, then dropped a perplexed glance on Jenny. "Royals," he meditated aloud. "It ain't in me to doubt the Old Man's weather nose, ma'am, but the wind 'pears a mite brisk up there."

She smiled innocently. "Well, you're in charge, Mr. Winston."

Later Cartwright appeared at the mate's side with a remark

about the way the ship pitched and rolled through the night. Mr. Winston agreed, saying a ship doing a full fifteen knots under royals should cavort a little.

"But Mrs. Broadwinder said that's what the Old Man wanted, so I'm hopin' he's restin' easy."

Cartwright wrinkled the crow's feet around his eyes. He could understand Philip's desire for royal sails, but with the knowledge that Philip was unable to think clearly he was wondering how Philip managed to convey his wants even to Jenny.

On the following day Jenny appeared on deck with Broadwinder's sextant. After requesting Sails to watch over the captain, she looked up at the sun, then at the instrument in her hands. Appearing somewhat bewildered, she said in the presence of Cartwright and the mate:

"I do hope I can remember a little of what Captain Broadwinder taught me." She smiled. "Now wouldn't we be in a fix if we got lost at sea?" With a remark about navigating by the stars, she swung the sextant to her eye, said something about her hazy memory of trigonometry and algebra, and began to work out a sight. She kept at it for some time, then resorted to chart work. When finished, she knew the position as figured to be correct, though it served her better to appear unsure.

"I'll need your help, Mr. Winston. You can judge better than I by the North Star tonight."

Flattered, the mate smiled.

Another day passed slowly. The ship ran under the maximum of sail on orders relayed to deck by the captain's wife, who looked more wan and upset than the day before. The discerning crew began to wonder about the captain, to talk among themselves. The bosun and Chips put them at ease by pointing up into the towers of sail, saying: "Who else but the Old Man would fly them rags to the weather?" Here was convincing proof that the captain wasn't too sick. But as another sunset followed with more of the same, the Old Man's kind of sailing without his appearance on deck, they began to wonder if his ghost was standing up there driving the ship on.

Jenny saw in their faces a growing puzzlement and one evening during the dogwatches served them a ration of the captain's favorite whisky: "Compliments of Captain Broadwinder," she said. "In appreciation for all you've done while he's ill." Cartwright admired her courage when the men smacked their lips and said it was "like the old Man, all right," for not two hours before he had seen her go pale when Philip stared out of feverish eyes and cried over and over, "There's the *Emperor*!"

Jenny had requested the stewards and everyone who helped with Mr. Fortune to refrain from any mention of what had happened to Philip. She knew the chief mate would force himself up and into a serious relapse. However, since bad news, like good, travels fast and into forbidden places, Ephraim Fortune somehow learned of the tragic happening four days later. After undue exertion, he managed to get on his feet. Three times he was thrown against the bulkhead of his stateroom by the easy roll of the ship and three times he struggled upward. At long last triumphant over the "devil of a deck," he smiled and got into his clothes. By that time he was too weak to go on deck, so he sat down and poured a stiff ration of brandy. It warmed him considerably. He indulged in another, then arose, steadied himself, and began working his slow way to deck. He paused often to rest, thinking of the surprise his appearance would cause up there but nothing of what four hours on duty would do to him. His captain needed him now and, prudent though he was, he would fly "Broadwinder canvas." A little giddy now, he grinned with fond anticipation and leaned against the handrail of the after companion while saying in undertones: "Run out the studding booms, lads! Put a reef in the fores'll Lively now!" He gained the deck and, at the taffrail, unobserved, stood a minute in appreciation of the familiar sights.

The steersman glanced at him and back at the wheel before jerking his eyes again to an apparition. "Mr. Fortune!" he cried, forgetting the lubber's line he was supposed to steer by. Before he spoked the wheel around the chief mate was moving forward to join the amazed second mate.

Ten minutes later he was seized by a hard chill and carried below.

Although Philip's fever had mounted steadily despite all that could be done to allay it, Jenny left him in Cartwright's care and rushed to Mr. Fortune. All that long night she and Cartwright alternately watched over the pair. When the first pink edge of day stretched across the eastern horizon, Jenny looked up to see Cartwright at her side.

"The mate is resting now," he said. "I'll sit with Philip while you get a little sleep."

He was kind and faithful, said her tired eyes. "Thank you. Just for a little while."

Placing a pillow at the back of an armchair, she sat down and was almost instantly asleep. Cartwright studied her face in quiet repose a long time. He saw her lips move and detected the trembling of her body as tiredness gave way to brief relaxation. She started often, and once her eyes fluttered open, only to close again when she found him at Philip's bedside. She came awake when early-morning sunshine flooded through the port. After studying the sea and weather, she told him she would return after a few minutes on deck. This she did.

Cartwright went on deck a little later, where Mr. Winston greeted him cheerily. "A fine mornin', sir, and us not more'n two days out o' Boston at most—and still ahead o' the *Emperor.*

"Aye, and it's good to know the Old Man's mendin' proper. I says to Sails when the cap'n sends word up a half hour back to steer her a point west so's to get the best out o' the wind that it beats all how he's a damn sight better deck sailor below on his back than me up here on my two pins."

Cartwright nodded his head. This time he knew that Philip Broadwinder had spoken no order.

34

☐ The *Calcutta Eagle* tore on through the day and into the night with all sail set and her pumps at work to empty the sea out of her hold. The second mate and Sails stood four hours on and four hours off. The captain's wife shot the sun and figured position, looked in on Mr. Fortune, left him with a scolding smile, and returned to her quarters where she knelt and prayed for Philip's recovery.

Eight bells, four o'clock in the afternoon, had just sounded when Tobias entered the cabin excited. Mr. Winston requested her presence on deck. A ship was breaking the horizon over the port quarter and, judging by her speed on a course identical to the *Eagle's*, the mate believed she was the *Emperor*.

Jenny sent the ship's boy to Mr. Winston with word that she would join him shortly, then turned a frowning glance on the ravaged face framed by a pillow.

"It's the *Emperor*," she said, as though he listened and heard. "I know it is, Philip, and we're so close, too close to lose this thing you want so much. But are you too weary to go on? What must I do, Philip?"

She left him. After long minutes on deck, she said: "Mr. Winston, Captain Broadwinder wishes the booms run out, and the moment the wind shifts due east, put it over the starboard quarter and sweat the gear for all she's got."

That evening she wrote into the log entry:

One day out of Boston, sighted the Emperor *astern. Captain Broadwinder growing steadily worse.*

An hour later Jenny stood in alarm at his bedside. Minutes before she had felt alone, weary, worried, and sad. Now she was frightened. Philip burned with fever. There was no calming him.

"Jenny! I was scared of the ice. Always was afraid of storms. You know it, Cap'n Contestable. Saw me, didn't you? Saw Jenny save the ship after I let her broach to. And now Jenny is at the pumps. It's my turn—soon as I run out the studding booms."

A low, desperate cry escaped Jenny. She dropped her head for a few seconds then shook wisps of hair from her forehead.

Philip threw the cold towels from his brow as fast as she placed them there. "Get the damned ice away from this ship! You, down there, Mr. Fortune, steer her off the floeberg! Lively!"

He settled back, coughing violently. When he spoke next his voice was low and he seemed very puzzled about something. "Why, Jenny?" he kept saying. Her soft replies went unheard. "Just when he had the race won," he said. Then he was asking why Tobias and Sails had boarded the *Emperor*. "On account of my reckless run through the ice, wasn't it? Tell me, Jenny."

He asked for water. She gave it to him. He lay still and silent for several minutes before reaching for her hand. "Jenny," he said in rational voice, "don't go away. Tell me what I said to you that night in Medford—when I asked you to marry me."

"You said——" Jenny faltered. "You told me I was created just for you, Philip; that you knew it the moment you laid eyes on me. And——"

"That I'd love you always and forever, didn't I?" With her reply, he said, "And I meant it. And I still mean it. Have I been a good husband, Jenny?"

"Yes, darling," she whispered. "Yes."

"Jenny, tell me the mermaid yarn."

Jenny's throat was dry. She tried to swallow, tried to speak. At last she choked back a sob and began: "It was a rough night and—and you were working the *Eagle* around for the lee of the island, searching for the pass. Back and——"

"Aye. Just when I had given up, the door to my cabin opens and there she is. Lovely, beautiful, all the way down to her scales."

A merry laugh escaped him. For a moment he was the gay Prince of Sea Captains. "Then she took the wheel, Jenny, and steered us right through the pass before the storm broke in full. I'll bet I've told it a thousand times. Got to believing it myself." He paused, staring at her.

"I love you, Jenny girl."

"I know, Philip."

"I loved you even when I wanted to spank the devil out of you."

"I know, Philip."

"Like the time I took you off the *Grace Darling*." He smiled. "You were a stubborn woman, Mistress Jenny."

"Because I love you, Philip. I——"

"Where is the *Emperor*?"

"Still behind us. I've been relaying your orders to deck, darling."

"My orders? I don't remember giving any."

"You did, Philip. Whether you spoke them or not, I heard and obeyed."

He thought about this, wonderment in his eyes. "Jenny." He fell silent a minute. "Jenny, I was terribly afraid of the ice. But I had to run it or forever know I was the man who couldn't save his ship when she lay on her beam ends in the storm. Do you understand?"

She nodded slowly, not taking her eyes off him. "I'm proud of you, Philip—for winning your battle, and for telling me about it."

"It's a load off my mind, Jenny. Now all I want to do is look at you a while. You're tired, but before you rest, would you read the Twenty-third Psalm to me?"

When she had finished reading she felt his hand, which had held hers tightly, relax. His eyes were closed and he was asleep, his breathing slow and belabored. She sat still, watching him and thinking of the past and praying for the future. She had no memory of drowsing off. She jerked awake, not knowing how long she had slept, knowing only that something was wrong. Somewhere a change had come over the world of ship and sea. She looked at Philip, wanting to touch him, to cry out to him, but she could bring herself to do neither. Her heart pounded in a chest suddenly gone hollow and her eyes grew wide with awe. He lay too still and white, the fever color gone and his skin was tight. "No! No!" Her voice sounded pitifully weak and lost, and a great and crushing hurt descended upon her.

Jenny pulled herself together and closed her eyes, knowing that when she opened them it would be the end of a horrible dream. But it wasn't. Philip lay still. She touched him. Philip was cold.

Not Philip. No, it couldn't be. She had known he was badly hurt, but she had never even thought of his dying. And now everything in her was spinning. Nothing made sense any more. She was aware of someone lifting her from the floor and placing her on the bed, of voices and more voices. She wondered about all the fuss, and then suddenly she knew the reason and asked the Lord to return her to a state of oblivion. But no such thing happened. The Lord was merciful, the Lord was unmerciful. He knew Philip's pain and He knew her awful hurt. She wanted to run away. There was no place to run to but to Philip.

She closed her eyes and tried in vain to believe Philip still lived. Why had God done this to her? She opened her eyes and stared at the lamp swinging in the gimbals. The ship sailed on. Why, when the world had ended? But it was only her small world. The bigger one observed no pause, but moved on, mockingly on, as if nothing had happened.

Her head turned. Bundled in oilskins, head bared, old Sails looked at her out of watery eyes filled with infinite sadness.

Chips wiped a tear from his leathery face. Tobias looked bewildered and held the ship's cat closer to his heart. Mr. Winston was stunned, frozen. Her glance fell on the shipowner. In George Cartwright's face she saw no sign of grief, only a great disturbance in his soft eyes and a grimness about the mouth. Perhaps it was grief, or pity, or shock, or all combined.

Then she saw something else in him as he stood still, his gaze on the men: strength. It was something she needed, something she must borrow from the one who possessed it.

It helped her rise and get to her feet. His hand at her arm was a gift for which she was thankful.

Cartwright felt the trembling of her arm under his touch and, knowing she was too hurt for tears, he feared for her. Then she paused near the captain's writing desk, turned her gaze on Philip's still face and stood a long time in silence before unlocking the drawer containing the logbook. Cartwright saw her steel herself for the ordeal as she opened the book. Her glance lifted to him and remained upon him as she seemed to be looking through and beyond him. He watched as she bravely made the final entry of the day:

The greatest captain of sail has spoken his last order. He passed into the great beyond at around six bells on the first watch. Captain Broadwinder had the Emperor well astern at the time of his passing. He never lost a race.

Closing the book, she walked to the bedside and looked down at Philip in death. She bent to the still face and planted a kiss on his forehead, then slowly raised the sheet to cover him.

The death watch began.

When the long, lonely night finally came to an end Jenny stood on deck gazing into the dawn. She watched the encroaching day snuff out the stars in the eastern heavens and pale the blue of nocturnal sky. The delicate pink of a seashell lifted above the horizon and threw the tint over the sea, up into the tall sails. This was the first hush of morning. It winged in gently at first in soft colors, then in mighty silence threw bolts and shafts of light upward and over the sea. The world would never stand still, and in the morning one felt God's promise more than at any other time. It was a time when hope soared in a mortal's soul.

Jenny bowed her head and moistened dry lips. She prayed in low tones that not even Cartwright could hear. He stood faithfully a little apart from her, always ready when she needed him. Slowly she lifted her head and thought of the maze of problems of the near future. Philip had never said he wished to be buried at sea. She wanted him at rest in Medford. She must soon decide. But there was a heavy tiredness upon her and her mind was a jumbled haze of questions that had no answers.

The ship? The race? The future? Where would she go and what would she do?

Life continued aboard ship. The helmsman struck the bell at the half hour. Mr. Winston was ordering the foreyards braced up, and smoke from the galley stove blew straight over the port rail. Blocks creaked overhead and the pumps continued to grind on. The hands stood at their stations, as yesterday and hundreds of yesterdays. They had taken their loss of captain more philosophically than Jenny had expected. Tears had rolled down cheeks, but there had been little wailing. Life ended in death.

The lookout's cry of land over the port bow reminded her that they would enter Boston harbor sometime in the afternoon. The end of a voyage, the end of a race. She looked toward the south, where the *Emperor* ran with all the sail and energy at her command. She lay five miles or more astern, though she was gaining a little.

"A race?" she said audibly, trying to reconcile the great effort of ship and men since Melbourne in her mind. For a moment it seemed very strange, and then she was not aware of any incongruity.

Mr. Winston and Cartwright were conversing now, puzzlement in their faces. They were looking at her, and she knew that some decision on her part was overdue. But decisions lay in some gray twilight of her mind.

Cartwright reached her side. Staring out over the sea, perhaps at the blur of land edging the horizon, he said, "Jenny, I must remind you of something." His pause eloquently described the pain this intrusion evoked in him. "The *Emperor* is gaining on us and—well, Philip's greatest desire was to win this race."

Jenny nodded, then lowered her head. Cartwright said nothing more, but stood patiently awaiting her reply. After a time, it came:

"Philip did win. It is written in the log."

Unable to comprehend her meaning, Cartwright looked perplexed. She offered no explanation; instead, she accepted coffee from the mournful steward and sipped in silence. Her brow knit as she looked up at the canvas flying, down to decks and again into the rigging. Cartwright knew that she was figuring sail versus wind, but what he had no way of knowing was her awareness of the moment that Mr. Winston was not getting the most out of the wind he sailed, or that unless the trim of sail aboard the *Eagle* was changed, the *Emperor* would probably catch up within a few hours.

Soon Cartwright forced himself to say: "Jenny, I must ask what every man aboard is asking—have you decided to bury Philip at sea?"

The answer finally formed on her lips. "No. I want him next to my mother in Medford."

She raised her glance and he met it. "What will you do, Jenny?"

"I'll return to Medford, I suppose."

He was thinking: Where she will need no widow's walk atop a house to watch for her husband's approach. What he said was: "One other thing, Jenny. Mr. Winston wants to know when he should fly the colors part way up the gaff."

This was the signal of death aboard.

Jenny looked back at the *Emperor* and said, "Not yet, sir."

The reply aroused his curiosity, though he held to silence.

A little later he took her to the saloon and told her in mildly determined words that she must eat something. Nor would he listen to excuses. She smiled at him, then ate lightly. When she rose, her hand fell to his arm.

"You've been wonderful, Mr. Cartwright."

"Thank you, Jenny," he said.

She went below. He was standing near her door when she emerged around noon. On deck, both felt the gloom aboard as mate and sailors stared at the *Emperor* now roaring abreast of the *Eagle*. Cartwright tensed and turned his frowning glance on Jenny. She appeared not in the least concerned. The same blank look, more an acceptance of the blow fate had dealt her, governed her expression. She gave no order to set studding sails or run the ship a point nearer or off the wind, things he had learned that she could do as well and as effectively as Broadwinder had done.

The cheers from the *Emperor*'s decks rolled across the

water. The hands aboard the *Eagle*, the mate, the shipowner and Jenny listened amid a deep silence and hurt. There was no Broadwinder aboard to cry orders that would put Mayo Keys astern. Broadwinder was dead.

The *Emperor* ran on, showing the *Eagle* her lengthening wake. When a mile or so of water separated the two ships, Jenny said to Cartwright. "Will you have the colors flown at half-mast?"

He knew why she had waited to do this. In all her grief, she had not wished to sail in unsportsmanlike manner. She had not burdened Mayo Keys with her trouble. He could understand this and admire her for it, but he could not understand what he knew now to be something she had planned along with that—to lose the race to Mayo Keys.

Why? Why had she done this when she could have as easily won?

The lookout on Telegraph Hill at Hull brought his telescope to bear on two ships breaking the horizon. The ship in the lead was winging fast for Boston Harbor. He started and gazed excitedly as it dawned on him that he was possibly viewing the end of the world-famous race between the Barking & Pevy *Emperor* and the India Commercial Line's *Calcutta Eagle*. If this were true, his perch on this day was the envy of every man in Boston.

The ships came on and he was thinking that the one in the lead carried the celebrated Captain Broadwinder. He was hoping as much, having a nice sum on the *Eagle* to win, when he made out the house flag of the vessel nearest him.

"The *Emperor!*" he cried in disbelief.

A little later he made out the *Eagle*'s house flag and then saw something that further shocked him. Her colors declared her in mourning.

George Cartwright stared ahead, knowing now that the news of the *Emperor*'s victory was being flashed to Boston by magnetic wire. He turned his gaze aft and pondered the whole thing. The fact that Jenny had deliberately lost the race on the last lap was no more puzzling than his strange lack of dejection at losing. She and Philip had together won the race. Then she had given up. And he, the shipowner who stood to lose thousands of dollars on the outcome, had chosen to help carry her burden. He did not regret it. In fact, he was glad.

Jenny had worked a great change in him. The Cartwright now entering Boston was not the same Cartwright who had sailed out of the harbor.

She stood at the taffrail looking out over the wake, as though she were staring back over the years, reliving memories astern in distance and time. Her large eyes lifted to the sky.

Cartwright moved to her side.

She would go to Medford, she had informed him. There time would heal the hurt. And he, the Cartwright who had learned patience among other things, would wait.

As he stood there, he seemed to know why she had not sailed on to win. It was not a sudden discovery, but one he had probably known in his mind and heart since morning. He realized also that he must and would forever keep secret the greatness of the woman who could have easily won the important race, but who chose instead to keep alive the memory of the celebrated Prince of Sea Captains without giving anyone cause for thinking his fame was due to her ability to fling sail in the Broadwinder manner.

Even now she was proving it, for the great racing *Eagle* that had torn across the sea lanes through storm and ice to make a fair wind to Boston was entering the harbor in the prosaic manner of other ships.

This was her salute to Philip, and with it she proved to the world there was only one Broadwinder.